Café Europa

Books by Ed Ifkovic

The Edna Ferber Mysteries
Lone Star
Escape Artist
Make Believe
Downtown Strut
Final Curtain
Café Europa

Café Europa

An Edna Ferber Mystery

Ed Ifkovic

Poisoned Pen Press

First Edition 2015

10 9 8 7 6 5 4 3 2 1

Library of Congress Catalog Card Number: 2014958207

ISBN: 9781464200489 Hardcover
   9781464203923 Trade Paperback

Poisoned Pen Press
6962 E. First Ave., Ste. 103
Scottsdale, AZ 85251
www.poisonedpenpress.com
info@poisonedpenpress.com

Printed in the United States of America

To Tibor Trencsényi
who shared his Budapest with me

Cast of Characters

Edna Ferber, popular short-story writer making the Grand Tour of Europe

Winifred Moss, embattled suffragette from London, England

Harold Gibbon, a yellow journalist in the employ of the Hearst syndicate

Endre Molnár, a rich young scion of an old Hungarian family

Cassandra Blaine, a beautiful American heiress

Marcus Blaine, a wealthy businessman from Connecticut

Cecilia Blaine, wealthy society matron and wife of Marcus Blaine

Mrs. Pelham, British-born chaperone of Cassandra Blaine

Vladimir Markov, Russian-born proprietor of the Café Europa

Count Frederic, an Austrian aristocrat in the Military Chancery

Baron Meyerhold, high-ranking Austrian investigator

Imre Horváth, an inspector with the Royal Hungarian Police

Jonathan Wolf, an American businessman in Budapest

Lajos Tihanyi, a deaf-mute Hungarian artist, a pioneering modernist

Bertalan Pór, Tihanyi's good friend and fellow revolutionary artist

István Nagy, an apologist poet for the old Viennese regime

Chapter One

Cassandra Blaine laughed too much. She tossed back her pretty head so that her golden hair caught the dusty shaft of brilliant sunlight streaming in through the open windows that overlooked the terrace. The Danube River shimmered below. Her delirious laugh broke at the end, so shrill it seemed dangerously close to hysteria. I'd known girls like her whose artificial laughter suddenly ended in collapse, girls who then confessed trivial sins no one cared to hear.

The few late-afternoon folks scattered about the café looked over, some amused, others annoyed, most indifferent. The beautiful heiress, young and privileged and frivolous, demanded all eyes find her, celebrate...smile...applaud. But her careless laughter rankled in the quiet Budapest café where customers whispered as they downed glasses of sherry or bitters. A table of American women, frail spinsters in amber beads and silk Spanish shawls, sipped strong coffee with whipped cream, the only sound the tinkle of spoons against cups. A wizened Hungarian in a black beret rustled the pages of a newspaper he'd taken from a bamboo rack. In the kitchen behind a closed door someone dropped a plate, and it shattered. A man's deep voice swore, a tepid German curse, followed by an English "Damn!"

"Edna, for heaven's sake." Winifred Moss touched my elbow. "You're staring."

"I know what I'm doing, Winifred. When people choose to perform, I watch them. I'm *supposed* to."

Winifred snickered. "You notice that all the wrong people have tons of money."

"And translucent porcelain skin," I added. "God's ways continue to mystify me."

Winifred sat back, pleased with her comment. Both of us watched as Cassandra's chaperone placed a censorious hand on the young woman's elbow and leaned in, whispering. An old woman, this pencil-thin companion, her gray curls worn under a frilly lace bonnet, her black cotton dress trimmed with too many schoolmarmish ruffles across the bodice. She obviously considered her position taxing, if impossible. Cassandra, her laughter abruptly stopped, glared back, her eyes bright with the power she exercised over the hired servant.

Winifred confided, a little too loudly, her brassy voice heavy with sarcasm, "That poor woman wishes she could slap that bratty girl."

The old Hungarian man, his pinched face buried in a newspaper, slid the sheets down and glared at Winifred, who could have cared less. She stared back, challenging. He grunted and looked down.

Of course, no one in the Café Europa recognized Winifred Moss, the famous—or should I say infamous?—suffragette, by way of the London battlefront. I'd met her two years ago when she spoke to a women's group in Chicago, invited by Jane Addams and Lillian Adler to address the question of the burgeoning women's suffrage movement in America. A rabble-rouser, this fierce, independent female, she took a soul off guard—at least she did me. Blunt, forceful, opinionated, she narrowed her eyes at a world that defined her as…well, inferior, second class, the drudge in the kitchen.

I saw a woman perhaps fifty, at six feet taller than most men, with a long, drawn, horse face behind thick spectacles, unlovely, but somehow…handsome. It was her eyes, I insisted—galvanizing, a hard-coal black that held you, froze you in place. Every so often, absentmindedly, she ran her fingers through her rat's nest pompadour, a stand of iron-gray hair that matched the black

Mother Hubbard smock she always wore. I'd liked her when we chatted briefly in Chicago, and thought her speech to the settlement house stimulating and relevant—though I still believed suffrage in America was a struggle impossible to win. I'd seen the red-faced drunken men with their hateful gestures and catcalls when women marched down Michigan Avenue for the cause.

"We have no choice," she'd told me then. Now, resigned, she sighed. "Such girls"—she actually pointed at Cassandra— "defeat our cause."

I sat back and wondered whether my brief sojourn in Hungary with the redoubtable Winifred Moss—twenty years my senior—had been a wise move. Two nights ago we'd taken the night train from Berlin, arriving early the next morning into picture-postcard Budapest with its fairy lights illuminating Castle Hill, its exotic Moorish architecture, its air redolent with perfume from the beds of lush-blooming roses.

I'd abandoned my mother in Berlin, an act of rebellion I'd doubtless regret, and at times I quaked at my rashness. We'd had a nasty, spitfire spat that left a bad taste in my mouth.

"You can't go gallivanting across Europe by yourself," she'd screamed. "What will people say?"

So be it. Touring Europe with Julia Ferber required Herculean stamina, patience, and an aversion to cold-blooded murder. In America my popular short stories, happily published in *Everybody's*, *Good Housekeeping*, and *Cosmopolitan*, gave me a name and bags of golden coins, and my mother had suggested...you and me, the two of us, mother and daughter, Europe. London, Paris, Rome, Vienna, Munich, Berlin. Well, she was still in Berlin—and she maintained that I should be at her side. At thirty, I was too old for rebellion—or was I? I knew we would do battle over my behavior. Perhaps I'd been hasty in agreeing to make the trip.

My mother had become suddenly—and noisily—fascinated by her oldest brother's family, pleasant enough folks, surely, but smug burghers, plump, red-cheeked, slap-you-on-the-back Berliners who circled Julia Ferber as though unearthing a rare gem. I found the hearty bluster of these Germans trying.

I sat for a portrait with painter Clara Ewald, an engaging older woman with a fiery but delightful tongue. I visited her small cottage nestled in the Bavarian Alps where, one afternoon, I met Winifred Moss, Clara's friend, who was stopping on her way to a holiday in Budapest. My mother had hinted we'd visit Budapest in hopes of connecting with family of my long-dead father, born in Oylso, near Eperye, a village outside the city. We'd received a letter from one of his distant cousins, inviting us to an afternoon visit. But Julia Ferber suddenly balked at leaving the coziness of German hospitality—at which time Winifred Moss, eyeing my mother with a baleful, unforgiving eye and spotting my own restlessness, suggested that I be her companion for a two-week sojourn in Budapest.

"A woman cannot travel alone without criticism," she told me. "Men don't realize a solitary woman, even with ostrich feathers in her hair and shiny brass buckles on her shoes, is an Edwardian Amazon."

Which was why, impulsively, I boarded the night train to Budapest, arriving in the picturesque city along the Danube early in the morning. The Marta taxi took us to the Hotel Arpad, a ramshackle dowager edifice—Winifred's choice, of course. A string of hotels on Maria Valencia Street fronted the Corso overlooking the storied Danube—the Hungaria, the Bristol, the Duna, and the Carlton—all sparkly and polished in the early-morning sunshine. Not so the shabby Árpád. Winifred often stayed there and found it "homey."

This ancient hotel of choice for English-speaking travelers—mostly journalists, businessmen, and a smattering of rich Americans on the Grand Tour—the Árpád overlooked the murky yellow river—the Danube was not blue, notwithstanding Strauss' lovely waltz. Elegant rooms with heavy but faded damask curtains and worn oriental carpets, creaky featherbeds that sagged in the middle, ancient white enamel faucets that creaked and groaned, and a bathtub so deep I considered requisitioning a fireman's ladder to descend and rise from it. The light fixtures sputtered and hissed, the lights dimmed and then brightened, and I fully expected to be wrapped in a blazing fireball in the middle of the night. But Winifred loved it—worshipped its echoey old rooms. I would come to cherish the place because such faded grandeur was as comforting as an old antimacassar inherited from your favorite grandmother.

Idly, the two of us drifted through our sightseeing days in and out of the threadbare Café Europa on the ground floor of the hotel. Its massive French doors opened onto a terrace surrounded by scarlet roses, acacia trees, and manicured shrubbery.

I understood that Winifred needed solace—succor. She was battle-scarred from her days protesting with Emmeline Pankhurst and the Women's Social and Political Union, a militant suffrage group brutalized by the club-wielding London police. Jailed, one of a group of women on a hunger strike, Winifred had been force-fed by sneering men, a funnel jammed into her throat, beaten, humiliated in her cell, forced to watch a friend sexually violated. During a protest march she'd been knocked to the ground by a policeman on a horse, and witnessed another woman, the sister of a member of Parliament, trampled to death. Stunned and shattered, she'd retreated, but I'd noticed her raw dislike of most of the men she encountered. She'd traveled to Germany and now Hungary to escape their faces.

Sometimes in a restaurant she cringed when a man rudely addressed her.

It broke my heart.

Now Winifred nudged me. "Your dreadful friend." She pointed to the open French doors.

Harold Gibbon was barking orders at some unseen person behind him, but stopped, flicked his head forward like a jittery woodpecker, and walked toward Cassandra Blaine. Something stopped him—perhaps the chaperone's imperious shudder gave him pause—so he veered away and slid into a chair at our table.

"Ah, Miss Ferber. Miss Moss. We meet again."

I glowered. "Sir, you were here at this very table for breakfast. Intrusive, opinionated…"

"Doing my job, dear ladies."

"The scurrilous Hearst syndicate…"

"My bread and butter." He grinned and withdrew a pad from a breast pocket of his wrinkled seersucker suit. A rose was pinned to his lapel, faded now, with a petal in danger of falling. He removed the summer bowler from his head and placed it on an empty chair.

A skinny, wiry man, shorter than my five-foot height, with jutting bone, freckled parchment skin, a pointy Pinocchio nose, and a Grimms fairy-tale chin to match, Harold Gibbon was that horrid new breed of yellow journalists invented by William Randolph Hearst—a mid-twenties city boy, brash, garish, gossipy, annoying, a second-generation Richard Harding Davis without the sartorial splendor. Harold was a gnat of the Fourth Estate, one impossible to swat. I'd met him two years earlier at the 1912 Republican Presidential Convention in Chicago when I'd covered the event for the George Matthew Adams newspaper syndicate with William Allen White and others—and Harold, the frisky newspaper reporter, interviewed *us*. Now, meeting him by chance in the Café Europa as we ate chewy bacon *pogácsa* and sipped black coffee laced with whipped cream, he'd assumed we were old friends.

"I scarcely know you, young man," I'd told him.

That had surprised him, his eyes bugging out, "But we *have* met."

"I meet many people, young man and—"

He'd interrupted. "But Americans gotta stick together in a strange land."

Now, leaning back in his chair, he grinned at us, a simpleton's look. "I'm starting to think I'm not wanted here."

Winifred had little patience with the pipsqueak. "Is there a reason you keep glancing toward Cassandra Blaine, Mr. Gibbon?"

"A cynosure, I'm sure you'll agree. And her upcoming wedding will be world news. If I can get past that dour guardian, I'll get me an interview." He beamed. "Another coup for me." He bowed.

"Is that why you're in Budapest?" I asked.

He leaned forward, withdrawing a packet from his vest pocket. Quietly, his eyes flitting around the room, he rolled a cigarette with one hand while fiddling with the monstrous ginger-colored walrus moustache he sported, so expansive it nearly touched the shaggy muttonchops he'd stolen from Grover Cleveland, though I doubted his knowledge of American presidents went back to the previous century.

"I'm here for *real* news, even though an American marrying into Austrian nobility might be a banner headline."

Winifred sneered. "How romantic."

Winifred, I'd noticed, had stiffened when the man joined us, closing up her face, her dislike obvious.

He stared at her, tickled. "Ain't it, though? Folks eat this malarkey up, truth to tell. Yellow-backed dime novel stuff. Graustark adventures in the feudalistic backcountry."

He leaned in confidentially. "I love it—really. Tinged with a bit of scandal, this wedding." He nodded toward the young girl. "Cassandra Blaine, only daughter of Marcus and Cecelia Blaine, wealthy Americans occupying the entire top floor of this fleabitten old hotel, though you rarely see them. Daddy is Connecticut insurance—vice president of Aetna, and a major stockholder of Colt Firearms in Hartford. Mommy is Newport and yachts and Mrs. Astor's Four Hundred in Manhattan. Living in Budapest for the past year now—just as I have, in fact. He's working with Hungarian investors on insurance opportunity, overseeing the construction of a building on Rákóczi.

"And fickle, spoiled Cassandra falls for the handsome Hungarian Endre Molnár until, at Mommy's command, she finds herself betrothed to Count Frederic von Erhlich, Archduke Franz Ferdinand's distant cousin, hunting companion, and all-around gloomy stick-in-the-mud. A marriage orchestrated in the ballrooms of Vienna, though probably not at Hofburg, the Emperor Franz Josef's private castle. End of story."

"No," I said, "it seems to me the *beginning* of a sad story."

"How so?"

I shot a look at the American girl with her elaborately coiffed hair studded with whalebone hairpins. Her arms covered with too many jangling gold bracelets, her diamond earrings glittering. She was dressed in an expensive Nile-blue chiffon day gown that exaggerated her narrow waist and high bust.

"From what little I've seen of Miss Blaine—two days now, occupying that same table under the cruel eye of her keeper— she's none too happy with an arranged marriage."

Harold smiled. "It's very popular in this part of the world. The transatlantic marriage of an impoverished nobility and nouveau-riche American girl."

"That's not my point, sir." I smiled back. "That young girl seems to laugh too much, and too loudly, mostly, I think, over nothing—or at nothing in this shadowy café that strikes me as worthy of such...hysteria."

Winifred was scowling at Harold. Earlier she'd told me—her voice harsh and cold—how much she disliked the brash young man, all breezy American strut and rah-rah-Teddy-Roosevelt-vigor. Now, rattling her coffee cup, she tried to dismiss him from our table. "Mr. Gibbon, perhaps you're sitting at the wrong table? Your nose for news fails you."

He wagged a mischievous finger at her. "Ah, the famous suffragette, arrested by London bobbies for assailing the prime minister, her picture in the *London Times*…and the American short-story writer, her too-serious picture recently in the *Talk of the Town*—sooner or later you'll both have a story to tell me." A heartbeat. He tapped his foot nervously. "The Hotel Árpád may have electric lights that sputter, windows that rattle in the night, mice scurrying in the old walls, and a hiccoughing telephone that goes dead when you need it, but it's a hotbed of gossip and intrigue and"—he pointed to Cassandra, who was frowning at her guardian—"front-page news back in the States."

"You never answered my question, Mr. Gibbon. Why have you been exiled here?" I stared into his eager, bony face. A ferret, I thought, some jittery little forest creature, all buck teeth and watery eyes. But I saw something else there: a cunning little boy,

Tom Sawyer whitewashing a picket fence perhaps, the unloved boy of the village who could be funny and charming—and wanted the world to look at him. That crooked smile under so emphatic a moustache and outsized beak nose. The flashing hazel eyes, unblinking, or blinking too rapidly, the sense of absolute wonder there. Wily, this reporter, and not to be cavalierly dismissed.

Harold was nodding at a portly man sitting nearby. "Simpson of the *New York Tribune*," he whispered. We watched as Mr. Simpson was joined by another man who was dapper in a summer Prince Albert coat, a pince-nez, an enormous cigar clutched in his fingertips.

"Important, that man." Harold smirked. "Or at least he thinks he is. Jamison. The *New York Times*."

Winifred sighed. "You visit Budapest and you are surrounded by Americans."

Harold grinned. "Sooner or later anyone hungry for English-speaking folks finds his way to the Café Europa." He pointed to a rack of international newspapers. "Sixty papers, mostly English, but also German, French. The *Morning Post* from London, three days late. Even"—a shocked look on his face—"the Hungarian and Austrian papers. *Budapesti Hirlap*. The *Vienna Reichspost*. The *Berlin Vorworts*." A heartbeat. "I've been here over a year now."

"So you said. But, once again, why are you here?" I probed. "Certainly that scoundrel Hearst didn't send you here to cover the morganatic marriage of Cassandra Blaine and Count Frederic von Erhlich."

He chuckled. "That's a bonus, really, though such marriages are stale news now." He carefully rolled another cigarette, taking his time, peering closely at the tobacco. "I'm here to chronicle the end of it all."

Winifred, impatient, rolled her eyes. "The end of what?"

He waved his hand toward the bank of windows overlooking the Danube. "The final days of the Austro-Hungarian Empire. The end of Franz Josef's long and awful sixty-something-year reign. Emperor of Austria and King of Hungary. The Serbian Question. Bosnia and Herzegovina, annexed in 1908 by Austria without so much as a by-your-leave, an insult to the Serbians living there. The Serbians hungry for vengeance. War. Serbia, a thorn in Austria's side. The rabble-rousers in the streets, the anarchists, the stink bombs, assassination of local officials, the—"

"And you're convinced it's ending?" I interrupted.

"The empire is a crumbling massive weight, the most untalked-about secret. Franz Josef recently had a bout of pneumonia, probably dying soon, and this...this Archduke Franz Ferdinand, a nasty piece of snobbery, ready to reign over its decline and fall. Read Gibbon—*Decline and Fall of the Roman Empire*." A foolish grin. "Another inquisitive Gibbon. I plan to write my own *Decline and Fall of the Austrian Empire*."

Raising his head, he sniffed the air. "You can smell the decay."

I smiled. "That's just this hotel crumbling around us."

"You seem so sure of things," said Winifred.

"I smell war now. Hearst smells war."

"Well," I said, "he did help to bring about the Spanish-American War—"

"Rumors, unfounded."

I went on, "Is that why you're here—to help push Europe into war?"

A mysterious smile. "They're doing a pretty good job of it by themselves, no?"

"But what's *your* reason?"

"I'm a restless man, a wanderer. I put my ear to the ground and listen for the drumbeat. It just happens that a man like Hearst—a man who believes in banner headlines—hires folks like me. I'm the kind of guy who looks at the world and says: *You, talk to me*." His eyes flashed. "Somebody's gotta be a war's Homer. Why not me?"

"Why Budapest? Why not Vienna?"

He didn't answer for a moment. Then, slowly, in a stage whisper, "Franz Ferdinand is very unpopular here because the Hungarians know the heir to the throne—*der Thronfolger*—despises them. Hungarians don't like being yoked to Vienna. After 1867 they coerced the emperor into a dual monarchy—Austria and Hungary, but that black-and-yellow Habsburg flag rankles the good Magyar patriot. Vienna is closed in tight, folks avoiding reality, lost in dreamy Strauss waltzes and strolling the Ringstrasse under the rows of lime trees. Here—well, people talk in private, huddle in coffee houses while they sip apricot *barack*. Perhaps the war will begin *here*."

Winifred was shaking her head. "True, Serbia is rearing its head these days, a country still angry about the annexation of Bosnia and Herzegovina. But a small kingdom, afraid of Austria's thrust and power?"

"Serbia wants a port on the Adriatic it will never have, though a Greater Serbia demands it. That upstart kingdom will never let go of its impossible dream. Serbia will always be the world's mosquito, insignificant, but eternally buzzing in your ear. Every so often you have to swat it."

I laughed out loud. "World politics in a nutshell, according to Mr. Gibbon."

"So," Harold continued, "I'm here to watch the world fall apart, bit by bit."

Suddenly, with an abrupt thrust of his arm, Harold waved across the room, snapping his fingers, and a man rushed to our table.

"Mr. Gibbon, sir?" The man bowed and stood too close to Harold.

"Dear ladies, you've met Vladimir Markov?"

Winifred and I shook our heads. I'd seen the café proprietor bustling about, a quick smile on his cherubic face. The roly-poly man, eyes enlarged by thick spectacles, in his late fifties, dressed in a vaguely funereal black cutaway suit, wore an elaborate scarlet cravat bunched at his neck, an incongruous puff of dandyish color.

He grabbed my hand, and then Winifred's, and kissed each. The Old World *Küss die Hand* rankled my small-town-girl

American soul. Winifred squealed, unhappy, and Mr. Markov, confused, apologized to Harold but not to us.

"A pleasure," I mumbled.

Amused by our discomfort, Harold grinned foolishly and spoke to Markov in German—which I understood. "American women cannot be touched." Then, surprising me, he warbled in rapid-pace Hungarian with Markov, who bowed repeatedly, answering him. "*Igen. Nem. Igen.*" Yes. No. Yes. "*Nem értem.*"

I'd mastered a smattering of Hungarian, an impossible language, I'd come to realize, though I struggled with a Baedeker phrase book at night in my rooms. A runic confusion, neither Germanic nor Slavic, but after a week or so of guttural German, blunt-edged, the spontaneous flow of Magyar struck me as melodious, each word accented on the first syllable—perhaps I was wrong—but with a lyrical power that soared, ending every periodic sentence with a whiff of marrow-deep melancholy.

Markov and Harold chatted on in Hungarian, the proprietor deferential in his repeated bowing, and both kept looking at Winifred and me.

"He offers you wine," Harold finally said. "For the beautiful women."

Winifred grumbled. "Then he'd best wait until they arrive."

Markov addressed us in choppy English. "This is home"—he waved chubby fingers around the room—"to the American and British visitor to our lovely Budapest." He snapped his fingers and an old waiter in a white linen jacket brought a bottle of Tokay and three glasses.

A slender boy, perhaps sixteen or seventeen, in dark pants and florid red cravat, stood nearby and waited, a pitcher of water cradled against his chest. Markov nodded. "György, come." The boy moved closer. "My wife's nephew, from Russia like me, but new here. And green as spring lettuce." He chuckled. "He has never seen Americans before he arrives a week ago. He stares with open mouth."

"We don't bite," I noted, smiling at the skinny boy with the prominent Adam's apple and colicky black hair a little too greased and polished. He bowed at me, tipping the pitcher so that the water spilled onto the marble floor and worn oriental carpets. Markov berated him quietly and then apologized—again to Harold—and the boy stepped back, scratching his neck nervously. Harold chatted in Russian now—another surprise—and burst out laughing. "Markov says little György is fascinated by Cassandra Blaine, the American girl with the golden hair. The laughing girl, he calls her."

Rudely, we all turned to glance at Cassandra, who was dipping a spoon into some chocolate ice-cream confection, and György, realizing we'd learned of his infatuation, turned scarlet and spilled more water. Lips pursed, Markov pointed to the kitchen door. The boy scurried away.

Markov spoke to Harold. "Too sad, my situation. A favor to the wife. You know how that is." He winked. "A peasant boy, used to cows and sheep and digging winter potatoes. The necktie—she is a noose on a young boy." He shrugged his shoulders, backed away, headed to check a large copper tea samovar on a sideboard.

"A good sort," Harold told us as he watched Markov pour tea. "A diplomat. He smiles at everything. You ask him about Franz Josef and Serbia or Albania, anything political, and he smiles and bows and backs away. He's Russian, so you never know what he's really thinking."

Winifred spoke up, a trace of pique in her tone. "Are you interviewing *everyone* for your own *Decline and Fall of the Austrian Empire*, Mr. Gibbon?"

He smiled and winked at her, improperly. "Well, anyone who'll talk to me. The landed gentry rule Hungary, even over the nobles. But the workers are the ones who'll tell you the true story. The unvarnished truth. The vendors in the flower market. The attendants in the mineral baths up on Mount Gellért. Newsboys hawking papers. The Gypsies in their camps. The Jewish storekeepers, the café owners, the grubbing artists."

"Jews?" I asked.

"You're in Judapest, ma'am. That's what the current mayor calls it."

I said, my voice hollow, "My sad father's home."

"Yeah, well, it isn't the aristocracy that's got the rhythm of this city, let me tell you. It's the old lady who wanders into the *gulyás* restaurant peddling her violets from Matra mountaintops. She understands that war's coming. The Gypsy violinist with his *czigany* music and rat-tail cigars. The Serbian men in scarlet capes and sashes."

"Yet you linger *here*, Mr. Gibbon. In this café. With us." I pointed to the expansive French doors, open now to the flagstone terrace spanning the quay that dipped down toward the Chain Bridge and the Danube.

"Café life, Miss Ferber. Look around you." He pointed to a man with a high flat forehead under slick wavy hair smoking a cigarette in an elaborate holder jutting from a goose-quill stem, wearing an ill-fitting jacket buttoned up to the neck and high-buckled boots.

"István Nagy, a poet. He's always here. He watches the foreigners. He hates us. He writes bitter art-nouveau verse about the fall from grace of the new man in the new century. The New World—that is, the rich Americans—comes to gloat at the *fin de-siècle* decay of an empire he stupidly adores. He longs for the days when Vienna was one grand ball that went into morning. The pre-Lent carnivals with masks and flirtation, Strauss waltzes played from the bandstand."

"How do you know this?"

He ignored me. "And there." He pointed to a corner table where two young men sat with an empty wine bottle, two glasses, and a chunk of dark bread, both holding sketchbooks. "The modern Hungarian artists, followers of that zigzag nonsense done by Matisse and Picasso and their ilk in Paris. The short one—the one who looks like a carnival clown with a lopsided grin—he's Lajos Tihanyi. His father was a friend of this café's owner. They linger here, him and his buddy, the tall lanky boy, Bertalan Pór, and sketch...us...everyone. That's all they do. They'll sketch you and you'll look like you've been twisted into a salt pretzel, your head not where it's supposed to be. Three arms, maybe. I don't know. People as cartoons. It's beyond me, but I'm just a working scribe. Tihanyi is deaf and dumb, so you will hear him sputter and groan, utter garbled sentences. Bit of a temper, in fact, easily rattled. He'll sneer at his friend, but this Pór is a calm sort—nothing gets to him. He smiles and makes peace. Frankly, I'd kill the clown."

Winifred held up her hand. "Stop, Mr. Gibbon. Please."

Harold arched his voice. "The avant garde, them two." He whispered. "Like everyone else, they're waiting for the death of Franz Josef. *Der alte Herr.*"

"Sir," I began, "you impugn…"

"We're a circus act for them, truth to tell."

I glanced at the two young men, both absorbed in their sketching, glancing up now and then toward the open doorway, their chalk rolling over their pads.

Suddenly, grunting, Harold jumped up, twisting his body like a wobbly top. Eyes wide and flashing, he stammered, "Guess it's time to question the lovely damsel."

With that pronouncement, blurted loudly enough to turn heads, he rushed to Cassandra's table. He stood so close to her that it caught her chaperone off guard. The old woman nearly toppled back in her chair. She squawked and put an iron grip on Harold's forearm. Harold, purposely ignoring her and half-bowing to Cassandra, blithely introduced himself—"Harold Gibbon, Hearst syndicate, reporter"—and requested an interview. Every eye in the café found him.

Cassandra, sputtering, looked to her chaperone and squeaked out a feeble, "Mrs. Pelham, you—"

But at that moment the redoubtable Mrs. Pelham, doubtless a veteran of caring for innumerable charges, deftly retrieved a summer parasol conveniently hidden, and jabbed Harold's side. He yelped like a recalcitrant puppy and backed away. Mrs. Pelham spoke through clenched teeth. "How dare you, you brutish mongrel?"

At which Winifred let out an unfunny laugh.

Harold slunk back to our table, slumped into a chair, and offered a grin to the audience he'd gathered. "You gotta try, no?"

"Mr. Gibbon," I began, "perhaps you should—"

But the giddy, ridiculous moment ended abruptly as a group of men entered from the terrace and stopped. Harold sucked in his breath.

"What?" I demanded.

"Endre." One word, hummed softly.

"Who?"

"Cassandra's lover. Her *old* lover. The man she abandoned after her horrible mother contracted her out to Viennese aristocracy and a pathetic, worthless title. A friend of mine. Endre Molnár."

The young man stood in front of his band of friends, all of whom had stopped their chatter, his eyes resting on Cassandra, who self-consciously touched her exquisite hair. Silent now, Endre watched her. He was tall and lanky and dark-complected, his black eyes set under a high forehead, his black hair swept back and down his shoulders—very Heathcliff, I thought. A swashbuckling moustache over razor-thin lips. A granite face, strong, rigid, shadowy. His smoldering stare radiated melancholy. Dressed in polished high black boots, blue trousers, and a white linen shirt that contrasted with his bronzed skin, he dominated the room, ruled the space. Every eye turned to him. Even Winifred, frowning at the melodramatic moment, stared.

One of the men with Endre leaned into his neck, but Endre shrugged him away, and spoke loudly in Hungarian.

"What?" I asked Harold, my linguist at hand.

"He said he belongs here—his friends come here."

Mrs. Pelham sputtered unhappily as the room watched Endre's rigid body. Even the two artists laid down their sketchpads, and waited. Cassandra Blaine, perhaps not realizing what she was doing, had stood, one hand gripping the table, her body swaying. Mrs. Pelham reached out, demanding the girl sit down, but Cassandra, a catch in her throat that we all heard, pushed her away. She sobbed out loud. Cassandra was staring at Endre, and he at her. It was marvelous, I thought, and melodramatically beautiful, this moment out of, say, an Offenbach operetta. Or even Franz Lehár's *The Merry Widow*, all the rage a few summers back. Or *The Gypsy Baron*. I expected to hear a plaintive Gypsy violin, maybe, a drumbeat, a wail from an unseen singer. A stage curtain, dropped.

But then, the spell broken, Endre turned away sharply, his face mournful but dismissive. A coldness there, calculated. And, in a flash, he disappeared back out onto the terrace into the late-afternoon shadows and golden sunlight glinting off the Danube. We stared, all of us, mesmerized, at the empty space.

"Well…" Winifred began.

Harold's head was twisting around like a dervish, unable to focus.

Turning, I spotted György standing by the kitchen door, dripping water onto the floor from the pitcher he seemed unable to control. I followed his startled gaze. In the shadowy entrance to the café, near the corridor that led to the hotel lobby, stood a tall, burly man with a dark beard, a derby on his head, arms folded over a barrel chest. I jumped. Though everyone else was gazing at the empty doorway to the terrace, the man was fiercely focused on Cassandra. My throat went dry, my heart pounded. The boy looked scared, which I understood because the man reeked of menace, danger.

When I looked back at the entrance, no one was there, just shadows and dim light. The man had disappeared. And for a minute I doubted what I'd seen there. But a shaft of fear passed through me as my eyes drifted back to the hapless Cassandra, crumpled over her table.

Chapter Two

Late afternoon in the café, we watched Markov switching on
lights, lighting the fat candles on the long tables banking the
open French doors, a woman in a housemaid's smock sweeping
the steps leading to the terrace. A slight wind blew in the sweet
scent of roses from the garden, mixing with the raw whiff of
river sludge. A lazy hum from the strollers along the promenade
on the Corso, the occasional piercing laugh, someone yelling
to a friend across the way. Winifred and I were loathe to leave
the room, caught by the narcotic rhythm of a café readying for
nighttime—the tinkle of unseen glasses and dishes, blackbirds
sweeping across the terrace and onto the locust trees, György
plucking dead blooms from a basket of blood-red Jacqueminot
roses on the sideboard.

Winifred and I passed into companionable silence. From my
seat, shifting a bit, I could watch the lights popping on up on
Castle Hill across the Danube, the grand Royal Palace gleaming,
the sweep of burnished gold and Italian marble on buildings
high in the Buda hills. A boy in a green canvas jacket shuffled
in and placed copies of *Le Figaro* on a table. At a nearby table
an old man closed his eyes, a smile on his face. Nighttime was
arriving in Budapest.

Vladimir Markov, hovering, put a platter of rye bread on our
table, each slice bearing a chunk of opaque lard speckled with
paprika and salt, an unappealing morsel Winifred and I ignored.
As we watched, three short men ambled in, instruments slung

on their backs. One man with close-cropped side whiskers wore a short jacket over an embroidered vest with silver buttons. Another, carrying a cimbalom, was laughing, a cigar stuck to the corner of his mouth. They began setting up on a small platform in a back corner. Dressed in a homespun jacket with white linen sleeves bunched at the wrist, the old violinist frowned as he tuned his instrument. A tzigane music man smoking a long pipe. Gypsy music.

Cassandra sank into her chair with her eyes closed. Winifred and I quietly sipped our wine.

Adjusting her shirtwaist, Mrs. Pelham stood, whispered something to Cassandra, and then left the room, headed into the lobby. She glanced back over her shoulder as she passed by our table, her face tight and lined, eyes steely. A supercilious woman, a sprig of white carnation pinned to her chest—a decorative accent that clashed with her steel-girder demeanor. But in that face I spotted something else: her unmistakable dislike of her petulant charge. Doubtless willful Cassandra, notoriously spoiled, was not what she expected when she assumed control. Mrs. Pelham looked like an American—though Harold informed us she was a British subject—because her stony face bore an old-time New Englander's puritanical resolve. That was probably why Cassandra's parents had employed her. Rockbound Calvinist, taskmaster, the frightening warden at a woman's penitentiary.

Who, I now believed, was failing at her appointed task.

Her raised voice drifted back from the lobby, a precise voice one uses on the telephone. She quickly returned to Cassandra's table, her jaw set, but flinched as the Gypsy violinist suddenly ran a tentative bow across his instrument, the discordant chord jangling. With exquisite timing, the overhead lights dimmed, flickered threateningly, then popped back on, and Mrs. Pelham drew her lips into a thin, disapproving line. But then so did I, believing the hotel would become a ball of fire as I slept unsoundly on the second floor.

Cassandra had crossed her arms defiantly, and Mrs. Pelham hissed at her. Two men sipping brandy near our table were frowning, and one smirked and told the other in German, "*Sie ist nur ein Fratz!*" She is a brat.

Within minutes, however, the room stiffened as a phalanx of six or seven men, shoulders touching, boots stomping, moustaches vaguely identical, dominated the doorway to the lobby. Near us Vladimir Markov gasped, tugged nervously at his scarlet necktie, and looked at a loss. His solution amused me—shrugging, he simply backed into the kitchen. A nervous hum swept the room. A table of old Hungarian women, resplendent in summer hats with peacock feathers, stood up, tittered for a moment, then lapsed into silence.

Harold, who obviously missed little, his eyes flitting here and there—the roving journalist on the prowl—bit his lip and beamed. He stuck his head between Winifred and me, like a bobbing puppet in a Punch and Judy street revue. "Lord! Count Frederic von Erhlich. Himself."

The count hesitated a moment, directed something to one of his aides—the moustache twittered—and strode forward. As he moved, people rose, nervous, stood at uneasy attention. Only the foreigners remained in their seats. I certainly wasn't called to military attention. His men blocked the entrance. Cassandra, watching her future husband approach, sat upright, ashen, but as if on cue, manufactured a little girl's obligatory smile, something done to please a demanding parent. Mrs. Pelham, already standing, seemed at wit's end, her fingers gripping the table.

The count stood before Cassandra. I saw a thick, stubby man, an oak tree stump whose ramrod stance made him appear taller. A wide, florid face, large dark eyes under bushy eyebrows, a small mouth with thick lips. A shaved round head. What startled was the moustache, salt-and-pepper, grandiose, a lacquered and twisted and manicured affair so slick and scalloped it looked like a pasted-on exaggeration worn by a vaudeville villain. A man in his late thirties, a veteran of some military frontier, he wore the regalia of an Austrian army man: high black boots so polished they seemed shellacked, belted brown trousers under a dark brown jacket emblazoned by a rainbow of celebratory ribbons and braids, and gaudy epaulettes bulky on his shoulders.

A strutter, this man, I thought, an overgrown boy looking for a parade to join.

Harold, always the gadfly, bounced up and sidled nearby, as one of the count's aides, watching from the entrance, made a loud, clicking sound, a warning. Harold froze, a sheepish grin on his face.

The count leaned into Cassandra's table, his back to fussy Mrs. Pelham, and said something to her. Belatedly, Cassandra stood up, performed a feeble curtsy, nodding at him. Like that, his mission done, the count swiveled like a child's mechanical wind-up toy, and left the room. Seamlessly, the aides separated as the count moved through, looking straight ahead, and immediately closed ranks behind him. The Hungarians in the room who'd stood up slowly dropped back into their seats. One woman fanned herself with a lavender-colored parchment fan.

Harold rushed back to his chair next to me and announced in a voice loud enough for the room to hear, "The count has to catch the night steamer to Vienna. Some crisis. He can't have dinner with Cassandra and her parents. He offered...no regrets."

Hearing his booming voice, Mrs. Pelham turned and glowered.

"Harold, please," I implored, "a little decorum, no?" I stared into his wide-eyed face, another little boy excited to be at the grown-up table.

"I've never *seen* him before," Harold blubbered excitedly. "This—this was unexpected and...and, well, unheard of. Titled folks don't hobnob in the Café Europa. They send their aides." A reflective pause. "Maybe the man has a bone of humanity in his body after all."

Winifred said snidely, "Well, I'd hardly call it hobnobbing, young man. He looked like he was dismissing his troops."

Harold burst out laughing and wagged a finger at Winifred's icy glare.

When I glanced back at Cassandra, now seated, she wore a relieved look on her face. Her pretty features softened, the wispy smile gone. She sat back, folded her arms across her chest and surveyed the room, as though for the first time realizing where she was. She stared at our table and then whispered to Mrs. Pelham, whose baleful eye deliberately dismissed us. Yet, stunning me, Cassandra locked eyes with mine—and for a second she smiled at me, as though we were old friends suddenly come upon each other in a strange country. Confused, I nodded back. She offered me a half-wave before looking away.

"Tell me about the marriage, Mr. Gibbon," I began quietly. Winifred groaned. "Really, Edna. Gossip?"

I ignored her. "Of course. People fascinate, no? Don't you read my short stories in *Everybody's*?"

She didn't answer and chose to glower at Harold. I knew Winifred didn't like him, a man constantly at our elbow, very much the irritant, but there was about him an innocence, the slack-jawed farm boy happy to be in the big city. I might enjoy his company, I realized—such a new American concoction: brash, confident, demanding, yet with that trace of Peck's Bad Boy, the neighborhood lad who steals an old woman's crabapples but makes sure she has firewood in the snowy winter.

"Well," he began, sitting back down, "it's one of the transcontinental marriages we've read about for years now, largely started in 1895 by Consuelo Vanderbilt and her imperious mother, Alva. American socialite, too much money, too few brains, unbridled ambition. A mother who feels she is *lacking* something—European certification. That is, a coveted title to emboss on your stationery. Royalty. Aristocracy. Looking back to good old Europe where the thrones are stored. So Alva finds an impoverished bit of nobility to marry, the Ninth Duke of Marlborough, and like that, her family is aristocracy. Rich and titled, though in a loveless marriage. The Duke gets railroad stock worth millions, courtesy of a matchmaker named Lady Paget. Everybody's happy because a struggling European noble can stay in the cold castle and look down on the rest of us. Of course, he now has a crass American countess at his side."

"Sham," Winifred muttered.

"Exactly, but Consuelo's marriage just got the international wheels rolling and spinning. A dozen such marriages that year alone. Since her marriage, it's been high season on the Atlantic. Lord, there's even a magazine called *The Titled American* that lists eligible but poor noblemen—bachelors. Winaretta Singer of the sewing machine magnates married a French nobleman."

Winifred was fidgeting in her seat. "What?" I asked her.

"In Britain today, in the House of Lords, probably one-quarter have American connections. Worse, when the American socialite Jennie Jerome roped in Lord Randolph Churchill, we ended up with the current Home Secretary, a rearguard politician named Winston Churchill."

"Why? What?" I asked.

She trembled, her eyes moist, which alarmed me. "He's notoriously anti-suffrage. If I may quote the powerful man: 'Women are well represented by their fathers, brothers, and husbands.'"

Harold snickered. "Well, no one said such mercenary unions produced children we could be proud of."

"But why Count van Erhlich?" I asked, puzzled. "If he's part of Franz Josef's family, the—"

Harold cut me off. "A family scandal, my dear lady. And the countess mother lacking hard cash. You see, the count's father, a cousin to Franz Ferdinand, was involved in some nefarious business dealings a while back and was caught embezzling funds. Red-handed. The story got into the press. Handed a revolver, his was a necessary suicide in his mountaintop cabin. So the haughty countess, struggling, a little bit stunned, maneuvered her only son—a confirmed bachelor—back into the good graces of Hofburg.

"Now he's a force in the Military Chancery, the *Militork-anzlerei*, a severe martinet whose military service—hence the uniform he always wears—gave him cover for his incompetence. But, I gather, old Franz Josef, tottering these days toward death, *likes* him. The old All-Highest doesn't like the heir apparent, Franz Ferdinand, with his marriage to Sophie from Bohemia. The emperor lives in the past—a man who won't ride in a motorcar and refuses to use an elevator, climbing six flights of stairs to his bedroom nightly. Currying favor, the count told Franz Josef that man was meant to ride horses—or to walk. The countess has always been an indulged favorite. Sycophants, both mother and son.

"Of course, her son will never be allowed in court with Cassandra, who must be relegated to a castle in Moravia, but the marriage is condoned because, well, his mother needs the cash to appear regal at the pre-Lenten balls in Vienna. And the count is...a shadow in the empire. He could never be admitted officially to court functions anyway because you need the quartering—unbroken descent from eight paternal and eight maternal ancestors."

"Cassandra doesn't appear too happy with it all."

"She has no say, although I understand she says a lot. A little outspoken, the Gibson Girl with the tennis racket."

I laughed. "You know, Harold, I wonder how you know so much."

He blinked rapidly. "I gotta know *everything.* It's my job."

I shook my head. "It's a sentimental tale out of some nineteenth-century romance by The Duchess. Rich American girl involved with cold-hearted European royalty. Humdrum bathos."

Harold's eyes became pinpoints. "Yeah, well, an American tragedy, really."

"I don't follow you."

Harold was wound up now, his voice rising. "Simple, really. I'm a romantic and there ain't nothing romantic about it. Think about it. *Nobody* ends up happy. And when the war comes, as it will, and shortly, trust me—you'll have an American girl left stranded in a cold mountain castle."

"Are you saying the count will die in war?"

"Of course not. Yeah, he *is* a part of the war—he *is* war, given his position—but the war will end ancient feudalism, shatter the royal houses, and crush empires. The Romanovs, the Habsburgs, the Hohenzollerns. Gone, gone, gone. One, two, three. No, the count will never be in battle, though he'll rattle his ceremonial sword when he leads parades and thunders praise on dead poor boys, but he'll just be a man stripped of his precious identity."

Winifred smiled. "But he'll still be rich, courtesy of American industry."

"But without a title he won't be—loved."

"Look." Winifred pointed to the doorway.

"The American peerage," Harold announced. "Marcus and Cecelia Blaine."

Cassandra's parents had come to gather her, though they refused to step into the café. Impatient, clearing her throat decorously, Cecelia Blaine caught Mrs. Pelham's attention, and the woman jumped as though slapped. She whispered to Cassandra, who appeared hesitant to move, turning aside and deliberately facing the wall. Mrs. Pelham, lips in a hard line, scurried to the Blaines and began her scattered apology before she even neared them.

Cecelia Blaine, dressed in a turquoise ruffled gown, a girlish pink silk shawl draped over her shoulders, was a big-boned woman with a long patrician face that must have been appealing—even striking—when she was a young debutante: a tipped-up nose over a cupid's bow lips, a narrow forehead that disappeared into a magnificent pompadour festooned with ivory hairpins and colorful aigrettes. Such a youthful look on a matronly woman suggested that she was a woman who refused age—and wisdom. A battleship of a woman, a force beneath the layered lace and magenta-colored ostrich feathers.

"Well, *demand* it," Cecilia hissed to Mrs. Pelham, speaking over Mrs. Pelham's shoulder in a voice thick and syrupy. "We have an engagement."

Tight-lipped, Mrs. Pelham sloughed back to Cassandra's table, delivered the demand, only to be rebuffed. Cassandra waved at her parents, dismissively, and mouthed the words, *Leave me alone.*

Marcus Blaine had little interest in standing there. He stepped back, ready to leave. A pot-bellied man with a round but determined face, dressed in a white linen summer suit stolen from Mark Twain, polished black shoes and pristine white spats, an incongruous bowler resting atop his bald head, he barely glanced at his rebellious daughter. Instead, his eyes took in the room in dismissive judgment. The shadowy corners, the threadbare oriental carpets, the old rose-colored damask draperies, and the quaint chromolithographs of old Buda and OBuda hanging lopsidedly on the far wall all suggested to him a place he cared not visit. He withdrew his gold watch fob and checked the time, stubby fingers circling the timepiece. A garish gold ring with an oversized amethyst stone on his index finger caught the overhead light.

"Enough, Cecilia. Leave her to her doom."

Harold laughed uproariously, and the man's eyes swept our table. A flash of coldness covered me, so intense his raw condemnation of what he saw. Riffraff, ne'er-do-wells, rag-tag sojourners in a shabby café.

When they left, Cassandra let out that same bubbly laugh she'd used before, but now it sounded hollow, shrill. A vein on the side of Mrs. Pelham's neck jutted out, throbbed. A strand of vagrant white hair had broken free from her careful bun.

"A curious mingling," I said out loud. "The Old World and the New. The Austrian count and the pompous American man of affairs."

Winifred turned to Harold. "The father never comes in here?"

"What do you think?"

"And yet he stays at the Hotel Árpád," I added.

"They occupy the top floor, all of it, a grand suite of rooms. They travel back and forth to America while he's orchestrating an Aetna building on Rákóczi. The last time they traveled, Cassandra refused to go with them because she'd met Endre and…well, love was in the air. They had no choice but to leave her in the care of Mrs. Pelham, which made her more contrary. The Blaines are fawned upon here, and Cecelia has a dislike of anyone who doesn't speak English. She has an American cook in their rooms, an American maid. Rumor has it Marcus is part owner of the hotel."

"How did Cecilia feel about Cassandra and Endre?"

"She went looking for a count."

"And found one," I concluded.

"Well, they're always standing around like potted plants, waiting to be spotted, hands out, last year's Prince Albert morning coat a little shiny in harsh daylight."

"Endre is a good-looking man," I noted. "Very dramatic in a swashbuckler way. A pirate on the high seas. The count, frankly, reminds me of a stolid pig farmer donning his Sunday best."

"Edna, really," Winifred admonished. "Sometimes you sound so…" She paused.

"Honest?"

"I was going to say giddy."

"But if Cassandra is so rebellious, why is she going along with the wedding plans?" I asked.

Harold shrugged his shoulders. "Because her mother has told her it's a contract that cannot be broken."

"Poppycock," I said.

"They've scared her, and the result is *that*." He pointed to the girl.

Then Harold left our table, first chatting with Markov, who'd come back into the room and was ordering around two of the older waiters. Next he sauntered to the corner where the two Hungarian artists were busy over their sketchbooks. Startled, both looked up as Harold occupied an empty chair. He engaged the tall one in a lively conversation, though the shorter man kept nodding his head. Harold burst out laughing, slapping his side, and the shorter man looked confused by his behavior, a flash of irritation in his eyes, but then he laughed. The deaf and dumb one, I realized. Harold was talking in German, which surprised me, given what I knew of the Hungarians dislike of speaking the language of the Austrians.

I heard him refer to Winifred and me—"the foreign ladies"—adding, in English, "so famous, those two. At least outside of Hungary." That made no sense, but all three men stared at us, with Harold, the cheerleader, pointing rudely. The tall man tore off a sheet from his sketchbook and handed it to Harold who rushed back to our table and thrust the sheet down before us.

"Look," he gushed. "From Bertalan Pór."

The artist had used a thick pencil to sketch Cecelia and Marcus Blaine at their most imperious—slapdash caricatures really, cruel but painstakingly honest renderings of the pompous couple. Winifred found herself smiling, and I joined her. Cecelia's nose was pointy now, pinched, upturned, with large, ocean-wide nostrils. Very Jonathan Swift. Her hair was a horrible nest of glittering baubles that looked like wild birds, caged. And Marcus, haughty with his dark dull eyes and cascading chins, grasped that elegant timepiece that seemed a body part peeking out the silk vest with the mother-of-pearl buttons.

"Good Lord," Winifred commented. "Bull's-eye, this sketch."

Harold was grinning at me, clearly up to no good.

"What?" I waited.

"Ah, Miss Ferber, the deaf one—his name is Lajos Tihanyi—impossible to remember, I know, unless you're…me…well, he wants to *paint* you. You! Your face, he says, is magic."

I groaned. "Will I end up looking like Cecelia Blaine?"

"No, he *likes* you."

"He doesn't *know* me to *like* me. This is ridiculous, Mr. Gibbon. What are they up to?"

"Well, it seems Tihanyi's father József owns a café nearby on Rákóczi at Szentkirály utca and is friends with the owner of this café. The father was a headwaiter at Weingruber's—and here, years back. Well, Tihanyi and his friend Bertalan are planning a book of sketches. You know, café society, Budapest-style. The Paris of Eastern Europe. Lively nightlife till dawn. Bertalan tells me there are over six hundred cafés and coffee houses in this city, small and large, busy all day and night. Filled at ten o'clock at night. Some haven't closed for twenty years, he says. Writers, artists, politicians—they spend all day and night at tables with Turkish coffee and wine and whiskey and newspapers—they're the real heart of the busy city. Gypsy violinists nightly. Revolutions begin in them. People fall in love. Well, this month they're here, Lajos and Bertalan, sketching the foreigners." He grinned. "Like you two lovely ladies."

Winifred looked at them. "Really."

"Impossible," I added. "What nerve!"

I turned to face the two young men, both staring back, eager but also uncertain.

"So it's all set," Harold concluded.

"Hold on." I touched his sleeve. "What's all set?"

"They want to make your acquaintance."

I shook my head. "Please. Not more of this kiss-the-hand blather."

"Well, you are in Europe, Miss Ferber."

I bit my lip. "I know where I am, sir. I excelled in geography at grammar school. Perhaps they don't understand common courtesy."

Harold laughed. "The squirrelly-looking one, this Lajos, wants to know if you've been to Buffalo, New York. I think he said one of his paintings was exhibited there a year back or so—or will be exhibited there. He's hard to follow."

"Tell him no one willingly travels to Buffalo. It's cold most of the year. Ice gets into the soul there."

I gathered my belongings, nodding at Winifred, and stood up. "Time to leave this place."

Yet I didn't move away. A breeze swept in from the terrace and I sighed.

Harold smiled at me. "Everyone lingers in the Café Europa."

"Is something going to happen here?"

Impudently, he winked at me. "Everything happens here. But you'll have to wait and see."

Chapter Three

Winifred touched my elbow and whispered, "Edna, don't leave yet. Look." She pointed.

Her words were interrupted by a sweep of violin music filling the room.

Harold shouted, "Ah, good. Now for some *czárdás* music. Hungarian folk music. And then some Gypsy music, melancholy and haunting."

I sat back down, thrilled.

The old violinist, his instrument tucked under his chin, began playing and singing in a voice that cracked and growled, lost notes, flattened them, but the passion was there, deep and throaty. The rhythmic Magyar tongue soothed, though the mournful tune made me flash to an image of my mother condemning my sojourn in Budapest, clicking her tongue at her errant daughter, suddenly a rebel.

At that moment an enormous man leaning on a gold-tipped cane slowly walked into the café. He settled into a chair near the platform, nodded as Markov hurriedly placed a bottle of *slivovitz* on the table, the fiery plum brandy that made me shiver with one sip. In a scratchy voice, quivering, he said, "*Köszönöm*." Thank you. Markov bowed and backed off.

Harold whispered, "János Szabó."

"And he is?" I asked. I watched the man adjust his gold-rimmed monocle.

"Nobody, really. He's in his eighties. He lives in the hotel, gets fatter by the year, and only comes to the café when his darling appears. So…"

"Mr. Gibbon, what are you talking about?"

The old man tapped his fingers on the table, impatient. He was wearing a long mulberry-colored silk dustcoat, stained and frayed, with dark gray trousers. He looked shabby.

"You'll see." A smug smile from Harold. "A man smitten twenty or so years ago in a Vienna tavern."

When the music stopped, there was a smattering of applause. A raised glass, a salute. Someone yelled out a request—or at least I assume it was, for the violinist nodded and began a rollicking song. A man at the table behind us punctuated the lyrics with his own off-key contribution. The violinist yelled and stamped his foot. Harold leaned into my neck and translated quickly.

"A drinking song." Harold paraphrased the words in a sing-song voice: "Away with sorrow and with tears, we fill our hearts with wine. No water for me. A Magyar drinks wine. A German swallows beer, but a Magyar hungers for the grape. With tears we sing…" He broke off. "A loose translation."

"Jolly," I told him.

"Drink up," Harold said. "Hungarians savor life lived with melancholy eyes."

Halfway through the song, the violinist stopped and bowed toward the doorway.

A woman approached the platform. The old man in the mulberry-colored coat bellowed out a name—"Zsuzsa, Zsuzsa"—and folks joined the sporadic applause.

She bowed toward Szabó, who raised his glass to her, but the smile on her face vanished as she spotted Cassandra and Mrs. Pelham sitting nearby. She hesitated, looked back over her shoulder as though debating whether to leave, but then, with a fatalistic shrug, approached the violinist who, of course, kissed her hand. The other two men kissed her hand. She expected it.

"The plot thickens," Harold told us. "Zsuzsa Kós, the cabaret singer and actress from the comic opera stage and the rowdy beer halls of Vienna."

"Are we supposed to recognize her?"

"Only the old men remember her now." He indicated János Szabó, whose face was bright red.

Zsuzsa was a fleshy, buxom woman perhaps in her mid-fifties, maybe older, a little haggard looking, but it could just be the garish red lipstick, the pancake powder slathered on her wrinkled face, lavish stage makeup probably worn to hide from sunlight. Poured into a snug canary-yellow dress, with a tattered hem that dragged on the carpet, a Moroccan shawl draped over her shoulders, she'd clearly never reconciled her weight with the wardrobe she'd kept from her days onstage. A sensual woman, clinking bracelets sliding up and down her arms, her too abundant dyed-blond hair a hayfield under the fringed mantilla covering her head. A Lillian Russell with a classic hourglass figure now gone to seed. Yet the old men in the room put down their newspapers and saluted her. Others applauded wildly.

"Years back she was famous in Vienna, popular at the Burg-theater, a confidante of Franz Josef's current mistress, Katharina Schratt. Songs were written for her—*about* her. You'd see her reading a French novel and sipping tea laced with rum at a table in the Café Central, or riding around the Ringstrasse in a fiacre drawn by a pair of black Russian trotters. Shopping for jewelry on Koerntnerstrasse for diamonds. She was the first to use blood-red lacquer on her fingernails, a *cause célèbre*, really."

"What happened?" I asked.

"Time, for one. You can't be young and pretty forever. And a falling out with some women in Franz Josef's circle, for another. Perhaps a snub to la Schratt. So she drifted back to Hungary where she was born, now lives off the courtesy of old admirers, a pittance here, pittance there." He whispered. "János Szabó pays for her tiny room at the Hotel Árpád." Then Harold swallowed his words. "There's a trace of madness, I hear—a slipping from reality."

Winifred sneered. "Is no one safe from your gossip, Mr. Gibbon?"

Eyes wide, bright. "No one. And no one should be. Gossip is the...spice of my life."

Winifred turned away.

"But she seems startled by Cassandra's presence," I went on.

"As well she should be. Zsuzsa Kós was the go-between employed by Cecelia Blaine to find a count or duke to marry her Cassandra. With Zsuzsa's connections, feeble though they are these days, and the fact that once a month she sings in this café, well…"

"And a pocket full of coins, I imagine…"

"…the union is blessed. Well, maybe not blessed—but, at least, happily contracted."

"But why is she startled to see her?"

He was nodding wildly. "It's a wonderful story, really. Cassandra doesn't *like* her, considers her a destructive woman, a grubbing conniver, a panderer. You know, they *had* been friendly here because Cassandra loved Zsuzsa's Gypsy songs. Zsuzsa is rumored to have Gypsy blood—you see it in the corners of her eyes, that wariness that allures. That was one of the rumors that got her exiled from Vienna, in fact. A taboo, that blood. Anyway, Cassandra believes Zsuzsa sold her out for hard cash."

I stressed my words. "She *did*, indeed, but I would think Cassandra would be angrier at her parents."

"Didn't you notice, Miss Ferber? She *is*. She won't obey them, though she knows she has to marry the count. But Zsuzsa is the face of crowns clinking in the pocket as well as back-room negotiation. And Zsuzsa, even at her age, is rumored to be a woman generous with her affairs, supposedly many of them, a woman not to be mentioned in some parts of polite society. Zsuzsa routinely lived with lovers—unmarried. What the Hungarians call *vadházasság*, a wild marriage. Cassandra repeatedly threw that in her face. They've had scenes—one nasty one in *here*." He chuckled. "Memorable. I took notes."

At that moment, her steps tentative, Zsuzsa approached Cassandra, but Cassandra waved her back.

"No," she yelled.

Confused, twisting around, Zsuzsa stumbled toward the platform, and the old man extended his hand, drew her up next to him. For a moment the look in her eyes was dark, but the violinist whispered in her ear. Her smile became bittersweet. Standing under those bright chandeliers up on that platform, she sparkled like old crystal struck by a shaft of afternoon sun. For a second I understood the beauty she once was. Drawing in her breath—I feared her generous bosom would escape the buttoned bodice meant for a more svelte performer—she sang. Beautifully, to my surprise and pleasure. She had a rich contralto, rough at the edges, raspy, but there was something—what?—absolutely heartfelt, sure, raw. She sang a melancholic ballad that played off the sad violin, a hint of tears in her thick whiskey voice, a lament that silenced the café. Even Vladimir Markov, repositioning a vase of flowers on an empty table, paused, eyes half-shut, his body swaying. He looked ready to weep. In fact, everyone looked ready to cry inconsolably. János Szabó sobbed out loud.

Then Cassandra spoke loudly over Zsuzsa's singing, deliberately rude, shattering the mood. Mrs. Pelham placed a hand on the girl's arm but Cassandra shrugged it off.

"I want to hear 'Alexander's Ragtime Band' now," she called out, naming that dreary American ditty then ubiquitous throughout Europe. "Come on along, come on along, it's the greatest…" All through my travels, it followed me like a pesky family dog. And now, to my horror, in regal Budapest. Zsuzsa narrowed her eyes. Tipsy and plagued by a trace of madness, she faltered, finishing her plaintive song so softly no one could hear her.

Then, like that, it was over. The one song ended, the aged chanteuse refused to start another. She glared at Cassandra as the violinist helped her join Szabó at his table. Quietly Markov, bowing, placed a glass of cognac before her. She smiled her thanks, though I noticed her hand trembled as she lifted the glass. Amazing. This woman, this once-celebrated performer in the dated dress, somehow demanded attention. She had glided across the floor with the grace of a Broadway ingénue. Zsuzsa would never relinquish the image she had of herself. She didn't have to. She had fashioned a definition of herself that satisfied. I *liked* that about her. Worlds apart, Winifred Moss, the independent suffragette, and Zsuzsa Kós, the unrepentant coquette, both understood what was needed for a woman to survive in a man's narrowly charted world.

Winifred was talking about Cassandra's errant behavior—"A hickory stick, mind you, that's what I'd recommend"—as Harold returned the drawing to Bertalan Pór and motioned toward us, which rankled.

Markov nudged the boy György toward Zsuzsa's table, a bottle of spring water in his hands. The jittery boy carried it as though it were some precious Arthurian chalice while Markov *tsk*ed. Just as he placed the bottle before Zsuzsa, who smiled sweetly at him, another man walked over, touched Zsuzsa on the shoulder affectionately, and sat down. She looked startled—and unhappy—with the interloper.

It was the elusive man I'd spotted earlier, the stranger who'd hidden in the shadows by the entrance, watching Cassandra. The man who'd disappeared into those shadows. Even the boy György had been bothered by the intensity of his look then. Now he was back. He called out to the boy in a brusque American voice, unfriendly. "Another glass. Am I invisible?"

Stumbling, probably not grasping the harsh English, György disappeared into the kitchen and didn't reappear. Meanwhile Harold was back at our table.

"Who is that man?" I flicked my head toward the burly man who was watching Markov approach with a goblet on a tray.

"Why do you assume I know everyone in the Café Europa?"

"Because you tell us you do."

He grinned. "My job."

"Sooner or later you're going to be in trouble."

"Then I'll write about it."

"I hope I don't regret my words, my dear Mr. Gibbon."

"Well, I never regret mine, Miss Ferber."

"And that's probably a character flaw you should work on."

He guffawed and banged the table, "Miss Ferber, you are something else." He winked at Winifred. "Ain't she, though?" Winifred ignored him. Then his face tightened. "Jonathan Wolf.

That's his name. A rich American who appeared here a few weeks ago." A puzzled look on his face. "He always sits alone. That's why I'm surprised he's there with Zsuzsa and Szabó now. Strange."

"Maybe not so strange."

"Why so?"

"I saw him watching Cassandra earlier from the doorway. And his look was icy."

My remarks confused Harold. He wasn't happy having missed something in the café.

"He's mysterious, I'll grant you that. One time I saw him approach Mrs. Pelham in the corridor, but she snapped at him. He was ready to *ask* her something. She had little patience with the man. I learned that he's from the East Coast. Boston, someone said. Lots of family money. A Harvard graduate. In the city on business, supposedly. Maybe he knew the Blaines back in Connecticut."

I sat back. "If so, he didn't look happy to see the pouting daughter sitting here carrying on."

Harold looked at us with mooncalf eyes. "Maybe she broke his heart back in the States."

Winifred said dryly, "Mr. Gibbon, for a hard-bitten reporter, you do have a streak of knight-in-shining-armor romance coursing through your veins."

Harold winked conspiratorially and wagged a finger at her. "That'll just be our little secret, ladies."

Chapter Four

Winifred and I strolled past the outdoor tables at Tabán, a tiny eatery on the Corso, steps up from the murky waters of the Danube. We'd been walking along the embankment, behind the wrought-iron railings, watching the sun glinting on the Buda hills. A serene June day, the air rich with the intoxicating aroma of baking bread from an unseen kitchen. A whiff of sulfur from the mineral baths across the river. A short distance away, the Hotel Árpád caught the midday sunshine, and its terra-cotta marble façade gleamed like an old earthenware pot. Earlier a light drizzling rain had fallen, and the landscape still glistened with beads of wetness. Idly, we watched Vladimir Markov throw open the expansive doors onto the terrace, and two waiters cleaned the slate-top tables and chairs, opened the huge striped umbrellas. When Markov clapped his hands, satisfied, the waiters left the terrace. Within seconds a man sat down at one of the tables and opened a newspaper. It was István Nagy, I realized, the poet we'd seen before, his face lost in the newspaper. A waiter poured coffee for him.

Someone called out to us in English. "Hello."

Seated in the shadows at Tabán, nearly hidden by an umbrella, Harold was waving frantically to us. A bottle of water and a carafe of coffee rested at his elbow.

"Hello, Mr. Gibbon," I answered.

He was sitting with someone whose back was to us, but at that moment the man turned, following Harold's greeting, and

I stared into the face of Endre Molnár. A cigarette bobbed in the corner of his mouth. Slouching in his seat, he appeared more relaxed than he did last night when he'd locked eyes with Cassandra. Now, a halo of cigarette smoke over his head, one arm draped over the back of a chair, his head tilted to the side, he looked comfortable, lazy. He smiled at us, almost bashfully, the corners of his mouth giving his bronzed cheeks boyish dimples. His huge moustache twisted like a disturbed caterpillar. I found myself contrasting him to the dour, stolid Count Frederic, and I understood to my soul Cassandra's dilemma.

"Join us. Please." From Harold. Endre nodded, though I noted hesitation in his eyes.

"I'd rather not," Winifred whispered to me.

But I was already headed toward their table.

Endre Molnár stood and bowed to us, and looked ready—eager?—to kiss our hands. Instead, stepping around the table, I slid into a chair. Harold, of course, was talking nonstop. He signaled to a waiter. Endre, sitting back, smiled indulgently, eyes slatted as he watched Harold rattle on. A sidelong glance at Winifred and me, conspiratorial, I thought—and amused.

Endre was a beautiful man. His long lanky body moved with the grace of a man comfortable with himself. A sudden turn of his head, the languid shifting of a raised shoulder, a finger tapping his knee—a man who understood that women enjoyed looking at him. That shock of brilliant black hair, so dramatically swept back from his forehead, that elegant Roman nose over a wide fleshy mouth. The way he slowly sat up, arching his back like a roused cat, spreading his long arms across the table, one hand absently reaching for a glass. The eyes held you, mesmerized. An Hungarian matinee idol, I thought, an intrepid horseman of the windswept plains.

Suddenly I realized what especially compelled: the lined, dark face was flawed—one eye was lazy, slightly closed, so that you were caught unawares. The exquisite Ming vase with a hairline crack that made you cherish it. I found myself staring, rudely, unabashedly, into that face. I couldn't help it. That lazy eye gave his glance a raw intimacy, a sensual—almost feminine—softness that warred with the ruddy Wild West moustachioed countenance. I wanted to reach out to touch that face.

Of course, I didn't.

Of course not.

I only wanted to.

Winifred was staring at me curiously. She'd glanced at Endre, dismissed him, and was content to glare unhappily at the rattling, chattering Harold.

For a few seconds the two men spoke in Hungarian. Harold's version was admittedly halting and scattered—Endre winced once or twice, though he found it amusing—but then Endre spoke in English, a precise British schoolboy English. "Mr. Gibbon is a fascinating man, yes?"

"Your English, sir, is…"

Harold broke in. "The result of being a student at Oxford."

"Of course," Winifred said.

"He tells me I talk like an American cowboy," Harold laughed. "A *csikós*, a horseman."

"Mr. Gibbon," Endre said directly to me, shaking his head at Harold, "wants me to tell him the end of the Austro-Hungarian Empire. *Finis Austriae.*"

"What?" I asked, startled.

Harold made a face. "I've known Endre here for nearly a year—a friend, I'd call him. We seek each other out for late-night romps to the wine cellars in the Buda hills. He thinks my idea of the coming war is faulty. But I need to quote him in my reports—in researching my unwritten book. He's a witness to the twilight of the gods. To tell you the truth, as a scion of the Zsolnay porcelain fortune down in Pécs, gold spilling out of his pockets"—he flicked his finger toward a smiling Endre—"drinks on him, of course, well, he understands the heart of the troubled economics of this land."

Endre shrugged. "Ah, yes, the *Götterdämmerung* so beloved of the decadent writers. My friend Harold Gibbon wants me to condemn our Emperor and King Franz Josef to oblivion."

Harold whispered loudly, "Endre is a proud Hungarian, a passionate Magyar. The moribund world of Vienna"—Harold pointed down the Danube—"is over, dead, weakened. Anemic. Franz Josef and his outdated army of horse regiments in an age of rat-a-tat machine guns. Lovely Budapest waits and waits for its moment in the sun. Remember that rebellion squashed in 1848. It's been one thousand years since Árpád crossed into this land. The Habsburgs stole the land from oppressive Turkey, and then *they* oppressed. Franz Ferdinand speaks of the Hungarians as traitors. The Austrian army orders its Hungarian recruits around—in German." Endre held up his hand but Harold rushed his words. "No, no, it is true, dear Endre Molnár. You know what I say about Vienna is true."

Endre looked embarrassed and lapsed into silence. Oblivious, Harold prattled on.

"Mr. Molnár," I began, "why do you put up with this impudent American?"

His eyes widened as he broke into a hearty laugh. "Are all Americans like my friend Harold?"

"Lord, no," said Winifred.

"Mr. Gibbon is a special breed," I noted, nodding my head at Harold, who was beaming. "Everyone's business is his own."

Endre smiled affectionately at Harold, shaking his head slowly. "But Americans—do they ask such…such personal questions?"

"Like what?" I asked.

Endre's deep-red color suggested he regretted what he'd just asked.

Harold blustered, "I was asking him about last night at the café—when he walked in and saw Cassandra Blaine sitting there."

Endre sucked in his cheeks, unhappy.

"Mr. Gibbon, please…" I said.

A waiter approached the table but Endre waved him away.

"Hey, just curious, no? I mean, Cassandra's behavior…" Harold shrugged his shoulders.

"She is a confused girl," Endre whispered. "I don't think…"

"She laughs too much, she cries a lot. She makes scenes in public. She teases you still, Endre. Last week, crossing paths with her and that…that hideous Mrs. Pelham, when you and I were having dinner in City Park, well, she…It's clear that she's thinking of you."

Endre looked serious, his voice dropping. "Dear Cassandra must marry Count Frederic."

Harold sat back. "Oh, I wonder about that. I see how she looks at you. Even last night."

Endre impatiently tapped an index finger on the table. "A woman must listen to her mother."

I interrupted. "Well, not always."

"Really, Edna," said Winifred, frowning.

"My mother is determined to keep me…unmarried."

Endre looked puzzled. "But why?"

"You haven't met my mother."

Immediately I regretted my remarks. An image of my long-suffering mother assailed me—probably at that moment discussing her errant daughter with the cousins in Berlin. I squirmed, uncomfortable.

Harold continued, "Hey, you forget that I watched the whole drama unfold. Cecelia Blaine frowned on you even *before* she decided she wanted her daughter to be a countess. Don't you remember how she shunned you last fall?"

Endre stood up, towering over us and said with an edge to his voice and a thin, forced smile, "We were talking about the end of the Austro-Hungarian Empire."

Harold wouldn't stop. "Hey, Count Frederic von Erhlich is a part of this sick empire. He's just as much a prig as his stiff cousin Franz Ferdinand, heir apparent to a corpse. A collector of instruments of torture, a man who seeks out palm readers for advice, a man who hates books."

Endre sighed and looked toward passersby on the quay. "It is not wise to talk ill of Franz Ferdinand."

Harold looked around him. "But all the Hungarians do—in whispers. Dual Monarchy, my foot. Slavery."

Endre took a step away from the table, his voice ragged. "Cassandra will marry Count Frederic and her mother will dance at court balls."

"Fat chance. Even Franz Ferdinand's wife Sophie ain't royal enough to be received before Franz Josef. Franz Ferdinand has to enter a room *alone*. The countess'll be at a ball but not in the palace—not with Cassandra, the American princess."

"That is because she is not..." He paused, a finger touching his moustache. "Never mind." He stepped away. "My friend Harold, again you invite me for coffee and I end up running away from you."

Winifred smirked, "Not an uncommon reaction to the man."

Endre Molnár bowed to the waist, formally, nodded at Winifred and me, winked mischievously at Harold, and left.

"Harold," I said, "must you alienate the people in whose country you're a guest?"

Harold grinned. "I understand Endre Molnár, my dear. Like other Hungarians, he is a radical at heart. He's waiting for the war. They wait for Franz Josef to die. No one yells, '*Éljen a király!* Long live the king!' unless ordered to do so. The fact that Cassandra will marry that fussy, pretentious Count Frederic— that pasteboard royal mask—only makes folks like Endre *more* radical. Sit with him late at night with a couple bottles of Bull's Blood wine from Eger, and he'll tell you his soul."

"I don't have time for such revelations," I said.

He snickered. "Well, I wasn't inviting you, my dear. Men have province where..." His voice trailed off.

"And so it goes," Winifred concluded.

But Harold ignored her. "I only got a few minutes before I gotta head to the telegraph office on Andrássy. The *New York Journal* needs my column."

I recalled meeting him at the 1912 Republican Convention in Chicago. He interviewed everyone, even me. "Edna Ferber just walked in...she's wearing pearls. 'Are those pearls real, Miss Ferber?' 'Yes,' she says. 'Of course, I paid $1.29 for them at Montgomery Ward...'" That paragraph followed by a revelatory quotation from Teddy Roosevelt about his newly formed Progressive Party. A satiric barb aimed at William Howard Taft. A smorgasbord of the sublime and the ridiculous.

So, perhaps, Harold Gibbon might be Hearst's most inventive reporter.

Preparing to depart, he couldn't resist a farcical account of his battles with the creaky dumbwaiter in his room on the second floor of the hotel. I'd already had my own battles with that contraption. In the ancient rooms everything worked...sporadically. Sometimes the telephone would—most times it didn't. "I called down to the kitchen for tea," Harold said, "and they send it up by the dumbwaiter. A bell rings. I open the door. The tea goes up half a floor, spills, the bell rings again, the tea comes back, most of it spilled."

"Well, I gave up," I admitted. "I feel I'm in a Gilbert and Sullivan operetta in this hotel."

He wasn't through. "I open the panel door and I hear someone in the kitchen complaining about me wanting tea so late at night. I hear Markov telling György he's an ass, just like everyone in Markov's wife's family, and he's not supposed to stare at the pretty girls with his tongue wagging out of his mouth. I missed most of it because it's a dialectical Hungarian or something, but György says he will marry a pretty girl someday and..."

"What is the point of this?" Winifred interrupted.

But I was laughing. "As I said, I gave up. I called down for coffee with whipped cream—ordered it in perfect German—and a strange voice says *'Ja ja ja, mein Herr'* and I scream, 'Herr?' and the voice says, *'Ja ja.'* I gave up. Then the bell rings and I open the door to find a tea biscuit on a tray. When I was first shown the room, the bellboy kept pointing at a garish painting of Franz Josef, eye level and out of place, the emperor an old balding man, and I kept saying, 'Thank you, thank you.' Finally, to show me, he unlatched the panel holding the painting and opened up the dumbwaiter."

Hurt, Winifred defended the hotel. "Franz Josef's redundant painting aside, the old rooms have...a coziness to them."

Harold grimaced. "When the war comes, those paintings of Franz Josef that seem to be in every room—mine shows him as a young man on horseback, which I believe he never was—will be gone. Burned in a pyre of celebration."

"And my cup of coffee will still be going to the wrong floor."

Harold waved his typed sheets at us. "I'm off. America awaits my words." He performed a little dance step, looking like a vaudevillian, and bowed.

Winifred grunted. "Edna," she said before he was out of earshot, "you find him amusing?"

"I'm afraid I do."

She shook her head. "A foolish man, and a dangerous one."

"Why do you say that?"

"He talks too freely with the Hungarians about Franz Josef, the Habsburg Empire, the war he expects. Franz Josef's agents are around. Spies everywhere."

"Are you serious?"

"The Austrians don't expect the Hungarians to be loyal to *their* empire. Yes, Queen Elisabeth loved Hungary, but an Italian anarchist killed her in 1898 in Geneva. Nowadays the Austrians hate the Magyars. Harold Gibbon, stoking the fire, is a trouble-maker. And someone could get hurt."

We lingered at the table, shaded under an umbrella as the heat of the day rose, and the tables filled up with folks. A young couple, giddy with each other, smiled over orange ice, the girl in a Capri blue dress, the boy in a suit with billowing trousers, a brass-studded belt, and glossy high boots. A man strolled by with a string of pretzels on a stick, calling out to passersby.

A lazy afternoon, my eyes half-shut.

"There." Winifred pointed. Nearby, debating whether to approach us, were the two young artists who were sketching in the café—and who shared with us that menacing caricature of Cecelia and Marcus Blaine.

Winifred, sitting up, waved them to our table. They hesitated, looked at each other suspiciously, and then walked over.

"What?" I asked Winifred. The invitation struck me as odd because Winifred turned away from men.

Winifred leaned into me. "The tall one—whatever his name—intrigues me with that drawing of those awful Blaines." She smiled broadly. "And I have a love of artists. Painters, well…" Her voice got foggy as she stared intently into my face. "Something you don't know about me, Edna." Then she confided, "In Paris Gertrude Stein showed me Picasso."

I had no idea what she was talking about—she'd mentioned a woman I'd never heard of. Modern art confused me, though I'd enjoyed the news accounts of last year's scandalous Armory Show in New York, with that scandalous *Nude Descending a Staircase* abstraction making clergymen across America sputter in their pulpits. Teddy Roosevelt, who wrote me gushing letters about my short stories, had condemned the invasion of decadent French art into America. I'd seen one painting by Picasso in a gallery window in New York, and it struck me as the work of a madman. Obviously Winifred Moss, my traveling companion, was a more complicated woman than the forceful, monomaniacal protestor for woman suffrage I'd come to know.

And, I soon learned, the two young Hungarian artists understood they'd encountered an advocate for their vision. Winifred, her voice animated, told us that her father had been an art historian at Cambridge, drummed out because of his passion for the new Impressionists. "Cézanne," she hummed. "My father met him."

Both artists were wide-eyed, staring at her.

The tall one introduced himself as Bertalan Pór, and I rehearsed the name in my head. He was a lithe, willowy man, dressed in a hard-pressed linen suit, a perfectly knotted purple bowtie. With his watery blue eyes and long bony face, a high forehead that exaggerated the sadness of those eyes, he struck me as patrician, an aristocrat in a way the brutish Count Frederic was not.

"I speak a schoolboy's English," Bertalan Pór admitted. "Learned in Paris, of all places."

But I found I could not take my eyes off his companion, introduced as Lajos Tihanyi, who could neither speak nor hear. "But," Pór added, "Lajos reads lips, understands German and some English, and will sputter sounds he believes are words he cannot hear. He *can* manage some words, though it seems his private dictionary." Then he sighed. "I need to warn you—he gets frustrated when he can't get across what he wants to say, and he…he gets moody, even angry. But just smile when he does that." He laughed and touched Tihanyi on the arm. "It's part of his charm."

Tihanyi, I noticed, was following the words closely, his eyes glued to his friend's lips, and he didn't look happy with him.

Bertalan Pór tapped a pad he'd extracted from a pocket, and said Lajos Tihanyi would jot down remarks. "In Hungarian or German, as you prefer."

Frankly, I preferred nothing at the moment, uncomfortable with the small man who stared at me with untoward attention, his head bobbing and his eyes amused. He was the one who wanted to paint me. Yes, me. Of course, I had little patience with that notion. In Bavaria Clara Ewald had executed a reasonable likeness—all my features positioned where God intended them to be. I would not be a part of any composition titled *Edna Ferber Descending a Staircase*.

Lajos Tihanyi had a disheveled look, his skinny body lost in a rumpled tan jacket, stained, with a thin scarf wrapped tight around his neck despite the day's sticky temperature. A jester's mobile face, with small squinty eyes and a slack mouth, a vaudeville comic up to no good—or looking to prank for fun. He reminded me of the old rollicking comedians of the New York Yiddish theater, all whoop-it-up guffaw and grotesque pantomime. Perhaps it was my own horrible bias. Poor Tihanyi grunted, gestured, rolled in his chair, at one point looking jealous of Winifred's attention to his friend. And yet, as I watched that sad-sack face, I discovered softness in his eyes, a faraway melancholy that utterly charmed me.

Winifred was talking rapidly in German, which I grew up speaking. She was looking at Tihanyi but speaking to Pór, curious about their work, asking about modern art in Budapest. I sat back, fascinated by her grasp of Parisian art movements. Both men had been part of a Hungarian group called The Eight, executing modern Expressionist works, Cubist art, heavily influenced by German and French avant-garde artists. A smattering of pioneer art had come to Budapest—Cézanne at the National Salon, Kandinsky and four Picassos shown at the Artists' Gallery. Kokoschko, Klimt. The names swept past me, a blur, meaningless. So somber had been my few days traveling with Winifred—the awful aftertaste of her agony in a London jail—that I marveled at her now—her vitality, her animation.

"Matisse," Bertalan Pór enunciated, reverently.

"Ah," said Winifred, as though saying *amen* at the end of a prayer.

Tihanyi's lips embraced the august name, though what I heard was a garbled blunt of language.

In 1907 Bertalan Pór had spent time at Gertrude Stein's apartment at Rue de Fleures 27, hobnobbing with Juan Gris, Picasso, and their followers. He'd learned English, he said, from Americans drinking in the cafés. And for a few months a nomadic Lajos Tihanyi had lived in the shadow of Matisse's home, though his being deaf and dumb limited his exchanges with the hardscrabble artists working and living at La Ruche. They'd returned to Budapest invigorated, banding with six other artists to exhibit at the Nemzeti Szalon. When Pór exhibited his paintings at the Könyves Kálmán Szalon, on the Váci, the Prime Minister Tisza publicly attacked his art, calling it degenerate, foul, unworthy.

Now he smiled at us. "The way to become famous is to have a politician condemn you."

Winifred was impatient. "You two are doing a book of sketches?"

Pór nodded.

"Why Café Europa?" I asked.

He smiled and glanced at his friend. "We are fascinated by the Americans. The busy reporters running around like wild birds."

"Like Harold?"

Again the hasty glance at Tihanyi who shrugged his shoulders, comprehending. "Americans have...let me say...Americans in Budapest...they swagger and they burst out and they...they are"—his accent got thicker, deeper—"the wonder of the New World."

I repeated, "Like Harold?"

"Harold the journalist is...is peculiar."

"Perceptive," Winifred noted wryly.

But Tihanyi nudged his friend and jotted something down on a strip of paper. Bertalan Pór grinned. "Like you, Miss Ferber." *Leek you Mees Fibber.* Swallowed, wonderful words. "Different, the look."

"Me?" I stammered.

"Lajos wants to paint you. In red."

"What?"

"He wants your face on canvas. You, in a red dress."

I smiled at Tihanyi. "Yes, the scarlet woman afoot in the Old World. Hawthorne would be pleased."

My remarks made no sense to the pair.

Winifred spoke up. "Your depiction of the Blaines was on target, Mr. Pór. You captured that rather stupid woman and that pompous man."

Pór rattled off a translation for his friend.

Tihanyi chuckled and pointed at his friend.

"Not all Americans are so...dreadful," I announced.

Tihanyi had been carrying an old leather satchel slung over his shoulder, cradling it in his lap when he sat down, and now clumsily extracted his sketchbook and flipped it open. The first drawing was startling—an unrecognizable figure, a slapdash jumble of blunt lines and chaotic swirls. I groaned—was this *Nude Descending a Staircase* all over again? But Tihanyi watched me closely, let out a gruff laugh and flipped the page. Staring intently into my face, he tapped a drawing. I was staring at Cassandra, her girlish beauty captured along with a hint of pouting in the puckered lips, meanness in her narrowed eyes. Hastily, eyes still on me, Tihanyi flipped the sheets, pointing, tapping another page showing a softer girl, one ready to cry. Another sketch—the secretive poet in the corner of the café, a man swathed in pastel scarves and arctic stares.

Bertalan Pór saw the question in my eyes. "István Nagy," he said. "Who hates us…and Americans."

"Why?"

"He is the darling of the art nouveau Austrian poetry of the last century. He writes pretty poetry about fragile girls with huge eyes lost in veils and garlands of flowers. We…how you say?…scare him…our new art…and Americans scare him. "He says the Americans will flood the Old World with their money disease. Franz Ferdinand, who has toured America, talked of the craziness of the Americans for the dollar bill."

"So this István sits in the Café Europa for *this* reason?"

"So he can write bad poetry about the loud Americans there." He laughed. "You can watch him…his lips…they curl…when an American yells at a waiter."

"Good Lord," Winifred said. She took the pad from the table and flipped back to the first drawing. "I like this."

"It's Lajos' self-portrait," he said.

Sharp, geometric lines, bug eyes, a crooked shoulder.

I kept my mouth shut.

Excited, Bertalan Pór suggested we accompany them to a gallery on nearby Váci Utca, where both had works on exhibit. Winifred was nodding up and down. Giving us no time to refuse, both men stood, and Winifred and I followed them out of the restaurant onto the quay.

On busy Váci Utca the aroma of coffee wafted from a café. A baker enticed us with warm Kaiser rolls displayed in wide wicker baskets. A grocer was hanging glossy strings of dried red paprikas and garlic from a clothesline. Nestled between a used book store with stalls spilling onto the street and a haberdashery advertising goods from Paris, the storefront art gallery was empty, dimly lit and musty. But as we walked in, someone snapped on an overhead light, and the narrow room was suddenly bright.

I blinked wildly because the walls were covered with canvases that startled. At least they startled *me*, a woman who favored the serene elegance of, say, John Singer Sargent. Elongated figures, garish misshapen heads, bulging eyes, splashes of vibrant color so bold they seemed blood-letting and barbaric, geometric angles passing for nudes, landscapes filtered through a drunken eye or a hashish-smoker's delirium.

Dazzled, Winifred and I hesitated in the doorway. This was a brave new world. Bertalan Pór, amused, nudged us in.

Winifred sucked in her breath, a smile on her face.

But our stillness was shattered by a lusty yell—Harold, out of breath, pushing behind us. "I saw you headed here and rushed…"

Winifred grumbled. "No one invited you, Mr. Gibbon."

He grinned. "But I'm expected everywhere."

Harold galloped past us, taking charge, and stood in the middle of the gallery, face to face with the young woman who'd switched on the lights. "What the hell is this? Someone's idea of a nightmare?" But he was laughing out loud. He swirled around, taking in the unorthodox paintings.

Lajos Tihanyi, puzzled by Harold's gesturing and strutting and the outburst in loud English, turned to Bertalan Pór for an explanation, but his friend looked to me.

Harold stamped his foot. "What in tarnation?"

Tihanyi's face tightened, a flash of anger in his eyes, a vein on his neck throbbing.

I smiled bravely. "Keep in mind that Mr. Gibbon is not an art critic. He knows little of culture. After all, he does work for William Randolph Hearst."

Bertalan Pór laughed and nodded at Tihanyi—a look that begged him to relax. Tihanyi breathed in. In careful, spaced-out English, Bertalan Pór said, "Then he is like most of Budapest— frightened of the new art, condemning this…new *vision*." He lingered on the last word, as if uncertain he used it correctly.

Stepping close to a huge canvas, Harold peered at a painting, which, I noted nervously, was signed by Tihanyi, and blurted out, "You know, before the coming of war there are always fireworks—flashes of anger and decay and smoke signals in the sky. The workers' protests. Breaking down the old guard. A slap in the face of tradition."

Harold, fingers tapping his chin, suddenly faced us. He pointed to Tihanyi's brilliant purples and reds. A portrait of a man whose wide-open eyes suggested astonishment at the world he found himself a part of. An emaciated man in what looked like a bolero hat, but the cubist angles reinforced the subject's smugness, his venality. "The end of the Habsburgs is *here*." He bowed to Tihanyi and Pór. "You, sirs, are the true revolution."

Bertalan Pór bit his tongue. "Yes, we are." Deadly serious.

Pór then enthusiastically showed us his work, an elaborate narration in a chaotic blend of Hungarian, German, English and, I swear, a trace of bungled French. He pointed to one painting— *The Sermon on the Mount*—that he said had been the subject of an attack on him a few years back. "A man cursed me in the street."

"A badge of honor, sir."

Pór bowed to Harold. Thank you. "*Köszönöm.*"

Harold's eyes popped. "Maybe *this* is what I should be writing about. The Hungarian artists who strike out at moribund Habsburg inertia with a paintbrush."

At that moment Winifred, gazing out the front window, started, and we followed her gaze. For a brief moment I caught the eye of the mysterious American from the Café Europa, that bearded man in the shadows, who sat with Zsuzsa Kos and János Szabó. The rich American from Boston—or so Harold suggested.

"Jonathan Wolf," Harold announced.

The man, peering in through the dusty windows, jerked back quickly, and disappeared.

"I'm being followed," Harold said, his voice unusually quiet. His head flicked back and forth nervously, and he bit a fingernail. "Yeah. There's a story there."

"But what?" I asked.

"I don't feel good about this. Not one bit." His eyes flashed with anger.

Chapter Five

The next morning, later than I'd planned, I entered the Café Europa to find Winifred already at a table, her hands circling a cup of black coffee. Markov, hovering nearby, signaled to one of the waiters who placed a cup in front of me, bowed, and asked in stilted English what else I wanted. I waved him off. Dark, bone-tingling coffee with frothy whipped cream, a concoction I'd become fond of and knew I'd demand in every American restaurant till the end of my days. I sipped the tangy brew, smacked my lips.

Winifred smiled. "The Hungarians call black coffee 'black soup.'"

"More like black mud."

Harold, sitting nearby at a table, had glanced up as I entered, nodding through narrowed eyes. He was scribbling on a pad, biting the end of a pencil with the dedication of a beaver on a log.

"So you've exiled dear Harold?" I smiled at Winifred.

She didn't smile back. "I didn't say a word, but my steely eye sent a message to the man."

"Sooner or later he'll be sitting with us."

"That's because he knows you favor him." She twisted her mouth. "Something I'll never understand."

"A character, I admit, but amusing in the way the family pet satisfies its owner."

She shook her head. "And I thought I'd mastered the cruel jibe."

I shrugged. "I meant my words to be kind."

"Edna, I travel with you because you don't suffer fools. You're a young woman, but somehow you've learned that lesson early on. It took me a lot of years to learn that—and time spent on a cold jail floor, held down by rapacious men."

"I'm so sorry." I shivered. "I can't imagine that."

She reached over to pat my wrist. "Don't feel sorry for me, Edna. Friendships fail when pity enters the picture."

Harold was sitting back now, arms folded against his chest, glaring at us, perhaps catching some of the conversation about him. Then, inspired, he scribbled furiously on his pad, then looked up to survey the quiet room. A few tables were occupied, one unfortunately burdened by the sour-looking poet, István Nagy. A snake-like man, dandyish in his fuchsia scarves and undulating *belle-époque* softness. Only his piercing eyes betrayed a petty character: hard, unforgiving. He caught me watching him and his face stiffened. Idly, I compared him with the two artists, Bertalan Pór and Lajos Tihanyi, who, despite their quirkiness and bizarre canvases, were welcome breaths of fresh air, vital young men in a hurry, racing to the horizon, spirited, robust.

Out of the blue, Harold announced to the room, "The topic of the day: the Serbian Question. My day, of course."

Winifred grumbled, "Madness in a young man is particularly alarming."

I addressed Harold. "What are you talking about?"

"The Austrian-Hungarian Empire doesn't know how to deal with little crazy Serbia, spreading venom, throwing stink bombs, assassinating aristocrats—as if that'll take care of things. Bosnia and Herzegovina be damned. Serbia, that Balkan powder keg, the streets filled with anarchists sailing merrily through the cobbled streets, looking for someone—sometimes I think anyone—to kill.

"I've been there—in Belgrade. Unlike the emperor who has no clue what is happening in his empire's far corners. Mud and pigs in the streets, ladies lifting their skirts to avoid the muck. King Peter Karageorgevich, a corrupt man, happy only in the brothels of Paris. Afraid of the Black Hand that put him in power. Young Bosnia—hungry for vengeance against the tyrant Austria. What to do if you're Austrian? *Alle Serben müssen sterben!* All Serbs must die."

Pleased with this insane oration, Harold stood and bowed, and somehow didn't look foolish doing so.

"Good Lord, Mr. Gibbon. Stop! So early in the day." I chuckled. "Politics is a bore this time of day."

"Politics pay my bills."

"But you talk of assassination and mayhem."

"A day of reckoning that's coming round the bend. Welcome to the Old World."

Too bombastic, his words sailing across the quiet café, doubtless his day's copy to be wired to Hearst. From his table István Nagy looked up from his desultory versifying, and grunted too loudly. An unhappy man.

Now, deliberately, Harold pointed at him. "The spy in the house of Magyar. The apologist for the cruel double-eagled monarchy."

Vladimir Markov, signaled by Harold, rushed to the table and placed a bottle of spring water on the table.

"Mr. Markov," Harold began, "a moment of your time."

Markov didn't look happy but moved closer and leaned in. "Of course." A thick English accent. *Ov corz.*

"You hear everything here, my good man. Perhaps you can shed some light on the question of the day. Franz Josef, when he's not dying and shunning Franz Ferdinand's unroyal wife Sophie, spends his days hating Serbia. What do you think?"

Flushed, Markov looked back to the kitchen door, as though seeking escape. He fumbled with a button on his black vest, and then checked to see whether his cravat was still knotted. For a moment he was silent. Then, stuttering, he answered, "I no discuss the empire."

Harold guffawed. "I love it. 'The empire.' That rumbling over-bloated entity, bursting with bile and pus and sewage, unhappy with the heir to the crown—aloof Franz Ferdinand, hidden away in his castle in Bohemia with that *hausfrau* no one likes. He hates Hungary, doesn't he? Good old Franz, tooling through Budapest in his Lohner-Porsche, scattering the chickens and calling the city a hotbed of dangerous men. And so the old Magyars despise him."

Markov flinched. "Sir, I am a foreigner living in this glorious city. A guest worker, I think you say." He slipped into German. "*Un arbeider.* A worker. Budapest is my home. Me and my wife who comes—flees—the mountains of Russia. The village there. A wonderful life here." He smiled uncomfortably. "Here—electric lights, the underground train. I love Budapest."

Harold flipped his hand. "Yeah, yeah, I get the message. We all love Budapest. That is, everyone but good old Franz Ferdinand. What happens to the Croats, Serbs, Bulgarians, Gypsies, Jews when he takes over for his uncle, who at this moment, I understand, is gasping for a final undeserved breath?"

Markov looked around him, locking eyes with István Nagy, who was listening closely. "Such talk is…dangerous, sir. I have a simple job…"

Harold looked at Winifred and me. "See? Everyone is afraid here. Everyone kisses your hand, bows like *you're* the king and queen, but first looks to see if you've got a bomb in the other hand." He roared at his own remarks.

Markov backed off, but not before catching István Nagy's eye. A low hiss escaped from the poet's throat. Finally, swiveling around so quickly he bumped a chair, Markov fled into the kitchen. Voices from inside: a woman's frantic voice, maybe his wife, quivering, questioning. Markov's own voice, laced with fear. The crash of glass dropped onto the tiled floor. A curse in Russian.

"You like to endanger that poor man's job?" I said to Harold.

He waved his hand in the air. "Really, Miss Ferber. I'm just doing my job."

"He has nothing to offer you."

"The man in the street—my take on things. The fact that he's scared to talk of how much everyone hates Franz Joseph is a topic unto itself. And so I report it." He stopped to jot something down, his face contorted with concentration. "The old pensioner sitting in City Park is a gold mine of juicy tidbits."

"A weasel," Winifred said too loudly.

"Someday you'll like me, Miss Moss."

"Not in the usual lifespan of any intelligent woman living in 1914."

An amused flick of his head as he tore off the page, crumpled it, and blithely tossed it to the edge of the table. A passing waiter deftly removed it, and bowed.

Winifred picked at a piece of the cherry strudel and twisted her chair so that her back was to Harold. "Our Soon-to-be-Countess Cassandra, that delightful young American, woke me up last night," Winifred began.

"Where?"

"You know that she and Mrs. Pelham, her dreadful duenna, have that suite of rooms at the end of my floor. Her mother and father are safely ensconced on the above floor, the entire floor. Their servants stomp a little too loudly late at night, by the way. Anyway, I was readying for bed, perhaps eleven last night, putting down my book, when I heard Cassandra passing my door. Despite Mrs. Pelham's pleading for quiet, Cassandra was retelling some joke someone had told her at supper. Laughing like a hyena, that girl, disturbing the quiet corridor."

"Well, she *is* spirited."

"I'd use a different word, dear Edna."

"Did you say anything?"

"No, of course not. With Mrs. Pelham grumbling—her rumbling was strangely more annoying than Cassandra's cackle—the two managed to enter their rooms without waking the entire floor."

At that moment Mrs. Pelham appeared in the doorway, one foot tapping angrily. She glanced behind her, impatient, and said something to a slow-moving Cassandra. Ever vigilant, Markov scurried to greet them, ushering the pair to the same table they'd occupied the day before.

Mrs. Pelham snapped her fingers, ordering tea for both, but Cassandra was shaking her head. "Nothing for me."

"Now, dear…"

An icy voice, cutting. "I *said* nothing for me."

Mrs. Pelham sat back, narrowed her eyes, and kept still. She addressed Markov, waiting by the table. "*Two* teas, sir. Acacia honey with tea." A long pause. "I have a spring cold."

Cassandra was dressed in a blue satin morning dress, her hair dressed in a pompadour with an abundance of ivory and silver hair combs. But there was something wrong with her face—yes, she'd powdered her cheeks, gently rouged her cheekbones, but unevenly, haphazardly.

Mrs. Pelham, drawing attention to her incomplete toilette, hinted that Cassandra had best return to her rooms—"Do I need to tell you again?"

Cassandra shrugged her shoulders and took in the room. The crowded café was staring, mesmerized by her entrance.

At that moment her eyes caught mine, and I saw curiosity there. She held eye contact with me. I didn't know how to interpret her startled look. There was irritation, yes, but hesitancy, fear, anger, a welter of flashing emotions the untutored girl entertained. Something was wrong. In that second I felt a jolt of electricity. It was as though she'd been given a secret she found baffling and was asking me for an answer. But that was impossible. Her lips trembled. My pulse quickened. What was going on here?

Winifred whispered, "Our spring daffodil is losing her petals."

Intrigued, Harold had put down his pencil, folded his arms across his chest, and blatantly stared at the young girl. He cleared his throat. "Ah, Miss…?"

I broke in. "Harold, no."

"What?"

"You're going to say something *I'll* regret."

He chuckled. "God, you're no fun, Miss Ferber."

"Allow someone her privacy."

"Then I'd be out of work."

"Maybe you should be," Winifred sniped.

He winked at me. "See? She's thawing already."

Winifred growled and stuck her fork into the cherry strudel. But at that moment the skittish György emerged from the kitchen with a tray, a pot of hot tea, cups, a basket of breads and biscuits. On his face that foolish country-bumpkin boy smile. He was nervous approaching the beautiful girl. His hands shook, and the teapot shifted. He began bowing before he approached her table, not the wisest behavior for a scattered young man toting a tray. Mrs. Pelham nodded at him as he placed it on a side table and lifted the teapot.

Cassandra cried, "I told you I *don't* want tea."

Mrs. Pelham breathed in. "I requested…"

"I don't care what you requested. Didn't you hear me say…"

The boy twitched, swung around, as though looking for Markov. He held the teapot in the air, suspended, hands shaking, uncertain what to do.

Mrs. Pelham tapped his arm emphatically. "Here, child."

György jumped as if slapped, and hot tea sloshed from the decanter, mostly onto the table and floor, but a few drops landed on Cassandra's sleeve. She screamed and threw out her arm.

The boy backed away.

Again, Mrs. Pelham touched his arm. "Leave it, young man. Do you hear me?"

Cassandra glared. "Speak English."

Unintelligible language seeped from his mouth—probably no language, this amalgam of Slavic, German, and English. The boy froze, his face crimson, his eyes blinking madly. I thought he might break down sobbing.

"This is unacceptable," I declared.

"Well, that'll end that boy's infantile infatuation," Winifred added.

Mrs. Pelham glanced our way. Harold frowned, tipping his chair so two of the legs were in the air.

Vladimir Markov rushed in from the kitchen. "What? What? *Was ist los?*" His glance took in the petrified boy and the by-now hysterical Cassandra who was waving her arm in the air as though it had caught fire.

"Him," she cried. "This...this child is allowed to dump boiling water on the guests. Is this how things are here?"

Mrs. Pelham reached out to stop her flow of words, but Cassandra pushed on. "I want him fired."

Markov said softly, "So sorry, dear madam. He is a boy. In training. My wife's..." He stopped. "My apologies, please." He swung around and gripped György's arm tightly. "Leave now." But György was stuck to the spot, though he'd begun swaying back and forth like an unstable toy. Finally Markov shoved him, smacking him across his skinny chest, and the boy grunted. Stunned, hurt, he walked away slowly, and my heart went out to him, an adolescent boy who found himself mired in muck. As the kitchen door slammed behind him, I heard a woman's voice, soothing, comforting, a run of Slavic words that ended in what sounded like a sob. The boy's or hers—I didn't know.

Infuriated, Harold stood up and addressed Cassandra. "Was that necessary?"

She drew in her lips, her eyes dark marbles. "How dare you? You gossipmonger."

Harold glanced toward the kitchen. "He's a boy."

"He's a servant."

Mrs. Pelham bristled. "Cassandra, my dear..."

"Enough," the girl snarled. "Drink your spilled tea and leave me alone."

The room drifted into silence, heavy and uncomfortable, broken by Cassandra. "I cannot sleep in this country. I want to go home."

Ms. Pelham ignored her.

Cassandra began to sob quietly.

Vladimir Markov was at a loss how to handle the woman, fidgeting, shifting his feet, watching her from across the room. Finally, with a shrug, he addressed Harold. "Sir, I told my wife her family should stay goat herders in the mountains. The goats...they do not care what you say to them."

The preposterous lines enlivened Harold, who whooped and banged on the table.

Suddenly Cassandra stood up and pointed out onto the terrace. Everyone near her followed the gesture. Zsuzsa Kós was standing by an iron grill near the garden in conversation with another woman, both in flowery summer dresses. Zsuzsa wore a monstrous hat with ostrich feathers and paradise aigrettes, something that may have looked natural in one of her old musical reviews but now seemed tawdry, best left in an attic trunk.

"You," Cassandra yelled. "You."

Zsuzsa didn't realize she was being addressed until her companion, probably sensing every eye in the café riveted on the pair, nudged Zsuzsa.

Cassandra ignored pleas from Mrs. Pelham and headed toward the terrace. "You! You betrayed me. You made believe you were my friend. The afternoons in City Park. The picnics on Margaret Island. Suppers at the Green Band. And then you sold me out for a few pennies."

Zsuzsa walked toward the opening but stopped, uncertain. "Cassandra, you foolish child." She spoke in German, harsh, bitter. "Leave me alone." Her friend pulled at her sleeve, but Zsuzsa shook her off.

Cassandra talked back at the tables in the café. "Everyone talks German. Whatever happened to English?"

Then Cassandra rushed at the older woman and slapped Zsuzsa in the face. It sounded like gunfire. Or the crack of thunder.

A horrible moment, raw, cruel, ugly. Cassandra faltered, overwhelmed by her own fury, opening her mouth to speak. Nothing came out. Rubbing her hand against her face, Zsuzsa let out a trapped animal's gravelly howl—I swear we all trembled—and then disappeared onto the quay. Her companion stood flabbergasted. Cassandra, penitent, waved sloppily at all of us, and then retreated to her table where she hung her head and sobbed.

I was surprised to see that Mrs. Pelham wore a tight-lipped, satisfied look that translated—*See, all of you. The American brat. See how my labors are rewarded. See what I have to deal with. Madness all around me.*

Cassandra looked up and caught me looking at her. I shook my head slowly as I tried to convey—what? My concern, my *worry* about her. No mother to guide her, as they used to say in Victorian novels. And I thought of my own mother demanding that I obey, stay at her side, comfort her. I grew dizzy.

For a second Cassandra shut her eyes, as if debating something. Then, startling her chaperone, she jumped up and mumbled something about leaving. "Have to. Have to. This place…"

She headed toward the terrace but staggered, as though drunk, one hand grasping a chair rail. She swung around and headed toward the door into the hotel lobby. She stopped, her right hand fluttering in the air, finally touching one of the gaudy hairpins. It slipped out and fell to the floor. She ignored it. Then, nearing my table, she toppled into an empty chair next to me.

Winifred gasped, but I remained calm. I had become part of the drama in the old café, but I didn't know what that meant.

"You," the girl got out. "The American writer. You write those short stories in the magazines. I've read…" She glanced at Winifred, but then turned her body so that she was facing me, leaning in confidentially. Close up, behind the sloppily applied powder and rouge, I saw a pale face, blotchy and streaked.

"What?"

"You. You watch me. You look at me as if I'm…" She stopped, at a loss for words. "Like I'm hurting. You see that. Your eyes. You are…"

"Edna Ferber, my dear."

She swung her head back and forth. "I know—I read a story…You…I need to talk to an American. I need someone who doesn't *know* me…I need to ask you…"

I touched her hand, resting on the table. "Of course."

"People say I'm a fool, but I'm not, really. You think I don't hear them talking here? A spoiled girl, just an empty…shell. But"—she glanced around the room, so many eyes on her—"I can't understand this world here, these people, these…My mother tells me…I can't make sense of things. I missed something. Maybe not. I don't know. I don't understand what Count Frederic says to me...his English is so bad...now Endre he..."

"Please," I began, but she held up her hand.

"I...My German is so bad. My French...my Hungarian is ten words maybe...I just want to hear *everything* in English. Is that so bad? I don't understand things any more..." She mustered a gaze so intense I jerked back my head. "How do I know what's happening to me?"

She broke down, sobbing into a sleeve.

Mrs. Pelham had been standing next to the table, rumbling like a stockyard bull. In the most emphatic English accent I'd ever heard, she swelled up and roared, "Stuff and nonsense, young lady." She pulled Cassandra's sleeve and hissed through clenched teeth. "Your mother will be horrified at this...this display of hysterics."

Cassandra allowed herself to be pulled out of the chair. As she was led to the doorway, she glanced back before disappearing into the hallway.

"My Lord." Winifred was bothered. "What was that all about?"

I was silent for a minute. "Something has happened to her."

"But what?"

"A spoiled, indulged young girl has suddenly looked into a mirror and doesn't like what she sees."

"She's just another vain, dreadful rich girl."

I shook my head emphatically. "Oh no. I don't think so, dear Winifred. This time she saw darkness that scared her."

"Her soul?" Winifred added, a remark that I didn't expect from her.

"No." I struggled with the words. "Darkness coming at her."

Winifred and I were two genial travel companions who'd come to Budapest to see the sights, but now, shaken, we sat wordless in that old café.

Our silence was broken by a loud voice. In a strained, phlegmatic voice, thick with bile, the poet István Nagy, his fingers idly twirling the fuchsia scarf that circled his neck, told the room in accented English, "Ah, the Americans. They continue to think that they discovered the Old World. We are their play toy to do with as they see fit."

Chapter Six

Late that afternoon Winifred and I returned from sightseeing at
St. Matthias Church in the Buda hills to find gifts waiting for us.
Bertalan Pór had delivered two exquisite drawings—simple but
delightful renderings of the Chain Bridge at the foot of Castle
Hill. Not realistic depictions, for the bright colored pencil strokes
exaggerated, but the opposite: a nighttime landscape captured
through the prism of hot fever. Arc lights threw ghostly auras
over the steel girders.

Winifred gushed her appreciation, muttered about Matisse's
reinvention of color and the wild beasts that were defining the
world of art. I simply appreciated the gesture, though I doubted
I'd display the drawing prominently back in helter-skelter Chicago.

A note accompanying the drawings invited the two of us
to join both men at five for coffee and pastry at the celebrated
Gerbeaud's confectionary on Vörösmarty tér. Written in formal,
respectful German, addressing us with the proper distance and
etiquette, the note seemed a royal writ, so careful the penman-
ship, signed first by Bertalan Pór and then by Lajos Tihanyi.

"Of course we will," Winifred told me.

"Isn't such an invitation a little awkward?" I asked. "I mean,
two men we scarcely know. Unmarried women in Budapest do
not go out unchaperoned with strange men."

Winifred pointed to the drawings. "Of course we know them,
Edna. And, yes, thankfully, they *are* strange men—otherwise
I'd shun them."

That made little sense, but I smiled. The confections at Gerbeaud's patisserie were legendary according to my Baedeker guide. I dressed in a navy blue Eton suit and a soft hat with a single rose pinned to the front. At five o'clock, promptly, Winifred and I strolled through two squares, past the Váci Utca, entered the eatery and were greeted in English by an effusive hostess.

"I thought we blended in," Winifred said. "I'm trying to look Hungarian."

I laughed. "It's the shoes, they tell me."

"Mine are cracked and worn at the heel."

"Exactly."

Gerbeaud's thrived on its Old World ambience. Mottled marble-topped tables surrounded by dark red velvet-covered chairs. Gold-gilt woodwork, gleaming chandeliers, a long glass-fronted counter with a mouth-watering display of frosted cakes and tortes. The aroma was intoxicating, the rich chocolate and vanilla cream puffs, the baked pastry, the steaming coffee drinks with whipped cream fizzed on top, the whiff of coffee ice cream served in deep, slender glasses. Waiters sailed by us with trays covered in tempting treats. A crystal bowl held mounds of chocolate truffles wrapped in silver. Tables were pushed close to one another, the heat of the day making the air thick. At the back of the room, a chamber orchestra played waltzes, but quietly, as if from a gramophone hidden in a distant room.

Although I was absorbed in the utter sweetness of the room, Winifred was telling me that the Hungarian artists were already at a table, both standing, with Bertalan Pór waving and at his side Lajos Tihanyi, a grin on his face, his hand raised in the air. Two genteel souls—nothing like the shrimp seated with them. A man who remained seated, though his hands fluttered in the air like manic birds of prey. Harold Gibbon, always the unwanted guest.

We joined them, enduring the classic kissing of the hand, the bowing, the stylized European civility long disappeared from America. I was starting to enjoy its ritual, though a part of me craved down-home Chicago brashness and swagger, folks bumping you on Michigan Avenue without so much as a how-de-do.

"Harold, you surprise me," I said to him.

He snickered. "I wasn't following you."

"No," Bertalan Pór said resignedly, "he was following us."

Lajos Tihanyi attempted some incoherent sentence, looked frustrated, and then scribbled in Hungarian on the small notebook he obviously always had at his disposal. Bertalan Pór took the torn slip from him and smiled. "My friend insists that Mr. Gibbon has a coterie of spies relaying the whereabouts of anyone he wants to visit."

Tihanyi guffawed. In his rumpled light tan summer suit with the oversized brown buttons and the white linen shirt, a size too large, he appeared a boy jester. But perhaps I was being unfair: Tihanyi, despite those intense but droopy eyes, so direct and deep under arched brows, had been born with the gargoyle face so that he'd always appear the buffoon. But no simpleton, he—truly the man defied his appearance. Those eyes told you he was seeing everything, analyzing, digesting, loving, celebrating. Nothing got past the man whose penetrating stare read someone's character in a heartbeat. It was easy to miss his intensity.

Bertalan Pór was dressed smartly in a Norfolk gray flannel jacket buttoned up to the neck. With his regal good looks and tiny Ben Franklin spectacles, he could also be dismissed as a Beau Brummell playboy, some wrecker of a fickle young girl's heart. But he, too, I realized, possessed fire in the gut.

And then there was small ferret-like Harold, head bobbing like a baby bird in a nest, happy to be noticed.

"I do have spies," Harold insisted. "You are all my spies. I watch all of you, and I'll learn the secret."

"What secret?" Winifred wasn't happy that Harold had intruded on this little visit. Since meeting the two artists, she'd brightened—and I was thrilled. Perhaps her horrors of London could be forgotten, at least for now. Her escape, I realized, was to lose herself in the echoey halls of an art museum. I knew she wanted to talk Art, capital A, hungry to discuss Gertrude Stein and Matisse and Expressionists…and nightmarish abstractions cavalierly plastered onto canvas. Selfishly, I was relieved to see the pesky reporter because he would save the afternoon from the all-consuming specter of Pablo Picasso.

Bertalan Pór ordered for all of us, and I marveled at the smooth, lyrical Magyar language. It seemed a gentle hiccough, the rhythmic emphasis of words like a ripple on still waters that drew you along. Words piled on—attached—willy nilly, it seemed, until you lost your breath. Impossible to learn, I'd been told, but I wondered. My German, fluent since a child, paled beside it. The Magyar tongue was the language of a Gypsy camp, the fierce horsemen gathered around a fire on the plains, the wild dancing of the *czárdás*, earthenware jugs of water, the violinist on the street corner…or had I simply appropriated such romantic imagery from the pages of my Baedeker and my sentimental imagination? No matter. That was why I'd come to Budapest—to sit in this splendid, expensive café and imagine myself in a lyrical Léhar operetta.

"What do you think of Café Europa?" Bertalan Pór asked us, speaking in stilted English.

"They like it," Harold answered for us, speaking in German.

"I can speak for myself," I said sternly. I deliberated. "It has the hominess of an old coat."

"Meaning?" The artist looked puzzled, but Lajos Tihanyi had read my lips, and scribbled on a pad. "She means," his friend read to us, "that you always know when you put it on how it will fit. And where the seams are giving out."

I laughed. "Exactly. It's the place Americans go to hear others talking American."

Harold added, "And to watch the Americans make fools of themselves."

"Cassandra?" Winifred asked.

"Not only her." Harold went on. "Even the British"—he glared at London-born Winifred—"speak more pompously to show the Americans how English is supposed to sound. The King's English."

"That's why there are folks like Mrs. Pelham in the world," I said. "The angrier she gets with her recalcitrant charge, the more British she becomes."

"Cassandra shames us all," Winifred remarked.

I took some issue with that. "She does like her hair-raising scenes in public places. But something else is going on, I'm afraid. Yes, she's a spoiled American brat—very much as that judgmental poet"—I hesitated and Bertalan Pór grumbled "István Nagy"—"so rudely proclaimed, a girl born to wealth but also to loneliness. An only child, sold like a carpet in the marketplace to the highest bidder. What we're seeing in the café is a young woman who doesn't know how to handle the world she is tossed into."

Winifred fretted. "She could say no."

I shook my head. "She doesn't have the vocabulary to say no. What she has is frustration and sobbing and hysteria and acting bratty…annoying those around her. A dutiful daughter who suddenly fears her parents. And probably the count. But I tell you—when I caught her eye this morning, I spotted something else there. Yesterday she was vain and silly. Today she was vain and silly, but now she's also frightened. That is one scared child."

Harold added, "You see things that no one else sees. Yet it doesn't help that she had this wild love affair with the dashing Endre, some cowboy hero out of a melodrama who swept her off her feet and took her horseback riding through fields of sunflowers at sunset. That's hard to leave behind for a stiff-backed aristocrat from a crumbling regime."

Winifred opened her eyes wide. "My, my, Mr. Gibbon. Once again—twice now—I do believe we're seeing a romantic under that lizard skin."

He frowned at her.

I raised my voice. "I insist Cassandra is a victim here."

Tihanyi had trouble following my impassioned speech, but he was nodding furiously, perhaps catching some of it. He spoke a garbled sentence that left his friend puzzled. Quickly he jotted something down on his pad and handed it to Bertalan Pór. His friend contemplated it but seemed hesitant about his translation.

"What?" I demanded, smiling. "Is your friend taking issue with me?"

He laughed. "To the contrary, Miss Ferber. He says this... this spirit in your face confirms his desire to paint you. In red."

"Stop. Really. A painting of me?"

"He insists your...passion demands it."

"He'll have me fragmented, one eye elevated above the other, my one hand in the air holding a hyacinth and the other in... in a buckled shoe."

Tihanyi obviously caught the tenor of my remarks because he laughed. He struggled to utter something, but I caught none of it. This poor deaf and dumb soul—no, I stopped myself. Not poor. Lamentable, really. For, in truth, here was a man who accommodated what he lacked with a grace and a power that overwhelmed.

His friend caught me watching Tihanyi's moving lips. "My friend lost his hearing and speech when he was eleven. Meningitis, I think you call it. He always drew, largely self-taught, and his father, a wonderful man, asked me, five years older than the boy, to tutor him. I'd been wandering in the cafés, selling my drawings to make money. I gave him Nietzsche to read." He winked. "Subversive. We both come from old Jewish families in the city. But his father fears his son will become Catholic—to convert. It's common among artists here."

He glanced at his friend. "And today we are the artists that so many in Budapest despise. The avant-garde. In 1910 an exhibition in Berlin was mocked and censured. Abused. Lajos' daring depiction of wrestlers—figures unlike any other on canvas—was seen as the end of life as we know it."

Tihanyi scribbled on his pad. Bertalan Pór read to us: "He says that was how we knew we were a success. The critics damned us."

Winifred was delighted by the conversation. "Freedom of the artist suggests freedom for the masses. Finally, for women. In England I founded the Artists' Suffrage League in 1907. Last year I was in Budapest at the International Woman's Suffrage Alliance Congress."

Bertalan was nodding. "Yes, suffrage for all." He pointed at Lajos. "We are members of the National Reform Club, dedicated to universal suffrage."

Winifred's mouth fell open. "Yes, I know them, I…"

She stopped because Harold groaned out loud. He had been following the conversation, but looked unhappy. Finally, he withdrew his pad from a vest pocket and jotted down some notes.

"Are we being immortalized?" I asked him.

"I was just reminded of something. Nothing to do with this… this art. I'm thinking of something Franz Ferdinand said to his friend, Kaiser Wilhelm. About the bond of the Aryan races."

"Not now," Winifred insisted, her voice hard. "We're having coffee and delicious pastry."

"There is only one topic in this part of the world. The Austro-Hungarian Empire and the Serbian Question. The anger of the Serbs. The Black Hand. Terrorists…"

I groaned. "For Lord's sake, Harold, a respite, please. Your book will wait. Your boss Hearst will dream up another war— let's say in Mexico. Sip your coffee. Listen to the music. Try the coffee ice cream with whipped cream. It's singular…"

A bell sounded. Conversation ceased.

Everything in the café stopped. Total silence. Even the waiters stopped moving and put down their trays. Two red-faced boys in Fauntleroy suits rushed to lay out a red carpet in the entrance, straightening the edges and then backing away out of sight. One solitary last tinkle of a spoon against the side of a cup. Then silence. Suddenly everyone stood up, at attention. The two artists nodded at us, compelling us to rise. So I stood there, a little foolish, anticipating some oom-pah-pah band to break into a brassy rendition of the national Austrian anthem, if such a patriotic song existed.

But quiet, eerie, certainly uncomfortable.

Though no trumpets blared, the effect of a royal entrance was evident. Harold quietly whispered that the Countess Carolina, mother of Count Frederic, had arrived in a carriage. Accompanying her was a bewhiskered old gentleman in a starched black cutaway suit, striped trousers, and a black vest. A carnation in his buttonhole. A military sash over his chest. A derby on his head. The imperious woman paused at the threshold, surveyed the room of standing subjects, and then walked to a table at the back, partitioned off from the rest of the hoi polloi. She wore an elaborate crepe de chine dress trimmed with sable. The crowd sat down, though the silence persisted for a moment. The countess, sitting with her back to the room, was immediately waited on, bowed to, whispered to, hummed to—a circle of waiters colliding like sun-drenched houseflies. The orchestra resumed playing.

A tiny woman, though broad like her son, the countess wore a preposterous hat of streaming ribbons and festoons and cockamamie feathers and doohickeys galore, a menagerie of sensation atop a head of spit curls the color of rust. She sat in a velvet chair—almost painfully, it seemed, an iron-stiff posture, hands dropped into her lap, head staring across the table at the crusty old gentleman who was doing all the talking, though he did manage to light a pipe. The smell wafted across the room.

Never one to be interested in the trappings of aristocracy—I always saw myself as a small-town working-class girl who wrote about working-class folks in the American heartland, the children of the American Republic—I was intrigued by this ritual of the old regime, flabbergasted, in fact, that a body of people would rise for a second-rate countess simply because she was a countess. And one whose husband embezzled funds that necessitated he kill himself. A scandal, so I'd heard. Even Bertalan Pór and Lajos Tihanyi, revolutionary artists whose mission it was to crack that nineteenth-century veneer of stale respectability—their paintings fresh assaults on representational art and life—stood out of respect.

But what followed immediately was disturbing. Within minutes, Cecelia and Marcus Blaine entered the room, followed at a distance by Cassandra and her chaperone, Mrs. Pelham. Obviously, protocol demanded that the countess not be seen entering with the American riffraff, moneyed though they were—and salvation for the impoverished household of that very countess and her retinue. Mr. and Mrs. Blaine were bedecked in formal toggery, she with diamonds and emeralds, in a crimson gown that matched the carpet on which the countess had just walked, and an ermine cape despite the day's heat. Her husband checked his gold watch fob self-consciously and fiddled with a top hat similar to one Woodrow Wilson sported at a convention. They tried to walk with a debonair air, as though to the manor born. It didn't work, quite. Instead, the two Americans looked like overfed burghers going to a potluck dinner at the grange hall— admittedly the pretentious, wealthy shopkeepers of the village, but drab folks, nonetheless.

Cassandra trailed after like the family pet, her guardian close by, her head leaning into the girl's neck. Surveying the room, Cassandra spotted our table. Surprised, she paused, ready to say something to us as she walked by.

But Mrs. Pelham, pressing forward, bumped into the girl's back, and uttered a distasteful grunt. "Move, child," she ordered.

Everyone looked unhappy. The countess, the old anony-mous man, the mother and father, Cassandra, Mrs. Pelham, all performing for someone not there. An obligatory afternoon at Gerbeaud's, lolling on the red plush seats, the old gentleman and Marcus smoking cigars, an afternoon perhaps calculated by the countess to show the power her title still held among the peons assembled for whipped cream and coffee ice cream. Let the rich Americans know what *they* were gaining in this dread-ful marriage.

Harold spoke too loudly. "A marriage made in hell."

"Harold, manners, please," I said.

He grinned. "Imagine Christmas Day at the palace. The countess on a throne and the Americans bringing frankincense and myrrh."

Winifred added, "Cassandra hiding in the water closet, weeping."

"Dreaming of Endre and those eyes of his," I added.

Harold grumbled, "Count Frederic has two eyes, too."

"Yes," I said, "but some men have...*eyes.*"

Winifred nodded.

Bertalan Pór cleared his throat and invited all of us—his glance even took in Harold, who he assumed was the obligatory American at any occasion—to his studio at our convenience. Tihanyi tapped his friend on the arm, and Pór added that Tihanyi would also like us to visit his studio.

"He lives nearby, at 12 Drava Street. A stone's throw."

Then, to my discomfort, Tihanyi pointed a bony finger that had some dried green paint at the knuckle, a scamp's smile on his face, and indicated with an elaborate movement of his arm that he wanted to paint me. He mimed a canvas and easel and... me, sitting still.

"In red," Bertalan Pór added, smiling. "He sees you in red."

A stir in the room as the countess, seated for a matter of minutes, perhaps changing her mind as royalty is wont to do, suddenly rose and headed out of the restaurant with the old gentleman. With scarcely any notice, the packed crowd stumbled to its feet, spoons dropped, napkins slipping to the floor, elbows banged, chairs dragged, so precipitous the woman's departure. Doubtless it surprised the Blaines because they also struggled to stand, perplexed looks on their faces, the husband whispering something to his wife, and, waiting until the countess was out of sight, began the march to the exit. It all seemed too awkward and unnecessary, capricious, especially the pandemonium it created in the café.

Cecelia Blaine looked back over her shoulder. "Cassandra, let's go."

But the young girl shook her head back and forth, her mouth set in a grim, petulant line. "I'll finish my coffee. After all, isn't that why we came here—to perform?"

Her mother stepped back but looked toward the front entrance. Of course, the countess was nowhere in sight. She seethed. "Right now. Do you hear me?"

"No."

"Now."

"I'll be back home in a bit."

"Don't talk to anyone, please."

Suddenly conscious of the customers gaping at her, Mrs. Blaine shuddered, appalled that the world would treat her so, and stormed out the front door, tugging at the sleeve of her befuddled husband. Triumphant, Cassandra sat back, though Mrs. Pelham was making a cacophony of short, jerky animal noises. An unhappy soul, that hired pasha.

Cassandra obviously had other plans. She took a sip of coffee, then slid the cup away and stood up. Mrs. Pelham smiled, as though her pesky pleas had brought about a change of heart in the young girl. Cassandra pushed back her chair, deliberated, and then turned to Mrs. Pelham. "Sit down. I have something I have to do."

Confused, the old woman sat back down, reaching for an enormous lace handkerchief to dab at the sweat on her brow. She stared, helpless and furious, at the back wall.

The young girl moved quickly toward our table and stood too close to me, watching. Her face was trembling, and her cheeks were moist with perspiration. With the back of her hand she dragged sweat from her face and then wiped the hand on her lovely tea gown. I was reminded of the rough-and-tumble lumberjacks in the back woods of northern Minnesota, where I'd once visited as a reporter. I'd watched one grizzled old axe man perform that very gesture, though his hand rubbed his denim overalls and not an expensive frock. I loved it, truly. But Cassandra, trying to smile but grimacing, leaned into me. "We meet again."

"Miss Blaine," I said quietly.

Cassandra eyed the others at my table, Winifred, Harold, and the Hungarian artists. No one said a word, focused on the hapless girl. "A moment of your time." The young girl waited a second, breathing hard. "Please."

"Please sit, my dear."

She slid into a chair, but turned it so that she faced me, her back to the others. Her head was a foot from my face, her dull eyes blinking madly. She whispered, though I'm certain everyone at the table could clearly hear her, especially Harold, giddy with the moment, who had leaned so far forward I feared he'd rest his bony head on her trembling shoulders. Winifred, cross, narrowed her eyes but sat back, arms folded over her chest. The two artists were baffled at the bizarre moment, and Lajos Tihanyi made a gasping noise. His face crimson, he looked angry, as though an interloper had disturbed his precious moment. Bertalan Pór put a restraining hand on Tihanyi's forearm. A crooked smile on his face. Its message was apparent: calm, calm.

I suspected Lajos Tihanyi was a man with violent spurts of fury, perhaps irrational and sudden. Flash floods of panic, always that lively and creative eleven-year-old boy, suddenly ailing. Bedridden, fed nostrums that did nothing, finally waking up deaf and dumb, a lad ready to strike out at a world he didn't understand. Probably a life in which chronic pain leveled him. Such juvenile bluster warred with his artistic temperament and innate intelligence—or maybe it fed into that creative juice.

"What?" I whispered to Cassandra.

"When you looked at me earlier, well, your eyes told me you understood…I don't know what but…Everyone else pities me or laughs at me and manipulates me or uses me or…You know…"

I began, "Cassandra, I *don't* know."

"Wait," she broke in. "I gotta talk to someone and there is no one else. The servants run from me." She looked back at Mrs. Pelham. "*She* tells my mother everything. She's a horrid woman who hates me more each day. She *pinches* me when no one is looking, and no one believes me. A tattletale, that woman. The British don't believe in secrets, I've been told."

From behind her Winifred raised her eyebrows, a slight smile appearing.

"But we can't talk here. I need…I'm lost, Miss Ferber. I read one of your stories in a magazine…like *Everybody's*, I think, about a lonely girl, a homely heroine you called her. You *liked* that girl. That girl, I felt, was me. And so…I'm lost. Help me."

I didn't know what to say. "But how can I help?"

Suddenly her voice became small, tinny. "I heard something. A secret. But maybe I didn't hear it. Maybe I was wrong. Shall I tell someone? You hear things in the hallways even if you don't want to listen. What to do? I speak such bad German. Or Hungarian. I don't know. Words and words and words...a mishmash. Help me. "

Fear gripped me. "Are you in danger?"

She didn't answer for a heartbeat. "Someone is always watching me."

From behind her Harold interrupted. "Tell us."

I fumed and shot him a nasty look.

Perplexed by Harold's interruption, Cassandra blurted out, "That man."

"What man?" I reached over and rested my palm on her hand. Her flesh was hot to the touch.

"He's always in my hallway, then disappears. That Jonathan. I asked about his name. I pointed him out."

"Jonathan Wolf," Harold said.

"What does he want from me?"

"Well, I've noticed him slinking about. True, but..."

Mrs. Pelham had stood, plodded over, and placed a hand on Cassandra's shoulder. "We must leave." She breathed in. "Now."

Bertalan Pór's eyes got wide, alarmed.

Cassandra stood up. She smiled thinly at Bertalan Pór and Lajos Tihanyi. A slight wave of the hand to them, and they mimicked her gesture. Both men instinctively stood up, ready to bow. I hoped they wouldn't reach for her hand, but she backed away.

"I'm afraid of everyone," Cassandra said. She looked at the two artists. "I don't know who to trust." Her voice rose, broke. "I'm afraid of people. The Hungarians."

She looked at Winifred, as though seeing her for the first time. "I don't know you."

"Cassandra, this is..."

Impatient, she interrupted, her voice hollow yet wistful. "I used to talk to Endre. You know, he listened with those eyes staring at me." Her own eyes got misty, cloudy. "He has those eyes that...invite you to *talk* to him. He talked to me in that quiet thick English he always uses. He understood things. He *listened*. Men don't listen to girls, but he did. Who'll take me seriously now? Everybody runs from me. You, Miss Ferber. Should I trust you?" Her thoughts tangled as she stared around the room. "Endre did...but I betrayed him. And he got angry with me. You could see it in his eyes. Dark, pessimistic, a voice that scared me. The Hungarians are sad...they cry...Even the men cry. He wanted to...to hate me. That scared me. So handsome, my Endre, but his look was...barbaric. American boys blush, stammer." Then she laughed. "Hungarian men are so beautiful, but they all believe you have to fall in love with them. They're foolish that way. When you do, they're like little happy boys. When you leave them, they become cold and dark. I don't know..." She breathed in, stopped. "I'm talking too much."

Shrugging her shoulders, she turned away and allowed Mrs. Pelham to push her out the door.

I called after her. "Cassandra, talk to me later."

She stopped moving and threw back her head, letting out that laughter I heard her use in the Café Europa yesterday. "Oh, Miss Ferber, Maybe it's too late. I'm always a day late with my wisdom."

Chapter Seven

"I'm worried." I looked into Winifred's face.

"Edna, you look ready to cry."

I closed my eyes.

We were walking back through the lobby to our rooms. I needed to dress for the evening: a concert of Béla Bartok's new composition, recommended by Bertalan Pór who knew the revolutionary composer, at the Royal Opera House, followed by dinner at Gundel's in City Park. A late-night stroll across the Chain Bridge to watch a fireworks display upriver, and then a good night's sleep. I'd laid out my pale blue silk embroidered jacket, the lovely black onyx shawl I'd appropriated from my mother, and a gray silk dress of lacy bodice and wraparound gauze. Very Parisian, I thought, very high fashion.

But Winifred's comments stopped me cold. Cry? Why would I? But of course I knew the reason.

"I'm bothered by Cassandra."

"It's got nothing to do with you, Edna." Winifred looked straight into my face.

"Of course it has. Think, Winifred. I…well…that scene at Gerbeaud's…the way she approached me…her reaching out to me. Something is wrong." I stressed my words. "She *told* me."

"She's a melodramatic young girl, used to attention."

"No, Winifred, I'm sorry—when she looked into my eyes earlier, she *told* me something."

Winifred smiled. "Don't become a patsy, dear Edna. Isn't it bad enough women are dismissed by a cold world? Would you have one of our own gender manipulate you?"

That rankled. "People don't use me, Winifred."

"Everyone uses everyone. That's the awful grease that propels civilization."

I hesitated. "This is different."

She had no interest in continuing the conversation. Purposely she strode ahead of me, stopping at the reception desk to ask for her mail. I headed toward the stairs. The elevator was an untrustworthy contraption like most inconveniences in this hotel, and I chose not to risk my life in that noisy, jerky box. Like the dumbwaiter, it would sail past your floor, stop at some midpoint, and the frightened occupant would pound on the door like a delirious patient in Bedlam.

Winifred, the intrepid explorer, trusted that she would have a smooth, uneventful ride. I liked to think of myself as one who enjoyed exploring possibility, the adventurer looking for stories. Winifred, the brave suffragette, simply liked to tempt fate, stepping into quicksand. I had covered the nasty, mud-slinging Republican Presidential Convention in Chicago in 1912 while she was being dragged by smarmy London bobbies into a cold jail cell. Both activities, I insisted, were fraught with danger and horror.

Harold was leaning across the reception desk interrogating the desk clerk, a string bean of a man who wore a monocle that slipped periodically from the bridge of his nose. Harold fired questions in Hungarian, but the man answered in monosyllables, his voice low and wary. "*Igen nem nem igen.*" Yes no no yes. I smiled. Harold Gibbon, never away from his job.

Back in my rooms on the second floor, I thought of Cassandra on the floor above me, guarded by the dreadful Mrs. Pelham, rooming one floor beneath the master suite of her parents.

I sat down to write her a note. Simple and declarative, if a little presumptive. "Cassandra, please see me as soon as possible. Tell me a time. Please answer me. Edna Ferber." I wrote down my room number. Then I added, "Knock on my door even if it is late. I don't care how late it is. Please." I underlined the last lines. Leaving the hotel, I asked the desk clerk to make certain Cassandra received it immediately. The look he gave me did not look promising. He squinted at me.

"You do speak English?" I asked. He nodded. Of course. "Can you get the note to her?" He nodded again.

I found it impossible to enjoy the evening. Winifred and I rode in an electric car, some weird high-wheeled box, vaguely like a hansom cab but with tufted plush seats and, to my wonder, a small glass vase with a single rose. Yes, the concert entertained me—how could it not? Novel, modern strains of Bartok filling the hall, even a vagrant piece of Endre Edy's celebrated verse put to music. All of it tantalized, though I didn't understand the Magyar tongue. A magnificent building with elevators of polished oak and a red velvet carpeted hallway. Dull gold stencils on the walls, a Renaissance building with frescoed ceiling, with monstrous chandeliers. A glass of cognac beforehand. Afterwards, a stroll outside, under a fittingly deep indigo cloudy sky.

As anticipated, the dinner at Gundel's in City Park was wonderful. I dined on cold Richelieu turkey with truffles, while Winifred ate Russian caviar on a silver plate with little strips of cured bacon rolled in paprika. We shared—and gushed unabashedly. Steaming black coffee with buffalo milk, a curious but potent combination. We slathered butter on the chewy rye bread with caraway seeds. Gypsy violinists strummed while a toothless old woman begged us to buy bunches of purple violets and cherries she'd picked on the banks of the Danube. "Blackbirds sing on the cherry boughs," the woman sang to us in German. Nearby a group of fussy men in Prince Albert coats frowned at us—two unchaperoned women sitting happily in a tavern. We ignored them.

We rode back to our hotel on the newfangled electric underground train with its varnished yellow cabs. A perfect evening—even the leisurely stroll across the bridge, tucked into a crowd of folks oohing and aahing at the fireworks that ended the day—but I found myself distracted much of the time. Cassandra, the vain young girl, a type I tended to avoid, was *hurting*. Her pain got to me.

Walking back to the Hotel Árpád, Winifred turned to me. "Edna, you didn't enjoy any part of this evening."

"Of course, I did."

"I could see you were distracted the whole time."

I got pettish. "Well, shouldn't I be?"

"I guess so." Sighing, she smiled thinly. "I suppose it's one of your attractive qualities, this empathy."

"It should be everyone's character, Winifred."

Again, that weary expression. "The world isn't built that way."

"Well, my world is." An edge to my voice.

Now she laughed. "I suppose you're going to have to be her savior."

At the reception desk I asked for my mail, hoping there would be a note from Cassandra. But—nothing. That bothered me. I asked the night clerk, who smelled like lilac water and looked freshly groomed, "Did someone deliver my note to Cassandra Blaine?"

He narrowed his eyes and checked the cubbyholes behind him. "Of course. Among the others that were exchanged this evening."

"What does that mean?"

He turned away from me.

Late now, darkness shrouding the patch of the Danube I could see from my bedroom window, I was restless, pacing the floor. The clock on the wall struck ten. Of course, it was actually closer to midnight. Sleep was impossible. I dialed the kitchen, was surprised someone answered, and requested a cup of tea with steamed milk be sent up. But the woman who answered kept repeating the word: *tea tea tea*. Then *milk milk milk*. I translated into German, and I could hear the tinkle of her laughter. *Ja ja ja*. All right then. In short order the bell rang and I clumsily slid open the panel door, unfortunately dislodging the garish oil painting of Franz Josef nailed onto it. It tilted to the right.

A cup of tea with a small pitcher of steaming milk was, indeed, there, accompanied by a tray with two glazed sugar cookies. Nice touch, I thought. From the open shaft wafted the faraway sounds of a girl's singing voice—light, airy, a tad melancholy. A Hungarian melody, perhaps, haunting and mournful. Was this the hotel's bonus? A lullaby before bedtime?

When I reached for the tea, the shelf moved, splashing steamed milk onto Franz Josef's craggy face. Wiping it off proved troublesome because the hot milk stained the emperor's bushy white whiskers. Now he looked as though his royal barber had executed a slipshod shave.

I drank the remaining tea and nibbled absently on a cookie.

Why hadn't Cassandra written back? Perhaps, it hit me, she'd come to my room when I was out on the town. She might have knocked when I was watching the fireworks. Maybe. Maybe not.

Uncertain, I dressed and hurried downstairs. Almost midnight now, stillness in the lobby. A different desk clerk was sitting on a chair at the corner of the reception desk, bent over, nodding off. He sprang to his feet as I neared, but I waved at him. "Please, no. Don't bother." But the look on his face suggested that a single woman strolling about the hotel at this late hour was unseemly, the stuff of scandal.

I had no idea what I was doing, save a desire to…move. To get some air. To trust my instincts.

Outside I stepped onto the quay, glanced down into the churning waters of the Danube. I watched nighttime revelers nearby, singing, tipsy, and happy. Lights up and down the Corso, cafés open, people spilling out. A city that never sleeps. Supper at eleven and socializing till dawn in the Gypsy cafés. The air harsh, vinegary, as wind rustled the river. A surprising number of folks walked about, though I spotted no single woman strolling by her lonesome. As I walked along the quay, two older couples, huddled into each other, paused to frown at me. A gaggle of rousing peasant workers headed home, dressed in scarlet and green embroidered jackets, bags slung over their shoulders. They eyed me curiously.

I lingered by a wrought-iron railing, staring up toward Castle Hill as nighttime lights flickered on and off. Below me a silent scow lumbered up the Danube, passing by, a solitary boater, a lantern making him appear shadowy. I watched him until he disappeared.

Exhausted now, still rattled, I walked back to the hotel, though I decided to enter through the garden by the terrace. Arc lights lined the pathway, misty haloes dotting the quay, but the garden was dark and shadowy. I stopped when I heard something. I glanced back toward the quay and for a moment I thought I saw Cassandra pausing under a light. A girl ran quickly, disappearing into the shadows. But was it Cassandra? Yes, I had that young girl on my mind, but there was something about the light striking those golden tresses…the way her head was thrown back, and a hint of laughter, forbidden, echoing in the dark night. Cassandra? Out there? Alone?

I hurried back to the quay, paused by that light, but no one was there. Then I heard the bubbly laugh again. Immediately I recognized it as Cassandra's soprano. Yet no one was around.

Foolishly, I yelled into the darkness. "Cassandra."

Silence.

The laughter was back toward the garden now.

"Cassandra." Nothing.

I walked on the pathway, slowly, hoping to spot Cassandra. From the garden I stared back toward the quay, lingering by a copse of trimmed hedges. Quiet now, the ghostlike streetlights eerie.

Nothing.

To my surprise Endre Molnár strolled by, paused under the light. He walked away, disappearing into the shadows, then immediately he was back, then gone again. He was pacing back and forth, I realized, waiting for Cassandra. Or was he? But now I heard her laughter behind me, near the French doors of the café, off the terrace. So brief a high-pitched laugh—or was it a cry? Rowdy roars from a coffee house yards away. I didn't know what to think. Perhaps Endre heard that sound because he started, twisted around, but then walked away, headed toward the steps down to the Danube. I waited. He reappeared. Foolishly I called out. "Endre Molnár."

At the sound of my strident voice—and not Cassandra's—he let out a grunt, and disappeared again. I waited, but he never returned to the light. Darkness in the garden—I felt chilled.

Around me all was silence. No laughter and no silhouette of a troubled Endre Molnár under an arc light, expecting an assignation. If, indeed, that were the case…

Whispering behind bushes. A man's throaty voice, hurried. A whiff of cigar smoke.

From faraway the garbled scream of drunken partiers.

Walking across the terrace, I opened the unlocked French doors and stepped into the café, dimly illuminated now by shadowy light from the lobby hallway and a wall lamp by the kitchen. Eerie, the café after hours, chairs up on tables, draperies drawn, a galvanized wash bucket with a mop by the music stand.

I moved toward the lobby, but someone was standing inside the entrance, backed against a wall as if not wanting to be seen. I screamed, not the most gracious move on my part, embarrassing. I had nearly collided with Mrs. Pelham who was hugging the wall, out of breath. She'd been gazing back into the lobby so she'd not expected me to collide with her. In the dim light I searched her face—stony, bitter, furious.

"Mrs. Pelham," I sputtered. "I'm sorry. I…"

She peered over my shoulder.

I began walking past her, but quickly she stretched out an arm and gripped my shoulder.

"What?" I felt afraid now.

She was trembling. She muttered in German.

I answered her in German. "Is there anything wrong?"

She didn't answer at first, and then squeaked out a choked phrase. "*Zuviel ist zuviel.*" Too much is too much.

"What is?"

I didn't believe she was speaking to me, but to herself, as if I were not there. Trancelike, she stared, unblinking. Her hand still clutched my shoulder as she slowly became aware of my being there. She gasped and dropped her hand, shoving by me, tottering through the lobby to the stairwell. Trailing after her, I saw her move up one stair at a time, keeping one hand on her hip, until out of sight. At that moment I realized she wore a shapeless white nightgown, though she'd thrown a jacket over her shoulders. On her head a white bonnet with ruffles. She was barefoot.

The desk clerk, startled by the activity, was ogling me as though I'd done something untoward to the old woman. Trying to think of something to say, I blathered nonsense in German, then segued into bits and pieces of English—I don't know why. I'm ready for bed. I'm tired. I'm being foolish. Enough nonsense. In the morning I would find Cassandra. Or Endre. Or—someone.

"Good night." I spoke too loudly. In one of the lounge chairs by the reception desk someone stirred. Vladimir Markov was slumped in a side chair, legs stretched out, fast asleep, a news-paper covering his chest. I noticed the scarlet cravat was untied, and the careful vest unbuttoned. Snoring softly, he scratched his head, opened one eye tentatively, unfocused, and sank back into sleep. I walked by him.

Another man was sitting by the elevator. István Nagy, the fussy poet. His face was buried in a book, eyes too close to the pages and he refused to look up as I passed. But out of the corner of my eye, I saw his head flick sideways, lips pursed, his body curled in. He swore softly in Hungarian, but swearing sounds the same in any language. You don't need a devil's lexicon for that.

Behind me the desk clerk wished me good night in Hungar-ian. "*Jó éjszakát.*"

I waved back at him.

Winifred rapped on my door the following morning. I was scheduled to meet her downstairs for breakfast at nine, so her knock was unexpected. "What?" I asked. "Is everything all right?"

She was shaking her head slowly. "Edna, you sleep through chaos. Something *has* happened. I don't know what, but my floor is swarming with people. Everyone is yelling in Hungarian and no one paid me any mind. I had to push through swarms of officious men, dozens, chests emblazoned with ribbons, all bumping into one another. A man dressed in scarlet and blue and gold—a Matisse painting, really—ordered me away."

"What's going on?" My heart pounded.

"Early this morning I woke to yelling in the hallway but ignored it. When it didn't stop, I cracked my door. Mrs. Pelham was stamping her foot on the floor, as though having a tantrum. She was poking a man with that infernal parasol she carries. He seemed scared of her."

"Can you blame him? She is a terror."

Winifred's words were whispered. "Cassandra Blaine, doubtless."

"Cassandra Blaine," I echoed.

The young girl in the midnight garden. An assignation? For a moment I felt a tick of excitement—had she found the spunk to slip away from Mrs. Pelham's awful authority—and flee?

"Endre?" Winifred wondered.

"Perhaps they've run away." I shivered, thrilled.

Winifred was nodding. "If so, she's turned the world here upside down. Crowds of men bumping into one another like wild dogs…"

"They don't like disobedience."

"A girl with gumption?" Winifred said, eyebrows raised. "I wouldn't have thought so."

But a flash of fear suddenly hit me. "Winifred, last night I saw the strangest…"

I got no further. Heavy footsteps thumped at the end of my hallway, as bands of frantic men rushed down a staircase. Behind them, walking with reluctance, was Mrs. Pelham. She dragged her feet, and the man with her kept nudging her, muttering at her.

"What in the world?" I looked at Winifred.

"Madness, this hotel."

I waited a second. "Let's find Harold."

Winifred made a face. "You're assuming he knows what's going on."

I nodded. "I'll bet he does." A heartbeat. "If he's not the one responsible for this nonsense."

Harold spotted us coming down the stairs. He was leaning against the reception desk, a cigarette stuck in the corner of his mouth. The tip of his beak nose was bright crimson, and his hair looked uncombed. The noise in the lobby was deafening, a roar that alarmed me. Harold maneuvered his skinny body though the blustery men, all talking at once.

"Follow me." He didn't wait for an answer but walked out into the sunlight. A line of police vehicles was backed up to the entrance. We followed Harold down the quay where he pointed to a bench. "Sit."

"For God's sake, Mr. Gibbon, such drama," Winifred said. "Just tell us."

I gazed across the Danube. In the morning it was shadowy with gentle ripples, flecks of gold punctuating the yellow waters. Two young boys oared rowboats beneath us, calling out to each other, playfully teasing each other. I couldn't look at Harold.

His words were laced with sadness. "Cassandra Blaine." A sigh. "Dead."

Winifred watched me closely. "Cassandra Blaine." Her voice broke. "Lord, I had hoped..."

I closed my eyes and understood that wave of fear I'd experienced. In a raspy voice, "I hoped, too."

Somehow I had known something was wrong during the long, sleepless night as I lay awake listening to the old hotel walls groaning and creaking. "Tell me."

"Early this morning a gardener arrived to begin work in the beds. There she was—Cassandra lying on her back in a clump of bushes, just outside the terrace."

"How?"

"Stabbed in the heart."

I shuddered. "How horrible."

"Who?" From Winifred, sucking in her breath.

Harold shook his head. "I don't know. I don't know if *anybody* knows anything. I did my best to eavesdrop but the authorities are closemouthed. This is serious business. The daughter of huge American money and welcome investment in Hungary. An heiress engaged to Count Frederic von Erhlich, whose connections stretch from England to Russia. The aristocracy. Another crack in the almighty empire. We're talking trouble here."

"What was she doing in the garden late at night?" Winifred wondered.

"Meeting someone." My voice was flat, metallic.

Winifred started. "How do you know that?"

I was silent, but Harold watched me closely.

He went on. "They think it was a robbery—they *hope* that. According to Mrs. Pelham, the diamond necklace she wore is gone. Her rings. The diamond ring from the count, in fact. Some nighttime bandits."

"No," I announced.

Both looked at me. "Really, Edna," said Winifred.

"No."

Harold squinted. "They found a note in the pocket of her dress. From what I could piece together, it was from Endre Molnár. Three words only. 'Midnight. Yes. Endre.' That's why she was there, sneaking out on the good count, safely blubbering in Vienna as we speak."

"Maybe," I said.

"Edna," said Winifred.

"Such a beautiful young girl," Harold lamented.

"She warned me," I said.

Winifred frowned. "Edna, you mean that silly babble in Gerbeaud's. I don't think..."

"She never got to talk to me."

Winifred looked at me, concerned. "Edna dear, I'm so sorry. I know you..."

I held up my hand. "I was in the garden at midnight." I shivered as fear gripped me.

Chapter Eight

"You were in the garden?" Inspector Horváth scratched his head, baffled.

Late in the afternoon I was sitting in a small, windowless room behind the reception desk, sipping a cup of tea provided by the kitchen, being interviewed by a small, compact man who identified himself as Inspector Ivan Horváth of the Royal Hungarian Police. Clean-shaven, with small twinkling brown eyes and thinning hair, Inspector Horváth had bowed and kissed my hand. I let him—after all, he was the police. There are stops on my contrariness, even though there was too much bowing and scraping, too much begging-my-leave and pardon-the-intrusion-on-your-holiday...I trusted none of it. Yet I immediately liked the earnest thirtyish man because he was so respectful. He kept apologizing. I liked that in a man.

"Yes," I said slowly, approximating his own rhythm of stilted English, "I couldn't sleep."

"You were looking for Cassandra Blaine?"

I paused. "I suppose so."

"But why? And so late?"

Carefully, methodically, I told him about my limited exposure to the temperamental young girl, what little I knew of her impending marriage to the count, and—I hesitated at that point, nervous—my fleeting eye contact with her in the café, that knowing—if difficult to explain—glance that suggested something was amiss. That look had been followed by the hasty, awful conversation at Gerbeaud's where she said she knew something. Or maybe not. She didn't understand something, but something *bothered* her. She wanted to talk to me.

"I sent her a note, asking to meet her as soon as possible. But I never heard back from her."

"So you went looking for her at *midnight*?" A slight smile as he stressed the last word, the *midnight*.

"I walked out on the quay, then back to the hotel through the garden."

"But you talked to her?"

"No, no. But I thought I saw her walking, running maybe, but I'm not sure...out on the quay...I heard laughter, maybe hers...lights from Castle Hill...I saw Mrs. Pelham in the hallway..." I stopped abruptly.

Endre Molnár, out there on the banks of the Danube. Midnight. Pacing back and forth. Waiting. Of course, I knew the Inspector had been told about the note found on Cassandra's body. From Endre, agreeing to meet at midnight. Three words. A clandestine rendezvous, forbidden. I didn't want to mention Endre's name, but of course I had to. Yet I hesitated. Endre killing Cassandra with a knife to the chest? It was impossible. Of course it was. Endre couldn't...what? I scarcely knew the man, though I was taken with him. That was dangerous.

Inspector Horváth leaned back, reached for his pipe and took a long time lighting his tobacco. He never took his eyes off me. He was unhappy being there, I realized, and perhaps didn't know how to proceed. Murder at the Café Europa? At the venerable Hotel Árpád, where old men quarreled over chess and American women insisted the cold sour-cherry soup be heated. A hideous murder? A beautiful young girl? An American? Wealth and position? A situation fraught with trouble.

He smiled at me, a halo of wispy smoke circling his head. "Just tell me what you know. Begin when you came downstairs and left the hotel." A heartbeat. "I don't wish to disturb you longer than necessary. You are...the bystander."

"I am that."

But the moment I began my narrative, the door flew open, and we both jumped. A tall, broad-shouldered man stepped into the doorway, his ferocious gaze darting from me to Inspector Horváth. With close-cropped white hair, a small salt-and-pepper cavalry moustache, a Van Dyke goatee over a stern mouth, the man clicked his heels and pointed at Inspector Horváth, who was immediately on his feet.

"Baron Meyerhold," the man announced, looking at no one. He moved into the room, adjusted his jacket, some military garb, I assumed, given the gaudy display of ribbons over his chest and the fringed red epaulettes gracing his shoulders. Burnished gold buttons gleamed, though none as shiny as his polished boots. He struck me as a buffoon from an Offenbach operetta. "Baron Meyerhold," he repeated, though I didn't know why. Neither Inspector Horváth nor I had spoken. I sat there, marveling.

Inspector Horváth bowed. "Sir." An exaggerated bow.

He was ignored by Baron Meyerhold. Horváth's neck was crimson now, beads of sweat on his brow.

"Ah, Miss…" He hesitated, uncertain of my name but not bothering to ask. "Miss…"

"Ferber." As chilly as I could muster.

Baron Meyerhold thundered his words, as if marshaling his troops. "I have just arrived from Vienna on orders from the Military Chancery. It is assigned to me the responsibility to conduct an investigation into this…unfortunate event. The dead American girl." He glanced at Inspector Horváth. "The involvement of Count Frederic von Erhlich, however distant, demands our attention. This matter cannot be left in the hands"—again he turned around to eye the embarrassed young officer—"of the local authorities. An American girl was betrothed to a member of the Habsburg family."

He licked his lower lip. Spittle formed at the corners of his mouth.

Inspector Horváth stepped away, uncertain of his next move, but the Baron pointed to a side chair and the policeman sank into it, looking crestfallen.

"Please sit," he said to me. But, of course, I was already sitting, so I wondered at his command of English. He spoke with a clipped British accent, stressing the wrong syllables. He must have realized his error because he offered me a sliver of a smile. I shuddered. He sat down in the chair opposite me. "The young officer will assist me." He nodded at Horváth, who did not look happy.

"Baron," I began.

He held up his hand. "Miss…"

"Ferber."

"Yes. How long did you know the dead woman?"

"I didn't know her."

"I am told you followed her into the garden."

"That isn't true."

"You were there."

"Yes, I was but…"

"At midnight?"

"I suppose so."

"You argued with her?" He swallowed. "Yes?"

"No." I breathed in. "Sir, if you let me say my story, I can clear up…"

"From what my aides have informed me on the train, there was anger earlier in the café. Something happened." He paused. "An excitable young woman."

I sighed. "I knew Cassandra Blaine, sir, but briefly. She impressed me as a young woman who was indulged, allowed a fiery temperament, but from our brief conversation I believed that she was troubled about something. She was afraid…"

He cut me off. "She was the intended of Count Frederic von Erhlich."

"And, frankly, sir, I don't believe she wanted that mandated marriage. It strikes me as medieval when marriage is predicated on an exchange of money and…"

He half rose from his seat. "Your comment is out of line, madam." He pointed a finger at me. I glanced at Inspector Horváth and detected a hint of a smile, which quickly disappeared.

"It is not your position to question an alliance that..."

"That to my American eye is preposterous."

His face got cloudy. "If *you* didn't kill Cassandra Blaine, who did?"

Wildly, my mind swept through thoughts of Endre in that dark garden, waiting, waiting.

"I have no idea, but of course I am not your murderer. I'm not one to attack people with knives. I'm a writer, sir—my knives are otherwise."

"I don't understand you."

I shook my head. "I did not kill Cassandra Blaine."

"You were seen socializing with Endre Molnár." He waited, a cruel grin on his face.

"Yes."

"You know of the failed romance—and the note he sent her?"

"I've heard."

"Did he talk to you about that note?"

"Of course not." I took a breath. "Sir, you seem to believe I have some larger role in this tragedy. But I assume your battery of investigators, disembarking from the night train from Vienna, will find the culprit."

"Who, I insist, is someone who visits the Café Europa." His eyes glanced toward the doorway, as if expecting such a culprit to sail in, confession spilling from his vile lips.

I waited a heartbeat. "Then you should have a simple job of it."

Flustered, he glanced toward Inspector Horváth who was suddenly fascinated with a loose thread on his lapel. His head cocked to the side, that same suggestion of an unavoidable smile. Baron Meyerhold glowered at him, as though blaming him for my errant behavior. He seemed deep in thought, began a question he didn't finish, then stood and bowed. "We shall talk further."

"I'm looking forward to it, sir."

He waited until I stood up and then waved me out of the room.

"I'm a suspect in a murder," I told Winifred when we met in the lobby.

"Impossible," she answered, dismissing the idea. "Have you seen Harold, by the way? He's wandering around the hotel, searching for answers. And he was looking for you." She cocked her head. "He's acting like a junior-grade detective. Sherlock Holmes with a Midwestern twang."

"It's not funny, Winifred. Cassandra is dead. That poor, poor girl."

She nodded. "Of course, I know that. But really, Edna, the idea that someone is accusing you of her murder is farcical."

I summarized Baron Meyerhold's bizarre interrogation, Inspector Horváth's respectful questioning, and my abrupt dismissal. We were sitting in oversized wing chairs in a corner of the lobby, sheltered from the reception desk by towering plants and an oriental screen, but Harold's booming voice disturbed us. For a tiny man he managed a loud roar. Excited, stammering, he asked the desk clerk where I was. The clerk glanced in my direction. Bustling, bumping into someone walking by, he found us. All a-titter, buzzing and nervous, he gripped his pad tightly in one hand, a pencil in the other.

"News, news, news," he bellowed.

"Mr. Gibbon, please. A little quiet," I begged.

He dragged a chair near us, though he turned to face me. "What in the world is going on? I've been hearing the strangest rumors, which I assume are true. I heard they're arresting you. What a headline! 'Edna Ferber, American short-story author, dragged off to jail.' You know, it has a certain ring to it. This fuddy-duddy Baron Meyerhold—I mean, I've met him before. In Vienna, a top-level scandal when one of the senior counselors was discovered selling secrets to the Russians and this Meyerhold confronted him, told the man he had best kill himself. A matter of honor. A gun placed on the man's dresser. It was…"

"Mr. Gibbon, no one is arresting me. And I'm not going to kill myself because of a nuisance like this…this pesky Baron Meyerhold."

"All right, then. Spill the beans, Miss Ferber. Tell me what happened. Everything, A to Z." He leaned in, his face close to mine. So I did, tersely, without embellishment, the stark facts. Harold demanded more juice, more sensation, hack tabloid reporter that he was, his eye on a bold headline in America, but I wanted my participation in this tragedy diminished.

Winifred tapped him on the wrist. "What have *you* found out, Mr. Gibbon? I'm assuming you know everything the authorities know."

He grinned sheepishly. "Not quite, but getting there. It's annoying how tight-lipped the Austrians can be."

"Do they know that Endre was there at midnight?" I asked, nervous.

"Of course. *He* told them, so I understand. His apartment is nearby, down on Andrássy, across from the Café New York, in fact, and someone alerted him early this morning. I thought that strange, but so be it. He rushed over, distraught. They tell me he was sobbing like a baby. I was hoping he'd come looking for me—but nothing so far."

"Poor Endre."

"Indeed," said Winifred. "He's in the thick of it, I'm afraid."

"I need to tell the authorities that I saw him last night, but—but my words…incriminate. I hate to…" My voice trailed off.

Harold was watching both of us closely. "They'll probably arrest him, though they'll do it carefully. He's from a well-known family—an historical family, as they say in Hungary—so the niceties have to be observed. Yet he's not too popular with the Austrian authorities, given some of his friendships. Frankly, this baron is a driven constable, a notorious military background—torture, so rumored—and a vicious temperament. Before his parents shipped him off to Oxford, Endre as a young student was somewhat of a rabble-rouser, a protestor in the streets with the peasants, arrested once, and the Austrians have his name in their books. The fact that he was Cassandra's *real* love counts against him—it seals his fate. You gotta believe that the count and his vicious circle will demand blood. Magyar blood. Innocent blood." He smiled. "If not American blood." He winked at me.

"I'm innocent," I protested.

Harold looked at me curiously. "That doesn't matter in a dictatorship. The prisons are full of souls crying out."

"Never mind," Winifred broke in, shaking her head. "Let's not scare Edna."

"It takes more than a strutting peacock like Baron Meyerhold to scare me. I interviewed hardened murderers when I reported in Milwaukee."

Harold gestured toward the café, which had been shuttered all morning. "The authorities have cleared out. Coffee?"

No one was in the large room. Vladimir Markov stood against the kitchen door, his face drawn. When we walked in, he approached us, bowed, and hovered over us as we took a table. He was shaking his head back and forth.

"Are you all right?" Harold asked him.

He shook his head vigorously. "Never all right, sir. The innocent girl is...dead...like that." He snapped his fingers. "Out there." He pointed to the terrace where some police officers lingered. Markov trembled. "Footsteps away from here. Who will come to my café now? No one. The people will go to the others. The Café New York where the young writers go. The Japan where the artists meet their friends. We are old...old. They will fill the empty tables of the smoky Fiume Café. This café is a place of tears, this old café." His voice trembling, he waved his hand around the empty room. "My life is this café, and now it is...this. The scene of a murder." He shuddered. "The dark Hungarians are superstitious. They believe in the Gypsy curses. The old women will walk by and close their eyes, make the sign of the cross. They will stay away. The American dies here. The Americans stay away." He threw up his hands in the air, grunted something in Russian, and walked away.

Harold brashly called after him. "Coffee, Mr. Markov, please. With whipped cream."

"Mr. Gibbon, give the man air to breathe."

Harold leaned into us. "There are so many rumors going around."

"Like what?"

"Hooligans. Roving bands of bandits from the dark caves deep in the Buda hills. There's been stories of tourists assailed, robbed of cash. Pickpockets. Angry peasants with pitchforks. That sort of thing." He whispered. "Gypsies slinking in the night."

"Do you believe that?" Winifred asked.

"Not on your life. A rich American girl wanders the quay or the hotel garden at midnight, planning an assignation, alone, without her dreadful chaperone, and she just happens to encounter a passing band of thieves? Never!"

"But I gather her jewelry was taken," I said.

"A masquerade."

"Then what do *you* think happened?"

Harold bit his lower lip and hunched up his shoulders. "I think the count had second thoughts and had her killed. That's why he's conveniently in Vienna. It would be embarrassing to call off such an engagement. I know that advisors in the inner circles didn't like his mother's plotting—after all, he was a bachelor who liked being unencumbered. Murder is…convenient. American brides are expendable."

I whispered back. "Stop this, Mr. Gibbon. Such talk is dangerous. Please watch what you say. You're impugning the integrity of a man of high station who…"

"Who is a militaristic, soulless creature."

"Stop, Mr. Gibbon," I pleaded.

He sat back, a smug look on his face. "Just an idea."

Winifred was frowning at him. "Which you don't really believe, young man. Do you hear yourself? You just want to foment trouble, stir the fires, all of which you'll sensationalize and wire back to Hearst, that yellow journalistic hack."

"He pays my salary, no?" He sucked in his cheeks.

Markov carried a tray to the table, apologizing. "The waiters they stay away today. No one comes to work. What am I to do?" He served coffee slowly, as if afraid he'd drop something. From the kitchen the boy György carried a pitcher of water, but Markov rolled his eyes, stammered. "György, this how you serve the people?"

Gyorgy wore his street clothes, a rumpled puffy white peasant shirt, open at the neck, and white pajama-like baggy trousers over worn boots. Markov pointed to his clothing. The boy sputtered, "I don't…" But stopped.

The lad looked sad, his eyes moist and swollen. Markov motioned for him to return to the kitchen, though György stood there, hangdog. "He drags along, the snail today. He says it is like an arrow to the heart, the beautiful girl gone." Suddenly he reached out and gripped the boy's shoulder affectionately. "There is sadness in the world, yes?"

György stared back vacantly, uncomprehending. "Uncle," he began, speaking in Hungarian, which Harold immediately translated for us. "Tell them about the door."

Markov jerked back, surprised, letting out a tiny laugh. "György, such gossip."

"You said…"

Harold sat up, boomed out, "What, György? Markov?"

"It is nothing," Markov answered in English. He looked over his shoulder toward the lobby. "No one talks to me so I wonder…how important."

"Tell us," I demanded, irritated.

"When I close up the café late last night, I shut the French doors to the terrace and garden. Always. As I am told to do. I *lock* them. It is night. There are dangers, no? But I couldn't sleep, so I sit in the lobby and talk with the desk clerk, Attila, an old friend. I drift to sleep. Two in the morning I wake up, walk back into the café, and the door is wide open. One of the doors is. I *know* I locked it."

I nodded. "Of course. I walked back in from the Corso at midnight—through that door. I gave it no thought."

"Someone unlocked it."

"Maybe Cassandra," I said, "as she headed to the garden."

"But she didn't walk by me as I sat in the lobby."

"Are you sure?"

A thin smile. "No, of course not. We made coffee in the back room, Attila and me. No one was around. Even István Nagy joined us, which surprised us. He does not believe in having coffee with the workers."

"Did you see Mrs. Pelham?"

A shake of his head. "No."

György was nodding his head and began talking in German. "Tell the police, Uncle."

Markov looked nervous. "I don't know…"

I raised my voice. "Of course you do. Maybe unimportant, but maybe not. Tell Inspector Horváth. He is the one…"

"I know the man," Markov said. "He stops in for coffee and to hear the Gypsy music with his beautiful wife. A friendly man. But the other man scares us, pushing through the kitchen, yelling, pointing fingers. No questions…just…ordering everyone around. 'Move! Move!' he yells." He grinned stupidly. "He makes me long for my Russian village."

"Did you hear anything last night?" I asked. "When you were closing up?"

He shook his head. "Silence. Darkness. When I saw the door was open, I closed it, locked it again. I thought I forgot, but I know I didn't. So I go home to my wife who is waiting up for me, and angry." He smiled.

"Someone came into the hotel," Harold concluded. "Someone walked in from the garden."

"Or *left* the hotel," I said. "Someone headed *for* the garden. It's impossible to know the answer."

"Had you seen Miss Blaine earlier that evening?" Winifred asked.

Markov considered, speaking now in his labored English and glancing nervously toward the doorway. Sweat glistened on his brow. "Very early, I think. But she didn't stay. She walked in from the garden, through the café. Zsuzsa was drinking with that strange bearded American who scares everyone. I worry because of the…the scene with Zsuzsa and the American girl the day before. The slap in the face. So sad, that." He leaned in, confided, "I don't want my café to be a place for brawls. But Miss Blaine walked over to say something, and I think they smiled at each other, but I didn't hear what they said." He turned to György, who was holding the water pitcher at a suspect angle, a fact that Markov noted with a flick of his hand. In German. "You hear anything, boy?"

György had been staring toward the terrace, bored, leaning on one hip and then the other, at one point scratching a pimple on his cheek. Startled, he rolled his tongue into the corner of his mouth and shook his head. "I stayed away from her, Uncle." A shake of his head, an aw-shucks smile. A speck of blood where he'd picked at the pimple. "I didn't want her crazy at me again." He sighed and muttered something in Hungarian, his eyes gleaming.

"What?" I turned to Harold.

"He says beautiful girls should never be made angry."

Winifred growled. "But that's the only fun some of us have."

Frowning, Markov pushed György into the kitchen. "Shoo, shoo." The corners of his mouth crinkled as he looked knowingly at Harold. "He is too young for Budapest."

Harold appreciated the line, barking loudly, "And the rest of us are too old for this city."

Markov looked puzzled. "What do you mean, sir?"

Harold didn't answer and turned away, which further confused poor Markov. He bowed and began inspecting the samovar on the counter. Harold spoke too loudly. "I'm guessing that poor Endre Molnár is somewhere in the hotel. He's gotta be a wreck of a man, haggard, tearful. I know that man—heart on his sleeve. But this martinet Meyerhold has sequestered him somewhere, probably grilling him, threatening, beating perhaps, covering him with his bratwurst breath, insulting his Hungarian blood so that Endre will show his hothead spirit. Meyerhold will get a confession out of him."

"But Endre didn't kill poor Cassandra," I announced.

That startled Winifred. "Edna, what? How in the world do you know?"

"In my bones, Winifred. In my soul."

She snickered. "You can never believe a good-looking man capable of atrocities, Edna."

"Not true. Daguerreotypes of John Wilkes Booth show a handsome man…if a little cruel in the eyes."

"Let me qualify that. Unless the evidence is overwhelming."

I smiled wistfully. "You don't know me, dear Winifred."

"I know enough…"

Harold broke in. "What are you two ladies gabbing about? This is not the issue—the man's good looks. You know, the police have that note from Endre, found on Cassandra's body. It puts him *there*." He actually pointed out to the terrace.

"No, it doesn't," I insisted. "It suggests his intention to meet her there. There is no proof he actually *met* her or *talked* with her."

"Tell that to the police, Miss Ferber. Hardly conclusive."

A garbled rasp sounded from the entrance, a barely-stifled sob. Zsuzsa Kós floated in, a large black silk handkerchief gripped tightly and held against her cheek. She stumbled near our table, almost toppling, as Harold rose to help her, but she waved him away. She tucked herself into a chair at a table in the far corner, buried her head on her arms for a moment, and then leaned back, staring up toward the ceiling. She was dressed all in black, a matronly funereal gown that swept the floor, a black cape lined with black satin dramatically slung over her shoulders, and on her head a monstrous hat constructed of ruffled fabric, enormous black silk roses, and dyed black ostrich feathers. The first keener at the funeral, and the most demonstrative. An inappropriate laugh, immediately suppressed, escaped her throat, followed by a full-throated sob.

"They say she's going mad," Harold told us.

"Shh." From Winifred. "A sad woman, she is."

"But slipping from reality."

Winifred then quoted a line from Shakespeare, which touched me deeply. "Leave her to heaven," she whispered.

Markov, approaching tentatively, offered coffee or wine but she held up her hand and mumbled something incoherent. Glancing at us, as though for help, he backed off.

To my horror, Harold bounced up, hesitated a moment, and then sailed over to her, pausing before her table. "My condolences," he said. "I know you two were friends who…"

She screamed, "Go away." In German. "You horrid little man."
"I only…"

She shrieked and Harold backed away, bumping into a chair in his path. For some reason he wore a goofy smile, an expression owing more to nervousness than celebration—the pesky little boy, reprimanded.

Seated back at our table, Harold leaned in, motioning us forward. "I already got stacks of cables this morning. Hearst, of course. He wants banner headlines—fire in the gut. The news was wired out of Budapest early this morning. This is a big story—and it may get bigger. This is scandal, writ large. The American princess and the Habsburg count. Ill-fated marriage. Blighted love. The dashing, moody Hungarian porcelain magnate. Impassioned, inconsolable, perhaps the murderer. The supercilious count who was spotted last night dining at Sacher's with a duchess from Saxony. It'll be in all the afternoon papers. Murder in the midnight garden. Moonlight glowing on the Chain Bridge. Roses making you dizzy in the garden. Heads of state will react. Lines drawn. Anger. Tempers flaring. My byline, of course. I'm here in the thick of it. This is my new story. Hot off the presses. Let me tell you."

"Harold…" I attempted to break in.

He ignored me. "The sinking of the *Maine* was nothing compared to what I'm going to say."

Chapter Nine

The following afternoon, sheltered beneath towering walnut trees, Winifred and I strolled on the gravel walk through the Zoological Garden after a lunch of *paté de foie gras* sandwiches at an outdoor eatery. The city was famous for this delicacy. For a while we sat on benches in City Park, though the quiet was disturbed because Harold—was that imp everywhere?—called out to us. In German, for some reason. *Grusz Gott!* God's greeting. We tried to ignore him, but he tagged after us as we got up to leave. He was spouting some nonsense about international conspiracies, the Frankfort bankers, and the danger of Tsar Nicholas' unholy alliance with Serbia.

Turning a corner, we spotted Jonathan Wolf sitting at a table, dining by himself and reading a newspaper. Harold stopped, mid-sentence, just as Winifred was pooh-poohing his political science, and pointed at the elusive American in our path. Under his breath, Harold hummed, "Jonathan Wolf. Somehow he's in this story. I don't trust that man."

"No, please." I touched his sleeve, but Harold bustled toward Wolf, who looked up, surprised and unhappy, at the intrusion.

"I'd like to make your acquaintance," Harold told him.

Jonathan Wolf ran his tongue over his lips, dabbed at them with a napkin, and put down his glass. He was debating what to do, but finally, measuring his words carefully, he nodded at the table. "Won't you all join me?" There was nothing friendly in his invitation.

Winifred protested, but to no avail. "Do we have to do this?" Harold grinned. "Of course, we do. Miss Ferber's face tells me she would love an introduction."

Admittedly, I was staring intently into Jonathan Wolf's upturned face, trying to size up the well-dressed man with the dark black beard, neatly trimmed. A tall man, broad in the shoulders, a wrestler's chest. A light tan Savile Row summer suit, expensive. A diamond stickpin in his lapel with a Phi Beta Kappa key beneath it. A straw boater rested on the seat next to him. Gray kid gloves lay on the table. A tall highball glass with brandy and soda, melting ice. A plate of mushrooms-on-toast. A cigarette stubbed out in an ashtray. Here was the comfortable man of leisure, on holiday.

Harold introduced himself, but that gesture was not necessary. The man cut him off. "I know who you are, sir." A smile difficult to interpret. "A scurrilous newsmonger from the tabloid Hearst syndicates. A man who annoys everyone. A tick on the belly of mankind." Harold bowed, smiling. "And these ladies are Edna Ferber and Winifred Moss, also guests at the dilapidated firetrap called the Hotel Árpád." He stared into Harold's face. "You have been dying to talk to me for days now."

"Well, of course," Harold began. "Everywhere we go, you're *there*."

Jonathan Wolf held up a hand.

"You grant no one privacy, Mr. Gibbon. That's clear from watching you strut around the café like a bantam rooster. No one can hide from you. No one can harbor secrets, even in so remote a place as Budapest."

Harold was irritated. "Do you have secrets?"

"Everyone has secrets. But some are trivial and mundane. Worthless."

"*Most* people's secrets," Harold noted. "But…"

"But obviously not mine—if I am to judge your inquisitiveness. You think that I have something to tell you."

"Do you?"

A sardonic smile. "I provide no answers unless you ask the right questions."

"And those questions are…"

"That's your job, sir."

This verbal skirmish ended as a waiter approached the table. "If we are to have this unpleasant conversation, let me offer you all some wine." He spoke to the waiter in Hungarian. "Of course, we'll have Tokay, the legendary grape every tourist demands. And rightly so. A favorite of mine."

Harold was impatient to get back to the conversation. "I'm by nature a curious man."

Wolf eyed him, but looked at me and then at Winifred. "You ladies choose to wander these lovely, ancient streets with your family pet."

That rankled Harold. "Hey, I'm a reporter."

He eyed Harold over the rim of the brandy he now finished. He chomped on an ice cube as the waiter returned with wine and poured it. Wolf's voice was laced with sarcasm. "And I'm not a reporter—nor curious." He sighed as he fingered his beard and then sipped the wine. "Ladies, please." I sampled the wine: pungent, rich, smooth, aromatic. I smiled. "I told you you'd like it. Everyone does. Even if they *don't*, they *say* they do."

That bothered me. "I never lie, sir." A charming smile. "At least about wine." Then, watching his face, I told him, "Sir, I've had Tokay before."

"Good for you then. A head start on excellence."

"You come to Hungary often?"

My abrupt shift in conversation didn't faze him at all. He grinned. "Are you working for Mr. Gibbon?"

I bristled. "I work for no one but myself. I'm trying to make idle conversation with a rude man who invited us to sit with him. Perhaps you should choose a topic that you approve of, sir."

That surprised the man, who tightened his lips into a frown. Then, unexpectedly, he smiled, sat back in his chair, relaxed his body. "Yes, I *am* being rude, Miss Ferber. My heartfelt apologies. I wasn't raised that way." He glanced at Harold. "It's just that—well, some folks rattle my chains, as it were. I'm a private person."

"I understand that exactly, sir," I said.

"It's actually a pleasure to meet you two ladies." He avoided looking at Harold. "I do know your enviable reputations."

"Apology accepted," I told him.

He took a sip of wine and seemed to be weighing his response to me. "But you are right. We are having a pleasant conversation—or trying to. To answer your question, yes, I visit Hungary often. I've often vacationed at Lake Balaton. A village. Almádi, in fact. A long, beautiful lake. Vineyards. Old peasant women sell poppy seed rolls in the park or carry green earthenware jugs filled with buffalo milk. Old men in faded hussar uniforms nodding on the benches. Delightful. I have good friends in Pécs." He reached out across the table, offering his hand to Harold, who was pouting. "Friends, sir?" Harold shook his hand.

"Edna and I have traveled to Budapest to see the sights," Winifred told him.

"My father was born in Hungary," I blurted out.

That intrigued him. "Really? Ferber?"

"Yes, a nearby village. A shopkeeper's family, I gather. In some ways this is a sentimental visit for me. My father often spoke of Budapest, a city that dazzled him, a place where…" But I stopped talking. Jonathan Wolf wasn't listening—he was watching Harold, who was eavesdropping on a conversation at a table near us.

A moment of silence, then he shifted the subject abruptly. "I'm here on business, in fact. I work for a company in Massachusetts planning some major investment in Eastern Europe. Based in Boston. Since I knew Budapest…and Prague, in fact… even the Croatian Agram…I was asked to…scout out possibilities." He was still staring at Harold.

Something was wrong. His words rang false, though I wasn't certain why I thought that. The breezy, casual speech had suddenly become staccato, rehearsed. A set piece delivered as a capsule biography to keep people away. Jonathan Wolf did, indeed, harbor a secret.

"And you chose the Hotel Árpád?" I asked.

He waited a bit. "For English-speaking contacts, of course. American businessmen. All Americans end up there—creatures of habit. I've been a guest a number of times, and each time I marvel at the decay—and danger. I ignore the intrusive image of Franz Josef staring at me as I wake in the morning." He laughed, though no one joined him. "And a curious room service that has a mind of its own. A plate containing a piece of crispy apple strudel sailing to floors other than my own." He shook his head back and forth. "But charming, no?"

Winifred was nodding her approval.

What I detected was a slight accent, barely suppressed under the rigorous Bostonian inflection. Jonathan Wolf, I concluded, most likely had been born in Europe.

"You were born in Boston?" I asked.

Amused, he was shaking his head. "Ah, more questions. A reporter, too?"

"Yes, indeed," I answered, a little hotly. "A product of Sam Ryan's afternoon *Appleton Crescent*, circulation under one thousand, more when disaster struck."

"And did it strike often?"

"Not often enough. I was fired after one year."

He waited a second. "Yes, I was raised in Boston. Boston Latin, Harvard. The full sweep of Brahmin acceptability."

"But you're not a Brahmin."

He didn't answer.

Harold was watching me, delight in his eyes. Partners, his look conveyed, in solving the mystery of the bearded man. I was still haunted by my first glimpse of Wolf as he stood in the shadowy entrance, watching Cassandra, a look not curious but—harsh, menacing.

"A hotel that was the scene of a horrible murder," I began, goading him. "That poor American girl. Cassandra Blaine. Had you met her?"

"Of course not." Said too quickly, and glibly. He was looking down into his half-empty glass. When he glanced up, I saw wariness in the corners of his eyes.

"So close to her marriage," I went on, driven. Winifred squinted at me: What? What? Really, Edna. I was used to her questioning looks—often withering—and her belief that I was too forward. Rebel though she might be in the war for suffrage, she still harbored conventions about proper conduct, which I didn't. After all, she was British. I...well, wasn't. The Atlantic Ocean had loosened some of the rusty bolts of respectability.

"What do you think happened?" Harold asked now.

A heartbeat. "I don't know. Gypsies, perhaps."

"That's an easy conclusion," I offered.

"From what I heard, it was a robbery gone bad." He fiddled with his pocket watch, anxious, and stared toward the sidewalk.

"I don't believe it." I locked eyes with him. "Cassandra was suddenly afraid of something. She *told* me so."

That news shifted his interest, and he tilted his head toward me, eyes questioning. "Afraid of what?"

"I wish I knew." I glanced at Winifred. "But it seems her presence in the Café Europa drew quite a bit of attention from folks. I recall seeing someone standing in the shadows of the doorway, his eyes riveted to her, and not too kindly." A disingenuous smile. "A large man, bearded."

I expected him to squirm, but he didn't. Debonair, slick, he smiled in recognition. "Ah, you have a wonderful eye, Miss Ferber. But perhaps a passing stranger might be fascinated by a noisy, frivolous girl who enjoys making scenes in public. As an American, I tend to dislike when my compatriots feel the need to behave childishly in foreign countries. Perhaps that stranger was simply looking at her with distaste. End of story."

"And yet this woman was to be married to an Austrian count."

He laughed out loud, and for too long. No one else did. Then, his tone sober, he said with marked annoyance, "Stupid, these transcontinental marriages. And with an impoverished count who thinks he has his finger on the pulse of modern Europe and its trouble spots. The age of feudalism looking up at the airplane in the sky with the wonder of a child discovering his big toe."

"So you're saying the count is...clueless about modern life?"

Harold warmed to the subject. "Franz Josef himself is without a clue. Here is a man who refuses to ride in an automobile—after all, it is a modern trapping, a death machine. A man surprised by rebellion in the provinces, who expects the enslaved Slav to bow before him. A man who..." Harold stopped. Jonathan's face looked stony.

"I take it you don't care for the Habsburgs?" he asked.

"What do *you* think of Franz Josef?" Harold countered.

"I really have nothing to say on the subject."

I smiled. "So you're not invited to the wedding that will never happen now?"

That surprised him. "I'm here on American business, Miss Ferber. I believe I already told you that."

"Yes, you did."

"Edna," Winifred began, "what are you getting at?"

"I believe Mr. Wolf is harboring secrets."

"And so the conversation comes full circle," he concluded.

No one laughed. Wolf glanced toward the street, his eye following a policeman standing by the underground stop. He pushed his plate away from him, drank the last of the wine, slapped some crowns on the table, and signaled to the waiter.

Harold hurriedly spoke up. "How long are you staying in Budapest, Mr. Wolf?"

A thin smile. "I guess the inquisition has another tiresome act."

We waited. Harold fussed with a napkin, then waved his hand at Wolf, his fingers resting near the man's sparkling diamond pin. "You're very much the cosmopolite, sir."

"A lovely word, but not really describing me. I'm a simple American businessman."

"You've already established that," Winifred said, her voice sharp, something that surprised me. Jonathan Wolf looked at her with an expression that suggested his only ally at a hostile table had drifted over to the opposing side, leaving him naked on the battlefield.

"Well, I was supposed to visit Sarajevo, but I've been warned against it. Too much trouble brewing there."

Excited by the sudden introduction of politics, Harold rushed his words. "I may go there soon—if given an assignment. Archduke Franz Ferdinand is scheduled to visit there shortly. With his wife, Sophie."

"A mistake, I would think."

"But Bosnia is an Austrian territory now."

"But it's filled with angry Serbians. Anarchists who resent the encroachment of the empire on their ancient lands."

"Ah, Serbia," Harold rhapsodized. "Their national anthem is a hymn to lost souls."

"Tell that to the Black Hand, those anarchists roaming the streets with bombs. With Franz Josef hostile to beleaguered Serbia, there's bound to be trouble, no?" He sat back, folded his arms across his chest. "According to what I read in the papers."

Harold beamed at me. "I told you so, Miss Ferber. War *is* coming."

But that remark bothered Jonathan Wolf, a quizzical look in his eyes. "Austria doesn't want war with Serbia. A colossal mistake, really. You're convinced..."

"Of course." Harold insisted. "But there are forces in Serbia that fund the anarchists' movements in Bosnia. *Narodna Obdrana*. The Union of Death. Responsible for the *coup d'etat* that killed King Alexander and Queen Draga in 1903. Barbaric thugs, hunting them down like dogs and hurling their naked bodies into the street. What's his name? A madman nicknamed Apis—the Bull, now Minister of War in King Peter Karageorgevich's reign. Dragutin Dimitrijevic, a monster. Assassination is the name of the game for the Serbians. But it's David and Goliath, really. Austria ruling from the Alps to the Mediterranean. Except that Austria is a lumbering giant, sickly, tired. And Serbia is a spitfire nation that will never win a war. It comes from having kings who were pig farmers who suddenly titled themselves royalty."

"Mr. Gibbon," I broke in, "another lecture on world politics? Do you ever rest?"

"Never."

"Well, maybe…"

Jonathan's face was animated. He considered Harold's words for quite a while and didn't look happy. "Not good for business—this war of yours. You appear to have some inside information, sir."

"I read the papers." He breathed in. "I also write for them. Remember Otto von Bismarck's prophecy—'Some damn foolish thing in the Balkans will mean war.' There are souls in Austria itching for war. For one, Count Frederic von Erhlich, Cassandra's intended. A foolish man."

"Mr. Gibbon reads what Hearst says about this region," I noted.

Jonathan Wolf laughed. "So Mr. Gibbon makes it up, and the world believes it. And then, oddly, even he believes what he just made up."

"I'm a journalist. I write the truth."

Jonathan stood up. "Pleasant as this is—and it actually *was*—I must be off."

Harold held out a hand, touched the man's sleeve. "Perhaps we can continue this conversation."

Jonathan Wolf shrugged him off, his expression humorless. "I really have nothing more to say about politics. You've heard the extent of my knowledge, coffee house chatter available anywhere in town—what the Embassy warns business investors about. I read the *London Times* and the *New York Times*. I tend to avoid the Hearst tabloids."

"Wise choice," Winifred quipped.

"But…" Harold insisted.

"No." Strong, deliberate, final. "Chitchat about politics—and the foolish game of war—well, it's idle talk over a fine lunch. This has been fun but really…unnecessary."

I spoke up. "Oh, perhaps you're wrong, Mr. Wolf. Perhaps there are things being said that are truly important."

He squinted. "That's makes little sense, Miss Ferber." A patronizing smile. "I trust your short stories make more sense."

I harrumphed, a Victorian exclamation I usually resisted because I always sounded like my hectoring grandmother in Chicago. "Goodbye, Mr. Wolf."

He placed his boater on his head, adjusted it, tugged at the lapels of his jacket, checked his necktie, and bowed away from us.

Absently, staring after Jonathan Wolf who was weaving his way through scattered strollers, Harold remarked, "I'll get to the bottom of that man."

"And what does that mean?" I asked.

"I don't trust him. He's lying to us. He's not here in Budapest on business. He's up to no good. My nose tells me that. He follows me sometimes, you know. I spot him watching me. He was playing games with us."

"I agree," I added. "There's something he's not telling us." I stared into Harold's eager face. "But be careful."

He grinned foolishly. "That's never any fun."

We walked back to the hotel, taking our time, enjoying City Park with its drooping willows and delicate acacia trees. Like a madcap schoolboy, Harold chased an electric trolley until he drifted back to us, out of breath but laughing.

"He'll never grow up," Winifred whispered to me.

"I hope not," I answered.

At the hotel we discovered a line of black touring cars stretched out in front of the hotel. A spiffy Graf & Stift roadster was positioned in front, followed by a fleet of cars, including a small truck. Bumper to bumper, the assemblage struck me as a freight train on some track. As we watched, porters loaded suitcases and trunks into the cars, methodically packing back seats. The cab of the truck was piled high with boxes, all tied with red canvas ropes. Functionaries, yelling orders, bustled about, distracted, flummoxed, and annoyed. A grim-looking man in a tweed jacket and British spats stood to the side and reprimanded a porter for dropping a box.

"So Marcus and Cecilia Blaine are moving out," Harold announced.

As we watched, two maids and a manservant dressed in uniforms lined up and then filed into one of the cars. A porter opened the doors of the imposing car at the front, and the Blaines, as though waiting for a stage cue, stepped from the hotel's front entrance. Looking straight ahead, neither speaking, they got into the rear seat. Cecilia Blaine was dressed in black, her face hidden by a heavy black veil. Her arms had elbow-length black gloves, and she gripped a rolled parasol. Despite the heat, she wore over her shoulders an ebony Spanish shawl trimmed with fur. Marcus Blaine, in a businessman's black suit and a formal black top hat that was more appropriate for an evening at the opera, nodded at the driver who moved the car into traffic.

The line of vehicles behind followed, a somber funeral procession that ignored crossing pedestrians and other cruising vehicles. A perpetual motion machine, that caravan, undeterred by courtesy and custom. The lead automobile almost sideswiped a shabby dog cart pulled by a team of black horses in yellow harnesses, and the driver, a thick, sunburned peasant with a long pipe in his mouth, cursed in delirious Magyar and shook his fist in the air.

Harold gave the benediction. "The American royalty headed back to America, lock, stock, and barrel."

"And Cassandra's body?" I asked.

He shrugged his shoulders. "Headed back to America for burial in the family plot in Hartford. Cedar Hill Cemetery, where the rich are buried."

A lump in my throat, sadness filling my heart. "Such a short, unhappy life."

"The rich don't cultivate happiness," Winifred said.

"Well," Harold told her, "of course they do. But they call it by another name. Money."

"And her murderer walks the streets of this beautiful city," Winifred commented.

I waited a heartbeat. "Yes, that's true."

Yet, quietly, I kept repeating over and over the same refrain, echoing in my head, beating against my heart: You've met the killer, Edna, in the hotel where you are staying. You will see that killer across a breakfast table at the Café Europa. Or on the terrace. In the garden. And then, in a moment of awful but exhilarating crystallization, I knew I'd stumble upon the answer. But when? How? I knew it was but a matter of days.

Later that evening I stood at the huge window in my rooms, my palm resting on the glass as I stared out onto the quay. A narrow view from my room, a sliver of pavement and streetlight and Danube and a hint of Castle Hill beyond. Moonlight softened the Danube, and the ghostly streetlight threw shifting shadows onto the pavement. I stood there too long, my shoulders aching, but I was captured by the postcard moment. A chromolithograph of a faraway land caught on a stereopticon. Ah, Budapest!

While I lingered there, my mind drifting, I spotted István Nagy sitting down on the bench, stretching out his legs, adjusting the scarf around his neck. He appeared to be staring back at the Hotel Árpád, or at least I believed he was, because his body was stationary, his head unmoving.

My eyes focused, sharp. What was there about that poet that rankled? Then, staring, I realized that Jonathan Wolf was walking by. He stopped a second, stepped back and obviously said something to István Nagy. Then he moved away but immediately returned. He was waving his hands in the air, pointing into István's face. The poet turned aside, his back to Wolf, but finally stood up. An awful pantomime, the two of them, with István now gesticulating wildly, head bobbing. Under the hoary streetlight both men seemed random characters on a stage, Rosencrantz and Guildenstern bumbling through a scene. Each gestured, each backed off. My face pressed against the glass, I wondered what was being said—and why. Suddenly Jonathan threw his hands into the air and moved away.

In a quick, jerky move, István lunged after the American and shoved him, propelling the man forward.

They both disappeared from my line of sight.

I waited.

A second later István came back into view, standing in front of the bench, alone now, but swaying back and forth, as though trying to maintain his balance. Then he stretched out his arms toward the hotel, in my direction. And though my own reaction was irrational and stupid, I pulled back quickly from the window as if to avoid being spotted. My heart was beating wildly. I felt frightened, but that made no sense.

Chapter Ten

The following evening, a warm night with puffy clouds against a lazy blue-gray nighttime sky, Winifred and I wandered through Váci Utca, mingling with the crowds who promenaded there, getting lost in the narrow mews and cobbled lanes. We bought postcards at a little kiosk by the underground train station. Peasant girls strolled by, each one in an embroidered jacket, each with colorful skirts over a dozen petticoats billowing out like old cotillion gowns on American debutantes. Legs covered in blue stockings. Arms jingling with bracelets. We stopped for supper at The Green Band, sitting at a table covered with a linen cloth so starched its edges were knife-sharp. The waiters, thrilled to be serving tourists, insisted we sample the *fogas*, a delicate freshwater fish from the Lake Balaton waters. Of course, we did—and oohed and aahed appropriately. A dreamy evening, happily spent away from the Hotel Árpád and its murderous echoes.

I'd spent the afternoon visiting a cousin of my father, an ancient woman living in Eperye, a village outside of Budapest. A short train ride from Eastern Station, and an afternoon of coffee and powdered sugar doughnuts at a little café high in the hills, accompanying an impossible conversation that was a labored mixture of German and Yiddish but mostly silence. I'd written her earlier from Berlin, and we'd had planned the meeting, but she had few memories of my father as a young man. She recalled a skinny, high-spirited boy, bashful and polite, a yeshiva boy, but then she acknowledged her memory might be of another boy in the village. We ended up staring at each other before I walked the kilometer back to the train depot and happily returned to Budapest.

"My father," I was telling Winifred, "never liked to talk of those early days in the village, just his delight in visiting Budapest as a young man. For him, America was his only conversation." I paused. "And yet America failed him. A struggling life, one bankrupt store after another." I took a sip of wine. "And an early blindness and then death. You travel across continents to find—emptiness."

Winifred nodded. "But he was a loving father."

I grinned. "And I was his favorite daughter." I tapped the table. "I insist on that—to the horror of my older sister Fannie." I looked around the restaurant. A beautiful place with potted greenery, walls tiled in white majolica tiles, discreet streamers overhead in the Hungarian colors—red, green, and white. "He never wanted to return to Hungary."

"But now you have."

"And I feel nothing of him here."

"Well, America gets in the blood."

"Does England get in the blood the same way?" I asked her.

"Not for me, I'm afraid. I'm the daughter of a vocal and much-hated militant suffragette mother, an amateur artist who talked only of the world—out *there*." She pointed into the heavens. "I'm just continuing her struggle."

"Someday."

"Soon."

"And your father?" I asked.

She smiled. "A quiet man who wrote essays about Cézanne and Monet. He died—hit by a runaway carriage. But I remember him as my mother's fiercest advocate."

"Then he was a good man."

Happy, we smiled at each other.

Back at the hotel, Winifred suggested a glass of sherry at the Café Europa, and I agreed. Our supper conversation, speckled with nightmarish images of my ailing, handsome father and the golden America he dreamed of, had left me melancholic. My mother was in Berlin, but was never a comfort to me: the judgmental eye, disapproving, demanding. Her hold on me was velvet, but unyielding. And my leaving her there was—treason. I quaked. Distance exaggerated my betrayal. I felt alone in the world, and somehow an aimless tourist abroad, a solitary woman with too many suitcases, the thirty-year-old spinster—images that struck me as a faded photograph in a vellum-embossed family album I never wanted to open.

Walking in, we spotted Endre Molnár sitting alone in the café, a bottle of wine before him, his shoulders slumped forward, elbows on the table.

Markov rushed to us, gratitude in his face, as though our random coins would be his salvation. He pointed to Endre, who had not looked up. All the tables around him were empty, and the lit candle on his table, flickering because of a slight breeze from the terrace, made his profile appear ghastly.

"Him," Markov pointed. "The sad man. Him. Sit with him. Please." Stuttered words, monosyllabic, pleading. He motioned us toward Endre's able, and we let him.

"Mr. Molnár," I began, and he looked up.

Endre offered a tentative smile and then closed his sleepy eyes. He leaned forward, gripping the wine glass so tightly I feared it would shatter. When he looked back up at me, that handsome face trembled, uncertain. A ghost of a smile, almost not there, appeared, then disappeared. He was dressed in a tight-fitting black linen jacket with polished gold buttons over a magenta-colored silk shirt, open at the neck. Billowing peasant-style trousers tucked into high red boots. Very appealing. I thought, though a tad dissolute and Bohemian. A slight beard stubble on his chin, the result of a failed morning shave, but the grand life-of-its-own moustache looked waxed and manicured. Even a grieving man must keep his priorities, and in this age of the tonsorially splendid moustache—from the walrus bushiness of an American president to the slick, toothbrush fuzz of a vaudeville villain—a man never forgot that caterpillar above his upper lip.

Frankly, I preferred the clean-shaven face of a Woodrow Wilson. I never agreed with Ella Wheeler Wilcox who insisted that kissing a man without a moustache was like eating an egg without salt. Clever, but faulty.

"Please." He pointed to chairs opposite him as he struggled to stand and bow.

Winifred and I sat down. "Should you be sitting here alone?" I asked.

A bittersweet smile. "I still expect to see Cassandra sitting there"—he pointed to the table near the terrace where she regularly sat, guarded by Mrs. Pelham—"making too much noise. The silly little girl who was never silly around me. A bright and charming woman, she was."

"Mr. Molnár, my condolences, sir."

He looked into my face. "There are times I burn with anger."

"Anger?"

"I want to strike out. To hit someone."

"But…"

He shook his head slowly, and the corners of his mouth twitched. "I have a temper, I am afraid. Hungarians are dark and moody"—he smiled wistfully—"as everyone will tell you. But the struck match sparks a bonfire. You will hear that about me." His eyes drifted from the terrace to the kitchen. "That is why so many people think I murdered Cassandra."

"Who thinks that?" Winifred asked, indignant.

"The police, I tell you. That…that dreadful man from Vienna. Baron Meyerhold. He has his men following me everywhere. They sit outside my apartment. They look through my mail as it arrives on the doorstep. He says to me: Confess, confess. And I say—to what?"

"Well," I said, "he is an intimidating man, a man I disliked immediately. I don't trust such pumped-up authority, all bluster and swagger."

"It's his job, he tells me. In the service of the Crown. The Military Chancery. And the American authorities—Washington. A senator from Connecticut is sending telegrams to Vienna.

William Randolph Hearst has trumpeted the murder on page one. Lots of angry ink, let me tell you. Vienna only cares because, well, Washington is sending up dark smoke signals. So now Count Frederic demands it. His honor, his integrity, his...love. But I don't believe that. The count has already forgotten this... this little interlude with the American girl he never even smiled at. A man without a soul, that one."

"That sounds so cruel."

"But true. Why else was she so...unhappy. You know, I saw the changes in her. When I met her, she was quiet, laughed lightly—never the brat everyone saw her as later on. When you laugh all the time, and so loudly, you..."

I finished for him. "You are telling the world something is wrong."

He nodded. "Yes. Yes." He stared into my face. "You understood that about her. You *saw* that."

"Mr. Molnár," I said after a bit, "Cassandra spoke to me in Gerbeaud's. For some reason she trusted me, and she wanted to talk to me. It never happened. She was frightened of something. Not just unhappy about a ridiculous marriage. But afraid. Something bothered her. I think she believed she was in danger."

He watched me for a long time. "Of course," he said matter-of-factly. "The person who murdered her."

That startled me. Winifred leaned into him. "What do you mean?"

"I mean, her death was not the result of robbers or Gypsies or...or bandits from the Buda hills who just happened to be in the garden so late at night. Ridiculous, such talk. She was going to meet *me* there. But such a meeting was unusual for her. Not a rendezvous you can time by a clock or date by a calendar—it was a sudden plan. Her idea—spur of the moment." He paused. "Maybe—because she *was* frightened of something. She needed me to help her." He trembled. "Something had happened to her. She sneaks away from Mrs. Pelham to meet me."

"Yes, Mrs. Pelham." I pictured that severe woman in the corridor, backed against the wall, watching, in her nightgown. The dangerous sleepwalker.

"Who is still at the hotel," Endre noted. "She is staying in one of the rooms, so I heard. Left behind by the Blaines like… like debris. Waiting for a new family to arrive."

"Really?"

"Like the count, she too forgets. But then she never liked Cassandra."

"Well, that was clear," I said.

"Cassandra told me. She told her parents how Mrs. Pelham pinched her. And they did nothing. They didn't care."

He poured some wine into a goblet and stared at it. But then he pushed the glass away. "Enough," he said to himself. "A man who drinks alone is dangerous. My head pounds from too much drink, and my eyes tear from sadness."

"You shouldn't be here," I told him.

His bleary eyes got wide, unblinking. "My apartment is a prison cell." A low, strained laugh. "Perhaps I'll be in a real prison cell in a few days."

"You did not kill Cassandra," I announced.

"Edna, really," said Winifred.

"Some things I know."

He smiled mournfully. "Well, thank you, Miss Ferber." He looked toward the kitchen. "But when I walked in here tonight, the waiters rushed away, muttering, watching, fumbling to get away from me. My dear Markov, that soul of diplomacy and someone I know for years, he talks to me with hesitation, looking over my shoulder as if waiting for Baron Meyerhold to rescue him from the crazed murderer. So polite, but in his eyes—you know, the…the fear that, yes, Endre Molnár, the rich Hungarian, may have killed the one he loved." He choked up. "Here in that garden I first said to her, '*Szeretlek*.'"

Winifred and I stared at him.

A crooked smile. "I love you."

I watched him closely. "Were you surprised to receive that note from her?"

"No." A heartbeat. "I expected it."

"What do you mean?"

"We did communicate, dear ladies, I confess. Now and then—but rarely. She'd slip a note to the desk clerk with my name on it. A few coins changed hands. Or I'd slip a note to her, though not recently. Not since the count and his dreadful mother arrived in Budapest this last time. She didn't dare. Mrs. Pelham was a fierce watchdog, a woman who ran with gossip. But we used to write notes—'Hello. How are you?' But that night I got a note. I think she was bothered after I saw her in here—when I stormed out like a madman. My fault—I was in a foul mood. She was acting crazy then. 'Meet me at midnight in the garden.' That's what she said." He punched one fist into the palm of his other hand. "A note now in the hands of Baron Meyerhold after his men searched my rooms. My note and hers. Two pieces of evidence. A death sentence in the Austrian Empire."

I shrugged it away. "That means nothing. An assignation. Two lovers...*former* lovers who..." I trailed off.

"Yes, a love that was over. But *not* over."

I thought of something. "Tell me something, Mr. Molnár. I know that midnight assignation didn't take place. I believe that. You know that I was there. I saw you pacing the quay. I saw you heading down the steps to the Danube. I think I heard her voice in the garden."

He watched me closely. "Yes, I waited but she never appeared. Or she came after I left—I didn't wait long enough maybe. Or"—he shuddered—"she was already dead in the garden. Crazy, I walked onto the Chain Bridge, lingered for an hour in the middle of the bridge, staring like a simpleton down into the Danube, even thought I'd hurl my body into the waters. But then I walked home."

"But," I began slowly, "you did meet in the garden *before* that night. True? That wouldn't have been the first time."

He watched me, a twinkle in his eye. "Smart American woman, you are, Miss Ferber. Yes. Midnight. Once or twice before. Some time ago, though. After she was lost to me—handed over to the count like a dress bought in a store. But only when Mrs. Pelham was fast asleep."

"She wasn't that night."

"No, she woke up and went to look for Cassandra."

"Maybe she murdered her," Winifred offered.

The blunt remark jolted us, and we sat there, silent, looking away.

Endre said nothing, but he bit his lip, his eyes getting moist again.

"Tell me about the other times."

Lowering his voice, he said, "Two times in the night garden. One kiss. One hug. Two times in tears. We both cried." Then he said something in Hungarian. It sounded like a poem, the cadence lilting, melodious. We waited. Then, finally, back to English. "I am sorry. It is a song I used to sing to her."

"Did she mention her upcoming marriage?" I probed.

"Of course. What other subject is there for a girl in captivity?"

"There's the hunger for escape. Freedom," Winifred answered.

Endre eyed her curiously. "Sometimes a slave loses hope." A sigh. "But yes—that was her dream, too."

"How?" From me.

"Well, in the early days when the betrothal was announced, she did talk of escape. She wanted to go back to America. She wanted to disobey her parents and rush back to America. She hated the count, she said. Whenever he looked into her face, she said he didn't *see* her. Each time with him was like a...a meeting. Contracts drawn. Papers signed, ink on the line. Cattle in the stockyard. Evaluated. Looked at. Nodded at. A price given. Her mother did all the talking. The countess barely spoke, unhappy with Americans, but resigned to her horrible fate—chained to an American bank."

"This all seems impossible to me," I exclaimed. "How could this possibly be a marriage?"

"It has nothing to do with love."

"Clearly."

"But I made a big mistake." His hand trembled, gripping the half-empty glass. "I told her she *had* to marry the count."

That shocked me. "But why?"

"Because in my world, this world—what the poet István Nagy would call the beleaguered Old World of Europe—you must *obey* your parents. Many families choose their children's partners. For centuries. It is...routine. Love is often not considered or expected, though our music and operettas talk of nothing else."

"Well, that's hardly your fault."

"She fought me. 'Help me escape to America.' Preposterous, I told her. A father's wishes. A mother's wishes. She cried, 'You and me. The night train to Trieste, over the Croatian mountains. We will hide in America.'" He chuckled. "'Montana' she tells me. 'No one goes to Montana. We'll live in a cabin in the mountains. They will never find us.'"

"Tell me, Mr. Molnár, she was unhappy. But I'm bothered that she was frightened the last day."

He shook his head vigorously. "That bothers me, too. She must have learned that she was in danger. That's why she turned to you in Gerbeaud's. But—what? And she was turning to me—at midnight." He pounded his fist on the table. "But they killed her first."

"Who?" I pleaded. "Who?"

Winifred spoke in a soft voice. "You must have given this some thought, Mr. Molnár. Who would do such a horrific thing?"

He ran his finger around the rim of his goblet. His voice became a whisper. "I believe it was an order from Vienna. From Franz Josef's court."

"The countess?"

"Lord no. She is a woman who values title but she covets money more. American money makes her dizzy with delight."

"But..."

Endre's face got red as he slammed his fist down on the table. "There are forces in Vienna that frowned publicly on the union." An unhappy smile. "Your Mr. Gibbon thinks along the same lines, you know. He blames Vienna for everything, including the bad weather." A long pause. "And some behind closed doors, I'm sure. I think...maybe...some insider, like the evil madman Count Conrad of Hotzendorf who calls for war with Serbia every day…maybe he sent someone to assassinate. Him—or another insider. I'm convinced Vienna is somehow behind this.

"Count Conrad despises Archduke Franz Ferdinand—not only because the archduke balks at war but because he married below his station. Unforgivable. Killing Cassandra was another way to avoid scandal in the future. The Habsburgs are not so generous with their titles as the British are. The English run to America, hands open, coats of arms offered as gifts." Endre glanced at Winifred, momentarily unsure of his words, but she nodded at him, agreeing. "What could the royal court do with such a marriage?"

"But you have no proof."

"Of course not," he whispered. "And spies are probably listening to me right now as I talk to you." His eyes swept the room. A sly smile. "Even such an obvious one like István Nagy." Then he stopped. "But now the matter is over. A convenient marriage, truly, but *frowned* upon."

Raised voices came from the lobby. A quick burst of drunken laughter, a girlish laugh. As we watched, Zsuzsa Kós poked her head into the café, then stumbled in. Harold Gibbon was with her, his gentlemanly hand tucked protectively under her elbow. His eyes got wide when he spotted the three of us, but he never stopped moving, leading a tottering Zsuzsa to a table by the kitchen. Endre's look alarmed me—utter dislike, a seething anger. Winifred was nodding toward Harold and said under her breath, "Astonishing, that hack. There is nothing that sap will not do for a story."

Harold's speech was slurred, bubbly. They'd been drinking, which explained their raucous chatter as they walked in. He babbled stupidly at the woman, waiting for her to say something, then gushing his response. An embarrassing display, I considered, and dangerous. He was playing some questionable game. I was certain of it. The fact that he consciously ignored the three of us in the nearly empty café, turned away from us as he ordered wine, underscored his deadly cat-and-mouse play. What was the man up to?

Zsuzsa laughed at something Harold whispered to her and looked in our direction, a coquette's look, her hands fluttering in the air. Catching my judgmental eye, she laughed harder. Her hand stroked Harold's forearm, lingered there. Harold leaned into her, sputtered some inanity into her neck.

Their conversation was a curious mix of English and German. What fragments I gleaned stunned me: Harold was drilling her about Cassandra's last days. Despite his blatant flirtation, he managed to lace his words with pointed questions.

"Tell me what she said. What do you think of Mrs. Pelham?" Zsuzsa mouthed her dislike. "How did Mrs. Blaine first approach you? Or did the countess request your…your introduction?" Harold, pouring wine from the bottle a waiter served, raised his voice and finally glanced at us. A conspiratorial wink. See me at my craft? Watch and learn, dear ladies. "What did you think of the countess? Of the count? What did they say to you?"

I signaled to Winifred. "Let's leave."

But Winifred was fascinated by Harold's cruel interrogation.

Zsuzsa, flattered by the attention from the young man, fluttered. "They all blame me," her voice breaking at the edges.

"But why?" Harold probed.

"Them. All of them. I talked to people in Vienna. A few letters posted—old friends at court who still talked to me. Mrs. Blaine talked to me."

"Did they pay you?" Abrupt, in her face.

A long pause. "Of course," in English. Then, through clenched teeth, a barrage of teary German. "How else can I live on in this fleabag hotel? The pittance of old men who remember me. Exiled from Vienna, a career shattered by gossip and innuendo. A wild girl from a Gypsy camp—that's what they said about me. Mocked, laughed at." Her voice cracked.

Harold patted her hand. "Who would do that?"

She eyed him suspiciously, tilting her head. A maddened woman's brief flicker of sanity. She looked scared. *Am I being made fun of?*

"You take advantage of a foolish woman, Mr. Gibbon."

"Why do you say that?"

"You are a reporter."

"But I'm an honest man, Zsuzsa dear."

"No men are honest unless they are forced to be."

"You don't know me."

"I know the way I've been treated."

"No, no," he said. "Your voice tells stories. When you sing…"

Then, to my astonishment, she stood, wobbled, gripped the edge of the table, and croaked out a fragmented song in broken English. What I heard was:

The Gypsy girl has eyes so black
Her hair is dark as night
She dances on the river bank
Until the morning light.

At the end, falling back into her seat, she waited.

Harold wore the sheepish look of someone not understanding what has just happened.

"Well?" she cried.

"I don't…"

She clapped for herself, feebly, and then she sobbed. Confused, Harold grabbed her hand and held it tightly. Looking into his face, she whimpered like a forlorn child. "Take me out of here."

"Zsuzsa, I wanted to ask you…something you said earlier… reminded me…so…"

He got no further. "You know, I never wanted to do it! I hated that girl. That Cassandra. She made fun of me. 'You tired old carnival act.' That's what she said. 'You old hag in a ripped gown.' I hated her."

Endre, bristling, stood up, but I put a hand on his arm. He sank back into his chair.

Nervous now, Harold mumbled something about leaving. "It's just that I was wondering…"

I shook my head. The dreadful journalist, unrelenting. A nose for trouble, that one. But I wondered about Zsuzsa's story. What part had she played in this sad tale?

What was Harold hinting at?

At that moment Bertalan Pór and Lajos Tihanyi walked in, paused at the threshold, eyes riveted on Zsuzsa, who was rocking back and forth at her table, hands flailing. Alarmed at the loud weeping in the empty café, Bertalan Pór nudged his friend. Lajos, the gesture communicated, let's leave now. Catching Pór's eye, I waved them to our table, though they hesitated, Lajos Tihanyi stepped back toward the lobby and pulled on his friend's sleeve.

Spotting the artists, Zsuzsa screamed at them. "Those two. They stare at me—at us—spies eating into our souls. You think I don't see their childish cartoons. They draw us as circus freaks. Ghouls, vampires. Their sketches make the world look like the bottom of hell."

Harold tried to quiet her but she shrugged him off.

Frozen in the doorway, the two artists watched as she came toward them. Staggering, she brushed against a nervous Tihanyi. Harold trailed after her and avoided looking at us.

Winifred spoke in a whisper. "That man has sold his soul to the devil."

"Yes, and at the moment it seems Satan has dyed straw hair and a face blotchy with soggy pancake cream."

Zsuzsa looked into Bertalan Pór's face. "Vultures," she mumbled. Her fingers tapped Pór in the chest. "Maggots on the carcass of the empire."

His face animated, Tihanyi was looking at us, so he missed her bitter words, but Pór flicked his head back, puzzled, and opened his mouth to say something. Nothing came out. Then Zsuzsa and Harold disappeared into the lobby, though Harold's persistent voice drifted back to us. "Dear Zsuzsa, I wanted to ask you…You said…"

Silence.

The two artists walked toward us and stood by our table.

Endre was fidgeting in his chair, his face crimson and his shoulders hunched up. It frightened me. He ignored the two artists who were looking at each other, Tihanyi mouthing some inarticulate syllables that suggested he was confused by what had just happened.

"Mr. Molnár," I began, "don't let that woman…" But I got no further.

Smoldering, he stood up, towering over our table. "That woman, that—Because of her meddling…She was the one who started all this…this tragedy…for a gold coin and a bottle of whiskey…A king's slave…" Seething, he caught my eye, bending his body so that his face stared into mine, his voice now a lethal whisper. "You know, I hated the count. That pompous ass, smug…There were times I wanted to kill *him*." He banged the table. "He should be dead, that man. Not Cassandra. There were nights I imagined a knife in his throat." He stopped abruptly, his words soft, swallowed. "The wrong person died." He heaved a sigh. "When Cassandra said yes to that monster, she asked for her own death."

He fled the room.

Shocked, we sat there silently, shaken, no one looking up.

Tihanyi pulled his satchel onto his lap. His friend gently touched him on the shoulder, a calming gesture I'd seen before. His eyes glancing toward the disappeared Endre, Tihanyi reached into his bag and withdrew a drawing. His fingers caressed it lovingly, protectively. Then, a whistling sound coming from the back of his throat, he slid it across the table until it rested before me. He tapped it—Look, look. It was a sketch of Cassandra, the look on her face captured at her most troubled. The facial features were contorted, exaggerated, ugly. No longer the pretty American girl, winsome and golden. Rather, here was a pettish girl, mean, hard. I'd seen that moment in her, and I didn't like it. Of course, I'd also seen the look that pleaded *help me*. But this drawing was haunting, twisted.

Then, taking it back quickly, Tihanyi slid another drawing across the table. This one was of Harold Gibbon. I hadn't expected that. Here was the reporter depicted at his most deadly, the ferret eyes, his beaked nose, the quivering moustache, the jutting chin. Unattractive, but largely true to the hungry man on the prowl, the reporter who wouldn't take no for an answer. I yelped, a foolish sound, so graphic was the stark depiction. My face tightened. Tihanyi made a guttural sound, unpleasant, and when I looked at him he looked angry, as though I'd insulted him. He drew his lips into a straight line, disapproving, and his hands shook. In German, facing Tihanyi so he could read my lips, I said slowly, "You have captured the soul of the man, sir. The face you draw somehow looks like his hail-on-a-tin-roof voice." Bertalan Pór laughed. Tihanyi's eyes flashed.

Tihanyi jotted something down on his pad and slipped it to Pór, who contemplated the Hungarian sentence. Finally he looked into my face.

"What?" I asked.

He quoted Tihanyi. "'I see what you hear.'"

Chapter Eleven

Seven a.m., still groggy from a restless night, I planned to gather Winifred, a woman who insisted she was up for battle at four a.m., and the two of us would have breakfast and then head to Margaret Island to wander the blue-velvet lawns in the rose garden, perhaps a mud bath at a hot springs spa, a luncheon of fresh-baked rye bread slathered with thick sour cream. A paprika salad with mocha coffee. A long day planned, away from murder and Harold Gibbon slinking around our lives.

Stepping off the landing onto Winifred's floor, I stopped, backed into the door, and hoped I'd become invisible. That voice. Harold's foggy voice compelled me to step back. Harold was standing in a doorway leaning into the doorjamb, whispering, laughing lightly. A very disheveled Harold, his vest unbuttoned, hair sticking out so he looked like a rowdy Katzenjammer Kid.

I stood there, frozen, feeling intrusive, my tiny body hopefully lost in shadows.

Then a woman's lazy morning voice, dragging and low, but peculiarly sensual—a vamp's practiced intonation, somehow not real but delivered with the assumption that men expected such tantalizing timbre after an amorous night. Harold's sweet departure, but an impatient one—out the door, get away from the moment, rush, rush. The woman's hand reached out and gripped his arm, but he backed away. Again the goodbye, louder now. He stepped into the hallway.

"Wait," Zsuzsa Kós implored, in German. "Please wait."

For a moment she was framed in the doorway, the overhead hallway light illuminating her stark face. Drawn, pale, her blond hair uncombed and wiry. A Japanese robe with hummingbirds and bamboo reeds was wrapped around her, but it sagged, dragged on the floor.

"Wait, my Harold."

Well, her Harold was not waiting. His night was over. A flick of his wrist in farewell, as though bidding adieu to an old college friend, a cavalier gesture that smacked of the new breezy American manhood—flippant Morse code, rat-a-tat farewells. The rendezvous forgotten within seconds.

Perhaps.

Peeved, a confused look on her face, Zsuzsa executed a feeble wave, bittersweet, and closed the door.

Stepping lively down the hallway, an enigmatic smile on his lips, Harold Gibbon ran smack dab into me, the schoolmarm eyeing him suspiciously. All I lacked was a hickory stick and a dunce cap.

He let out a melodramatic bark. "Waaah!" A lovely sound, barnyard and earthy.

"Good morning, Mr. Gibbon." My sweetest voice.

Mouth agape, he waited, something he'd refused to do when implored by the abandoned Zsuzsa. Wait, please.

He stammered, "Miss Ferber, what are you doing here?"

An untoward question, I considered, given his presence in the aging songbird's rooms.

"Mr. Gibbon." I walked toward him.

"Miss Ferber." He was nodding like a caged bird.

"Working so early in the morning?"

A thin, raffish smile. He looked over my shoulder toward the landing. "Well," he said, "I am always the consummate journalist."

"A credit to your profession," I remarked, striding past him, then turning to watch.

He skedaddled down the hallway. I swear I heard him laugh out loud as he bounded down the staircase.

Of course, within the hour, as Winifred and I sat in the café having coffee and poppy seed rolls, Harold rushed in, promptly insinuated himself at our table without an invitation and, ignoring me, addressed Winifred. "Don't believe a thing Miss Ferber has told you."

Winifred eyed him sternly. "Edna does not lie."

"She may not fully understand…"

I smiled. "You are such a man of the world, sir."

Winifred went on. "The news of the day suggests there is no bottom you will not search for, Mr. Gibbon."

He reached for a roll in the basket on the table, crumbled it between his fingers and chewed on a piece, swallowing loudly. "Let me explain. Nothing is ever as it looks."

"Of course it is," I insisted. "That's the pleasure of discovering a two-bit Casanova in the middle of an indiscretion."

He bit his lip. "It wasn't the middle, I'm afraid. But the unfortunate conclusion."

I held up my hand. "Mr. Gibbon, a little restraint, please." I smiled. "I'd rather not know of your nighttime roaming, sir."

He leaned in. "It's like this…You see…"

"Nothing will stop him," Winifred said to me, throwing up her hands, a twinkle in her eye. "Social decorum easily dismissed, and two proper Victorian ladies are treated to one man's idea of titillation."

He raised his voice, ignoring her. "It's like this. Listen. You gotta hear me out. Hearst wants a series of articles on the Cassandra Blaine murder, especially with the Habsburg angle. Everything else has been put on hold. My *Decline and Fall* has to wait."

"Which necessitated you sharing room with an aging cabaret singer?"

He wore a hurt look. "Zsuzsa, it turns out, talks too much when she's a little tipsy. And she's…well, a bit of madness is seeping in these days. Well, you've seen her in here in that woeful state—her boisterous singing, yelling, conversation A real charmer."

"You obviously find her so," I said wryly.

"She can give me secret information. Great stuff. It turns out she knows all sorts of clandestine Habsburg scandal and nasty gossip and...and international rumor. She's a goldmine. Pure gold."

"I realized that when I first saw her shrill yellow hair."

He waited a bit, eyes unblinking. "Now you're being cruel. I expected a little more decency from you, Miss Ferber. She's a lonely, sad woman, abandoned. Do you realize that János Szabó, an old admirer who's a retired Hungarian vintner, himself without much, pays her hotel bill? Such an act of kindness. You've seen him in here. But she has little else—no money really. He hands her crowns."

"How ignominious, really," I said archly. "In some circles there's a name for that."

He was getting hot under the collar. "You don't understand the peculiar rhythms of old European life. Life isn't flash-in-the-pan footlights here. Folks venerate legendary performers who blazed their way on stages thirty years back. Some old-timers remember them fondly. Their days of rollicking youth and... and dance hall intrigue and beer hall sensation. Europeans have long memories. Americans forget yesterday's news."

"Tell me, Mr. Gibbon. What is the basis of *your* veneration?"

He leaned in, confidential. "Frankly, she misread my attention last night, my idle interest, my..." A shrug of his shoulders.

"Flirtation? Please, Mr. Gibbon, we witnessed your primitive courtship ritual."

"You know, she carries with her a reputation for being a celebrated and great"—he swallowed and looked away, a mooncalf glow in his eyes—"romantic."

"Ah, the power of euphemisms," I blurted out.

A bittersweet smile. "She surprised me...warm and tender and—and, well, downright lovely. She took me by surprise."

Her fingers tapping the table, Winifred was frowning. "Enough of this cheap revelation, sir. Now, foolishly, you're trying to convince us that this sad tryst of yours was done in the name of journalistic investigation."

"Well, yes. Tidbits about life in Vienna and the royal court. Did you know that there's a ghost in Franz Josef's Hofburg—*Die weisse Frau*—the white woman, who mourns and cries and… Franz Ferdinand hates Wagner and Jews and frowns on liver and boiled beef…and Queen Elisabeth encouraged her husband's affair with Kathi Stratt…and the account of Cassandra's murder in the German-language *Neues Pester Journal* here in Budapest made no mention at all of the count and the planned marriage… none. None! Did you know that? I had to rush to my rooms this morning to jot it all down."

"Trivial, such hogwash. Do you think America wants this scandal as headline?" I asked.

"I *know* so. Hearst *demands* it. Ordinary Americans are hungry for these royal tidbits. Democracy only gets a person so far when it comes to excitement. But you know, it somehow all ties in with my larger purpose in Budapest—my chronicle of the end of empire. The coming of the horrible war."

"How so?"

"The count was part of the Military Chancery, ineffectual though he is, probably a wooden figurehead much mocked by his underlings. I wouldn't be a bit surprised. Anyway, he still has a role to play in the game of war."

"What does that have to do with his attempt to marry an American heiress? Surely you're not suggesting that Cassandra Blaine is connected to the demise of the Austro-Hungarian Empire."

That gave him pause. "Only that such a marriage suggests how weakened the aristocracy has become—how desperate. It suggests a crack in the surface of things."

"Quite the stretch, Mr. Gibbon."

Winifred was watching him closely. "You know you're a weasel, Mr. Gibbon."

He laughed loudly, delighted. "You're not the first person to call me that."

"Then perhaps you should listen to those souls. Mend your ways."

Brushing her comments away, he went on, excited. "You know, I can even expand these juicy articles into a best-selling book, something thrown together before my major opus, my *Decline and Fall.* Let me see—*The Count and the American Heiress.* Nice title, no? I can see the movie now. D. W. Griffith will direct it. Mary Pickford as Cassandra. Me—as myself."

"*Mr. Gibbon and the Goddess*," I suggested.

"Hearst wants me to get all the gossip."

I laughed out loud. "Hence an all-night rendezvous with the dissolute beer hall singer."

"Exactly." He reached into his back pocket and took out a crumpled edition of the *New York Examiner.* With a flourish, he pointed to the bold headline. "My scoop. My words, but the Chief wrote the headline himself."

An incendiary headline: "Franz Josef Ignores Murder of American Heiress."

"How does he—you—know that?"

He grinned. "Let's just assume Hearst knows everything." Harold jumped up and pushed back his chair. "I have work to do." He glanced toward the kitchen. "Zsuzsa told me that one of the porters, leaving work late that night and stopping to smoke a cigarette out on the terrace, swears he heard two men whispering behind a wall. Drunken whispers, he thought. He heard only two words: 'This time.' In German." Harold's brow furled. "Or something like that. Or he thought it was German. And then, as he lingered on the quay before heading home, watching a boat chug up the river, he saw a big man wrapped in a cape, a hat pulled down over his face, stagger away, drunk, bumping into a railing. A man who turned his head away as he passed by."

I was interested. "At what time?"

"He leaves the hotel at ten. So, early—long before the murder."

"That could mean nothing," Winifred said.

"Or everything," I commented. "Harold, did the porter tell this to Baron Meyerhold?"

Harold grinned. "No one tells that scary man anything. To

talk to him is to invite questions about your own soul. Meyerhold will persecute the innocent simply for the pleasure of it."

"Then…"

"But he did tell Inspector Horváth, who's a Magyar and a member of the Royal Police. The Hungarians work with Meyerhold, but with reservations. They don't trust him. Which is why the case won't be solved early—or at all. No Hungarian willingly steps into the path of the dreaded Baron Meyerhold."

"Obviously the Hungarians are a people with exquisite and perfect judgment."

Harold laughed and backed off. "Do you hear the clock ticking? The empire is listening to the death knell." He jerked his head back and forth. "Tick tock tick tock. Listen. Ain't it beautiful? My ticket to fame. Franz Josef is writhing with dysentery or some other royal virus, days to live, gasp gasp gasp. Is that the ghost of my dead son Rudi? Who walks there? And Franz Ferdinand is scheduled to go to Sarajevo on St. Vitas Day, a Serbian holiday, to review Austrian Army field exercises. Appointment with the grim reaper. An empire with an insatiable desire for death. For Franz Josef's eightieth birthday, you know, Serbian dailies praised would-be assassins outright in editorials bordered in thick black, and insisted every Serbian has a duty to go to war with the 'monster' Austria. Happy birthday, old man." Harold stomped his foot. "What a great time to be in Europe!" He bowed, retrieved his feathered slough cap he'd placed on a chair, and sailed out of the café.

Winifred narrowed her eyes. "I can't believe I'm saying this, but—it's Zsuzsa I feel sorry for now. She's been hauled into that messy spider's web."

Vladimir Markov was standing some ten feet from us, shifting from one foot to the other, nervous, arms folded behind his back, his head dipped into his neck like a wary bird.

"Mr. Markov, is there a problem?"

The man hurried over to us but looked quickly toward the lobby. "A minute of your time, dear ladies. But I feel I am being…how do you say it?…indiscreet. It's forbidden for the staff to engage the guests in my problems."

"Heavens, no, Mr. Markov," I said. "Please sit. Perhaps you offer some relief to the balderdash we've just sat through."

"Ah, Mr. Gibbon." He lowered his voice, again glancing toward the departed Harold. "A fine, fine man, no?"

"The best." Winifred blurted out the words. "Hearst's finest."

Again I invited him to sit with us, but he shook his head. "Of course not. So inappropriate. My employment, you see. My place here. I feel…"

"Please, tell us."

"You are the good friends of Mr. Gibbon, yes?"

"No." Winifred exploded. "A fellow American, a subspecies usually kept in the family attic."

That confused him and he didn't know what to say, his brow wrinkling. But I smiled. "Ignore my friend. She's being funny. Or trying to be."

"The kitchen…it is all frantic and…workers bumping into things…dropping plates and…"

"And this is Harold Gibbon's fault?"

He nodded hurriedly. "Perhaps you can talk to him. Tell him to stay out."

"Lord, what's he up to?" Winifred asked.

"For him, it is like the sad murder happens just now. He rushes in, runs around, asking everybody questions. Many don't speak English, of course. He tries German, Hungarian, Croatian, Russian. Everything. 'What do you know? Tell me. Tell me. Do you see Zsuzsa Kós in the afternoon the girl dies? What about this…this Mr. Wolf, the American who looks at everyone? The scary man with the beard.' He asks what words Miss Blaine said to the staff, anything, everything, scraps of conversation. 'Tell me now. Did she say—Good morning? Good night. Hello. Mean, happy, bad, good?' It is craziness. And so no work gets done. They stay away. The dishwasher quits. Everything is upside down now. I am at my wit's end, dear ladies."

"I don't think we have any power over that man," Winifred said.

I softened my voice. "I'll speak to him, Mr. Markov. But he is a stubborn man. A reporter, and a driven one."

"Thank you." He bowed. Then, an afterthought. "A dangerous man."

That startled me. "Why, for heaven's sake?"

"He accuses the cook. Ivo Merlac. A young man, a foolish man who drinks too much and fights in the streets, but a man who minds his own business. My best baker." He smiled. "The best doughnuts. Powdered. You know—delicious. But when Mr. Gibbon runs through the kitchen, banging his way like a drunk himself, well, he sees poor Ivo sitting and reading a newspaper. A Serbian newspaper. *Trgovinski Glasnik*. So common in Budapest, of course. So many Serbians here—he *knows* that. The man comes from Mostar. An honest Muslim, that man, though not religious. A drinker. He thinks nothing of the… politics, believe me. When Mr. Gibbon he spots the newspaper, he yells at him. He yells about politics and murder and Bosnia and…war…and…"

"Good heavens." I glanced at Winifred.

"He has scared everybody in there." He pointed back to the kitchen.

"Ignore him," Winifred advised.

Markov shook his head. "But that is impossible. The man is like…like a mosquito buzzing around the head all night and you can never swat it."

"Try." From Winifred, her mouth in a sardonic line.

"Tell me about this Ivo Merlac," I asked.

"Because of Mr. Gibbon, the Royal Police stand in my kitchen. Mr. Gibbon he talks to somebody. They come here. This Ivo is a man who scatters his crowns on drink." His voice dipped to a whisper. "He plays cards and spends his time with the lost girls on Magyar Street. Yet he calls himself a Muslim. It's not my business. Really. But Mr. Gibbon follows him around, talking in German, in Russian, in what he thinks is Serbian. 'Where were you that night? Where were you when the Croatian house painter assassinated Baron Ivo Skerletz?' A stupid question, yes. Ivo stared, frightened. What does Ivo know of Croatian killers? But Baron Meyerhold tells me Ivo was in jail the night the girl was murdered. So it cannot be Ivo. I ask Mr. Gibbon, 'What reason has Ivo to kill her?' 'He's a drunk,' he says. 'Serbians kill everyone.' He says Ivo follows her to the garden. She runs, he stabs. But Ivo is in jail. Still, Mr. Gibbon comes back again."

"Pay him no mind," I advised.

Markov shrugged. "Then he starts to talk of the coming war. 'What war?' I say to him. No one wants war. This"—he waved his hand around the room—"will be no more. Politics is...is for people with money. The landowners. The rest of us...huh! Nothing! But he scares everyone. Franz Josef will declare war on Serbia. Serbia will fight Austria. My country Russia will join Serbia. Germany will jump in on the side of Austria. Everybody. Alliances. England. France. Italy. This or that. The whole world upside down. He makes us dizzy. So my wife starts to cry, scared out of her mind. 'We are Russians in Hungary,' she tells me. 'We will be the enemy.' So my wife...she leaves two days ago, headed home to her village. She believes Mr. Gibbon—and is scared."

"Will you stay?"

"This is my life, good ladies. I love Budapest. This is my home for so many years. I returned to Russia to find a wife, but I rushed back here. My home. Mr. Gibbon...he makes everybody run. Two workers leave yesterday, take the train to Moravia. There will be no war. Serbia is...how you call it...the braggart. Huff and puff."

"Your nephew György, the handsome boy..." I began.

He rolled his eyes. "The clumsy oaf. A boy unable to learn. He tags after my wife, packs his clothes in a bundle on a stick like a Gypsy in the fields, and goes back home with her. He is afraid they will take him into the Austrian army. I am left with no family here. No one." He smiled. "György, though a simpleton, was my wife's blood, and so my family. Gone."

"I'm so sorry, Mr. Markov."

"If war comes, I will be a prisoner."

A group of young women, dressed in summer frocks and giggling about a boat ride down the Danube, interrupted us, and Mr. Markov straightened, sucked in his breath.

"Don't listen to Mr. Gibbon," Winifred said. "He is hoping for a war because it's the story he is writing."

"But that makes no sense."

"He thinks if he talks enough about the coming war, his words will make it happen."

Astonishment in his eyes. "He has that kind of power in America, that man?"

I smiled. "Well, he thinks he does."

Markov edged away, moving toward the young women who were taking off their summer bonnets. A smile on his face, a gentle bow, gracious. He looked back at us, then stepped toward us. "I come to Budapest as a young man because I find a postcard in a market stall in Kiev. The bridges, the river, the lights on the Buda hills. A postcard. Magic, all of it." He frowned. "But I discover no city is really a postcard, though it always will charm you. Let me tell you something. Budapest is the lovely woman who likes to whisper in your ear."

Chapter Twelve

"Twilight of the gods." Harold paid no attention to Winifred and my admonishments. "Hey, I'm just doing my job." Ten o'clock at night, late for me, the quay bright with halo-like streetlights, Castle Hill behind us sparkling with illumination. A cool breeze drifted off the river. We were sitting on a bench over the Danube, the hotel behind us, and Harold waved his arm back to the hotel. "Markov, like so many others, refuses to hear the war drums beating."

"Nevertheless," I repeated myself for the umpteenth time, "you're bothering the workers at the hotel. Leave people alone."

"They have a story to tell. And now that I'm exploring the Cassandra Blaine murder, it's imperative…"

"It's imperative," Winifred broke in, "that you conduct yourself with civility."

He grinned with a shrug. "I never learned how."

"I'm not surprised."

"Mr. Gibbon. Harold." The line between formal address and casual friendship had begun to blur days ago. "Nevertheless…"

Harold was finished with the topic. He peered up the quay. "Where are those two infernal Hungarians you ladies have chosen to befriend?"

"Bertalan Pór and Lajos Tihanyi are lovely young men…"

"Who draw those odd paintings. All the portraits look like paint-smeared freaks in a sideshow."

"Admittedly, not my taste," I went on. "However, they are sweet men."

"One of them can't talk or hear. How much fun is that?" He clicked his tongue. "Men aren't sweet, Miss Ferber. Women are."

I caught his eye. "You should know, dear Mr. Gibbon."

Winifred grumbled. "Sometimes the inability to talk or to hear can be a blessing."

Harold guffawed. "I'm starting to like you, Miss Moss. You ain't the tough soul you insist you are."

"I actually do *like* people, Mr. Gibbon."

He laughed louder. "There you go again."

The two Hungarians emerged from the shadows, Bertalan Pór calling my name and apologizing for being late.

Winifred wasn't too happy with this evening's excursion, though she'd come to like the two artists—because, in fact, they *were* artists. The night's adventure was Bertalan Pór's idea, this questionable ramble into the dark Budapest night, his insistence that no one could understand the rhythms of the old city without soaking in the intense life of the cafés and night streets.

"Budapest comes alive after dark," he told us. "No one sleeps." I gathered that he and his artist friends—names that meant nothing to me, like Béla Czobel and Róbert Berény and Odön Márffy—spent nights awake, crawling through the café life. At two in the morning the artists met at Japan, a coffee house on Andrássy near the Elizabeth Ring, smoking cigarettes, sipping wine, playing cards on the raspberry-colored marble tables.

But, he said, there was a different world in the city that was taboo, a neighborhood no tourist ever visited.

Winifred nodded at that statement. "Probably with good reason."

Of course, Winifred balked, finding the idea suspect—and dangerous.

"We will take you there," Bertalan Pór said. "You will understand something else about this city. The heartbeat."

I was intrigued, the old reporter in me beckoning.

"We'll be killed," Winifred told me.

I didn't answer.

Of course, as we lingered in the lobby of the Árpád, I contrived last-minute entreaties to a reluctant Winifred—she was carrying a flimsy summer parasol and didn't appreciate my glib comparison to the fierce Mrs. Pelham, a woman probably fast asleep at that hour in some small room at the back of the hotel.

"Hey, I know the districts," Harold informed us. "The late night cafés. The real seedy night spots where the girls dance the Maxixe and ragtime. Even Chicago."

"Chicago?" I asked.

"No, Csikago. A down-on-your-luck working-class neighborhood in the Eighth District, pickpockets everywhere, schemers, shifty-eyed souls, where the miscreants congregate. It's called that because folks think of the American Chicago—they picture a tumble-up city, bursting the seams, ramshackle tenements, hastily thrown up, grubbing Slovaks and Bohemians and Gypsies slaughtering cows in their backyards."

"Yes," I said grimly, "it sounds like my old neighborhood back in Chicago."

Which was why he insisted he accompany the four of us. Bizarrely, Winifred seemed relieved at his presence, as though another body, even squirrelly little Harold Gibbon, would guarantee her safety in the dark, uncharted streets.

So we wandered. The two artists maneuvered us down Andrássy, a wide, lively street paved with hard wooden blocks to soften the *clop clop clop* of horse traffic. We turned a corner and stopped before a storefront window. An artists' supply store, canvases and brushes and palates decorating the dusty window.

But there was also one gigantic painting framed in a gold gild, prominently displayed. Bertalan Pór pointed at it. "Mine." In English. Then, glancing at Lajos Tihanyi, he smiled. "Mine." A swelling of pride in his voice, and Tihanyi chuckled. An unlighted display, unfortunately, but light from the streetlamp helped me to see a huge canvas of dour figures, their clothing executed with brilliant if muted color—melancholy blues and reds. "My family," he announced. "A picture much talked of a couple years ago." He pointed to the leaning figures who looked vaguely ethereal—and unhappy, the mother with arms folded over her chest. Doubtless they were unwitting models for the bizarre and strange son of the household.

"And they're still talking to you?" Harold asked.

Tihanyi had been facing Harold and read his lips. Frowning, he turned away, breathed in, the muscles his neck bulging. A hiss escaped his throat. He stomped his foot on the pavement.

Bertalan tapped him on the shoulder. "You need to understand the American humor," he said in careful English.

Tihanyi shook his head, unhappy.

"Harold has no humor," Winifred told him.

"It's lovely," Harold went on, looking at Pór. "A Sunday album portrait."

Bertalan Pór looked at me. "And the American sarcasm."

"Yes," I sighed, "we're good at that, especially when we're insulting our hosts."

Bertalan Pór laughed and began walking away.

For nearly two hours we strolled by the cafés that seemed to populate every corner of the city. We skirted into a packed coffee house called Orpheum, pushed our way through the sweating, chattering crowd.

A church clock tolled midnight. "A midnight city," Bertalan Pór said to us, and I flashed to Cassandra Blaine in that midnight garden. Yes, Budapest flowered at night, the vibrant cafés bursting until dawn, but Cassandra had been alone outside the hotel—with the person who took her life.

Bertalan Pór secured a table in a corner.

Harold spent much of the time flitting among the tables, restless, his eyes dancing. He knew so many people, nodding to this one, chatting with that one. Backslapping, joking, whooping it up, buying drinks to toast whole tables of folks. "*Egészségedre!*" he screamed over and over. "To your health!" A man in a scarlet cape sent over a small tumbler of some drink, and Harold grinned widely. "It must be drunk without pausing, all of it." And he did so, dramatically upending the glass and downing the whiskey. He shivered and roared, and the crowd laughed. A few applauded. Of course, he stood and bowed.

While we sat in the coffee house, he disappeared for a while, roaming the streets, seeking adventure. He'd dart out and then back in, sliding into a seat at our table, sputter something in Hungarian to the artists, then speaking to Winifred and me in English. "You wouldn't understand. You have to be Hungarian."

"And you are?" I countered.

Tipsy, swinging his arms in the air, he announced, "Living in the shadow of an oppressive empire, you must be the oppressed people you are with. Today it's the Hungarians. I am a Hungarian. And proudly."

Winifred shook her head and he winked at her.

"Really, Mr. Gibbon. Such conduct would *not* be permitted in America. You do not wink at women."

"Hey, it ain't permitted here. They got more rules on proper conduct here than in that wild frontier we affectionately call America."

"Midnight," Bertalan Pór intoned again. "Time for the season in hell."

His words made Winifred jump. "Edna, I think…"

I didn't answer.

"We promised you Chicago."

Of course, Chicago to me was Lake Michigan, Lincoln Park, Maxwell Street's Jewish bazaar, my grandparents' old home on Calumet, sumptuous Sunday dinner with savory pot roast and parsley-speckled potatoes. An afternoon stroll on Michigan Avenue with a beau. A baseball game at Wrigley Field.

Harold sang out. "The real Budapest."

We wandered through smelly backwater streets, lit by sputtering gas and torches. Fires roared in rusted woodstoves inside alleyways, the stink of old wood burning. A few cafés with gaslight and candles had open doors, hucksters in front pointing us in. Factory workers with cigarettes and pails huddled on narrow lanes. A broken-down peasant cart rumbled by, the horse in tattered rope harnesses strapped to a crooked shaft.

A nightmarish scene out of Hogarth, this Eighth District, this make-believe Chicago. At midnight, at one a.m., probably even at four a.m. and at breaking dawn as the milk wagons lumbered over cobblestone, the gloomy streets and dark alleys were packed. Vagabonds ambled by with burlap bags slung over shoulders. A slatternly woman crouched in a corner, a toothless grin, her straggly hair bunched up under a bonnet, a lit fire in a barrel throwing ghastly shadows over her shrunken face as she offered gnarled apples from her lap. The sickening scent of burnt coffee wafted from an open doorway.

Harold was like an errant boy on holiday, skirting around plodding horses and carts, bumping into people, disappearing, popping back up at our elbows, grinning. I watched him rush pell-mell up a street, turn a corner, out of sight. Then he reappeared, letting out an Indian whoop. No heads turned, and that surprised me. He rushed back to us.

"I have a favorite Gypsy café up ahead. Come on."

He skipped ahead.

A band of dandyish lads, bedecked in ascots. tight black trousers, and high red leather boots, hissed at an old man pulling a horse into an alley. Loud, shrill prostitutes, their satin bonnets ablaze with red and gold ribbons, winked and smiled and invited. One girl, perhaps fourteen, maybe fifteen, circled the handsome Bertalan Pór, whispering sweetness to him and sneering at Winifred and me. Another leaned into Lajos Tihanyi, touched his cheek, and he seemed ready to follow her to the ends of the earth.

Bertalan Pór whispered to us, "My Lajos has a weakness for pretty girls."

Winifred shook her head, disgusted by it all. But not I—I sneered back at the cheerful girls, savoring all of this. I came from the real Chicago and had been a reporter in beer-sodden Milwaukee. Ladies of the midnight road were no match for my brutal gaze. The girls snarled, slid away.

"There are streets in London," Winifred began, but got no further. A chubby man in a winter cap, a gash across his face, begged her for a crown, holding out a grubby hand. She yelped and pushed past him.

Bertalan Pór watched us nervously, and then whispered, "Perhaps this is not…"

I held up my hand. "No matter, sir. We are fine."

Of course, Winifred wasn't. She nudged me. Go now. Leave. Now. Now. Edna, really.

Harold circled us, disappeared, reappeared, led us to the café he favored. Inside we sat and listened to a fat Gypsy violinist with wild, long black hair, a sunburnt man who thrilled with his nimble playing. I found myself tapping my feet. Harold poured wine for us.

At one point Harold left us again, dashing out, and Bertalan Pór asked me about him. "Ignore him," I said.

"It is hard to ignore the family cat that eats the grass that makes it dizzy."

I laughed. "Yes, Harold, the frenzied house cat."

A swarthy man with a brilliant black moustache, his puffy white shirt and crimson bandanna pulled low over his forehead, struggled to address us in German. He'd read our palms. Glorious fortunes, he hinted. His wide smile that revealed a blackened front tooth.

Harold returned, his pockets filled with honey walnut rolls, freshly baked, intoxicating, sweet. He handed one to each of us. I sipped wine and nibbled on the bread. Heavenly. Light and sugary and crusty, a sinful confection.

"Let's go." Harold said.

For a few minutes Bertalan Pór and Harold argued with the tavern keeper about the charges. Exorbitant, Pór yelled. Watered-down swill at double the price. Everyone yelled back and forth until, both sides relaxing, an amount was agreed upon, the requisite coins handed over, and we left. Behind us the barkeep's wife hurled curses at us.

I heard one word distinctly: "Americans." *Ameericuns.*

A filthy child, a girl perhaps five, lay on a piece of cardboard, hand outstretched, begging. Nearby her mother, a Gypsy in rags, pleaded with us, pointing to the child. "Dying, dying, my little girl. Dying." In German. She offered nostrums to cure whatever ailed us.

A man slithered alongside Bertalan Pór and offered obscene French photograph cards, fanned quickly in front of his face.

Somewhere, unseen, from a high open window, the sound of a Gypsy violin, mournful and lovely. A girlish laugh broke at the end. An old Gypsy woman pushed though us, making me jump. Behind her trailed a young boy with dark and brooding eyes, his long hair tied with a loose string at the back, an earring in his ear, a boy maybe seven, maybe eight, a cigarette hanging from his mouth, the red tip glowing in the dark.

"Chicago," Bertalan Pór whispered again.

Lajos Tihanyi watched everything closely, his face gleaming, his hands twitching. His eyes blinked wildly, like a Kodak snapping photographs, doubtless pictures he'd depict on canvas later that night in his studio.

Chicago. Pulse and throb and roar and scream.

A man and woman brushed past Harold, knocking him to the side. Harold immediately lunged after the man, grappled with him, and adroitly extracted his own wallet from the man's inside vest pocket. The man was bigger than Harold, but not ready for the spontaneous reaction, as Harold pummeled him, spinning him around, cursing him. A kick to the kneecap. The couple fled and Harold, triumphant, held up his wallet as though it were a trophy.

"I've been in Budapest a long time," he announced. "I'm nobody's fool."

A midget, round and bald, with a falsetto laugh, set balls of twine on fire and hurled them into the air, laughing darkly as they bounced off the pavement. A band of tough boys, all in shiny black trousers, loose peasant shirts and slough boy caps tight over their boyish curls, threw pebbles and coins at him, aiming for his head. He bowed and caught a fiery ball with his outstretched hand as he lunged for the meager pittance.

Chicago.

I'd had enough, this ill-considered romp as a voyeur, "Let's leave," I insisted.

Harold, his face aglow, was restless as we walked back to the hotel. He darted ahead, hung back, bellowed, sang, grumbled, disappeared. The two artists watched him closely, and I noticed Bertalan Pór smiling. Lajos Tihanyi, however, looked frightened of Harold.

"Thank you for a lovely evening," Winifred said to them as we stood on the quay in front of the Árpád. I shook my head.

"You did not enjoy yourself," Bertalan Pór said slowly. "I am sorry."

But I spoke up. "Actually, I did. Although I'm enjoying it more now that we are standing in front of the hotel and there is no one hurling fireballs over my head."

Harold was a hundred yards away, walking back to us.

As I stepped toward the hotel, I heard him cry out, a wounded animal bellow that made us spin around toward him. To my horror Harold was crumpled on the sidewalk, his body twisted with his knees pulled up to his chest, his head flat on the pavement. Two men stood over him, shadowy silhouettes in the dim light, one of them fiercely kicking him in the side. Harold rolled away, screamed, and covered his head with his hands. One of the men swiftly kicked Harold's head.

I was screaming as Bertalan Pór and Lajos Tihanyi ran toward them, but the two men, alerted, dashed away and rounded a corner. Bravely, Pór gave chase, pausing barely a second by the writhing Harold and then disappearing into the next street. Lajos Tihanyi was kneeling by Harold, his hand resting on Harold's shoulder. Winifred and I, both moving like reluctant sleepwalkers, shuffled toward Harold who was now sitting up on the sidewalk, both hands holding a bruised and bloody head. Tears streamed down his cheeks.

"Harold, what?" I asked, but he stared vacantly at us. Then, as though losing power over his body, he sank back to the sidewalk, his legs stretching out before him, his shoulders flat on the ground, his head lolled to one side.

"Are you all right?" Winifred whispered. "Say something."

At that moment Bertalan Pór returned, panting, out of breath, and he spoke in a raspy voice. "Gone, both of them. Hooligans."

Lajos Tihanyi was frantic, heaving and making a gurgling sound. His friend watched him closely.

"Austrian officers," Bertalan Pór told us.

"What?" From me, rattled.

He pointed to his own jacket. "One man was wearing an old regiment jacket. I recognized it."

Harold was muttering something as he tried to sit up.

"Don't move," Bertalan Pór told him. "We will get help."

"Warned me. Cursed me in German. Leave Budapest now. Mind my own business."

He struggled to stand and Bertalan Pór helped him. "Then they weren't just bandits," I announced.

Harold was shaking his head. A smear of blood over his left eye, a clump of dirt on his chin. A deep gouge on his neck, dark blood staining his shirt.

Suddenly a smile covered his features. "The murder."

"What are you talking about?" I asked.

"The murder." His bruised fingers touched the wetness on his forehead. "Or my remarks about Franz Josef. The end of the empire." A puzzled look on his face. "Or both. I'm an enemy of the empire."

"We need to get you to the hospital." Bertalan Pór tucked his arm under Harold's shoulder. But the injured man shrugged him off, lumbering ahead, wobbly, headed into the hotel. The two Hungarians looked at each other, confused, but both stepped behind Harold, almost touching him, as though to catch him should he topple. Harold moved slowly, dragging his feet, but he never stopped chattering. This conspiracy, that one, this intrigue, this news story, that sensational headline. The hated military stalking him. All nonsense, of course. Bertalan Pór signaled to Winifred to rush ahead into the hotel to call for help.

"Hospital," he whispered.

As we neared the entrance of the hotel, a porter rushed out, stumbling after Winifred. We were a motley crew—Harold staggering, Lajos Tihanyi's head bobbing up and down, Bertalan Pór's face set in a stern steely look—and my expression one of utter alarm.

"Help is coming," Winifred announced.

Behind the porter stood some men who'd been lounging in the lobby, one with a cigar bobbing in his mouth. Another still held a newspaper, folded back. Among them was Jonathan Wolf, who stood back at first, but then moved forward, offering his arm to the teetering Harold.

"Tell me what happened," he said to me as he reached for Harold's arm.

Eyes dreamy now, his speech slurred and lazy, Harold managed to open his eyes to face Wolf. A stark look of recognition. With a trembling hand, he pointed at the man. "Don't you come near me. How do I know they weren't acting under your orders?" With that, he passed out, slipping out of Bertalan Pór's tenuous hold and crumpling up on the steps.

Chapter Thirteen

Early the next evening I sat alone at a table on the terrace. Winifred had spent most of the day in her rooms, ill with a headache and insisting she'd never recover from last night's ill-advised romp through the nether regions of tenderloin Budapest, an unfortunate evening capped off with the brutal assault on the gadfly journalist.

"I'll lie in bed with chocolate and cherries and a cold compress on my head." She winked at me. "This is all your fault, Edna dear." But she smiled. "At my age I should only be in the street with a placard for suffrage…in the company of hundreds of other women. That's dangerous enough." She jokingly pointed a finger at me. "You will always be a woman who steps lively into dangerous territory, Edna."

"Thank God," I'd countered.

"I hope you never regret those words."

So I sat alone and grieved and considered…and thought of Harold…and of Cassandra. But my thoughts kept drifting back to Jonathan Wolf. He was a piece of a puzzle that wouldn't come together. He was like a low-hanging sun in a tropical sky—always there, a brilliant ball of red fire whenever you turned your head.

Idly, I sipped coffee, dipped a spoon into a bowl of coffee ice cream, though I'd lingered so long at the table the dessert had melted. I tried to focus on the newspaper, the *London Times*, but the black-and-white print blurred, swam before my eyes. The headlines alarmed me. So much of the world was focused on the region where I now sat with coffee and ice cream: the futile and desperate balance between the Habsburg, Hohenzollern, and Romanov dynasties, each one seemingly hell-bent on its own destruction. Emperor and King, Kaiser, and Tsar. Anachronisms, all of them. Imperial and royal monarchies, failed. Puffery and ego and ceremonial braid. *Kaiserliche und Königliche Monarchie.* The newspaper shorthand: *K.u.k.* Cluck cluck cluck. Barnyard chatter.

Stop, I told myself—my mind wandering. During my recent stay in Berlin, I'd undergone a sea change. Germany had always felt like an ancestral home—from the comfortable distance of Chicago. We spoke German in our parlors, we cooked German food. But close up, Germany swelled and gloated...a land bubbling with sentimentality and gnawing rage. I imagined an unseen voice whispering in my ear. "Come, Edna, come *Julchen*, get out of here. Get out!"

The Romanovs in Russia were cardboard cutouts from a child's book. Grubby peasants looked in on gold and silver, out of reach, blinding them. And Austria-Hungary, the stern though trembling hand pointing at its far-flung regions—from Hungary to Bohemia, to Moravia, to so many other lands, unaware that the edges of the wonderful tapestry were always the first places where the unraveling began. Maybe not unaware—but indifferent. But...so what?

I sat there and asked myself: So what? Yet Harold made it his business to pinch and prick and shove the underpinnings of that Austrian Empire. He held a mirror to its wizened face. Is that why he had been beaten, threatened? Austrian spies reported the annoying American who seemed determined to foment trouble?

Baffling, all of it.

The waiter hovered nearby in a rigid Prussian stance, arrow straight, waiting for me to look up. When I did, he bowed and asked in garbled English whether I wished anything else. He was not Markov or any other familiar servers I'd come to recognize, but a thin blond, blue-eyed young man, boyish, though with a jagged blood-red scar on the side of his mouth that gave his face a peculiarly sardonic cast. I shook my head, no. Another bow, lower, a clicking of heels, and then he left me alone.

I'd spotted the poet István Nagy sitting a few tables away, his profile to me, his gigantic Aubrey Beardsley nose tilted up. As the waiter walked away, the poet turned to me, eyes squinting and then conspicuously dropped back to the sheaf of papers spread out on the table before him. He held a pencil in the air, poised as though waiting for heavenly inspiration, then tapped it against his pale cheek. But his poetic muse seemed absent at the moment, so he sat back and contemplated the Danube. But as I watched, he flicked his head toward me, checking on me, then away—more than once. An unsettling monitoring of my activity. What part did he play in this café drama?

I'd never looked closely at him. A stringy looking man, perhaps in his late forties, maybe older, wearing intricate layers of clothing, despite the day's heat. But dated, even to my American eye—a waistcoat draped over his shoulders, unbuttoned, his arms not in the sleeves, a brocaded vest studded with silver buttons inlaid with flat pearls, a garment that smacked of diplomatic courts of a half-century before. The cuffed old boots, the mocha-colored trousers, the checkered scarf wrapped around his neck as if to ward off chills from the river. That sculptured profile exaggerated his hawk-like nose, very British decadent, a thin moustache lost under its mountainous proportions, and a stubby Van Dyke goatee, carefully manicured. His brown hair, tinged with specks of white, grew over his shoulders, the last refugee from some Bohemian quarter of a distant past. He was an art-nouveau cameo etched against the Danube.

He kept watching me, though furtively.

Inspector Horváth and another man crossed the terrace, headed into the hotel lobby, and spotted me. "Miss Ferber," he addressed me, bowing.

"Inspector Horváth."

A slight smile. "You remember my name?"

"Of course. You impressed me, sir."

He bowed again deferentially. "An honor."

"You were told about last night's attack?"

"Yes. In fact, I am here to interview your Mr. Gibbon."

"Well, he's not mine, let me assure you. I gather he's resting in his room. He returned from the hospital this morning, head bandaged, a black-and-blue welt on his chin, but probably filled with the same dogged determination to tempt fate again. His wounds will be battle scars. We'll have to read about it."

Inspector Horváth's smile suggested he'd not fully comprehended my words.

I'd seen Harold briefly that morning, shuffling in, an attendant leading him to the elevator. Standing in the lobby, I'd called to him, but he avoided me, bending slightly, his head dipped into his chest.

"I don't like it when visitors are so...so assaulted in our streets."

I frowned. "We don't much care for it either."

His engaging smile, a bow, and he headed to the hotel.

István Nagy gargled aloud, though he sounded as though he immediately regretted that indiscretion.

"Sir?" I called to him. He refused to look at me. "Sir? You seem to find my brief talk with Inspector Horváth disagreeable?"

He shot a stern glance at me. "You presume too much."

"Oh, I don't think so, Mr. Nagy."

"The petty lives of Americans, especially the rich ones who visit our country, do not interest me."

"I don't think you're telling me the truth. I've seen you inside the café, leaning to the side, fearful that you'll miss some scrap of gossip spoken at a nearby table."

He bristled, pursed his lips. "I sit quietly and write my poetry."

"Yet you sit in a café populated by Americans and British." I smiled. "Are you honing your English-language skills?"

"My English is serviceable, madam." He offered a sickly smile. "As you can of course hear at this moment."

"I'll grant you that. Where did you learn English?"

"In England, which is why I speak English. Unlike you Americans who speak...wild Indian."

I chuckled. "Ah, as a boy you must have consumed Beadle's dime novels. Deadwood Dick and that sort. Cowboys and Indians and Buffalo Bill and…"

"I read Shakespeare," he interrupted me.

"Another wild man if there ever was one."

"The American movie sweeps over the young people of Budapest, madam. Sweltering halls with giddy men and women watching your idiotic Charlie Chaplin and galloping Wild West romance, all to the tinkle of a maddening piano."

"So you sit in that darkened hall and believe you're seeing the real America?"

"I don't go to such movies, madam."

"But you've become a social commentator on them, no?"

That bothered him. He turned away.

I stood up and walked to his table. "We haven't had a conversation, sir, though you seemed to have listened in on many of mine…and that of my friends."

He refused to look up. "Nor do I plan to have one now."

He infuriated me. At that moment, watching the beads of sweat form on his brow, the tendons on the back of his wrists tremble, and hearing a deep intake of breath, I suddenly understood something. Perhaps István Nagy was not a bystander to the tragedies and comedies that happened in the Café Europa. Perhaps he was a player. But what did that mean?

I sat down in a chair opposite him. "May I join you?"

He was furious but spoke in an even, steely voice through clenched teeth. He tugged at the scarf around his neck, exaggerating the movements like some *fin de siècle* British esthete performing for friends—or trying to escape from my intrusion by choking himself to death.

"I rather you not, madam."

I ignored that. "Perhaps we can…" I stopped because he raised a hand, palm out, fingers spread out. He started gathering his pads, tucking his pencil into a vest pocket.

"Are you aware, Miss Ferber, that in Europe it is considered improper for an unaccompanied lady to do what you're doing—uninvited, you sit with a gentleman. Do you understand how that looks?"

"Of course I do."

"Perhaps in America where there are no rules of conduct such behavior is acceptable."

"No, actually it isn't. The unchaperoned lady is a badge of dishonor in most places. So be it. My mother would be horrified at my behavior. She'd *agree* with you. Applaud you, in fact." I waited a heartbeat. "But, yes, even in America unchaperoned women do not behave so...indecorously."

"And yet here you are at my table."

"Sad, isn't it? I've obviously displayed moral lapses in more than one country."

"You make light of it all."

"Sir," I got serious, "I'm deeply aware of the archaic conventions of the day, especially regarding the proper conduct of women as regulated by short-sighted men." I chuckled. "But I'll let my friend Winifred Moss address *that* issue. She's much more in tune with the ugly strictures men place on women. But, truthfully, I am hoping you can give me some answers."

"About?"

"About Harold Gibbon and Cassandra Blaine and...and Zsuzsa Kós...the whole..."

He narrowed his eyes into slits. "I'm a simple poet. I write *nouvelle chanson* about the courts of love. The *Jugendstil* or what you Americans call art nouveau. The slipping of winter into spring. The maiden in a field of summer flowers. The..."

"Very nice, I'm sure. Lovely. Delightful. Yet events are happening that need to be looked at."

"By you?" His voice broke and his eyes grew cloudy.

"Why not? I'm a reporter."

He groaned. "Americans in Budapest are always reporters or...rich women in silk and fur." A rumble from deep in his throat. "Now I see the two can be one and the same."

A twinkle in his eye, his pale lips turned up briefly, a nod of his head. What was clear to me at that moment was that István

Nagy, despite his protests to the contrary, welcomed this conversation. He *wanted* it, naysayer though he was. That baffled me, and intrigued. Something would be said here. He signaled to a waiter who returned with a bottle of wine and another glass, though Nagy had said nothing to him.

My tone was conciliatory. "Sir, you're an habitué of the café. You are obviously comfortable there. You see what happens. You must have opinions on the murder, on the attack on Harold Gibbon, on whatever happens."

He pointed. "Let me tell you something, Miss Ferber. I adopted the Café Europa years back—long before its unfortunate discovery by the Americans and the British. The old, creaky hotel became a—muse. Yes, a muse for me." A sliver of a smile. "I'm charmed by its failings, its faded glory. Even though the lights dim too often, and sputter, hiss, making my heart quake. As a young man, fresh from a sojourn in Vienna where my first poems were published in a literary journal, my first poems, I found a comfortable table *here*."

"Vienna? But you're Hungarian?"

"My mother was from Vienna. An old Austrian family. Von Hofmann. Very respected, moneyed. My father was a professor in one of the university departments. A Magyar who loved Vienna. He died happily there."

"But you returned here to Budapest?"

He paused. "None of this is really important, Miss Ferber."

"It's conversation."

He drew his lips into a thin line. "I've discovered that nothing is ever *just* conversation. Behind your American vernacular is always some nagging question or suspicion or insult."

I smiled. "Never *just* idle curiosity?"

"Not in my experience. Americans are wily and smug, a deadly combination."

"Agreed. But such a combination makes for intriguing character, no? Perhaps we all become minor characters in a Henry James novel when we step onto European soil."

He raised his eyebrows. "What is it you wish to ask me, Miss Ferber? The sun will soon set and I prefer to contemplate the Hungarian sunset on the Danube in silence—the somber, wistful, echoes of a past on this lovely river."

"Probably a past that never existed."

A sardonic smile. "It only matters that it lives in my memory."

"True." I leaned in. "I've seen you talking with Jonathan Wolf, sir."

The abrupt shift in conversation registered not one bit. Nonplused, that same smile stuck to his face, he waited a moment. "That man bothered me as I sat alone. Once again, an American who does not wait for an invitation." He eyed me suspiciously. "I suppose it's a national characteristic. Every plot of land on this earth is his territory, occupied or not. Ever since Teddy Roosevelt presumed to send that mythic white fleet around the globe, insisting it sent the message that America had arrived on the international landscape, well, Americans place their bodies wherever they will."

"So Mr. Wolf is not a friend?"

"I scarcely know the man. I've seen him lingering around the hallways, sheltered by what he thinks are invisible doors, watching, watching."

"I did see you talking to him that night as you sat on a bench on the quay."

That stopped him. "Really? Were you hiding in the bushes by the locust trees?"

"I saw you push him."

A long pause as he considered what to tell me. Finally, sighing, he said, "He disturbed my silence."

"So you shoved him?"

"He asked too many questions."

"About what?"

"Well, if you must know, and obviously you do, since Americans have taken all rudeness as their province, he first feigned an interest in my verse, his being supposedly a lover of Dante Rossetti and that circle."

"Really?" That surprised me.

"Amazing, wouldn't you say? And he looks like any wealthy American on the Grand Tour, buying folk baubles he'll display back in America as relics of some fabled European past."

"Yes, the same past you entertain in your mind."

For the first time he offered a real smile. "Touché, my dear Miss Ferber."

"That was it—that talk of poetry?" I smiled. "That's why you shoved him?"

"Of course not. I'm not a foolhardy man. Mr. Wolf has no good intentions in Budapest."

"What do you mean?"

He stared into my face. "He purposely goaded me. A remark that I—I might be a spy. That's when I shoved him."

"A spy?"

"For the Austrian military."

"Are you?"

"He's a mad man."

"But that was it?"

A puzzled look covered his face. "Bizarre, his questioning, I must say. He asked about the hotel guests."

"Like?"

"Like the Blaines. He saw me saying good morning to Marcus Blaine. That pleasantry stunned him, I gather."

"Mr. Blaine?"

"He didn't return the greeting, as I recall. But Jonathan Wolf wondered about our…friendship. Of course, there is none."

Blaine? That flummoxed me. What was Wolf up to? "That seems absurd."

"Exactly. If you must know, once again, I suspect that he's not an American, despite the tailored clothing and bundles of dollars he sends flying into the Hungarian economy."

"That surprises me."

"Score one point for me then."

"What proof?"

"None. He has a slight accent that suggests he's from Eastern Europe, though it's been polished and honed."

"Hungarian?"

"One wonders. That, or Slavic. Perhaps German."

"What else about him?"

He waited a moment, glanced toward the Danube. The light was shifting as twilight neared. A rosy haze at the horizon, a patch of cobalt blue around the wispy clouds high in the sky.

"I believe he's an Italian anarchist."

"Mr. Nagy, why?" My voice rose. "I can't imagine an anarchist looking so…"

"So splendid in a suit?"

"Well, yes."

"I know in America—and even here, sadly—the cartoonists depict the anarchists as grubby socialist Muscovites in peasant garb, running through the streets with lit bombs in their hands. Left-wing Jews."

I smiled. "Yes, I've seen such cartoons. We had a Haymarket riot in the States—horrible—and the cartoonists did just that."

"Anarchists are the true spies, my dear lady."

"And they're in Budapest?" At that moment I felt that Nagy didn't believe what he was telling me—it was some foolish lie calculated to get me to react. An Italian anarchist? Jonathan Wolf?

He went on. "You forget, an Italian anarchist killed our beloved Empress Elisabeth as she strolled a river bank in Geneva. There are troublemakers everywhere, especially in the empire. With the crisis with Serbia looming, they lie in wait. They look for opportunity. You do know that there have been attempts on Franz Josef before. On other members of the royal family. A Bosnian Serb threw a bomb at Franz Ferdinand already. The brutal Young Bosnia, insane radicals. The ultimate prize is the old man himself. Franz Josef. That would be cataclysmic."

"You are an apologist for the old regime, I take it."

"I am loyal to the Habsburgs. They civilized our lives, even here in rebellious Budapest."

"But not modern."

"Modern?" A mocking tone. "You mean automobiles and the like? America insists the world mimic its love of foolish invention. Someday America will ruin the world with its noisy contraptions. Without a royal family, an emperor, we flounder, slide back into the Dark Ages. Chaos."

"And how do you fit into the scheme of things?"

"I hope I am the bard. The empire's Homer, though not of epics but of simple elegiac lyrics."

"Odes to the end of something?"

He grimaced. "Now you sound like that pesky reporter, Mr. Gibbon."

"He predicts a war shortly."

"There will be no war. None. The world fears the awesome Austrian army. Serbia squeals like a cornered pig in a sty—which, by the way, is where they discover their monarchs—but Austria-Hungary is mighty. A day's skirmish perhaps, the Serbian weeps and licks wounds, and Emperor Franz Josef dines that night on consommé, partridge, and caviar."

"All civilizations have a golden age and then become decadent. It's the sweep of history, no?"

"You're a poor student of history, I fear."

"Alexandria, Rome, Greece, others."

"We are not corrupt from within."

"Mr. Gibbon believes…"

He held up his hand. "Please."

"What do you think happened to him last night?"

"An American flashing money in a bad neighborhood where only miscreants reside. What else could happen?"

"But he was warned to leave Budapest."

He deliberated that. "I've been told that's what he *says* was told him. Frankly, he's a man who craves sensation. A gossipmonger, hungry for attention. Booming American headlines. He probably hired those hooligans to pummel him."

"Bertalan Pór ran after them and says one at least wore remnants of the Austrian military guard. I'm not certain…"

Again the hand in my face, but now there was a flash of anger. "That horrible Hungarian. Him and that...that circus performer, Lajos Tihanyi, hands gesturing, his mouth mumbling sounds a caged monkey would be embarrassed to utter."

My smile was beatific. "For all his being deaf and dumb, sir, he manages to express himself beautifully, especially with his art."

The man rolled back, tickled by my remarks, a laugh escaping his chest. "You call that art. A tribe of Negroes splashing colors on a canvas. Another symptom of a wayward society stinking with the manure of France."

"I admit these artistic currents today confuse me—but they don't *alarm* me. Abstractions, geometric patterns, black crosses, this Kandinsky, this Malevich, this Matisse in Paris—we have to allow the contrary vision, no?"

Emphatic, sneering: "No."

"So much for expanding one's vision."

"That's not vision. That's distortion, purposeful or willful destruction of a tradition. We already have too many of these embarrassing exhibitions in Budapest, let me tell you. The Vienna Secession. Oskar Kokoschka and his dabs of obscene paint. I've walked by the windows of galleries—impossible, destructive. Bertalan Pór and that defective he's friends with— they *kill* art. Gertrude Stein and that mob of scribblers who cannot parse an intelligent sentence."

Though I felt no need to defend my Hungarian friends, I said, "Perhaps they are the pioneers. Perhaps they see something that will be commonplace a hundred years from now, something accepted as natural and right and true to some artist's soul."

"For Lord's sake, Miss Ferber, do you hear what comes out of your mouth?"

That rankled. "I don't speak unless I have something to say."

"American cockiness."

"Perhaps you should imbibe a bit of American stamina and brio and...and zest for life. This languid posturing of another century gets to be wearing on the nerves. Like a fussy cat that keeps pawing at you."

His eyes got wide. "Yes," he said in a world-weary voice, "the American invasion of the world. Look how it ended with the American heiress."

"That's cruel, no?"

"But true. Cassandra Blaine and her parents sweep into an old city and decide to buy it for their occasional humor."

"Still, Mr. Nagy, you must agree that a young girl shouldn't die because of the sins of her ambitious parents."

"You saw that girl, Miss Ferber. Too loud, too insane, her laughter over nothing funny."

"Again, no reason to be murdered."

He debated that. "But don't you realize cause and effect dominate the sweep of history? Her father bustles about, the man of affairs, masterminding the building of a structure to house an American insurance company. No one in Budapest really needs that. Hobnobbing with women with titles and history, a mother suddenly wants her own blue blood, not the thin red kind she inherited. So easy to arrange a marriage. Everyone's doing it. When Consuelo Vanderbilt listened to her mother and married that dirt-poor Duke of Marlborough, immediately every rich mother from a prairie state shed her buckskin and gingham and swam the Atlantic for a tiara and a title."

"Again, not Cassandra's fault."

"She has to assume some blame, no? She was a woman in her twenties—not a giggly girl playing hoops. Her marriage was one more metaphor of the new stupid American greed. America is money. Simple as that. Money. Not art nor music nor literature. You *have* none. You have stockyards and gold mines and—and rustlers. Everything is *bang bang bang*. The Colt .45 and the rifle. Cassandra's father sits on money made from killing people in your Civil War. *Bang bang bang*. You are all cowboys who became the Indians. Red skins, all of you. Not bows and arrow, Miss Ferber. *Bang bang bang*. Shoot up the world. Hold up the world. Give me your money or I'll shoot you.

"Yes, the good Count Frederic von Erhlich is poor, the result of his father's indiscretion. And his mother the countess less than wise. But that wedding could *never* be. The empire crumbles under such temptation."

"You've thought this through, sir. And you got your wish. The wedding will not take place." I breathed in. "But tell me. Who should the count marry now?"

He actually gave the idea some thought. Then, nodding as if he'd solved a riddle, he said slowly, "His station."

"What?"

"Someone from his class. With equal parts nobility and lineage."

"And if such a lass is not available for purchase?"

"Crass, Miss Ferber."

"Good. I was afraid I was too subtle with you."

He lapsed into silence, but he was furious. Color rose in his neck, an eyebrow twitched, the eyes darkened. "Americans will never understand marriage."

"It's not a difficult concept. Boy meets girl, boy..."

"Stop, please."

"Are you married?"

"Of course not. I..." He tapped the sheets on the table. "I have my poetry."

"What is *your* station in life, sir?"

He waited a long time. "You're mocking me, Miss Ferber. I'm not a fool. To the contrary, I see the future clearly—and it isn't pretty. Luckily I have enough family money to avoid mixing with the world—out there." He crooked an elbow and wagged a finger at the quay. "I may worship the past—look back to previous centuries with sadness—but I believe I *understand* the future. Not your Bertalan Pór and Lajos Tihanyi and that bunch of misguided Hungarians panting like dogs before a perverted French master. They stink up the streets. Oh yes! I see the future."

"And just what do you see?"

"All *this* will disappear. The idea of stations will disappear. If there is a war, people like me will disappear." He pointed to Castle Hill. "All that beauty will disappear. An anarchist's bomb will end it all." A sickly leer. "The deformed and the invalids will rule the world."

I lifted my chin. "Quite the picture you paint, sir."

"Your odd Tihanyi will be our Prime Minister, Miss Ferber."

"Cruel again, Mr. Nagy."

"Oh, I hope so. Perhaps you're a woman who understands cruelty, Miss Ferber. You're young but you'll have your battles royal as your life goes on. The world fascinates you—but also irritates. I suspect you'll destroy a few souls."

I started to speak but he rushed on. "Like most Americans, you are afraid of silence. You know, one of our writers, Gyula Krúdy, has a character say, 'Everybody who still wants to live here after Franz Josef's death is a fool.'" He bowed slightly. "Well, I'm that fool. We are headed for a century of disaster. I feel it in my bones. Everyone will be an anarchist. Or a socialist. Americans will own everybody. Gypsies will head parliament. Jews will slaughter Christian babies for blood ritual. Good men will have to shake the hands of Jews and Gypsies. Unthinkable. Automobiles will run over innocents. Airplanes will fall into houses. Stars will fail to shine. The sun will be dimmed. Women like that fire-breather friend of yours, Miss Moss, will lead the charge. Can you imagine that catastrophe? Women will *vote*."

He stressed the word, an awful curse. "Women will whip men for their own pleasure." He was out of breath now, panting, sweating, paralyzed with his own dark vision of the future.

I stood up and bowed with a flourish: "It sounds like something to look forward to."

"Destruction, Miss Ferber?"

"Voting, Mr. Nagy."

Chapter Fourteen

Mrs. Pelham gasped when Harold Gibbon walked into the café a short time later. Sitting at a table near her, waiting for Winifred to join me before we left for supper, I watched Cassandra's erstwhile hired companion—the prim watchdog who'd failed at her task—gingerly sipping a glass of red wine. She been there for a half hour perhaps, escorted in by an overdressed Russian man wearing too much gold chain and too many diamond rings, his hair slicked back and glistening, a man in his forties. Mrs. Pelham, to my surprise, was glibly chatting in Russian and English, but forced to slip back into her native London speech when words failed her.

This encounter was obviously some sort of employment interview, as I gathered the Russian would be bringing his family from St. Petersburg shortly, and he worried about his headstrong seventeen-year-old daughter, Natasha.

"A firm hand, that's what I provide," Mrs. Pelham advised. He nodded at her. She smiled back at him and sipped the wine.

Annoying, all of it. When she first strolled in, she caught my eye but quickly averted her glance. I saw anger and suspicion—and, for no good reason, warning.

When Harold stood in the doorway for a moment, surveying the room, it was, I supposed, a purposeful entrance. With a bandaged head, bruises on his face and neck, he looked the veteran returning from a war, save for his grin. He spotted me and waved. Then, to my consternation, he spotted Mrs. Pelham, who'd suspended her conversation in mid-sentence, slack-jawed, staring at the wounded man.

"Ah, the delightful Mrs. Pelham. The lady's companion who courts death."

That made no sense, and the Russian, glowering, watched Harold through half-shut eyes as he struck a match and lit a cigar. Mrs. Pelham's expression froze.

Harold looked back over his shoulder toward the lobby, calling out in Hungarian. He turned sideways as Endre Molnár joined him. For a moment the two chatted quietly, Endre's face glum but Harold's typically impish. Endre was dressed like an enterprising American businessman with a black suit, gold velvet vest, and an ostentatious gold watch fob. Very dashing, I had to admit, though the grandiose European moustache still had a life of its own, its shellacked edges turned up like tusks.

"Miss Ferber." Both men bowed at me, though Endre Molnár's was genuine courtesy and Harold Gibbon's smacked of parody. I invited both men to sit at my table.

"Mr. Gibbon," I began, "you look like the first casualty of that war you predict."

"So you remember my prophecies."

"They're a little hard to forget when you trumpet the idea constantly. Usually at this very table."

Endre Molnár laughed. "Mr. Gibbon believes war is a game. We Europeans understand it is unavoidable insanity."

"Not a game," Harold went on. "A strategy played out by the greedy."

"How are you feeling?" I asked him.

He shrugged off my remark, though he placed a hand on his bandaged head. "Women look at me with sympathy."

"If that's what you insist on believing."

Endre was shaking his head. "Your friend does not take this assault seriously, Miss Ferber. Perhaps you can make him understand." He glanced toward the terrace. "There is danger out there."

"Hooligans," Harold interrupted. "Mountain brigands venturing into the city to rob the tourists."

"But what about the warning, sir?" I insisted. "That you leave Budapest. That's hardly the request of a simple robber."

He weighed the strength of my words. "I know, I know. But maybe I *imagined* they said that. I wasn't exactly in control of the moment. And I know that Bertalan Pór believes they were sent by disgruntled Austrians who balk at my message. In so many dispatches I wrote about the death of the empire. Last week's column made a dire prediction about Franz Ferdinand's fate. I predicted his death. The Austrians, irate, wired Hearst—make the scoundrel Harold Gibbon back off. The ambassador sent an indignant letter. Hearst loved it—published their cable."

"More bold headlines, Mr. Gibbon?" I teased.

He beamed. "The only kind the Chief enjoys. In fact"—he paused, reached into his back pocket and extracted a newspaper—"you can see for yourself."

Dramatically, he waved the front page before our eyes. The usual garish, house-on-fire headline: "Hearst Reporter Brutally Attacked!"

Harold's fingers tapped the paper. "Me! The reporter has become the story. Hearst is drunk with it. He's sent wires all over the place." Another dramatic pause. "Me!"

He pointed to a small, grainy photograph of himself—Harold as the young journalist in a stiff Eton collar, Ben Franklin eyeglasses perched on his nose. "Me! Washington, goaded by the Chief, has been hammering at Baron Meyerhold. No progress in solving Cassandra Blaine's murder, of course. What an embarrassment for the Austrians! And now—me!" A sidelong glance at me. "If I didn't know better, I'd think the Chief himself paid hooligans to attack me. It's sort of the thing he'd actually do—*create* the story, not report it."

"Harold, is he creating a war in Europe?"

Harold's smile was disingenuous. "No, but he encourages folks like me to help it along."

I pointed to his bandaged head. "Good job."

"I'm not a popular man in Vienna."

"Which is why you are in Budapest," Endre Molnár added.

"But perhaps you'd best return to America," I told him.

"Never!" he roared, his serious tone at odds with his playful demeanor. "Have you lost your mind? This is the hotbed, everything I work for. Here. Right here. The first shot will be fired in due time, and I want to be *here*. Austria continues to squeeze the poor Serbians."

"But," I tapped my finger on the table to make a point, "let's hope the first shot is not aimed at you."

"Hey, I'm too small a target. It'll be like shooting a schoolboy skipping down the street."

Endre turned to me, concern in his eyes. "Your friend has refused to talk to the police. Inspector Horváth of the Royal Police visited but was turned away. That was not wise. I know Horváth as a good man. A man I often play cards with at the National Casino. He is concerned…"

"Nothing to say. This is all part of my job. It's what I do, you know. I stir up a hornet's nest, and the wild insects buzz and hum and flit. And I get the story."

"Well, this time you *are* the story," I told him. "How much does it hurt?" I waved at his head.

"It's nothing."

"Really? A small price you pay for being the story?"

"Great, ain't it?"

"Not really," I answered slowly, biting my lip.

Winifred joined us, and Endre Molnár jumped up, bowed, held out a chair. Harold, his mind off somewhere, remained seated. Winifred frowned at him. "Don't bother to get up, Mr. Gibbon."

He didn't answer.

I told Endre, "Miss Moss and I are going to the Opera House. Maria Jeritza in Puccini's *The Girl of the Golden West*. Seven o'clock curtain. We'll sup afterwards at the Lake Restaurant."

He smiled. "Ah, you are becoming Hungarians."

Harold was paying no attention to us. "You know what I find interesting?" he broke in. "That pompous investigator, Baron Meyerhold, hasn't been around lately."

"How do you know?" I asked him.

"I have spies in this hotel. They tell me everything."

"Well, clearly not everything."

He made a face. "They tell me what's important. In some quarters I'm seen as a prophet of the end of Austria-Hungary. I'm not fond of Serbians, that much is true, though I don't like the Austrians bullying them around. But I do like the Hungarians. Hospitable folks, most of them."

"Except for the ones who beat you in the streets." My face was set.

"Austrians," Harold whispered.

Endre looked nervous at the shift in the conversation. "Mr. Gibbon, you are doing it again."

"What?"

"Talking too liberally about politics."

"That's what I do."

Endre leaned in, confidentially. "But Baron Meyerhold has visited me any number of times. In my rooms."

That surprised me, and alarmed. "And what happened?" My throat dry.

Endre deliberated what he wanted to say. "He says very little, in fact." A raffish smile as he touched the edges of his moustache. "He mentions my wealthy family. My distinguished father. The internationally renowned pottery we produce. The coveted name of Zsolnay. A signature of Hungarian art, known worldwide. That's how he talks of it. 'You, sir, a delightful man of affairs.' Flattering, humming along, unctuous, believing none of it." He twisted his head to the side. "My father has influence."

"So he'll not arrest you?" I was relieved.

He shook his head. "Not so simple as that, dear Miss Ferber. Vienna would love to see the whole tragedy ignored, forgotten. But the Americans are insistent on some resolution of this murder. The American government listens to Mr. Blaine who is a powerhouse in your country. Aetna Insurance. Colt Firearms. The rich upper crust. Newport society. Dinner at the White House. A telegram from Teddy Roosevelt. William Randolph Hearst trumpeting the story in the newspapers, courtesy of..." He stopped and stared at Harold.

"Because of me." Beaming, bowing.

"So the American Embassy demands an arrest. Baron Meyerhold conveniently believes I am the man who took poor Cassandra's short life away. But he's caught between American and Hungarian influence. Of course, he despises Hungarians, but he is politically astute. Inept, but not a fool, that man."

"A horrible combination."

"He's feeling the pressure from America." Endre looked at Harold. "From your Mr. Hearst. Those headlines speak of scandal, cover-up, incompetence. Not good. And this latest attack on you, Harold, will bring him back to my rooms. As I said, an incompetent man, spinning in circles and hoping he'll fall into a confession." He laughed. "He's afraid of America."

"He should be," Harold said. "President—Hearst."

"Yes, even the Hungarian and Austrian newspapers are afraid of Mr. Hearst. He hammers and steams and pounds his fists." He wagged a finger at Harold. "The editors here don't know how to translate his explosive American idioms, but they understand the fury."

"So the Baron doesn't know what to do?" I asked.

"A messy murder—an American."

"So nothing will happen?" The prospect of a murderer going free gob-smacked me.

"No," Endre went on, "ultimately I will be arrested. But in terms acceptable to Hungarian authorities. Somehow I must be discredited, some manufactured scandal perhaps, something anti-Hungarian. Someone reports that he heard me curse my country in a late-night tavern. The newspapers report it. Some trumped-up nonsense that will have the Magyars nodding and saying—Ah, too bad, a true son of Hungary lost his way. Take him away. Chain him."

"Horrible," I protested.

"But a fact of life in a corrupt world."

"Hey, I got a question about the note you received from Cassandra that night." Harold punctuated his words with his fist on the table.

"What?" Endre asked, puzzled. "What are you talking about?"

"It's one fact my spies can't help me with. And something the police haven't paid much mind to. The note Cassandra sent to *you* that night—the invitation to meet her in the garden."

Endre looked pained, turning his head aside and staring out the terrace to the Danube. "What does it matter now?"

"Oh, but it does, my friend. How did you find that note?"

Endre didn't want to discuss it, but he sighed, resigned. "Someone slipped it under my door at my apartment. Not in the box at front. Under the door. I admit I was surprised."

"Why?"

He smiled, his moustache twitching. "Earlier notes from Cassandra were left discreetly in the front box. But this time someone walked into the hallway—to be certain I received it that very night. I was there, in fact, but heard nothing. When I walked past my door, I spotted the note on the floor. From Cassandra."

"And you answered it."

"Of course. The note they found on her…her body. I said I'd meet her as she asked. I left it with the clerk in front."

"That's my point," Harold stressed. "Cassandra would have asked the day clerk or the night clerk, one of the porters, even a bellboy, to deliver the note."

"And?" I asked, impatient.

"And no one has admitted delivering the note. I've checked— my sources. Cassandra gave it to someone *not* connected to the staff. Someone she trusted."

"Mrs. Pelham?" I wondered out loud.

"I doubt it." Harold glanced at the table where Mrs. Pelham sat with the Russian, her back turned from us. When I glanced over—we all did, unfortunately—she must have sensed that she was being discussed. She swung around and glared, but only for a brief second. Frowning, she emptied the last of her wine. The Russian was signaling for a check.

"Could Cassandra herself have slipped out and left it?" I asked. Silence, long and uncomfortable. "Maybe," Harold acknowledged. "Unlikely, but possible. She was known to slip away from Mrs. Pelham's brutal eye now and then."

Endre laughed. "Yes, she did. We did meet secretly."

"So it is possible." I looked into Endre's face.

"She wouldn't walk into the building—too daring. Even if she did, wouldn't she have knocked on the door?" he asked. "A quick comment—meet me tonight. Then rush off. Impossible."

"No," I concluded, "someone in the Blaine household—a maid perhaps, or the valet—could have done it—in defiance of her parents' rule. Dangerous for them, but maybe Cassandra bribed one—or pleaded. A few gold coins pressed into an eager palm. Or, in fact, perhaps one of the servants might have sympathized with her."

"But the household staff is gone now." Endre shrugged. "It's impossible to know."

Harold was quiet too long. Finally, swallowing, he grumbled, "It's driving me crazy." Another long silence. "But I do have a suspicion."

Then, like an apparition, floating and swaying, Zsuzsa Kós drifted in from the terrace, her arms outstretched dramatically, her head thrown back. From her lips a plaintive humming. A stage entrance, I thought, Salome with the gaudy veils and noontime yellow hair. She called out Harold's name, elongating it so that it became a spooky chant. A mourner's keening. *Harrrooollld.* We all started, shifted in our seats. No, that wasn't true. Harold didn't move a muscle, eyes focused on the floating woman. Endre and I—and I think the rest of the café—watched her awful performance. Again, in English, a long wail. *Wooounded my prince.*

Well, her wounded prince was having none of it. An icy stare, chin jutting, fingers gripping the edge of the table.

Zsuzsa had doubtless learned of the assault on her midnight lover.

Dressed in a turquoise-colored gown with a gold shawl covering her shoulders, an enormous hat of feathers and veils atop that golden pompadour, she struck me as a woman from a French melodrama—or a sleepwalking Marie Antoinette headed for the guillotine on that fateful day. A sweep of fluttering arms, a twirling of her body, a tossing of her head—syncopated movements designed to make her a cynosure on the stage. Or, in this case, the dimly lit Café Europa.

She approached the table, stood over Harold, waiting. He refused to look up. Quietly, she reached out, and her fingertips touched the bandage on his head, lingered there for a moment, and then she drifted away, her shawl falling off her shoulders and dragging behind her.

Salome of the seven veils. Or, at least, one veil.

Winifred poked me in the shoulder. "Splendid, no?"

I was speechless.

Then she was gone, disappeared into the warm Budapest night. We waited.

"As I was saying," Harold began.

Endre interrupted. "Mr. Gibbon, surely you…" His gaze followed the disappeared Zsuzsa. "What?"

Harold shook his head mechanically, his voice booming now. "As I was saying." But then he said nothing more.

I smiled at Winifred. Harold Gibbon, suave but bogus *bon vivant*, suddenly bested by the sad cabaret singer. The price, I supposed, he paid for investigative reporting deep in the night.

"Mr. Gibbon, the wages of sin…" I began. His glare stopped me.

A waiter placed a bottle of mineral water on the table. Vladimir Markov, emerging from the kitchen, approached and squinted at Harold. "A bromide, sir?" he asked. "A headache."

Harold shook his head. "Very kind, sir, but no."

Markov bowed and stepped away, but Harold called him back. "Mr. Markov, has that Serbian worker returned to your kitchen?"

"Sir?"

"The one who was drunk the night Cassandra Blaine was murdered. The one taken to jail."

Markov turned pale, stammered. "Of course. A good baker, that one, and..."

"I'd like to question him. Ivo—his name, right?"

Markov bit his lip. Winifred looked at me and shook her head. She raised her voice, "Mr. Gibbon, could you please not terrorize the kitchen?"

"I'm doing my job. I have a few questions for my article. I need an outsider's perspective on the annexation of Bosnia and Herzegovina—the Serbian point of view."

Markov spoke up, "But, sir, he's a baker, not a...a politician."

"Still and all."

"And he was born in Budapest. He is Hungarian."

"Yet he speaks Serbian."

"Most people in Hungary understand it a little bit. Many speak it. You know the Serbian Orthodox Church on Szerb Utca where many devout, good Serbians pray. I can speak the language, sir. A little. *You* speak it, no?"

"Nevertheless." Harold touched the man's sleeve. "Sit and talk with us a bit, good sir. Indulge me."

Markov looked toward the lobby, his voice dropping to a ragged whisper. "You would have me fired, Mr. Gibbon." Breathing in, a rasp at the back of his throat, he shot a look at Winifred and then at me. "Dear ladies, the other day when I spoke with you, that brief conversation, meaningless, but confiding with guests, forbidden, my words, someone tells the owners. Someone listening—though we were alone." He hurriedly glanced toward the entrance. "I have been spoken to by the man who pays my wages. A violation, such...friendliness. My job is to serve. So I have been warned. My job is in danger."

"The hell with that," Harold snarled. "I'll talk to people. I know people."

But Markov was already backing away. "No, please. My job. This is what I have. Now that my family is back in Russia in a village, my wife is gone...no money...sir."

He kept backing up, a few steps at a time, until he finally disappeared into the kitchen.

"Mr. Gibbon," I implored, "could you please leave the man alone? Your quest for information is relentless."

"It's my..."

"Job," Winifred finished for him, her voice too loud in the room.

At that moment Mrs. Pelham was leaving, but she paused, deliberated, and then announced in a loud, very British voice, "Americans should never be given passports. They are children, always. And children should never leave their homes."

Harold burst out laughing, and even Endre, surprised, smiled. Mrs. Pelham barged out of the room, trailed by the Russian who had no idea what had just happened.

Standing, Harold announced he needed to lie down, and Endre offered to escort his friend to his room. Winifred and I were left alone at the table, looking at each other with wide, bright eyes. "My lord," I began. "Harold does stir up some pots."

"He started to say he had an idea."

"Yes, a suspicion about something. But what?"

"The murder?"

"Or the death of the empire?"

She laughed. "Harold on the track of solving something?"

"But he seems not to be able to put the pieces together."

She nodded. "Is it possible that Harold may have discovered something and not realized its importance?"

"Well, maybe he can't see the whole picture."

Again, the throaty laugh. "And we can?"

I smiled back at her. Perhaps that will be my task.

Yes.

After all, Harold wasn't the only American reporter in town.

Chapter Fifteen

The garden alongside the hotel's terrace was filled with late-blooming red roses and oleander, so the air was rich with a heady perfume. So potent the scent that I got momentarily dizzy, my eyes watery. I wondered about the night Cassandra was murdered in this very garden—the late night quiet, the bracing cool air, the faraway hum of the Danube, and the intoxicating power of the flowers. Now, in the middle of a quiet morning following a heavy rainstorm at dawn, the garden glistened as if all the green leaves had been painstakingly polished. I sat on a wrought-iron bench and faced the hazy sun hovering over the river.

I also faced Lajos Tihanyi who was standing ten feet from me, his stare penetrating, a sketchbook on a portable easel. He was drawing me. So intense was his concentration that I immediately thought of a classic painting: *Aristotle Contemplating the Bust of Homer.* No Homer here, to be sure, but a self-conscious American short-story writer trying to look winsome and fetching. Neither trait I'd ever allowed myself.

Of course, I'd refused to model for him. Over and over. To paint me in red—his redundant plea. I also knew that he and Bertalan Pór had quietly sketched Winifred and me—and, to be sure, everyone else, including that rascal Harold Gibbon—as we lounged in the Café Europa. With no effort made to mask their activities, they peered and stabbed at their sketchpads, then peered again, smiled at each other, squinted, and waited for us to sit still. I suppose we accommodated them, or at least Winifred did, given her joy of being with the pioneer artists, wanderers out of some paint-smeared French atelier that housed Matisse or Juan Gris or…maybe Picasso. We freely let them.

But Tihanyi wanted a longer session, his subject posing in the garden against a backdrop of leafy green branches and gray tree bark. Me, in a red jacket. As I told him, I owned none because such a vibrant color always struck me as too exhibitionist. The scarlet woman, targeted. But on the morning I agreed to sit for an hour, without talking—or with little talking—the hotel clerk handed me a package that contained a gorgeous crimson jacket, deepest red with tints of rose and gold. A little snug in the shoulders, but it did fit. And I had to begrudgingly admit that I felt grand in it, the Chinese emperor's newest concubine. The Jewish slave girl on the Nile, outshining Cleopatra on that lumbering barge.

Alone, the two of us, I was alarmed at first, given Tihanyi's difficulties with speech. He sounded words that were unintelligible to me. I wished that Bertalan Pór were there, and he shortly was, rushing in from the quay as though he'd missed an engagement. But I'd not been bothered by Tihanyi's quirky mannerisms, the two of us somehow finding an easy, emphatic way to communicate. He had a smooth companionability, a gentility I'd noticed in so many Hungarians, a masculine self-assuredness infused with the soft solicitousness a person associated with women. A startling juxtaposition, that combination, exaggerated by the clownish-looking man in the baggy jacket and the slough boy cap, a man who gestured wildly. I read his every gesture perfectly. He understood that. I liked him tremendously.

Bertalan Pór lingered at the edge of the garden, his own sketchpad tucked into his chest. At one point he said something to his friend, coming up close to him, though the words, spoken in Hungarian, were laced with laughter. Tihanyi pointed his pencil at Pór, then winked at me. A little disconcerting, I thought, because I always demanded to know what was being said about me.

"What did he say?" I asked Tihanyi, but I regretted my words. Did I expect him to answer? But, in fact, he did, a mannered pantomime with his hands and facial expressions, even a low hum from the back of his throat, a routine that suggested he was having a wonderful time—that he'd gotten his wish. Miss Ferber, the American short-story writer, was sitting in a garden where the scent of roses and oleander overwhelmed. I smiled.

"I don't like my portrait being painted."

"Then you are not an egoist," Bertalan Pór said.

"Oh, but I am, sir. Anyone who dares to put words to paper or oil to a canvas has to be an egoist." I paused. "Or a downright silly fool."

He laughed. "We are all fools."

"Thank you," I quipped.

Both men laughed.

Bertalan Pór confided, "In 1907 the artist Berény displayed his portrait of me at the Salon des Indépendants in Paris. I watched as visitors pointed at me and laughed. A critic called it 'filth-smeared Gauguinism.'"

I frowned. "I fear the same reaction will greet a portrait of me"—I paused—"in red."

But Lajos Tihanyi's face suddenly tightened, and he made grunting, unpleasant sounds. He snapped his brush in two. I started but didn't move. Zsuzsa Kós had entered the garden from the side, pausing a few feet from me, staring at me, staring at Lajos Tihanyi, narrowing her eyes at Bertalan Pór. A purplish color rose in her face, and her eyes flashed.

She moved slowly but finally positioned herself between me and Tihanyi, her arms folded over her chest as she glared at the hapless painter.

Bertalan Pór said something in Hungarian, and she flicked her head toward him. Anger there, raw hurt.

"What?" I sputtered.

Zsuzsa spoke to me in English, heavily accented, but her intent mightily evident. "You? You, the muse for the Hungarian painter?"

I wasn't amused by her attack, but kept still.

Lajos Tihanyi grunted. Bubbles of spittle formed at the corners of his mouth as he gargled out some nonsense syllables. He stamped his foot like a pouting child.

"I have been painted by the great Gustav Reich who painted Lola Montez. My portrait hung in the window of a gallery in the Kohlmarket. In Vienna. The Imperial Gallery begged to buy it for their collection. Only the Hungarians ignore their own singer."

Dressed in a simple periwinkle-blue morning dress with a white lace headscarf covering her golden hair, she twisted around like a dance-hall coquette, then posed, her palms placed under her chin. Then she approached Tihanyi's easel and peered at what he'd drawn. Laughter rose in her throat as she pointed. "This…this is not art."

"Please." Bertalan Pór sidled up to her. "This is not your moment, dear Zsuzsa Kós, you who've had so many beautiful moments."

It was, I thought, a beautiful line, and a moment especially for me as I sat in the perfumed garden.

But Zsuzsa raged, swinging her arms at the drawing, and Tihanyi, appalled, stepped back, his hands in front of his face. Zsuzsa stared over our heads toward the late morning sky and cried, "They are saying it's my fault, the murder of that girl. You think I don't hear the ugly whispers in the café at night. Murder, murder, murder. The folks turn their heads on the street. They point at me with anger. 'She, our Zsuzsa, the songbird, she led the American girl into murder.' They tell me I am to blame. If I hadn't introduced her to the count, she'd be alive, that girl. Me—blame me."

"Miss Kós," I began, but she wasn't talking to us. I realized then that I was watching the aging entertainer slipping away from reason, the frantic, faraway eyes of a prisoner isolated too long in a cell. "Miss Kós," I began again, "perhaps some coffee?"

She snapped out of her trance. "I know things."

That jolted me. "What things?"

She laughed rashly as she glanced at Tihanyi's drawing. Her hand reached out as if to tear it to shreds. But Tihanyi pushed by her, blocking the drawing, and Zsuzsa stumbled, nearly toppling into some bushes. She righted herself with the help of Bertalan Pór, and shrieked a torrent of Hungarian.

The effect on the volatile Tihanyi was immediate. Wild-eyed, arms flailing, he barked at her, his body swaying. Bertalan Pór tried to grasp his shoulders, but the painter was incensed now—he breathed fire, his cheeks dotted with red, his hands banging against his chest. Alarmed, I stood up, ready to flee these two impassioned Hungarians, but Zsuzsa suddenly stopped her own fury, backed away from the agitated artist, and stumbled out of the garden. Lajos Tihanyi, exhausted, sank to the ground, his body quaking, his shoulders slumped. He was sobbing.

"Well," Bertalan Pór nodded at me, "we witness the artistic temperament. The sad old singer acting out her loneliness and… and my good friend…the painter who will someday cut off his ear in the grand tradition of…" But he stopped. Abruptly Lajos Tihanyi stood up, hastily gathered his easel and canvas, crammed his brushes and paints into his field box, and stormed away.

At the edge of the quay he turned, calm now, his face serene, and he smiled at me, bowing low. He uttered incomprehensible syllables at me, impossible to grasp, though Bertalan Pór understood. "He apologizes for his behavior, but his art is all he has."

I doubted whether Tihanyi's utterances conveyed that noble sentiment, but I nodded back, content.

"And," Bertalan Pór went on, "You and your friend Winifred Moss are invited to his studio this afternoon at four to see his work."

Again, I nodded.

Then he quietly went after Lajos Tihanyi.

Minutes later, sitting in the lobby waiting for Winifred to join me, the desk clerk left his station and handed me a letter. "For the Miss Ferber." He bowed as I smiled at his English. "It arrives moments ago on the morning post."

Winifred joined me as I was opening the letter. "My mother," I told her, "writing me from Berlin."

"Good news?" she asked.

I frowned. "I rather doubt it. It *is* from my mother."

Winifred blinked. "Edna, really."

I read the letter quickly and looked up. "She's not joining me in Budapest."

"Well, you didn't expect her to, right?"

"True, but she's not happy in Berlin, it seems." I ran my eyes down the page. "A disagreement with a cousin, though she doesn't go into details. Some nasty words exchanged." I looked up at Winifred. "I'll hear about it for years to come." But the last paragraph caught my attention. "A visit to her oldest brother Isadore ended with someone hurling an anti-Semitic slur her way. She says she called his name out in a restaurant, and I guess his name is commonly used by some provincial Jew haters in beer hall comedy skits. Can you imagine that? It really unnerved her. So she was told to whisper his name." I ran my tongue into the corner of my mouth. "My mother doesn't believe in whispering."

"That's preposterous," Winifred said. "I never heard of such a thing."

"So she wants to leave Germany as soon as possible."

"Why not come here then?" A chuckle. "The Hotel Árpád will gladly dim the lights for her."

"No, she's headed to Paris, our final stop, and she wants me to join her there within the week. Three days from now, in fact."

"But your plans…"

"Are never a concern to her."

"What will you do?"

I sighed and folded the letter back into the envelope. "I believe we have an engagement this afternoon at the studio of a rather bizarre Hungarian painter whom I've come to like." I tucked the letter into my purse. "I'm rather looking forward to the visit. Perhaps later on you and I can take in some theater and a late-night supper."

At three o'clock Bertalan Pór appeared in the lobby to escort Winifred and me to Tihanyi's atelier. Dressed in a spiffy formal jacket with an elaborate necktie and carrying a pair of white linen kid gloves, he looked ready to attend a fancy cotillion and not a messy workaday artist's studio. "Afterwards, we go to tea or coffee," he told me as I greeted him. "And some cake." He pointed to his clothing. "Afternoon tea in Budapest is a formal occasion. For Miss Moss we drink tea *a l'anglaise* at five o'clock." Winifred whispered at me. "And we're dressed for a boat ride on the Danube."

Bertalan Pór shook his head back and forth. "Of course not. The American women in Budapest dress for dinner when they rise in the morning. They always look like…Paris."

"Flatterers everywhere," I commented. "I like it."

"It is necessary," he added, a remark I had trouble interpreting. But I followed the young artist out onto the quay. We walked down from the landing and onto the Váci Utca, then turned onto Rákóczi, and finally into a small street that seemed more alley than passageway. Bertalan Pór pointed to the large windows on the second floor of a grim, soot-covered brick building. "Up there."

"Up there" meant entering a dark stairwell with only a sputtering electric light bulb on the first floor, none too helpful as we climbed the narrow steps, creaky and sloping. I caught Winifred's eye. She was blissfully happy. Of course, she was—she loved those grubby Parisian artists in their gas-lit garrets and their paint-splattered lives.

The door was open, and the stinging assault of turpentine and dried paint wafted into the hallway. But I also heard a man's cheerful voice, laughing loudly at something, the rich rolling Hungarian cadences filling the room. Tihanyi Lajos, it seemed, had another surprise guest. Endre Molnár, also dressed in elegant attire, was leaning against a back wall, contemplating a painting hung there. When he heard us, he swiveled, delighted, and ushered us into the spacious room.

A cluttered shambles of a room, though Winifred scooted about admiring it all. Canvases and pads stacked up against the walls, four or five paint-blotchy palettes hanging off nails, easels holding incomplete canvases. A bank of windows on one side let sunshine flood the rooms, giving everything a lit-by-fire feeling. A comfortable space, I thought, and wholly Tihanyi's. His Expressionistic art assailed you at every turn—staggering geometric angles fused with brilliant hues of primary color. Portraits and landscapes, but of men at their most vulnerable, rolling farm fields at their most fantastic. This was no country other than one that brewed in his fevered imagination.

He bowed at us, excited, and immediately led me to a table on which was a scattered collection of drawings of—me. Yes—me. Me, in various poses, caught unawares in the café or on the street. Laughing, somber, lazy, dull. Me, posed decorously in the morning garden. Me, looking fierce and driven and a little world weary. Me, looking sad and lonely. Or ready to wither an annoying soul. Sketches of me, drawn in red crayon. The red jacket, collar turned up or flattened. Bothered, I said nothing though I was certain my confused expression revealed my astonishment. Try drawing *that*, I thought. He waited and I begrudgingly offered him an anemic smile that satisfied him.

Endre Molnár was watching me closely. "We are seen only through Tihanyi's special prism," he told me. "He aims to catch the soul. Look what he did to me."

An easel turned away from us held a completed oil painting, oversized, brilliant in royal blues and forest greens, melancholy, sad, yet a spurt of liveliness. So like the Hungarians—weeping made them feel alive. Endre Molnár, posed in a black Prince Albert coat, a diamond stick pin in burnished gold, his untamed moustache a blue-black sweep of color. His rigid jaw line sharp— a geometric slash. Aggressive, Alpine shoulders, pointed. But Tihanyi had purposely exaggerated Endre's one lazy eye, magnifying it so that it gave the portrait a vaguely oriental cast. Utterly and unabashedly charming, the painting. Riveting. I fairly lost my breath. So handsome, so magnetic, so—so enticing.

I struggled to speak. "You posed for…"

He broke in. "Sooner or later everyone poses for Tihanyi." He locked eyes with mine. "You know that Armageddon our friend

Mr. Gibbon announces with some regularity—well, that war is waged in rooms like this. A Hungarian critic has called this art 'a declaration of war.' The artists are the ones who shatter the comforts of the few."

Bertalan Pór nodded toward the sketches of me on the table. "Next you sit in the studio here."

I agreed.

But I found myself wandering back to another table strewn with the sketches the two artists had made in the Café Europa—and, I supposed, other cafés. The work-in-progress for their planned art book. Dozens of sheets, pencil sketches, half-finished, finished, abandoned, labored over. Works by both of them. There were many of Winifred, some so sad it hurt to look at them—the artist caught the pain she carried with her from England. But another showed her laughing in a way I'd not seen—utter joy, vibrant.

"Everyone in the Café Europa?" I asked them.

"The ones that intrigue," Bertalan Pór noted.

I spread them out, this varied panorama of faces and tables and chairs. Bottles of wine. A lithe waiter with a tray held high in the air. The Gypsy orchestra and the intense violinist. Zsuzsa Kós slumped at a table. Folks I didn't recognize. Many of them. And Cassandra and Mrs. Pelham. Over and over, a sweep of images both flattering and ugly, the sordid personality and the beautiful. I tapped one of them.

"Jonathan Wolf," I announced.

Endre looked over my shoulder. "Harold insists he's a spy."

Frustrated, I looked into his face. "Yes, I know. István Nagy told me Mr. Wolf called *him* a spy. He also said Wolf's an Italian anarchist." Endre's eyebrows rose at that statement. "But for whom? For what purpose?" The drawing showed a man with a Rasputin stare. "Madness, all of it."

He shrugged. "Harold's fancy perhaps. Maybe Wolf is only a rich American, a lone wanderer through Budapest streets."

"No," I said, "there *is* something about that man. He's always near when something happens. Frankly, I don't believe such moments are purely coincidental. He's not what he demands we believe him to be."

Lajos Tihanyi had been reading my lips, his face concentrating on mine. Finally he said something softly to Pór, but his friend looked perplexed at the stammered words. So Tihanyi jotted something on a slip of paper and handed it to him. He read it and smiled. "Lajos insists Wolf has the face of someone from Gypsy villages in Transylvania."

Tihanyi was nodding, and Bertalan Pór added, "Lajos watches every face he meets. He sees everything. In one minute he reads your soul. In a second he knows whether he should *like* you."

"I remember his words: 'I see what you hear.'"

Tihanyi, comprehending, sputtered happily.

As I peered at the drawings before me, so many focused on the Café Europa, my heart began to pound. There had to be some clue buried in the blunt pencil lines and bold charcoal smudges—something that told me something I needed to know. Cassandra and Mrs. Pelham at that table, a series of drawings, different moods, postures. What? I believed the answer to the murder had been captured by Lajos Tihanyi and Bertalan Pór as they sketched away. I had no idea why I thought that, but it held me. Staring down at the drawings, I had no idea where to begin looking. My mind swam.

"And now," Endre was saying, "we will go to New York."

Winifred glanced at me. "New York?"

Endre laughed. "Budapest's New York."

I rolled my eyes. "We've already been to your version of Chicago, sir. I still have heart palpitations and recurring dizzy spells. Perhaps it is best if…"

He was shaking his head. "New York is the café of choice these days. Not the intimacy and old worn fabric feel of the Café Europa, to be sure. New York is where everyone goes at five for tea or coffee. Or a glass of Tokay. Our table awaits us."

Bertalan Pór offered his arm to Winifred, who was touched by the gesture. Immediately she began asking about his days studying at the Acádemie Julian in Paris. He mentioned that a short time ago in Munich one of Tihanyi's paintings was rejected from the show—labeled *entartete kunst*, degenerate art—and so immediately Pór withdrew his own paintings.

"The brotherhood of artists," he told her. "Our Prime Minister István Tisza attacked my exhibit in Budapest." He grinned. "Expected, yes, but it still is hard to get used to—such dislike."

Thrilled, Winifred talked in a hushed but lively voice. She looked—softened. Yes, that was the word that came to mind. This hard-bitten soldier of the suffragette wars in England, so bruised and battered by the mocking, scurrilous men on the sidelines of her protest parade—this war-torn warrior of a noble cause had come to own a hard face, especially when men approached her. And rightly so. She understood her enemy.

And yet I'd seen her smile slightly as Harold Gibbon danced around her, teasing, impudent. And now, in the company of the courtly Hungarians, these talented and gentle forecasters of another future, she softened, responded to them. Winifred Moss was being brought back into a loving humanity. Wonderful to watch, I thought, and necessary.

Winifred walked at a brisk clip as we headed to the café.

New York was a modern coffee house connected to an American insurance company. "Not Marcus Blaine's," Endre quietly informed us.

An intimidating place, this New York, with its Gilded Age abundance. Slick marble floors and columns, huge gilt mirrors, blazing chandeliers, gold leaf trim everywhere and—horror of horrors, a pedestrian replica of the Statue of Liberty under a huge Stars and Stripes. New York, indeed. A palace built to overwhelm, which, of course, had the opposite effect—you cringed at the opulence, the sheer ugliness of unfettered riches. Crowded, a blue haze of cigarette smoke hurting your eyes, steamy, the smell of sweating bodies. The heady scent of thick red wine and too many cigars. Chess, checkers, newspapers, talk, arguments, politics, love, hate, a slap in the face, a hug in the corner, an illicit touching of the Gypsy waitress as she shuffled by with a tray of whiskey and soda. Yes, a celebration of life, I supposed, some usurping of the glitter world of, say, Paris or even New York itself without the carefree, devil-may-care abandon. Here the nagging melancholy inborn in the Hungarian lent the room a wistful, bittersweet beauty.

Delightful though our coffee was, especially in the company of these deferential gentlemen, my mind kept reverting back to Tihanyi's studio, that helter-skelter mess of drawings spread across that table. Scenes from café society. But something else—scenes from the characters in a murder. The dead and the—the what? The killer? A strand nagged at me, rumbled in my head, and, distracted, I found myself staring across the crowded café, hardly paying attention to the casual talk about café life, the globules of caviar slathered on thick black bread, the sumptuous chocolate cream cake called Rigó Jancsi, and even the pleasant Gypsy music.

Endre Molnár hired an open car, rather extravagant, and the five of us went to City Park for an evening of Tchaikovsky, though sitting next to the deaf Tihanyi diminished some of the pleasure for me. When it ended, Endre escorted us to Magyaros, a greenery restaurant at Deák Square, where we had cold sour cherry soup, followed by chicken *paprikás* with dumplings, eating outside under leafy chestnut trees. A crowded restaurant, a haze of cigarette smoke drifting into a hard blue sky. At midnight the car delivered us home, the two artists choosing to walk the short distance to their apartments. But as the automobile turned a corner, we noticed a sleek black town car parked in front of a villa set back from the street. As the car slowed, Endre nodded toward the occupants, then stepping out.

The countess and her son, Count Frederic von Erhlich—he sharply dressed in his decorated military uniform, she dressed in a black velvet gown with jeweled piping—both paused a moment on the sidewalk. A streetlight made them seem resplendent characters in a Viennese operetta. Attendants bowed and scraped, but the countess, covering her face with a veil, moved through them, never turning her head. In a hurry she called her son's name without turning back to look at him, but the count lingered by the open door of the town car as a woman emerged. A tiny capon of a woman with a plump, round face, she said something to the count. Reluctantly he reached for her hand.

Endre cleared his throat. "The Duchess of Saxony."

"I don't understand."

"A widow two decades the count's senior," he added. "An unhappy woman who has shopped for a husband in the marketplace."

"You're saying?"

Endre swallowed. "Rumor says that the count is already betrothed to the woman."

"Money?'

He snickered, but then seemed sorry he spoke. "Lots of it. Tons. But a nasty woman with a profane tongue, unhappy, blistering. Servants run from her, weep, hide. Her cruelty is legendary. She's never forgiven a slight—and everything is considered a slight. But very respectable German aristocracy. A mountain castle. Essen steel money."

"So everyone wins." Winifred's words were dry.

"All except poor Cassandra." I said.

I immediately regretted my words.

Endre's face sagged and his hands trembled.

Chapter Sixteen

Moments later Winifred and I sat on a bench on the quay watching a steamship move quietly up the Danube. Endre Molnár left us in the lobby of the hotel, but we weren't ready for bed. The night had been too lustrous. The company of Endre and the two painters, coupled with that robust supper at Magyaros, capped off with a glass of sherry at a small café where everyone greeted Endre enthusiastically, left us unwilling to end such an evening. So we drifted out through the terrace and sat on a bench over the river, facing Castle Hill, shimmering with light. A glorious night, a slight breeze of the river, the bellow of a whistle from a passing boat, the *clop clop clop* of a two-horse fiacre passing by, and the throaty roar of a lumbering town car's engine. In the distance the whine of a tram's brakes. Anachronistic, this city, like most modern cities—the horse and the machine crossing paths in the bustling metropolis. A night chill made me shiver.

"Time for bed," I told Winifred, rustling in the seat.

She nodded, yawned.

A few stragglers strolled by, the sound of a woman's voice reaching us.

"Zsuzsa," I said. "God no."

Winifred peered through the darkness, down along the railings of the quay. We could see two indistinct figures moving slowly toward us, one silent, one talking loudly with arms gesturing toward the other. Zsuzsa and Harold. Only one voice—Zsuzsa's. Harold walked a step or so ahead of her, as though hoping for separation, but as they neared us, Zsuzsa reached out and tugged at his elbow. He flicked her off.

"Harold," she cried, louder now. "You run from me."

He was watching us now, his body turned sideways, facing the hotel. "Tell me," he said to her.

"But you keep asking questions."

Winifred frowned. "This cannot be good. I don't want to be here. "

But I watched closely and tried to catch every word.

"You told me you saw something."

She chuckled. "I see so many things. So many."

He raised his voice. "Tell me. I hate your infernal secrets. You play games with me, dear Zsuzsa."

"Men love my games. They…"

"Maybe they *used* to love your…" He stopped. He must have seen something in her face because he stepped back, mumbled what sounded like a feeble apology.

"You want me to…"

"What I want, dear Zsuzsa, is for you to tell me what you saw. In City Park maybe. Somewhere. *Something*. You told me…"

She giggled again and missed a step, rolling against his side. "The night is so chilly."

He threw his hands up as though to catch her, but no—his movement was one of surrender. Hands up in the air. "All right, all right."

"It's so late, dear Harold." A hand reached out in the dark and touched his cheek.

He backed away, darted ahead like a scurrying rabbit, then stopped. He looked back at her, twisted his head left and right. When he glanced at Winifred and me, both of us frozen on that bench some yards away, he breathed in deeply, offered us a half-hearted smile. Helpless, that look, because he didn't want an audience, the Greek chorus of steely-eyed spinsters.

"Please, Harold." Begging in her voice.

He remained stony, arms folded over his chest. When she approached, she dipped her head into his neck and whispered something. He turned to face her, his body tense, and mumbled something to her that I missed. But I caught the tone—biting, raw.

Zsuzsa let out a choked sob, and then, twirling around, she slapped him in the face and stumbled toward the hotel.

Sheepish, Harold stood over us, waiting. But we said nothing—what was there to say?—and then, bowing dramatically like a rebuffed knight from the ancient Courts of Love, he declared, "Sometimes I don't like myself." He waited a second. "I suppose you two don't believe me, but it's true. Sometimes I wonder why I do the things I do."

◇◇◇

In the morning in the café Winifred remarked that she'd heard Harold's insistent voice in her hallway late last night. "Act Two of that tragedy," she added. "The bedroom scene. A reprise."

"Harold is playing with fire, Winifred. He wants information that he assumes she has, though that's questionable. Zsuzsa talks too much and to everyone. That's dangerous these days, but most folks probably believe it's all stuff and nonsense. The aging cabaret singer struggling for attention, slipping into her own fantasy world. A woman afraid to face nighttime—afraid to face the morning sun. Except that Harold believes she has a story to tell. So he's going at it the only way she'll accept—flattering her, wooing her, celebrating her…allure."

"Allure?" Winifred's eyebrows rose. "Really, Edna."

"You know, there's something sad when a beautiful woman gets old. For years, back in gay old Vienna, Zsuzsa lived on admiring glances from men. The pretty young singer, heralded, toasted. Lord, some old fool pays her hotel bill nowadays, true? Old camp followers of the sultry singer. A cabaret voice, satin and silk gowns, feathers in her hair. And she *was* beautiful—she *still* is under that powder and dye. But when she looks in the mirror she wants to remember that young girl, stunning."

"And that's where our scamp Harold comes into the picture."

"Exactly. A moral lapse on his part, I grant you."

"Maybe it's fair—each gets what each wants."

I shrugged my shoulders. "He wants information which he believes she has—but playfully holds back from him. She wants someone to pay attention to her. Or love. She hungers for love. Someone to hold onto at night."

Winifred shivered. "Really, Edna. The words that come out of your mouth."

"But both lose in the end because each act is selfish."

She mimicked Harold. "'I'm a reporter.'"

"And he is, and a good one who'll use one ruse or another to get his story. Who thrives on getting the scoop. The almighty scoop. You forget that I was a reporter once."

She smiled. "But you never batted your eyelids or smiled at... William Jennings Bryan to get an interview."

I smiled back. "How do you know?"

Harold appeared, his morning coat rumpled and his hair plastered down so slickly that he resembled some villain from a Broadway melodrama—Do not hiss the villain, please. Without preamble, he slid into a chair opposite me, and smiled widely, a huckleberry grin that exaggerated the freckles on his face.

"I know what you're thinking," he grinned.

"I always hate it when someone presumes to understand what is going on in my head." I smiled back at him.

"You think I'm a cad."

Winifred nodded. "I *know* you're a cad."

Harold shrugged it off. "Anyway, here's the plan for the day."

"What?" I asked, bewildered.

"You know, everything is starting to fall into place, I tell you. Things are cracking. I mean it. It's like electricity in the air. Don't you feel it?"

"Mr. Gibbon," I stressed, " you need to be more specific. Isn't that one of the tenets of news reporting? A quick review for you: who what where when—why are you so evasive? Perhaps your boss, Mr. Hearst, failed to properly instruct you."

He looked at Winifred and winked. "She's a hard nut to crack, wouldn't you say?"

"Mr. Gibbon," Winifred said sharply. "You assume that the women you encounter fall neatly into easy categories."

He frowned. "I don't know much about the women, I will tell you, but we men are simple folk. We don't have that much variation."

"So we agree on something," Winifred noted, a hint of a smile on her lips.

"I can tell you're starting to like me." He wagged his finger at her.

"I'd be more concerned with having the world respect you than worry about liking you."

"I want to be loved."

"Don't we all," I interjected.

"I don't." Winifred startled both Harold and me.

Harold, however, was rocking in his chair. "You do stun a man, Miss Moss."

"I try."

"But you're lying."

Winifred was silent. So was I—the moment was awkward.

I began, "What's this about a plan for the day—one that seems to involve Winifred and me as accomplices to your madness?"

"Things are popping now. I learned something that—well, something that may be the answer to all our questions."

"The only question I have," I interrupted, "is what you're talking about."

His hands reached out, as though ready to embrace the world. "I'm seeing the large picture now. Cassandra Blaine...a dizzy heiress...gone...a minor player maybe writ large...pouf! Like that! Endre Molnár *not* seeing the bigger picture. Not understanding the power he had if only he'd understood what was happening to her. *Around* her. Maybe if you're a native of Budapest, you can't see what is happening in front of your eyes. That's maybe the reason Endre didn't—well...The world around us here in Budapest. The courts in Vienna. In Serbia. In Bosnia. In Russia. Even in France. Everywhere. Even America. Americans don't have a clue. My problem is that I've been looking at the narrow picture. Really. I got sidetracked by the murder of Cassandra Blaine. Not that it isn't important. But the answer is with the count—*that* man. Count Frederic von Ehrlich. In fact, it all ties in."

"How so?" I wondered. "Mr. Gibbon, you're talking in circles. Either you know something or you don't. Tell us now."

"I'm still debating that. It *has* to tie in. All of it."

"How does it have to?" I breathed in. "What are we talking about?"

"There has to be...symmetry in life. Her murder is a petty little happenstance, easily dismissed. A dot on the distant horizon. An outpost on a world map. But it's like a stone, a pebble really, tossed into the churning waters of the yellow Danube. The ripple effect. Budapest to Vienna."

"Again you answer nothing."

"Because I'm not ready to tell you."

"And when will that be?"

"Tonight. We'll meet, the three of us. After I tie up some loose ends."

Harold was purposely mysterious, which rankled. He tapped his chest. "Evidence here." He opened his jacket and we saw the dog-eared edges of a sheaf of papers bound with twine.

"Now." I was determined.

"The real story is Budapest." He waved his arm toward the river.

"What does that mean?" Winifred asked, exasperated.

"The heartbeat of this great city. Look around you. The United States of Austria-Hungary. Look around. A city impossible to read. The Magyar wanders among a dozen minorities, pushing, shoving. It's easy enough to get lost in Budapest. A Gypsy plays his violin on a street corner for tossed coins. A Croatian peddles straw baskets in the flower market. A Moravian repairs the wheels of a dogcart. A Serbian bakes apple nut roll in the bakery on Drava. The German cobbler watches you from his storefront. The working stiff—that's Budapest—the milling crowds. The Jew manages the monies of the snobbish nobility.

Even your artist friends Pór and Tihanyi, Jews, yes, Budapest-born, but I'm thinking of the grubby poor, beggar Jews, gnarled hands outstretched. The Moravian peasant pulling a wagon. The Austrian bankers with their monocles and Altesse cigars. Look around you. The politicians are…*snoring*. All these people"—he got wide-eyed now—"so it's easy to hide here. How can you spot your enemy when everybody around you is different from *you?*"

"And such a motley arrangement leads you to—solve Cassandra's murder?"

"No, not really. Or maybe yes. What I'm saying is that the city—the empire—is rife with difference. *Seething* with difference—resentment, anger, distrust. Strife, lies, a Babel of tongues, odd and primitive customs, people hiding behind shuttered doors, scheming in the long night. The stranger among us. The bomb thrower hands you your morning *Magyar Hirlap*. Watch out! The man who sells you cheap Russian icons on the Corso may be a spy in the pay of—of your enemy."

"You're talking in circles, sir." I fiddled with my coffee cup, impatient.

"I am one step away from an answer. This will all be in my book."

"Ah, the book. *Decline and Fall*," I announced.

"The end of it all," he trumpeted.

"And our parts in this puzzle?" I asked.

For a moment he looked deep in thought. "I need to put things in order—to hear *your* take on things. I'm not writing a *word* until you tell me I'm not a fool."

Winifred started to say something, but stopped, wisely.

"Us?" I asked.

"I need to watch your faces when I tell you."

"I'm not following you."

"The world listens in on my conversations. This afternoon I plan to meet with some Bosnian Serbs living at the edge of the city, huddled alongside a Gypsy camp. They will tell me—confirm, I hope—what I have learned. The whispers in the Serbian language newspapers. I've been told the radicals publish hidden coded messages in *Trgivinski Glasnik.* They meet in secret, their members swearing oaths under human skulls hung on crosses. What I just learned last night. A suspicion. A sighting. Dangerous. Formidable. Impossible. Stupendous."

I laughed. "You sound like a midway barker at the Chicago World's Fair, sir."

"The town crier."

"And then what?" Winifred asked.

"Then I write the explosive article and you will treat me to champagne and pastry at Gerbeaud's."

"Tonight?"

"Meet me in Buda at a wine bar near Mount Gellért, an ancient cave sunk deep in the bowels of the city, ice cold, underground. Seven o'clock. I'll be back in town by then." He took out his pad and scribbled an address down. "Here. Wander the narrow twisted lanes with the secret gardens and the dark courtyards and the spooky limestone caves, a world once the home to filthy thieves and crazed hermits. You need to experience one of the wonderful secrets of Budapest. The deep cold cellars in the Buda hills."

"How do you know we'll show up?" Winifred asked.

Harold was standing now, already stepping away. "Because I see Miss Ferber's face. A hungry look, yon writer Edna Ferber. Lean and hungry. She wants answers to things."

"And you'll provide the answers?"

"Yes. Tonight. Definitely."

Bowing grandly, he disappeared out through the terrace.

At seven o'clock Winifred and I descended into the cool depths of Budafók, a wine cellar in the Buda hills. We expected to see Harold Gibbon waiting for us at a table, but the dark, cavernous room had a few men in working clothes hunched over bottles of wine. Two were playing a noisy game of checkers. A stark room, to be sure, seemingly cut out of granite eons ago, jagged rock and damp walls. But two American women stepping into its depths startled the proprietor, who had no idea what to do with unchaperoned women in summer dresses and flowered hats. We spoke in German, telling him we expected a third person. His rapid nod was not happy. He kept looking at the tables of gaping men, as though for help.

"Mr. Gibbon," I added.

His face lit up. "Ah, the little rabbit that hops from table to table."

"Yes, that sounds like him." From Winifred.

"A wonderful man."

"The best," I added.

Winifred wanted to leave, but I insisted we have some dark ruby Bull's Blood. "We'll never descend to this rung of Dante's hell again."

So we ordered, and for some reason spoke in whispers as though we were in a monastery, so solemn the cavern, so clammy the walls.

A pretty peasant girl served us, her hair plaited into a long, long single braid interlaced with green and blue ribbons.

"Edna, I read Harold's latest column in a newspaper this morning," Winifred was saying. "A copy in the café, doubtless left by the man himself. Inflammatory, war mongering, spiteful yellow journalism. I must tell you—he writes with a kind of bombs-bursting-in-air prose. He's in love with the exclamation point. He talks as if the war is days away. His writing is all Gatlin-gun sentences, bam bam bam, take your breath away. Serbia sending troops to the borders. Anarchists with bombs on every street corner. He claims he's seen such rag-tag miscreants running past him as he walked by the Franz Josef Bridge."

I sighed. "He makes it up."

"What?"

"He confessed that to me in one of his candid moments. Well, actually he told me that he *embellishes* the truth that he sees." But I laughed. "Hearst demands that he employ explosive prose, the fiery anecdote. Why else would they keep him here in Europe? He writes his exposés with the blunt hail-on-a-tin-roof prose of, say, O. Henry concocting an ending for one of his short stories. The punch and thrust at the end."

"He's a fiction writer then."

"He is that."

"A liar."

"He is that. But all fiction writers are."

She smiled. "Where do you go to find truth these days?"

"Not in a Hearst paper."

She drew her lips into a razor-thin line and spoke softly. "Sadly, I lived through that in London. The hostile reporters covering our hunger strikes, the marches, the protests before the Prime Minister. So much of what was reported was false—and purposely cruel. The same ugliness over and over—smart, dedicated women depicted as sinister fire-breathing dragons once they stepped away from the cozy hearth and their husbands' rods. Our worst foes were the women themselves, frightened by the news accounts, as if the right to vote would somehow turn them into—men."

"I know—the Fourth Estate is still a male enclave." I shook my head. "Yet I admit Harold is good at what he does."

"That's not a compliment."

"I know." I looked around the dark room. "He's not coming."

"And he's supposed to reveal something to us."

I gathered my gloves and my purse, tightened the shawl I'd worn around my shoulders. "We need to get back."

Outside, the fading daylight threw mottled shadows across the narrow street. "There," Winifred pointed. "Finally. Harold Gibbon."

We watched, annoyed, as Harold engaged someone in a lively talk on the corner, his notebook out, his pencil running over the sheet. But at the moment that he turned away from the old man, tucking his notebook into his breast pocket, another man approached him from across the street. A young man with a bushy beard and bulky leather headgear, dressed in a peasant jacket of winter sheepskin, embroidered in green and scarlet. A performer? An actor from a street revue? What? My mind raced. It's June, it's too hot, it's ridiculous, it's—

It made no sense. Harold didn't move, watching him, probably wondering that same thing. The man yelled something to Harold, but I couldn't tell if he replied. All I heard was a rush of frantic words—Hungarian? Slavic? what?—from the man. Harold turned in our direction, spotted us perhaps twenty yards away, and held up his finger—Be right there!

He broke into a run, lopsided, the frenzied, loping run of a child who didn't know how to run.

In a flash the bizarre man drew a pistol from his pocket, aimed, and fired one shot at Harold. Harold screamed, twisted around jerkily, and struggled to stand. The man fired a second shot, and Harold grabbed his neck, toppling against a wall, slipping down.

One more shot, close range, the man standing over Harold.

Then, leaning down, he reached into Harold's vest pocket and extracted a sheaf of papers. He shook them, as if they were tainted with blood.

A low moan from Harold.

Casually, the man turned and walked away, disappearing into an alley.

Frantic, Winifred and I rushed to Harold, standing over him, out of breath, dizzy, helpless. A gurgle from Harold's throat.

Winifred cried out.

I crouched down on the grimy sidewalk, my knees buckling, the hem of my dress catching on a crack and tearing, and managed to lift Harold's head off the pavement. Distraught, numb, I cradled his head in my lap, my hand resting on the side of his face. He was staring up at me, but the light in his eyes was dim, faraway. His eyes closed, then opened wide, and I saw astonishment and fright and bewilderment. His lips moved slowly, a jumble of words slipping out.

"What?" I begged. "Keep your eyes open. Please, Harold... please."

But his skin was ashy now, clammy, and one of his hands twitched against my side. Blood was seeping out of the front of his vest, a bluish red blot that grew larger and larger, floodtide.

Blood oozed onto my dress, dripped onto my hands. My fingers touched the side of his neck where a gash of blood spurted. My desperate, futile touch to stem the flow. His lips moved mechanically. His eyes held mine, panic there, confusion.

"Harold, please. Oh God. Keep your eyes open."

A gurgling hum from the back of his throat, low, dreadful. Gasping, struggling, halting.

"What?" I begged.

I leaned close to his face and smelled raw fear. His nostrils swelled, begging for air.

"What?"

Into my ear he mumbled one word. "Zsuzsa."

I blinked wildly. I hadn't expected that.

Again. "Zsu…" He struggled to finish.

I looked up and caught Winifred staring down at me, horror on her face. She was moaning.

We stayed like that for a few minutes, maybe more, an awful tableau that seemed like suspended time, the three Americans frozen on that dark Budapest street as heavy clouds moved across the pale moon in the sky and night shadows enveloped us. I didn't move, I didn't want to, I could never move again. My throat dry and my lips trembling.

I watched Harold's face, a feeble rasp escape from his chest, and slowly, horribly, the brilliant life he savored left his body.

Chapter Seventeen

You wake in the middle of the night, your eyes pop open, and you tell yourself you are having a nightmare. Because you can see it so clearly, though the images twist into screaming demons, into impenetrable walls, into surging rivers, into blood so scarlet you gasp at the horror of it. You lie there, sweating in the hot June room, a window partially cracked, but you hug the covers. You tell yourself—yes, a phantasmagoric pyrotechnic nightmare. Something you ate. That overly rich liver paté you sampled at supper. That was it. Of course. But then, sitting up, staring across the dark room, focused on that garish painting of Franz Josef hung on the dumbwaiter, off kilter now, so intrusive—Why do his eyes follow you in the dark? Is there no escape from the madness of this bloated empire?—the truth overwhelms you. You struggle to breathe, gasp. And then, because there is nothing else you can do, you sob like a helpless baby. You think—can I ever stop crying?

Because Harold Gibbon has died. Because you were there to hear his last breath. That choked, gargled word. You were there to see the eyes become glassy and dull. The fright passing with the light. Because you held his head in your lap and felt the spirit leave the man. Because...

A pall shrouded the Café Europa at night. Winifred and I had avoided it during the day, Winifred sheltered in her rooms, shocked and unable to talk. At one point I took a long walk across the Chain Bridge, but the loneliness of that trek—alone as people bustled past, laughing, talking, happy—depressed me horribly. I returned to hide in my rooms, a dish of bacon biscuits and hot coffee safely and miraculously maneuvered to me via the dumbwaiter—as if the gods took pity on me.

Inspector Horváth interviewed me earlier, and then spoke to Winifred. He'd stared, wide-eyed, as I described that horrific final scene, and Harold's muttering that final word: "Zsuzsa." Gracious, deferential, the inspector's voice trembled as he jotted my words down. Yes, I wanted Harold's murderer caught, but that seemed impossible. The bearded man dressed in that preposterous garb—a disguise, Inspector Horváth guessed—had blended back into the Budapest underworld of dark streets and unlit alleys.

But eventually, hungry for companionship and soothing voices, Winifred and I drifted down to the night café, only to discover a pall covering the room. Hungarian cafés and coffee houses burst with nighttime noise, celebration, laughter, card playing, violins, and Gypsy song. But not this café—at least not this night. Somehow word of Harold's murder had filtered through the walls where English-speaking visitors congregated—and they stayed away. Hotel guests stood in the entrance, deliberated, then headed away. Cassandra Blaine and now Harold Gibbon, both fixtures in the old café, two souls who had dominated that room. A few tables held newcomers, and a few stalwart Hungarians.

István Nagy occupied his accustomed table, a book propped up before him, but I chose not to look in his direction. Why? I supposed he'd gloat, be offensive, remark on the double murder as some fortunate and expected poetic metaphor for the decline and fall of his beloved feudalistic world. I was not in the mood for his elegiac verse. Never in the mood for those art nouveau confections, effete and irrelevant, thin as mountain air. So I sat apart from him, my back to him. When I looked around the room, I noticed he'd left.

Vladimir Markov stood with his back to the kitchen door and watched a waiter serve the few of us. Sadly, eyes half-closed, he surveyed his depopulated kingdom. If he rued the loss of business—and his continued employment—after the murder of Cassandra Blaine, well, the death knell had rung loudly and emphatically with the loss of Harold Gibbon. In his dark black suit, accented now with an elegant black necktie, he looked like the final mourner at a funeral, loathe to leave the waxen body. A flick of his head, an audible sigh, and he disappeared into the kitchen.

Winifred surprised me. "I finally liked him." She sighed. "Harold."

A hesitant smile. "It took a while."

"He charmed me, I suppose, because at heart he was a decent man."

"And he wanted you to like him. That's why he teased you all the time."

"And now he's gone, that spirited young man." A crooked smile. "Men never tease me. It makes me lose balance."

My voice was mosquito thin. "I expect him to waltz through the doors, brazen, annoying us, filled with crackpot theories of this or that."

"Maybe they aren't so crackpot after all."

"Meaning?"

"Maybe he did know something. He said he had something to tell us last night."

"And he never did." I shook my head. "Never."

"That's why he was killed."

I stared into her face. "How do we find out what he knew?"

"We don't," she said slowly. "Then they will kill us."

"No, they won't."

She smiled. "Edna dear, there probably have been folks who wanted to kill you over the years."

"True, but they haven't." I cocked my head. "I fight to the death."

"You're cocky." A bittersweet smile. "So American, really."

"I take that as a compliment. I have a charmed life."

She waited a heartbeat. "But I'm sure Harold Gibbon believed his life was charmed. He thought he could walk through fire."

That gave me pause. "Fire," I echoed. I looked down at my hands. They were pale, gripping the edge of the table.

A rustling in the entrance. "Oh lord, I'm not ready for this," Winifred grumbled.

Zsuzsa Kós stood there, dressed in black funereal weeds, excessively so, I thought. Black everywhere, layers and layers of it, head to toe. A gigantic hat, dripping with black veils. She appeared the grieving caricature, though I supposed my depiction unfair. How was I to know her grief? To understand it. As she paused there, contemplating the sparse room, hers eyes searching for something, she emitted a shallow cry, and she watched us.

"But I am," I told Winifred. "I've been waiting for her."

That last word echoed in my head: *Zsuzsa Zsuzsa Zsuzsa.* Harold Gibbon's valedictory cry. A punctuation mark on a lifetime. It had to mean something.

I motioned Zsuzsa to our table. Though she hesitated, one hand gripping her neck, she walked toward us.

She sat down. "I need to be with someone." Her first words, chocked and raspy, in halting English. But then she repeated them in German.

I knew Winifred had little patience with the woman, someone whose exaggerated look alienated her. A figure easy to parody perhaps. Zsuzsa struck Winifred as the antithesis of the emancipated woman she'd struggled all her life to establish. And yet... Zsuzsa was here, and grieving. And, more so, her name had been the last word spoken by the hapless Harold. What did that mean? Because, of course, it *did* mean something.

"The police have been questioning me," she said in slow, almost inaudible German. "The Royal Police. That Inspector Horváth, a sweet man, a flatterer, perhaps an admirer. But that Baron Meyerhold was with him, a hideous man with that fishy breath and marble skin, watching me, eyes hard as nails. He looks at you and you want to confess—but to what? To what?"

I stared into her ravaged face. She'd slapped on some peach-colored powder, sloppily applied, cracking at the corners of her mouth. "Harold's last word was your name, Zsuzsa."

She actually shrieked, which made Winifred jump. "I know, I know. Do you think I can get that out of my head? I'm tortured by it. Why, why, why? they ask me. Tell me, tell me, tell me. Over and over. They beg me. I sit up in bed, and I say my name out loud. I don't know."

"Are you sure?" I probed.

She paused, her eyes narrowing. "Do you think I'm lying?"

"No, no, of course not. But there is a chance that you *know* something but don't realize that you know something."

"What does that mean?" Bewilderment in her eyes.

"I don't really know. But Harold Gibbon must have told you something. He told us that *you* had told him something. He had a secret to reveal. He knew something."

Helpless, shrugging, her head flicked to the side. "But what? Yes, we talked, I told him things." A sardonic chuckle. "He always said I talk too much." She whispered now. "He told me I was a mad woman, yes, but a lovely one, madness giving me a devil's charm. But I talked too much. It could be dangerous. But he said I told him something that made him *think* of something… but who knows? I used to go on and on. I was afraid to stop talking because he would go away. Leave me." A deep sigh. "And now he has."

"Talk about what?" A long silence, all of us watching one another. Finally, breathing in, I said, "Tell me."

She waited, debating what to tell us. "What can I say? I don't know what to say. What is important? What is not? I see how the world looks at me. Other women. An old hag, the pathetic singer relying on the old toothless men. A silly figure of fun. The crazy woman. Hello—look at Zsuzsa. Look at our Zsuzsa. Mock me, they all do. I'm the cartoon in the daily *Hirlap*. Zsuzsa Kós, the beautiful singer straggling back into Budapest from the royal courts. Tipsy on wine the old men feed her. They say it in *front* of me."

I broke in. "We don't condemn you."

Her voice became a bitter rumble. "Hah! Everybody condemns me. The world needs people to make fun of. I learned that lesson years ago. A wonderful singer, she is, but her light dimmed, well, so fingers point at me. Look at her! Look at her!"

"Zsuzsa," I began, "tell me about Harold Gibbon."

A mischievous twinkle in her eye. "Ah, my Harold."

Winifred groaned.

"Tell us." My voice soft, reassuring. "Tell your story."

"Harold." Her voice became wistful. "How he lied to me! That darling scamp making appeals to my vanity, that man. Wooing, whispering. And at night the sneaking in, the visits. Yet he came to care. He had some—real affection. I felt it. That I *know*. I'm a woman who can tell." She laughed out loud. "I had my affairs of the heart so many years ago. Men flatter and promise and sing and dance around you. He did that, too. 'Talk to me.' Always the same line. So I talked to him. I lied to him. I made up stories that were better than the lies *he* told me. We lied at each other." She paused. "Do you know why?"

Winifred and I both nodded. "So he'd come back," I told her.

She smiled. "Smart lady. Yes, of course. But at one point I saw something different in him. I told myself that a part of him loved me…that he *cared* for me…He didn't plan it—what man does? Especially a funny reporter like Harold. A man who was happy only when he was running away from things. But we came to have…something. That funny thing that women understand and men never will."

"Feelings." I glanced at Winifred.

"Yes. That's it." Zsuzsa sat back, her eyes misty. "I'm not a young girl anymore. He was a man maybe thirty. Maybe younger. I never knew. I asked him but he always laughed."

"Yes, a young man," I told her.

"He could have been my son."

"You never married?" Winifred asked her.

A high, arch laugh. "The chances I had as a young girl in Vienna." She teared up, reached for a handkerchief in a pocket, dabbed at her puffy eyes. The thick, peach-tinted powder smudged around her eyes.

"Tell us."

A thin smile, a faraway voice, melancholic. "I was a beauty, you know. The little Hungarian girl from Gyoma. Some nights, weeping, my mother whispered about Gypsy blood, but my father beat her then. This was how those rumors drifted to Vienna—the attacks. On Sundays in that village I sang, and then I fled to Budapest. I sang and men pursued me, and then I was in Vienna. I sang in the beer halls and then in the cabarets. In an operetta. I acted onstage in glorious costume, diamonds in my hair, on my fingers. I sang—how I sang! My picture in the newspaper. On the arms of handsome men. And then I became friends with Kathi Stratt who soon became the mistress of Franz Josef. A selfish, stunning woman, but one who liked me."

Zsuzsa smiled at her memories. "Plump like a barnyard capon. How we laughed! Secrets shared. The dinners, the concerts, the affairs of the heart. I sang and sang. I acted. I was toasted, feted. Dancing at the pre-Lent balls. It was all a blur of champagne and flirtation and—and dreaming. Men begged me to marry them. A viscount, in fact. A Russian nobleman, drunk with me. He spilled emeralds into my lap." A long silence.

"And then?"

"And then, of course, the fall from grace. Young girls, jealous of me. Husbands who got dizzy around me until their wives would spit in my face. The careless mistakes, something said one night after a little too much slivovitz. Words come back to haunt you, don't they? Apologies afterwards mean nothing. A foolish slap in Demel's coffee house. Suddenly ten years have gone by, and I disappear from invitations, from teas. From invitations to Sacher's where everyone went to be seen. I end up singing in the grimy beer halls again, followed by some old men who still remember the young Hungarian girl who first came to Vienna."

"Then it was over." I stared into her trembling face.

"Over. Like that." She snapped her fingers and one of her gaudy rings slipped down to her knuckle. Her fingers were so skinny. "I drifted here and there, a woman now forty, then maybe fifty, dragging her tattered gown through the streets. And then I have to come back here, and so many Hungarians treat me like a traitor. She sings for the Austrians, they say. So I live here and there for years, older and older, desperate, living on the crumbs from an old man—others—who remember that pretty young girl. A crown tossed my way when I sing in the Café Europa—the only place that lets me sing my Gypsy songs."

But something was shifting in her as she rambled. Her drifting evocation of her past strengthened her voice, her chin upturned, her eyes bright. Staring at her, I saw that feckless girl, innocent, tackling the world out there. The young girl with the God-given voice and looks who jumped head first into the whirlpool of Viennese stage life, and blossomed. Staring at her now, I saw that girl, but I realized she was still a beautiful woman. Behind the garish makeup and deep wrinkles and tattered dress and those awful spun-gold tresses—behind that hideous mask was a glorious woman. I regretted seeing her as parody, some throwaway woman, superficial. Rather, she had about her some simple dignity that she'd earned, step by step, song by song, in tackling a cold world that used her and then pushed her out.

"Good for you," I said to her. But my words startled her. Squinting, wariness in her eye corners, she looked to see if I mocked her.

But Winifred, closely following the tread of her story, was nodding at her, and her words echoed mine. "You won your battles."

"What?" She was confused.

"You triumphed," Winifred said.

"But look at me now."

"Miss Kós, it only matters that you waged a war and won. Even if the world moved on."

Zsuzsa didn't follow our conversation, but grasped the tone. She smiled, her eyes wet.

I wanted to shift the talk. "So Mrs. Blaine asked you to find a nobleman for Cassandra?"

That puzzled her. "No, that's not how it was."

"I thought..."

"It was the other way around, really."

"You mean the count asked you to find a bride—an American bride?"

She shook her head vigorously, and laughed snidely. "No, never. The count lives for horseback riding, pheasant hunting, cigars, and mountain retreats. Marriage...never in the plans. His mother, the countess. That scheming, greedy woman...she meets me here, in fact, in my rooms, private, hidden in veils, incognito as you say, and implores me...'There is a wealthy American girl in the hotel for a year. Her rooms are down at the end of your hallway.'"

Winifred talked to herself. "So it wasn't Mrs. Blaine? I thought I'd heard...I mean, I thought *you* said..."

Zsuzsa grinned. "I *had* to say that. To tell people that it was the American who asked me. I was ordered to by the countess herself. Yes, Mrs. Blaine was eager—I'd heard stories of her interest in—titles. 'Americans are so common,' she said to me. 'We need royalty.' That sort of thing. I have no connections in Vienna now—over, done with. No one would listen to me. But it was the countess who approached me first. She says. 'Arrange it.' She offers me a pittance, really, but promises my return to Vienna. A return to the courts and the balls and the..." A sob. "She lied, of course. She knew I was friendly with the American girl. We talked here in the café. She liked when I sang my songs. No, no. It was the dreadful countess, impoverished, needy, hungry, who sought me out."

I looked at Winifred. "But Mrs. Blaine agreed."

Zsuzsa swallowed. "Because she is the American version of the countess: position, status, the...the stares from the poor people when you get into the town car or the carriage with the lanterns. I introduced the two women to each other in a park on Margaret Island. That's all it took. Mrs. Blaine slipped me American dollars."

"So that's how it happened." I sat back.

Zsuzsa leaned forward, as if ready to confide a secret. "Of course, the Countess von Erhlich asked so many questions about Mrs. Blaine beforehand. What her social status is in America.

What she is like, what she wears, where in America is the mansion, where is Newport, does she know the President, does she have dinner at the White House, on and on, a gossip, hungry for fabulous stories."

"But the count could care less?"

She bit her lip. "No, that was interesting to me. The one time I met him—he is distant and refused to look into my face, peasant that I am—the one time he talked about Mr. Blaine, the father."

"What did he ask?" Winifred asked.

"Too many questions. Money. Money. Money. Where does it come from? How much? Does he own Aetna Insurance? Money, money, money. Does he own the famous Colt Firearms in Hartford? Why is he the one they send to Budapest? When I go to America, will they understand that I am a Count?" She looked into my eyes. "He scared me. 'Does he have a gun?' he asked me. 'A good hunting rifle? They make the famous Colt .45, no? I am a well-known hunter.' I tell him—how would I know that? Why would he want to know about a gun?"

"Nonsense," I said. "All of it."

"So I make the introductions, and Cassandra begins to hate me because she hates the count. He is not a man easy to like, of course. A dreadful man, stuffed full of himself. His mother's son. But is that my fault? She accuses me of selling her into slavery. One time I tell her that her parents are the slave dealers—they never looked at her, cold, cruel people—and she starts to cry. I tried to be friends but that couldn't be."

"We saw how she behaved," I told her.

"She says—everyone then says—the great Zsuzsa Kós is slipping into madness...she screams over nothing...she imagines things..."

"What did Harold say about that arrangement?"

"He talked to me after the contract was made. Before that, he ignored me. I had no story to tell him. That's when he saw me across the room...only then. After that, he talked to me because he wanted to get stories from me. You must know that Harold had a cold side, heartless. He could be warm and lovely, he could dance around you to make you laugh, but then he could close down his heart and turn from you."

"Do you think the murders of Harold and Cassandra are related?" I asked so suddenly she started.

"Oh, no. But—but why? What makes you think so?"

"You have to wonder, no?"

"But how?" Winifred asked me. Her face quivered. "Harold was delving into the decline of the empire, meeting with all sorts of people, walking into dark neighborhoods, stirring up rivalries, trouble."

"And Cassandra was lamenting an upcoming marriage." I sucked in my breath. "It does strike me as farfetched." I paused. "But she was marrying into that ruling class."

Zsuzsa was nodding. "Harold died because he was playing with fire." Then her eyes got wide. "I remember one of the last things he said to me. We were talking about that horrible man, that Jonathan Wolf. He said that Wolf was not the man he said he was—he needed to be watched. 'But why?' I asked him. And he didn't answer me. But later he said he overheard a conversation of the American with one of the porters, both speaking in Serbian. 'So what?' I said to him. I speak Serbian. Many Hungarians do. There are Serbians all over. Then I remembered that I'd greeted the Serbian woman who sold violets in the café, and this Wolf yelled something in Serbian at me. When I answered him, he looked...satisfied."

Zsuzsa wore a perplexed expression. "I got confused by it all. Harold and this man Wolf. They don't understand that in Hungary everyone speaks many languages. It's not...America. There you just speak English and...and what? Apache? Cherokee? Geronimo? I don't know. That's what Harold told me. Was he lying?"

I smiled. "Yes, that sums it up."

Zsuzsa tugged at the sleeves of her dress. Her plump upper arms had pushed against the seams, splitting the fabric in places. She pulled her shawl tighter around her body, gripping it with her fingers. "I need to go. I need to be away from here." Her smile was sad. "You are kind women, you are. Most women refuse to sit with me."

"But why?"

"They see a harlot."

"Good Lord," I said.

"I was a singer. Men loved me." Her voice dipped, mournful. "A figure of fun." She said in hesitant English, "A laughing stock." A chuckle, back to German. "An American word Harold taught me. A word for my tombstone. But I tell you something. For a short time, for a couple of days, Harold made my life... fun again. Dangerous, but fun. He made me laugh. He showed me the young girl that I used to be. That springtime in Vienna. He helped me remember *that*. Thirty years ago. He made me stop hating myself when I looked in the mirror. He made me dance around my room like a girl ready for her first dance." She grimaced. "Even with dear Franz Josef staring at me at eye level."

Winifred smiled. "I've thrown a blanket over that portrait. I don't need that old man watching me sleep."

I rushed my words. "What do you mean by 'dangerous'? Why was it dangerous?"

She considered her words slowly. "Harold said knowing him was dangerous. He said he was being followed by agents from Vienna." A swallowed sigh. "And he was right. They assassinated him."

"Assassinated?"

"No one is murdered in this part of the world. They are assassinated."

"Cassandra Blaine?" I asked, confused.

She tapped her fingers on the table. "Assassinated."

Chapter Eighteen

We lingered in the garden of the Lake Restaurant in City Park, staring across the small table at Endre Molnár. We hadn't seen him since Harold Gibbon's death, and his written note insisted we meet here and not at the Hotel Árpád.

"Such sadness for me there," he ended his letter.

So Winifred and I called a taxi and arrived to find him already seated in the loud, crowded restaurant, a bottle of wine before him.

"I've sent notes to Bertalan Pór and Lajos Tihanyi," he told us. "We must be together, all of us."

That surprised me. I had not expected him to invite the two artists, but of course, he was a frequent visitor—and agreeable model—in Tihanyi's studio.

The striking man looked tired, pinched lines around his mouth, his magnificent moustache a little droopy, a sad-sack look. A web of spidery lines surrounded his cloudy eyes. It was the face of a grieving man.

Awkward silence as we stared at each other.

"I know Harold for over a year," he began. "He encouraged my courtship with Cassandra, though I think it amused him at first, the romance out of a children's storybook. He was always the reporter, but he became a loyal friend. Sometimes I think I don't understand the Americans visiting Budapest, but then there was Harold—funny, delirious, joking, deadly serious, noisy, a man to raise a toast with for any occasion. A man who remembered my name day and sent me wine and cigars."

Winifred said nothing, though I watched her gaze off over the heads of the crowd, her eyes lost on something in the distance. She looked stricken. Harold's death had an impact on her I'd not anticipated. I thought she might cry now.

Endre watched as the waiter poured each of us a glass of wine. "A lovely sweet wine from Szeged," he told us. "A particular favorite of Harold's." His voice shook, broke at the end. He raised his glass for a toast, though his words were swallowed, soft. "To Harold Gibbon."

"To Harold." My words caught in my throat, hollow.

Winifred raised her glass. Still she said nothing.

We drank in silence.

"I was visited by someone from the American Embassy," he said finally. "A man named Morris Jamison who took the night train from Vienna in order to talk to me." Endre hardened his gaze. "He wasn't very kind."

I swallowed, nervous. "What did he want?"

A wistful smile. "He wanted me to confess to a murder."

"Cassandra?"

"Yes. But then he mentioned Harold's murder."

I fumed. "Impossible. Incredible. What in the world is going on?"

"Within the hour he returned with Baron Meyerhold and some other men, though I was warned first by Inspector Imre Horváth who, I believe, is fearful his office is in jeopardy. Horváth has a loyalty...to me. But Baron Meyerhold stamped his feet like a frustrated child and mentioned over and over that the Americans demand an arrest soon. Demand now—his words. The killing of Harold Gibbon is scaring them. There are cables flying back and forth to Washington, to Vienna, to Budapest. Two American deaths in Budapest. Hearst himself is applying pressure, heads rolling. Hearst's headlines scream for justice. After all, Harold was one of their reporters."

"Hearst must be going insane," I said.

He nodded. "Our newspapers copy the headlines from his papers. They quote Hearst: 'Washington Demands Arrests.' So says Hearst. So many people believe all of America is pounding its fists at Vienna and Budapest—the man in the street, angry. You can't kill Americans and get away with it. Hearst is sending other reporters, we hear. That news put some fear in Baron Meyerhold's voice." He grinned. "A pleasure, spotting that weakness in the man. He's a man who refuses fear in himself. I imagine he is afraid of Americans." He caught my eye. "The world is afraid of Americans. They—how do you say it? They speak softly and carry a big stick."

"Ah, our Teddy Roosevelt."

"But most people say the Americans talk loudly."

I clicked my tongue. "But we're so wonderful as companions. Genial, wouldn't you say?"

He twisted his head to the side. "Americans are a mystery to us. They slap our backs and shake our hands as if they wanted to snap our wrists off. They use the familiar pronoun when they address us, especially in German. They start to call you by your first name almost immediately."

"Not all of us."

He bowed. "Present company excepted."

I had long been tempted to call him Endre—he had a kind of American boyishness I found charming—but resisted. I understood protocol. "Yes, we Americans are *peau rouge*."

He looked puzzled. I told him, "So many people I meet think America is the Wild West. Cowboys and Indians, even in the midst of our skyscrapers. Buffalo Bill and his show traveled through Europe. Even Budapest, I understand. So Americans are—red skins."

"The tomahawk." He enunciated the strange word slowly.

"Shoot 'em up." But I stopped joking. "Why haven't you been arrested then?"

He waited a bit, sipped his wine. "Well, it's not only the Americans who question what the Austrians are doing. Inspector Horváth tells me that the count and his mother are demanding

I be arrested immediately. They claim it's an embarrassment to their name—that the fiancé of Count Frederic von Erhlich is murdered and the obvious killer—the hotheaded jilted lover, the wild Hungarian horseman—is allowed to roam the streets."

"You mentioned this American Jamison accusing you of Harold's murder. Why would anyone think *you* killed poor Harold? That makes little sense to me."

"The authorities believe Harold gathered evidence that implicated me in Cassandra's murder. That he had the proof in his pocket and I had no choice but to kill my friend."

"Ridiculous!" I stammered.

He laughed. "You say that because you two are my advocates."

"We are that," Winifred said emphatically.

I nodded.

"And I was on Castle Hill when Harold was murdered."

"What?" My voice rose, a little too high. "What?"

Endre smiled at my concern. "Yes, a visit with friends. I *do* know people in Budapest. I live here. I was a few streets away, in fact, but headed home. I actually heard the police whistles, saw some men running."

"Running away from the street?"

"No, toward what was going on. But I paid it no mind. There are brawls outside the wine bars all the time. Tired, I headed back home. I only learned of Harold's death the next morning when a friend telephoned me." He closed his eyes for a moment. "I sat there in my chair, stunned, chilled. It just seemed impossible."

"So is your being accused of his murder."

"Anything is possible in the land where justice is arbitrary."

"Then why haven't you been arrested?" I asked, my tone hot.

"Ah, my dear ladies, another example of the arbitrariness of justice. Money—my family's. You understand that my family is rich. And the Zsolnay name is internationally acclaimed. Lord, Franz Josef himself eats his fancy Belgian chocolates off a gold-trimmed platter from my family's factory. Or so the rumor goes."

"Money talks," Winifred said. "Some clichés are always true."

Endre breathed in, looked around the room suspiciously. "But only for so long. As I told you before, the lies must be carefully constructed before I am taken away. But the scheming has started. I am being watched now."

I jumped, a reflex I found rather unattractive in myself. My head spun around, but all I noted was the noisy, happy crowd. No one was watching us. "What?"

Endre grinned. "You react like a protective mother to save her little boy. I'm flattered." With his hand resting on the table, he pointed toward the entrance, to the right of a bank of shrubbery. Subtly, or so I hoped, I shifted my head, feigning laughter, and glanced in that direction. Two men were focused on our table, both with cigarettes dangling from their mouths, both pretending an engrossing conversation.

"How do you know?"

"Of course, I know. The empire is so weak and afraid it fears every little crack and rumor and…indiscretion."

"A waste of time."

"Empires squeak and hiss when they die. They don't roar."

"Nice idea, but intrusive nevertheless." I paused. "Is this Jonathan Wolf a spy for Vienna?"

The question took him by surprise. "I've wondered about that. Too suspicious a man, that one. But he is too…*obvious* to be a spy, no? It is like he is *trying* hard to be unnoticed. And oddly I feel as if I've seen him before. Yes, yes, he's around the Café Europa too much, but of course he's staying at the hotel. *I'm* around too much—and I don't rent a room there. It is just that he looks suspicious. That, to me, is a sign he is innocent of charges." He laughed. "I don't know. There is nothing worse than a Hungarian who betrays his own people to Vienna."

"But Wolf is an American."

"He says he is."

"You doubt that?"

"He's Hungarian." Said emphatically, his eyes locked on mine.

"There is so much I don't understand," Winifred said.

I nodded my agreement. "But how do you know?"

But Winifred suddenly asked, "What about this István Nagy?"

"An anachronism, that one," Endre maintained. "If there is a spy in the house, it is…well, I can't say for certain. But he has made himself the watchdog for the empire. That fussy Hungarian had a moment in Vienna years back when his poetry was popular with the academy. Now he is living on some family money. Some say he reports everything to the authorities. But what does he *see*? He despises the new currents of Hungarian—European—poetry and art and music. Bertalan Pór and Lajos Tihanyi are enemies knocking on his door. Bertalan Pór has a wonderful sketch of him in the café: moody, bitter, sly, pretentious. A few strokes of charcoal and the man is on the page. They confuse me, those two, but they also amaze."

"I like them," Winifred said.

"István Nagy also believes Americans are to blame for everything." Endre was smiling mischievously.

"But he struck me as harmless," I said.

Endre got serious. "No one is harmless these days. The misspoken word, the gesture, the brief conversation on the street…"

I shivered. "Spies."

"Exactly."

"Zsuzsa?" I wondered.

"One of the true innocents, I insist. I was wrong when I said no one is harmless. Poor Zsuzsa is, but sadly. A woman still with fire in her eyes and belly, but smoldering. The throbbing Gypsy blood in her veins, if the old stories are to be believed. A woman I fear is slipping away because there is no other road for her. She blames herself for Cassandra's death." He blushed. "I feel guilty for the way I attacked her in the café. Blamed her. I was wrong to do that to such a sad and lonely woman. She struggles to live. I was a little drunk and I…you know…"

"You were grieving, Mr. Molnár."

"But I was wrong. I was…"

I interrupted. "And now she probably blames herself for Harold's death. The two were…" I hesitated. "I mean, Zsuzsa and Harold…"

Decorously, Endre nodded. "Everyone knows of their *affaire de coeur*. On her part. Maybe his. Over a glass of *barack* Harold did confess to me a growing fondness for her, which"—a wonderful grin—"surprised even him." He stopped. "I have no right to talk to you of this. Improper of me. My apologies."

"But it's what we want to hear."

"Perhaps you Americans are like the French. You hunger for scandal."

"But madness in her?" I was bothered. "We had a talk with her that told me she has moments when she sees herself…well, honestly."

"But she spends too much time in her own head, that lovely woman. And the echoes there confuse her."

A long silence followed, all of us lost in our own thoughts. Finally, my voice creaky, I asked him, "What will happen to you if there is a war?"

"Ah, the echoes of dear Harold still carry on." But he deliberated, glancing sideways toward the entrance where the two men stood, statues, unmoving save for the chain smoking. "If war comes, I will fight for my country."

"Hungary?"

"It's part of the empire. I have no choice." He whispered, "But I confide to you only—I despise the empire. My beloved Hungary is treated like an unwanted child forced to sit in the corner. In the Imperial Army all orders are given in German only. Magyar—it is forbidden. And in so many places. Hungarians only speak German when they *have* to." He smiled. "To communicate with Americans, for example. Magyar is the ancient beautiful language of the plains and the horsemen and the poets. It is treated like the speech of a gutter rat."

"Maybe there will be no war." I glanced again toward the entrance.

"No, I'm afraid Harold was right. War—and soon. You can hear the drumbeat under your feet. The bodies will fill up the fields of Kerepesi, our cemetery. The old emperor doesn't want war, but the military—Count Conrad who believes war is a man's duty, and even our fabled Count von Erhlich—they ready the military with glee and sweat, and the Serbians continue to spit in the face of disaster."

"Horrible, all of it."

He sat back. "But there is a chance I'll miss the war. There is a chance I'll disappear into Austria's death prisons, staring at the damp walls and begging for bread, and then I will die."

I closed my eyes. This lovely man, so passionate and vibrant— despite that mountainous moustache that admittedly was starting to grow on me—a good man who would be lost. Like Cassandra and Harold. Lost in the unrelenting sweep of troubled days.

Endre's eyes got dreamy and faraway. "Remember me."

Bertalan Pór and Lajos Tihanyi arrived the moment we were leaving the restaurant, as we casually strolled past the two watchers who now stared, suddenly enthralled, at their scruffy boots. They'd been arguing, the two artists, I could tell, because Tihanyi was gesturing furiously, sputtering mouth noises, jabbing his hand into Pór's shoulder. Bertalan Pór, looking at us apologetically, kept shrugging him off, and finally strode ahead, leaving the other man pouting, hands on hips, sucking in his breath noisily.

Pór bowed to us. "My friend refused to leave his unfinished canvas, and when I remind him of this…this invitation"—he bowed to Endre—"he stabs at the painting, ruins it, tears it, and splatters paint on his shirt."

Lajos Tihanyi was now standing at his side. "*Kérek*," I said in my best fractured Hungarian, and Tihanyi's eyes got wide with surprise. *Please.* Or at least I hoped that was the right word, though I saw Endre smile.

"He's like a child, this one," Pór went on. "But he is my good friend." A half-hearted smile toward Tihanyi. "And a talented artist, one I taught to draw so many years ago. So I suppose there must be…" He stopped and then spoke his final word in Hungarian.

"Allowances," Endre translated.

"The soul of the artist," I said.

"Is like a brat in the schoolyard," Bertalan Pór finished.

"And you?" I asked.

A mischievous smile. "I bang the wall only in the darkness of my small rooms."

"Doubtless a pleasure for the neighbors," Winifred told him. He laughed out loud and pointed a finger at her. "The price the world pays to have an artist in it."

Endre said his goodbyes and headed off to meet a friend at St. Lukács *fürdö*, a thermal mineral spa in Buda. Immediately, stumbling over his English, Bertalan Pór began talking about the illustrated book he and Tihanyi were assembling: the impressionistic or satiric sketches of café society in Budapest. Winifred asked a ton of questions, and Bertalan Pór sidled next to her, the two of them chatting away like old friends. Tihanyi, calm now, brushed against his friend's shoulder, attempting to comprehend, now and then uttering a sentence in what I assumed was his skewered Hungarian. I felt the outsider, though once again I found myself wondering about those sketches. So many of them, especially the ones drawn at the Café Europa. At the back of my head ticked an idea—look at them, examine, explore. Something might be there. A key to murder.

Lost in thought, I lagged behind the three, and watched the curious dynamic before me. Winifred was in her element. It gave my heart a start, that beautiful tableau. The woman found in Budapest a haven. Bertalan Pór as kindred spirit, a fellow lover of the art she championed. Watching them now, I experienced a tinge of jealousy, so intense their intimacy, that shared communion, that sympathetic bond. I lacked that. So, watching Winifred and Bertalan Pór chat, speaking over each other's words, I chided myself for being so petty. Here was an impossible salvation for the beleaguered Winifred Moss. These men—and I included Harold in that group—had helped soften her edges, and not in any patronizing way, some ugly stroke of masculine authority. Rather, the opposite—sharing perhaps, and thus salvation for the woman who fled her country because she'd decided she had too much hate in her. She was discovering the spark of life again. These were wise men, Tihanyi and Pór—and, I insisted, the lamented Harold Gibbon, imp of the perverse at the dinner table.

It gave me pause, such thoughts. Away from my mother, I felt—adrift. But then, an unexpected tick inside of *me*, I felt a wave of freedom wash over me.

I was an outsider here, but no matter. So I shooed them on, and the last thing I heard was Winifred's uncharacteristic laughter as they turned a corner.

Alone, joyously unfettered, I wandered the streets, stopped for a lemonade at a small booth on a street corner, and then sauntered leisurely through a small park near the hotel where I spotted Jonathan Wolf sitting on a bench under some beech trees, his head buried in a book. I stopped walking, but I knew his being there had to be pure happenstance. For once he was not the mysterious man on the edge of all our lives, but a man in the park reading a book. As I approached him, he looked up and closed his book. I glanced at the cover. A title in Hungarian.

I stood over him, imperious. "You're Hungarian."

He shook his head back and forth. "I'm an American."

"I don't believe you."

He pointed to the bench, and I sat down.

Quietly, he repeated, "I am an American."

"Who are you?"

His fingers drummed the book and he laughed out loud. "I tried to make myself invisible, but I did just the opposite. Everyone wonders about me."

"With good reason, sir. You spend much of your time spying on us." I faltered. "Or perhaps I'm wrong. But at crucial moments you've been spotted close by."

I sat on the edge of the bench, away from him, but turned to face him. He was debating what to tell me—that I could clearly see. His brow furrowed, his lips drawn into a tight line, he watched me closely. Finally he sighed and looked over my shoulders, choosing his words carefully. "I am not Jonathan Wolf." But then he backtracked. "Actually I am, but…"

"Sir," I broke in, "what lunatic talk is this? Just who are you?"

"I need to trust you."

That startled. "What?"

"I *can* trust you, Miss Ferber. I know that now. Too much has happened. I do have a confession to make. Yes, my name is Jonathan Wolf but not in America. You see, my real name is Ivan Farkas, which, translated from Hungarian into English, is, in fact, John Wolf. Stupidly, visiting here, I thought I was being clever. No one would catch on to my little joke."

I was confused. "But why, in God's name? So you come to Hungary and assume an Anglo-Saxon name—to disguise your Hungarian name?"

"The fact is, I was born in America to Hungarian parents. My father is a diplomat—*was* a diplomat in Budapest before emigrating decades ago. The rumors are true, at least some of them—I've heard them all. Yes, I did go to Harvard, and I do have a family business. And I *am* here on business. But my business here is really in the employ of certain Hungarian colleagues who have an interest…"

I held up my hand. "I'm not following any of this, sir."

"Everyone thinks I'm a spy."

"And?"

"Well, I am." He chuckled to himself. "I am. You're a savvy lady, Miss Ferber. I've watched you and your friend, Miss Moss. You don't miss much."

"Well, obviously that's not true. I've missed a few pertinent facts about your biography—and occupation."

"I *am* a businessman here, but…" He put the book down on the bench and scratched his head absentmindedly. "I've visited Hungary before, of course, so I was asked by some connections to see if I could pinpoint some shady business dealings here. So I'm a different sort of spy. Not the kind you're imagining. I can tell you about it now because it's over—my spying. You see, there are Hungarians—friends of mine—connected to Marcus Blaine's investment interests in Budapest, and there were irregularities, questions. Folks thought he was not—well, honest. There was money missing. A lot of money. Money sent back to America by way of someone else in Budapest."

"So you were sent to the Hotel Árpád…"

"To spy." He laughed. "Casually, unofficially, hopefully unnoticed. Lord, I failed at that task. I'm not good at being a spy—clearly. You caught me watching Cassandra Blaine. At first I thought she was involved. Your Harold Gibbon suspected me from the first, but he thought I was involved with politics. That's what everyone thinks in this part of the world. But not quite."

"Did you learn anything?"

"Yes, I did, but it doesn't matter now. Marcus Blaine has left Budapest and is back in America. Tracks have been covered. But he was definitely up to some shady dealings. My Hungarian friends have lost their investment. But there is nothing that can be done about it now. Mr. Blaine is a very clever man. So I have no purpose here now." His eyes darkened. "But I sensed Mr. Blaine was making deals with Vienna—with the royal court, in fact."

"What do you mean?"

"Yes, he was betraying his Hungarian partners—but I got an inkling that he was trying to buy influence with the Austrian court. Secret meetings. But"—he sighed—"that's over now."

"Why are you telling me this?"

A long pause. "Harold Gibbon's murder. You know, I first suspected he was working secretly with Marcus Blaine, a courier of sorts, but that became an impossibility. He was just too honest about things—and too much a maverick. Lord, I don't think even Hearst could contain him. I learned that fact early on. Blaine may have been embezzling cash on his own, some curious sleight of hand, but odds are he had an accomplice here. Some underling. No matter now. But I came to admire Harold Gibbon. So, frankly, his murder compels me to talk honestly with you. That has become my only interest now."

"You thought Harold Gibbon worked with Blaine? Amazing."

"At first, yes. In watching Gibbon, hoping I'd see him working something with Blaine, I also sensed that others were watching Gibbon. It didn't dawn on me at first, but suddenly I felt—the man is living dangerously. And I wanted to help somehow. But then it was too late. He was dead."

"Tell me what this all means." Anxious, dreading his words.

"No, no, don't look so alarmed." He interlaced his fingers, wrapped them around one of his knees. "What little I saw—spied on—made me realize that Harold Gibbon was right. War is on the horizon. But Marcus Blaine also knew that—hence his secreting of monies. He had stopped making payments and was pulling money out of Hungary. I suddenly realized how dangerous it was to invest *here*. Harold's political views resonated with me. In America friends of my father have interests in Serbia, in Bosnia. Of course, also in Hungary. There's a distrust of Austria and the minions of Franz Josef. So it served our interest if folks believed I was a spy for the Habsburgs. There is an undercurrent of anarchism afoot in Hungary. My job was simply to listen—to see who Blaine spoke to. Dealt with. His contacts. Perhaps befriend him, though I learned that was impossible. But someone was obviously warning him about the impending war. He was betraying his Hungarian partners."

I shook my head and smiled. "So you were never a spy for political reasons."

"No, of course not, though it all comes back to politics. I've tried to be rude to folks—to keep them at a distance. Especially with Harold Gibbon—I didn't want him too close." A sheepish grin. "You saw that first hand. I was rude to you and Miss Moss."

"Yes, I remember. You were hardly a gentleman. Unforgivable, frankly."

"I'm sorry."

"I doubt that."

He laughed. "I'm bad at spying. I'm obviously bad at apologizing."

"Keep at it. You may get better. Most men take a while."

"I thought if people believed I was a political spy for the Austrians, no one would pay attention to my real activities. István Nagy spotted me and assumed, like him, I was spying for the empire—another factotum of Franz Josef. At first he distrusted me—he actually shoved me one night. But lately he whispers secrets to me, mostly ridiculous. He tells me Bertalan Pór and Lajos Tihanyi are traitors."

"I still don't know why you are telling me all this."

"Because of the murder of Harold Gibbon."

I sucked in my breath. "How so?"

"I was watching him. I could see him slipping into trouble. A gadfly, it was obvious he discovered something important."

"But what?"

He shook his head sadly. "He kept that news secret. The reporter in him. Waiting for the big scoop. We did have a few conversations, and I could tell he was following a lead."

"What about the murder of Cassandra Blaine? Are the two murders tied together?"

He didn't answer. "Inspector Horváth believes they are."

"Why?"

"I have nothing to say about that."

"Now you're being mysterious."

He laughed. "Well, that seems to be the image I have created here in Budapest. In my feeble attempt to be anonymous."

"Tell me."

"There is nothing to tell. Yet."

"What do you want from me, sir?"

"Since I've been here, two Americans have been murdered. The crimes must be solved. My own sense of justice demands it. I've been watching you, eavesdropping on your conversations." He smiled. "I've actually been closer to you than you often realized. Anyone connected with the Hotel Árpád and the Café Europa—and thus Marcus Blaine—had to be watched. Of course, I didn't suspect you or Miss Moss—you both arrived too late on the scene..."

"And illegal acts make me break out in hives."

"Good to know. But I did learn something about you. You have a curiosity about what's going on—and a fierce loyalty to Harold Gibbon. I think you can help solve the murder. I *know* that you are planning to do so."

"Ridiculous, sir."

"No, not so. I'm not a fool, Miss Ferber. I've heard you questioning folks. But you need other eyes. This is alien territory for you, the young American short-story writer with the keen eye, walking the streets of Budapest."

"And you're those other eyes?"

"Among others." He stood up. "I trust you, Miss Ferber. You now know my secret. We'll talk. Keep in mind that everyone is a suspect."

"Everyone?"

"Perhaps your Endre Molnár, whom your eyes follow with loving regard, is the murderer."

"Never."

"I knew you'd say that." He laughed. "Even Mrs. Pelham. I overheard her wishing Cassandra dead. But we often say that about people we hate."

"You could be the murderer, sir."

"That's true."

I watched him closely. "You could be lying to me now."

A twinkle in his eyes as he ran his fingers through his beard. "That's also true."

He walked away.

Bothered, I stayed by myself in my room, refusing supper with Winifred, avoiding the lobby. I didn't know what to believe now, so rattled had I become after that brief, ambiguous conversation with that mysterious man in the park. Jonathan Wolf—or Ivan Farkas. Could he be trusted? Why seek me out for that serendipitous revelation of his identify? I didn't know what to believe, though I suspected vast spaces of that man's story begged credulity.

Yet somehow he happened onto an idea I knew to be true—my own resolve to solve this murder. *This* murder? Which murder? Harold Gibbon, of course. But maybe also Cassandra Blaine's horrible death in the hotel garden. Because, indeed, I was now convinced that both murders were interlocked in some maniacal, dreadful way. But how? And why? Why?

So I needed to sit in my rooms, quiet, quiet. I munched on soda crackers and read the day-old *London Times*, retrieved from the café. But the day's news was too distant with nothing of the vortex of anger and distrust and duplicity that seemed to rule this part of the globe. Austria-Hungary, the empire and the kingdom, both misnomers perhaps because empire and kingdom suggested allegiances, loyalty, fealty. What I sensed was fomenting revolution and dissent undermining the starved, decadent landscape.

But then it was late, my eyes heavy, shutting. Outside my window a driving rain had begun falling, splatters against the windows, loud, sloppy. A strong wind coming off the Danube whistled through the shaky sills of the old loose windows. A pane rattled, a curtain moved. I shivered. When I went to call for tea, the telephone line connected, then broke. Silence, dead. I tried again—nothing. Yet sitting there, debating, the bell for the dumbwaiter chimed, though I knew it could not be for me, but the portrait of Franz Josef shifted as the creaky cable lifted to an upper floor. Then nothing. I swore those imperial eyes sought mine, held them, accused. His horrible whiskered face became Jonathan Wolf's shadowy face—or that man now named Ivan Farkas. The shadows in the room shifted, played games, disturbed me. All of a sudden the overhead light dimmed, flickered, sputtered, then blazed back on. I breathed in. Then I heard an electric buzz, smelled something burning, a raw, sulfuric smell, and the room went dark. I sat there in the awful darkness, and I wondered if I was witness to the end of the world.

Chapter Nineteen

Ivan Farkas came to Lajos Tihanyi's atelier. That was my doing, though I wasn't certain why I extended the invitation so cavalierly. Obviously Tihanyi was rattled because his mouth noises escalated and his face contorted as he stormed around the room.

"I'm sorry," I kept saying, turning to Bertalan Pór, imploring him to explain my behavior to his friend. But Bertalan Pór looked helpless and unhappy, choosing to sit in a chair by the bank of windows and stare vacantly down into the street below.

No one was happy with me.

I'd spent the first two hours in the studio with Tihanyi and Pór, acquiescing to Tihanyi's request that I grant him a mere two hours in his studio. I liked his ramshackle but appealing work space with its heady hint of turpentine, old rags, oils, sweat, and old clothing. A painter's lair, that comforting, large room, a kingdom of one man's passion. I sat quietly on a stool, my body slightly inclined to the left, tucked into the red jacket given to me earlier, and holding a preposterous daisy that immediately wilted, replaced with a second, and then a third. I hated daisies, a bloom I associated with Pollyanna maidens, but I wasn't the artist.

He'd already transferred outlines from the various sketches he'd made earlier, including the rough painting he'd done in the hotel garden. The figure I glimpsed on the canvas looked—well, intimidating. A woman determined, forceful. My face bony and stark. Of course, it didn't look like me, a point I immediately made to the artist, who ignored me. I supposed it wasn't my prerogative, my captured image. What mattered was Tihanyi's skewered view of me, some Expressionistic—how glibly I now hurled about that meaningless word!—rendering of a woman he saw as independent, fierce, determined. Perhaps a little maddened. A woman he deemed worthy of oil and canvas. Me. Miss Ferber, thirty years old, sitting on a stool in a Hungarian atelier, painted by man who couldn't speak to me or listen to my reservations. Perhaps he preferred it that way.

Meanwhile, Bertalan Pór sat sketching in a corner, rarely glancing up from his sketchpad, at one point brewing a pot of tea when I was granted a respite, but otherwise silent. Winifred Moss arrived after the first hour, was greeted enthusiastically by both men, but especially Bertalan Pór, who fawned and hovered and insisted she comment on the art. But even Winifred was surprised by my announcement that I'd invited the newly dubbed Ivan Farkas to the studio.

"What are you up to?" Winifred asked, smiling slightly.

"We had a talk yesterday. I thought about it last night as I stumbled around my darkened rooms, and I've decided to trust the man."

"I repeat: what are you up to? That look in your eye."

Bertalan Pór kept shooting questioning looks to Tihanyi, and muttering in Hungarian. I could see Tihanyi frantically attempting to read his friend's lips, which he did—though he was baffled by what he read. He'd dart glances at me, sipping the hot brew, and shake his head. A whistling sound escaped that sad mouth.

"This is Ivan Farkas." I introduced Jonathan Wolf when he had climbed the stairs and stood in the doorframe.

No one knew where to look.

"Come in, please."

What startled me was that Ivan Farkas was now clean-shaven, revealing a sharp jaw line, a Roman nose, and the most unexpected dimples in his cheeks. He looked boyish now, and very

American. He stroked his naked chin with his fingers, as though trying to understand who this new man was. It made me nervous. "You also know him as Jonathan Wolf. He has a story to tell us. And, I believe, we have things to tell him—all to the end of solving Harold's murder."

Winifred yelped, startling herself. And Bertalan Pór, jotting the tenor of my words down on a slip of paper, showed it to Lajos Tihanyi.

"Miss Ferber has chosen to believe my story, and I've come to trust her instincts. And those instincts suggest the three of you"—his glance swept from one to the other, held brief eye contact—"are to be trusted. You knew Harold."

I stressed my words. "And Cassandra, don't forget. You watched her in the café. I refuse to let that girl be forgotten."

"She won't be," Farkas told us.

He quickly summarized the tale he'd confided yesterday in the park, his role in monitoring the unethical Marcus Blaine. He drifted from German to Hungarian to English, an amalgam that was effective, crazy though the speech was. But I could see that Winifred and the two artists were still wary of the man, their faces rigid, eyes focused, waiting, waiting. "The murder of these two Americans haunts me. Hence this meeting."

"Why here?" Bertalan Pór asked,

"Away from the hotel and the café," I told him.

"What about Endre Molnár?" asked Winifred.

A heartbeat. Then Ivan Farkas said in a low voice, "There is always the possibility that he is the murderer."

Hotly, I stammered, "Impossible."

Ivan smiled. "I believe that, too. My instincts say he is a fine man, honest, decent, and suffering these days."

"Then why?" I looked into his face.

"The only thing I can say with certainly is that the five of us are free from suspicion."

Bertalan Pór arched his back, lifting up his head so that the overhead light brought his face out of the shadows. His look aristocratic, proud, with that high forehead, chiseled cheekbones, and swept-back blue-black hair. "But we do not know about you, sir."

Ivan grinned. "Ask Miss Ferber."

Everyone looked at me. "I could be wrong, a misguided fool, suckered in by this glib-talking man, but my instincts say no. I…"

Winifred Moss finished for me. "Trust him."

I nodded. "I do."

"Are your instincts always right, Miss Ferber?" From Bertalan Pór.

"So far." But inside I quaked. Maybe not, maybe not.

Ivan contemplated the large room, his eyes surveying the art hung on the walls and on the easels, canvases and drawings spread over the tables. He looked puzzled. "I'll never understand the new world," he concluded. "To me, it's like the symbolic year 1900 signaled to young folks that there had to be a radical shift in everything. The old order passes and the new is alien to me. The airplane, the automobile. *This!*" He pointed at a particularly bizarre canvas, a landscape of peasant huts and farm fields but splashed with brilliant unreal color, blotches of paint so gaudy they seemed slathered willy-nilly on the canvas. But then, looking into the faces of the two young artists, he beamed. "But somehow it all seems right—now that I stand here and look at it."

He was stalling, perhaps unsure of how to approach the problem.

I took over. "Another reason I wanted Jonathan—Ivan—to be here was to look at the sketches both of you accumulated for your book. Ivan has been in the Café Europa often, he's watched the people there, he understands things we may not understand, and maybe he *sees* things we don't. I'm not seeing something, and I think—I *insist*—something is *there*."

I indicated the chaotic stacks of sketches strewn on the library table by the window, and we all glanced at them. They seemed Biblical grails of wonder now, revelatory talismans of coded meaning.

"I know Inspector Horváth," Ivan said. "In fact, I met him in America—but that is another story. A good man, hampered by Austrian regulation and outright bias. But a dedicated man. I told him I'm coming here today."

That news alarmed the two Hungarians, Tihanyi nodding his head vigorously.

"What did he say about that?" I asked.

"He says maybe the Americans can solve the murder of the two Americans. Maybe the reason for the murder is not something in Austria-Hungary, but the solution looks back to America."

That idea stunned me. Something in America? What? Cassandra and Harold? Strangers back in the States. Well, virtually strangers in Hungary. How could that be? But perhaps Inspector Horváth was privy to something I'd not considered.

"Mrs. and Mrs. Blaine? Hearst?"

"I don't know. But perhaps we need to look at the count and his mother."

"For heaven's sake," Winifred remarked, "what for? I don't see the connection with Harold Gibbon."

"Perhaps there isn't one," Ivan told her.

Winifred was looking at Ivan intently, her face suggesting she had reservations about him. Nevertheless, I'd invited him—assumed his integrity. She respected my decision.

We sat at the table, with the exception of Lajos Tihanyi who refused to leave his place in front of the painting he was executing. Luckily, the easel faced away, so I could see the artist and not the splash of red that was an embryonic Edna Ferber portrait. I did notice Ivan looking at it before he sat down, choosing not to comment, but I thought I detected a bemused and not very salutatory look on his face.

While we settled in, Tihanyi dabbed at the canvas, a brushstroke here, a correction there. When I glanced back at him, he wore a quizzical smile, and he looked content. I suppose the troubled, unfortunate artist always found his particular peace in front of an easel. That was good. Of course it was. Like my Oliver typewriter and me back at home, a comfortable sight, if trying and taxing. My kingdom there, ruled benevolently. I created my world and peopled it. So, too, this Hungarian artist.

For a few minutes Ivan Farkas rifled through the piles of sketches, but he didn't look happy. He kept moving them back and forth, peering at them, squinting, but I could tell he was not seeing anything there. There were just too many of them spread across the table. Perhaps my idea was a faulty one. Perhaps Tihanyi's and Pór's sketches were nothing more than colorful vignettes of a thriving café society, a kaleidoscope of varied faces lingering long hours in smoked-filled and aromatic coffee houses.

"Let's talk of what we know," he began, sitting back and disregarding the stacks of drawings. "Harold Gibbon was dancing around too many fires, I think. So he probably made enemies. Who foremost?"

"The Austrians," I volunteered. "The empire. Harold prophesized doom and destruction for the empire. He wrote about the coming war. That had to rankle Vienna."

"And the Hungarians?" Bertalan Pór asked.

I shook my head. "No, I can't believe that. He wanted to be in Budapest because he loved it. He thought the Hungarians were treated unfairly by Vienna. He befriended Endre Molnár."

"No Hungarian would kill Harold," Bertalan Pór announced fervently. He banged the table with his fist. Tihanyi, peering around his easel, made a rasp noise.

"I believe that," Ivan said. "Miss Ferber, tell us your thinking."

I deliberated. "I start with Harold's last word to me. His final word. Repeated twice. A name. 'Zsuzsa.' A woman he believed held the secret to whatever he was looking into. A woman he purposely wooed, perhaps foolishly, though perhaps not, but a woman who admitted talking too much. A woman also who might have known something and not realized its importance."

Winifred was nodding. "Zsuzsa's focus is on her own loss and sadness. She looks back to her heyday in Vienna and gets lost in the memories."

"It seems to me that Harold was trying to tell me that Zsuzsa had told him something, and at the moment he died he understood that she was *right* about it. But when I approached

Zsuzsa, she begged ignorance. And I don't believe she's lying. I don't think she knows."

Ivan clicked his tongue. "I've watched her. I've sat with her. The conversations I've had with her are depressing—even a little chilling." He sighed and avoided looking at us. "She told me a woman must always look good for a man, no matter how old she is. Not for herself—but for a man."

Winifred broke in. "Her first mistake."

Ivan went on. "She hungers for kindness."

"Don't we all," I added. "But it's interesting that she used the word 'assassination' when she talked of Harold's death." Then I remembered something else. "She also used it with Cassandra's murder, but she added that all murders in the empire are assassinations."

"A melodramatic woman," Bertalan Pór added. "A woman who lived a high style—intrigues, love affairs, royalty and politics and…"

"And," I broke in, "high drama. When she was important." A wry chuckle on my part. "In her world only important people are assassinated."

Ivan Farkas twisted his mouth into a wry grin. "It's a comfort knowing that my murder would be…commonplace."

"Don't joke about such acts," I insisted. I shivered. "There is too much death around me already. Too much loss."

"I'm sorry." Blunt, direct, but there was no apology behind the words.

"What did Zsuzsa and Harold talk about that last night? It was so crucial that Harold told Winifred and me that he was ready to reveal something that night when we met on Castle Hill."

"And never got the chance."

"So only Zsuzsa knows," I concluded. "And I've already talked to her." I nodded in Ivan's direction. "You need a conversation with her, sir. I suspect that she responds better when in the company of attractive men. Me, the dowdy American writer, well, she could look around me. You, sir"—I grinned—"especially clean-shaven and looking very much the matinee idol of a rousing Broadway review, well, I think she can suddenly remember patches of that lost conversation."

Ivan Farkas raised his eyebrows as color rose in his cheeks. "Matinee idol? Me? Ben Hur in a chariot dragged across the footlights?"

"Really, Edna." Winifred was shaking her head, though her lips twitched slightly in a reluctant smile.

"Don't be that pleased with yourself, sir. I don't consider a swaggering James O'Neill worthy of his picture on a tobacco card. And he's popular these days on the boards in America and has long been a rah-rah-rah heartthrob for women."

None of this banter was making sense to Bertalan Pór, whose head bobbed up and down in an attempt to follow the loose-jointed American exchange.

But Ivan agreed. "I'll do it." He bowed to me awkwardly—like a ham actor in the stage version of *When Knighthood Was in Flower.*

"I want to step back a moment." I looked at Winifred. "I want to review Cassandra's behavior that last day. What do we know? I recall her at Gerbeaud's, seeking me out, begging for a meeting, telling me she was afraid." I stressed the word. *"Afraid."*

Winifred was nodding her head. "Keep in mind I heard her the night before. With Mrs. Pelham, the two returning to their rooms at the end of my hallway. Cassandra was laughing loudly at some foolish joke. She sounded happy. Not a care in the world. The usual frivolous Cassandra." She frowned. "Oblivious of the noise she was making in a late-night hallway."

"So," I concluded, "something happened to her. But what? The next day in the café she was moody, sad, confused. By afternoon she was afraid. By midnight she was dead."

"Bad news?" From Bertalan Pór.

"What happened overnight? In her rooms. A visitor? Something Mrs. Pelham said—or did. We really don't know much about Mrs. Pelham."

"Or early the next morning as she readied for breakfast. It didn't have to be overnight." Winifred bit her lip. "Someone she met—or saw—as she left her rooms."

"But she was with Mrs. Pelham."

"So what?" I said. "The horrible woman slept in the same suite. No one could enter without her knowing."

"But Cassandra was famous for slipping out. Probably when Mrs. Pelham closed her own door and slept."

"So we have no way of knowing," Ivan said.

"It comes back to Zsuzsa," I said.

"Zsuzsa," Ivan echoed. "And not the most reliable witness to events."

I sat up. "What about István Nagy? The poet. He's a curious character in this mix of things."

Everyone shifted uncomfortably. Bertalan Pór blurted out, "What? That failed poet?"

"He knows something," I announced. But in saying that, I paused. "I don't know why I said that. Only that my conversation with him lingers with me—I feel he told me something that fits into this puzzle."

"What?" From Winifred, frantic.

I struggled to remember. "I can't get it yet. It's a piece that eludes me."

"And Endre Molnár?" Ivan asked.

"What about him?" I countered.

"You answer a question with a question, Miss Ferber. That's very American."

I shrugged. "There is no question, sir. At least about this. Endre Molnár is not capable of murder."

"But he knew both the victims. He was intending to marry one. He befriended the other. Of everyone involved, he was closest to both victims. Think about that."

"No matter," I insisted. "He was in love with one and loyal to the other. That says something about the man."

"Love rejected and a friendship betrayed are common reasons for murder. It's the stuff of books, no?"

"You test me, sir." But I smiled at Ivan. "But there are just some things I know in my soul."

Bertalan Pór was nodding. I realized that Lajos Tihanyi had left the easel and my unfinished portrait and was standing near us. A clicking noise escaped his throat as he pointed to the stacks of drawings, and his friend acknowledged his gesture.

"Take the drawings, Miss Ferber, his and mine, the ones from the Café Europa, and look at them in the quiet of your rooms. Perhaps your eye can see something no one else can."

"Yes, of course."

Both men gathered the drawings and tucked the huge pile into an overstuffed black cardboard portfolio. Bertalan tapped it. "I will leave it at the hotel for you." He held the bulky package in the air and grinned. "Perhaps this heavy package is weighty with meaning. Maybe the name of the killer is in here."

Lajos Tihanyi mouthed something at me but I didn't understand. Helpless, he looked to his friend, who was smiling. "Remember Lajos' words to you some time ago." He winked conspiratorially at his friend. "'I see what you hear.' Words to remember."

What had Tihanyi seen as all of us huddled at the table and discussed the murders? He'd stood at the easel, jabbing at the painting with a thick brush coated with blue paint. When I rose to leave, I stood before the canvas. He'd stabbed at the lines, exaggerated the colors, gave my eyes a determined, stark look. A woman with a purpose, and not necessarily a healthy one. He saw me looking at the canvas and sheepishly moved in front of it, blocking my view. Then, to my surprise, he took another brush, dragged it across the palette, and smeared long streaks of thick white paint across the portrait, crisscrossing it, obliterating it.

I cried out.

Bertalan Pór touched my elbow. "All that means is that he now has a new vision of you."

"What? Erased from life?"

He laughed. "No, a woman powered by imagination."

After an early supper with Winifred, I sat at the desk in my rooms, the drawings spread out before me. So intense was my perusal, so focused my gaze, that I began to drift into a stupor.

There was simply too much to consider, drawing after drawing, both artists rendering the ebb and flow of café life.

People—Mrs. Pelham, István Nagy, Zsuzsa, Zsuzsa's rotund patron, scurrying waiters, the desk clerk popping in for a coffee, Harold Gibbon, Winifred Moss, Jonathan Wolf now rechristened Ivan Farkas, Endre Molnár. Suddenly I wondered what poor Harold would have thought of Wolf's redefinition of himself. Thrilled, doubtless, with a cable sent back to Hearst at a dizzying speed.

Pictures of me—plenty of me. Too much of me. Vain though I might be, my redundant image rattled me after a while.

Dozens of people I'd never seen before, sketched briefly but effectively, a few dramatic lines capturing a mood or gesture or sensation. Brilliant, all of them.

And the objects: the damask curtains that moved with breezes off the Danube, the way the huge chandeliers overhead gleamed, the crowded tables, the bamboo racks of newspapers, clouds of blue-gray cigarette smoke, the bar with glasses and bottles. A world contained here, and tantalizingly revealed.

It struck me all of a sudden, as I moved slowly from one to the other, that these were isolated frames from some D. W. Griffith movie, the reiterated *click click click* of a camera capturing persons moving and talking. In one series a waiter could be seen staring out of the kitchen door and then stopping at a table as he moved into the room, then approaching another table, and finally bowing at the entrance to the terrace as he greeted a guest. An anonymous man, dressed in a uniform, doing his job. Step by step. Charlie Chaplin jerkily sauntering across the floor.

The lights flickered and I cringed. The desk clerk had assured me the problem with the electricity had been repaired, and I'd have no more nights plunged into darkness. Of course, I didn't believe him. Hotel clerks the whole world over were practiced in the fine art of kneejerk lying. But the lights stayed on, and I lay in bed, eyes closed, reassured by the lamp on the nightstand. Franz Josef stared back at me, unfriendly. The man never looked happy. All that garish braid and colorful decoration—the moustache tipped up at the edges. The grand old tyrant with the evil eye and the archaic brain. What hack painter had been commissioned to paint that redundant visage on canvas after canvas, unaware that his pedestrian hand would ruin the nights of the hotel's guests?

Finally, I switched off the lamp and reviewed the drawings in my head. But suddenly, ruminating about that imperial painter and court factotum, my mind inadvertently riveted to the salon poet, István Nagy, another court functionary. István Nagy, always watching what happened in the Café Europa, not trusting the people around him, a spy in the house who was looking at all the wrong people, his facile judgment at the ready, there, always there, always.

And in that moment I knew.

Chapter Twenty

János Szabó, Zsuzsa's portly patron, the old wheezing man with the gold-tipped cane and the Turkish cigarette smoked in a long ceramic holder, decided to celebrate Zsuzsa's twenty-fifth anniversary as a singer and actress. He'd first seen her perform at the Vienna Music Hall in June of 1889, Zsuzsa as the pretty maiden enchanting before an applauding Viennese crowd with Gypsy folk songs. He was there, he insisted, and she'd brought him to tears. Drunk with her fresh beauty and her songbird's trill, he'd sent her blue violets and Belgian chocolates the next night. She'd touched his cheek affectionately. He was a younger man then, of course, a Hungarian vintner doing business in Vienna, and her plaintive, melancholic ballads brought him back to his father's village a few kilometers from Lake Balaton.

To honor his beloved Zsuzsa he would have her perform, and he would let the champagne flow. A tribute, he said. He abandoned his corner table and chose to sit in front of the small platform where the old violinist was playing softly. Szabó's face was beet-red and shiny, his brow sweaty, and he told everyone who walked in what a magical night it would be.

Zsuzsa Kós walked in on the arm of Ivan Farkas, wide-eyed, blinking furiously. Behind her, Endre Molnár appeared. Ivan glanced back and nodded at him. Zsuzsa missed a step and Ivan balanced her, leaning into her, whispering something as he led her to Szabó's table. The old man struggled to rise to bow and kiss her hand but finally settled for a bowing of his head. Ivan and Endre then joined our table. Bertalan Pór and Lajos Tihanyi walked in, startled by the crowd, but I motioned them over. Earlier I'd hired one of the red-capped messengers who hustled around Budapest to deliver a note to Bertalan Pór, an invitation to join me at the Café Europa that evening. I wanted both artists with me because I had a plan.

István Nagy sat at his usual table and looked up when Zsuzsa walked in, but his eyes locked on Ivan Farkas. When he realized that the clean-shaven man was Jonathan Wolf, he half-rose from his chair, then sat back quickly, his face tight. Frowning, he surveyed the room and caught my eye. He shuddered, a response I didn't appreciate. I was hardly his nightmare. Although perhaps I was—would be.

Mrs. Pelham came into the café on the arm of the same Russian she'd accompanied before, but this time a young girl was with them, a raven-haired child of perhaps fourteen or fifteen, dressed in a canary-yellow gingham pinafore with yellow ribbons in her hair. Only her eyes betrayed her dislike of her new keeper—they flashed and turned away. But her father acted oblivious, joking with a stony Mrs. Pelham and snapping his fingers the moment he sat down, yelling to Vladimir Markov in Russian that he demanded slivovitz for himself and sherry for Mrs. Pelham. Markov nodded at a waiter who hurried into the kitchen.

Ivan whispered to me, "After our talk this morning, Miss Ferber, I spoke with Inspector Horváth."

"And?"

"He's following up on what Zsuzsa told me."

Winifred was curious. "What's going on?"

I ignored her, looking back into Ivan's face. "Zsuzsa doesn't understand what happened?"

He shook his head. "She simply told me everything she could remember, but she can't understand the pieces."

"I thought so."

Ivan raised a finger and the waiter rushed over. "I gather we're supposed to be drinking champagne," he told us, "but I prefer some good old Hungarian brandy."

I agreed. "Champagne, to me, is ginger ale with an attitude."
He laughed and gave an order to the waiter. "Champagne
makes me foolish."

"I don't believe you've done a foolish thing in your life, sir."

Amused, he pointed a finger at me. "I bet people say that
about you."

"I hope they do."

Markov hovered nearby, pleased. "János Szabó plans an
expensive night at the Café Europa."

"So people are coming back after the murders?" I asked.

The word bothered him, and he glanced across the tables,
fearful that my words would drive customers out the door. He
shrugged. "A little. New guests to the hotel wander in. Tourists
ask me about boat excursions down the Danube, to the baths.
It's a relief, I have to tell you. New news takes the place of old
news." He leaned in, confidentially frowning. "The owners tell
us not to answer the guests' questions about the murders. If
questioned, we must discuss the beautiful weather."

"Bad for business?" Winifred commented.

Markov stepped back. "And here I am doing that very thing,
something forbidden. With my family gone from Budapest—a
letter from my wife says György has fallen in love with a village
girl—I talk to the walls." He bowed. "My apologies."

"Life moves on," I said. "A cliché that rings horribly true."

Endre looked downcast, his head dipped into his chest, and
I sensed he'd begun his evening drinking at another café. His
eyes gleamed, his speech slightly slurred. His face sagged, there
were deep lines around his eyes, and he'd failed to groom that
handlebar moustache with his usual fierce attention.

"Are you all right?" I asked him.

Twisting his head to the side, he gave me a weak smile. "A
long, sleepless night, Miss Ferber. Every hour I stood at my
window and stared into the quiet street. I nod off, but wake
suddenly, dreaming of Harold Gibbon. I can hear his voice."
He swallowed. "You know, that excited, nervous voice of his. I
keep expecting him to point a finger and lecture me."

"About what?"

"About the end of things."

"Meaning?"

Quietly, he pointed to a small table by the entrance, shielded by some potted plants, lost in shadows. There, to my amazement, sat Inspector Horváth, not in his official uniform, but in a black cutaway suit, very formal, a careful black cravat at his neck, a summer boater resting on the chair next to him. With him sat a beautiful woman in a rose-colored silk gown, brilliant rhinestone hair combs in her pompadour. Her hand rested lovingly on Horváth's arm. While I watched, Horváth said something to her that made her laugh.

"So? A husband and wife in the café for the evening."

"He is here to arrest me."

I jumped. "Mr. Molnár, no. You have an imagination. He is a friend of yours, no? Even...even police can spend the evening in cafés, no?" I smiled. "I'm sure his wife demands it."

He glanced back at Inspector Horváth who was talking softly with the woman.

Ivan spoke sharply to Endre. "True, a police officer is never away from his job. He has no choice." Then, laughter in his voice, he added, "Even when he has a beautiful distraction at his side."

Shaking his head vigorously, Endre eyed me. "Look, Miss Ferber. I've heard rumors. I am to be taken away."

"Baron Meyerhold?" I asked.

"I understand he's somewhere in the building." From Ivan.

"But why?"

No one said anything. Lajos Tihanyi, brushing up against Bertalan Pór, jotted something on his pad. Then, surprising me, he leaned forward and touched Endre's forearm, tightened his grip, his eyes filled with compassion. Pór spoke for him. "You are not a killer." A wink at me. "My friend says he believes Miss Ferber is always right."

I nodded at him. "I love a man who has the right attitude."

"Or one who so easily surrenders to you," Ivan added.

Suddenly, the violinist dramatically concluded his song with a flourish, yelling in Hungarian. A party of patrons roared approval. Markov smiled. "Ah, this is the moment old Szabó weeps for."

Zsuzsa stood up. For a second she looked disoriented, her head flicking back as she acknowledged the scattered ripple of applause. She squinted as if the light blinded her, her eyes out of focus. Panicked, she sucked in her breath. Laughter from a back table—a young girl flirting with her boyfriend. Zsuzsa glanced back at them, bit her lower lip nervously. Perhaps she thought folks were mocking her, so used was she to believing that. Perhaps she thought others would laugh—or heckle. But as she stepped onto the tiny platform, turning to nod at the old violinist, she looked scared. She whispered something that elicited a smile from the violinist. He whispered something back, and I could see her face change. At that moment, looking out at the people gathered at the tables, she smiled.

It became a rare and unexpected moment. Zsuzsa shimmered. She glowed, radiant. Under the shadowy light you didn't see the tears in the ill-fitting gown, nor care about the plumpness of her arms or waist or neck. Or, for that matter, the messiness of that beehive golden hair. What happened, I supposed, was one of those precious times in which the world catches fire. The planets shift, the moon circles the sun, and the earth trembles beneath your feet. Exaggeration perhaps, I freely admit, but Zsuzsa embraced the moment as though, indeed, she were that young, untutored peasant girl with the Gypsy soul who sang her heart out on that Viennese stage.

The room got eerily quiet, save for the muffled sobbing of the old man at his nearby table.

Zsuzsa began slowly, softly, almost afraid of her voice, but then she built, triumphant, and though her voice was raspy, whiskey-soaked, and phrases were botched or missed, though she hummed lines she once knew, it didn't matter. Zsuzsa understood to her soul that she was shining.

I held my breath, listening. Yes, it made no sense to me, the lilting, rolling Hungarian cadences, but it didn't matter. She sang as a woman possessed, in thrall. Yes, perhaps a little maddened because at one point, stopping, she threw back her head and screamed, some campfire howl that made the hairs on the back of my neck rise.

Endre, near me, gasped.

Winifred clutched her throat.

Only Ivan Farkas, mesmerized, stared straight ahead, the look on his face a mixture of wonder and surprise, but also question.

She roared through the song, hesitated, and then sang the same song again, confusing the violinist who'd stopped playing. She went on and on, without music, her voice a dark wail sweeping down from the mountains and across the cold Hungarian plains.

Sweating, swaying, laughing a little too crazily, she ended with a whimper, her face awash in tears, and she stood there until the violinist extended a hand and led her to Szabó's table.

It was, frankly, a performance that stunned and silenced the room. She glanced around as though waiting for thunder and lightning. None came. She sobbed then, big sloppy tears. But the silence didn't last. Rhythmically, slowly, an old man clapped, then another joined in, then others roared, louder, harder, until the noise swelled. The crowd stamped feet, whistled, went wild. Someone, delirious, smashed a wine glass against a wall.

Zsuzsa sobbed.

János Szabó sobbed.

Endre's eyes teared up. Standing, he tottered toward the platform, reeling a bit, a cockeyed smile on his face. He paused by Zsuzsa's table and bowed to her. Her face streaked with tears, she reached up and touched his face.

"Magnificent," Endre said in a voice loud enough for the room to hear, and then, his voice cracking, he sang a few lines of some Hungarian song, finishing with a long hum. As he ended, she hummed with him, and then others joined in. I had no idea what was happening, save that the Hungarians in the room were caught in the spirit of the moment, and the humming grew, intensified, exalted. Bodies swayed and glasses were raised. Folks saluted one another.

Bertalan Pór hummed with the others, though he did stop to whisper to Winifred and me, "A song of lovely patriotism." He quickly translated, "Liberty and love, two things I must have. A lyric from our revolutionary poet, Petőfi." He glanced at István Nagy, who was also humming. "But a song to bother the Austrians. Forbidden."

Endre stepped onto the platform and the violinist, sitting down with his own glass of wine, greeted him and reached for his instrument, but Endre waved him away. He turned to face us. "Tonight," he began in English, "we celebrate the wonderful Zsuzsana Kós, our beloved Zsuzsa." Another round of lukewarm applause. Endre clapped his hands. "She has always brought us to tears of joy," he went on. "And tonight, hearing her sing for us, that passionate voice, we understand the soul of the Hungarian—a deep and warm melancholy in the blood. We sing our songs of love with a tear at the throat." And, as if to prove himself correct, he wept.

János Szabó raised a glass with a trembling hand. "The young man is Hungary."

Surprising me, István Nagy echoed the word in a soft voice that only I heard, "Hungary."

Endre glanced back at the table where Inspector Horváth and his wife were sitting. Melodramatically, his voice quivering, he called out, "I also salute the memories of two Americans, Cassandra Blaine, the woman I intended to marry, and Harold Gibbon, my dear friend. Lost, the two of them, from this very café and from our lives. Lost..." His voice trailed off. Then, rousing, "Murdered. Murdered. Murdered."

A buzz swept through the room.

Nervous, I glanced at Inspector Horváth who was paying special attention, turning slightly away from his wife and fixing his eyes on a slobbering Endre.

Ivan Farkas rustled in his seat, cleared his throat, and called out to Endre. "Sir, perhaps you..."

Endre's voice got hollow, strained. "Tonight I will leave you. I've been told that the Americans and the Austrians have decided to name me the murderer of these good people."

Someone in the café screamed. I realized, to my horror, that the unpleasant sound came from—me. Every eye turned to me, disapproving, curious.

"Really Edna." From Winifred, touching my sleeve.

I sloughed her off and stood up, not certain of my next move.

"Mr. Molnár, you did not kill those two people."

Behind me I sensed quick movement, a scraped chair, a glass dropped. Inspector Horváth had stood up.

"I need to say something." Breathing in, I surveyed the room. I opened my mouth but nothing came out. Ivan Farkas smiled at me, nodding. A heartbeat, then, "The cloud of suspicion around Endre Molnár needs to disappear."

Winifred reached over to grasp my elbow. "Be careful, Edna dear."

I ignored her, focused on a floundering Endre, then leaning against a chair. "Let me begin by saying that I am troubled by one omission in all the investigations into the two murders. Who delivered the note from Cassandra Blaine to Endre Molnár's door? A question that Harold Gibbon asked. Who slipped it under his door? Probably not Cassandra herself. Maybe Mrs. Pelham."

The woman called out, "I never. This is a carnival show you put on here. How dare you?"

"Oh, I dare question everything, dear lady. But I doubt if you would violate orders from her parents." I smiled at her Russian boss. "Such a good servant, this lady."

The Russian man grumbled, looked unhappy.

I glanced back at Inspector Horváth. "And the authorities have found no one who admitted delivering that note, which makes me wonder. That note informed Endre Molnár of Cassandra Blaine's plan to be in the hotel garden that night. But obviously it also let the bearer—and possibly the killer—learn than she would be alone. So…my question again—who?"

I waited. The violinist, holding his instrument, inadvertently plucked a string, and someone yelped. Behind me a woman tittered, nervous. But then the room went still.

I took a few steps away from the table and faced the room.

"One of the big questions, to me at least, is whether the two murders were connected. It seemed preposterous at first, but perhaps not. After all, Harold Gibbon, an integral fixture of this café here, had become intrigued by the young girl's murder, spurred on by Hearst back in the States. So he decided to investigate, to write a series of explosive exposés. That was his big mistake. Who were these people? he wondered. Mr. and Mrs. Marcus Blaine. Rich and vain and stupid Americans in Budapest. Perhaps he uncovered something questionable about the American investments here. Or Mr. Blaine's shady dealings with the Military Chancery in Vienna."

I glanced at Ivan Farkas, who smiled back at me. "Or the count and his controlling mother. The ridiculous arranged marriage. Connections with the royal family in Vienna. And another thing—in talking with me, Zsuzsa termed the killing of Harold Gibbon an assassination. A reasonable judgment, I thought, since Harold Gibbon was into politics. But then she also remarked that Cassandra was assassinated. Perhaps simply a slipshod use of language, but it got me wondering if the murder of Cassandra could have been political in nature. After all, the young woman hardly had a connection with the internecine and Byzantine politics of Austria-Hungary. But the marriage of an impoverished—but well-connected count—to the American heiress might have larger implications."

I paused, reflected. Ivan Farkas was watching me closely. When I hesitated, he nodded his head, encouraging me.

"Yes, Harold Gibbon was a fly in the imperial ointment, buzzing around, trumpeting his views on the coming war and the end of empire. But he was not alone in such conversation—not the first by any means. An annoyance perhaps, and most likely monitored by agents of Franz Josef"—I surveyed the room— "doubtless here today, squirming and trying to memorize my treasonous words. But I believe the marriage of the count and Cassandra had to be stopped. It was too dangerous."

Mrs. Pelham stood, glanced toward the entrance, but the Russian put out his hand, touching her elbow, and she settled back in the seat. Her steely eyes accused me. I read her lips. "Unseemly, this."

Probably true, but I was now in it, and focused. Endre Molnár, lazy-eyed, was gripping the back rail of a chair tightly, alert, wary.

"If that's true, then Harold's murder was related to Cassandra's—the result of his investigating. I had to consider another factor. My friend Winifred Moss related that the night before Cassandra died, she was entering her rooms with Mrs. Pelham, and she was happy—loudly so, annoyingly so. She woke my friend up by her laughter."

Mrs. Pelham bristled. "I…"

I held up my hand. "Let me finish. Please. Cassandra was happy. Or, at least, joking about something with Mrs. Pelham. In high spirits. Yet the next day in the café she was dour, worried, fretful. At Gerbeaud's that afternoon she sought me out and told me she didn't understand something—something that clearly frightened her. What had happened to change her so radically? From happy to frightened in one night. Something in her room perhaps? Hardly possible with Mrs. Pelham there"—the woman's face was purple now—"but perhaps something Cassandra wouldn't discuss with Mrs. Pelham, a woman she didn't like. Yet Mrs. Pelham had her own room, her door shut. Cassandra had left her rooms before—probably with Mrs. Pelham snoring just yards away."

"I never!"

"My theory is this: Cassandra heard something she didn't quite grasp. Like so many of the guests here, we've battled with the dumbwaiter to the kitchen and that infernal painting of Franz Josef staring us in the face. When I called for tea, I sometimes heard talking below, garbled, muted, faraway. One time someone nearby sang a song. Scattered words in Hungarian, but other languages. German—the one I understood. An English word now and then. Perhaps Cassandra accidentally opened the panel to hear something said *about* her—some danger to her. Some loose tongue, unaware of how voices carried up the shaft.

Some plot. Maybe bits and pieces of it. Something didn't come together for her. Just enough words to confuse her, frighten her, make her moody the next day. Make her seek me out. Me, a stranger, but someone she felt she could trust."

From the corner of my eye I sensed Inspector Horváth shifting his body, arms folded across his chest. "Miss…" he began but stopped. Then in a quiet voice, "Go on."

"Someone in the kitchen scared her. That's what I believe happened that night. So it came to me that someone else in that kitchen might have delivered the note to Endre Molnár's room, someone Cassandra trusted as a confidant."

Vladimir Markov, standing against the kitchen door, listening, suddenly blurted out, "Impossible, good lady. Never. Such a…violation. I wouldn't allow it."

"Violation, indeed," I answered, "but that's the answer. Who? Of course, I thought of that young boy with the infatuation, your nephew, György, a careless lad, though pleasant, now back in his native Russian village. He'd do it for her."

Markov was nodding vigorously. "A naive boy, that one. The pretty girl teased…she…"

"She also announced that she wanted him fired, remember that?"

Markov sputtered. "But a foolish boy. Perhaps he did such a stupid thing."

"Actually, Vladimir Markov, I think Cassandra entrusted the deed to you. The one person she trusted. You probably delivered notes for her before. You, who flattered and tried to please us all."

He stomped his foot. "She never asked me. I swear." Wildly, his head flicked around.

"One other point I need to make now." I glanced down at Bertalan Pór and Lajos Tihanyi. "My talented friends here, two wonderful artists, provided me with another idea. "Last night, poring over dozens of their sketches drawn in this café, a collection of moments and people that fascinated me as I looked for something. But what? All these faces stared back at me. Nothing came to me. But then, stepping back, I examined the drawings again. The kitchen staff is represented in so many, but how? A face peering from the small kitchen door window, over and over, eyes focused on Cassandra's table. A waiter in street clothing standing at the terrace entrance and looking into the room. Two waiters whispering in a corner. Background figures in the drawings, for the most part, but one figure in particular watching Cassandra at her table."

Markov sputtered, "Ah, Marac the baker. I told you…"

"No, sir. György, that seemingly innocent boy. Oddly in two pictures Lajos Tihanyi caught a rather hateful, almost maniacal, look on his face. Almost caricature, I thought. But something there—something else going on. Those drawings made me reflect on little innocent György. I remember how after the murder he babbled about unlocked doors, the need to tell the police—all talk that shifted suspicion away from him."

"A farm boy…" Markov threw his hands into the air.

"But another idea came from you, sir." Now I looked directly at István Nagy, whose eyes grew wide with alarm.

"I beg your pardon. This is all nonsense."

"You, sir, gave me a motive. In your rather sad harangue about America's place in the world and the disappearance of an old, cherished life, you condemned Mr. Blaine. And I remembered another comment from Zsuzsa that the count had a ton of questions about that rich American man—not the wife nor the daughter. The father. Yes, Mr. Blaine was here to establish a branch of his insurance company. But easily overlooked was that fact that he also was a gun manufacturer. Colt Firearms Industries. Important. Mr. Nagy, you said, 'America is all *bang bang bang.*' Guns. Lots of them. And Mr. Blaine had them."

I paused, then went on. "What I'm saying is that Harold was indeed right—there are anarchists running around the city with their plots and schemes and assassination plots. The Back Hand, that Serbian band of thugs hell-bent on battling Austria-Hungary because of Bosnia. War *is* coming—thank you, Harold Gibbon. And should the American heiress of a huge American firearms company marry, the empire would perhaps have an advantage—or so some evil mastermind might have believed. Some rabid anarchist. The Austrian army is outmoded, old-fashioned. A modern army needs weaponry, perhaps help from Colt Firearms in Connecticut. Perhaps Mr. Blaine's secret meetings with Vienna…So the marriage had to be stopped—for political reasons. Such a union could be deadly for Serbia. So it *was* an assassination."

I stopped, looked around the room, waited.

Ivan Farkas stood now, and I waved my hand toward him. Take over.

He stepped close to me. "My real name is Ivan Farkas, not Jonathan Wolf, as many of you have come to know me." István Nagy sputtered, his mouth agape. "Yes, it is true that I am in Budapest on business, but my purpose here was to investigate—to monitor—possible discrepancies in some business dealings. Some embezzlement. And yes, I became aware that Mr. Blaine was up to no good—something also going on with Vienna. My investigations led me to observe…well, some suspicious behavior. What I mean is this—largely because of my time in the Café Europa but also because of Harold Gibbon, I started to examine the world through his political eyes. He made me look at the bigger picture here. Mr. Gibbon had a way of focusing all experience through that prism, and while many turned away from him, nevertheless, he had a point—and a valid one. Yes, the demonic Serbian Black Hand is infiltrating every corner of the empire. Radicals, young men, some barely sixteen, firebrands, dangerous. Here, too, in Budapest. So the highly-publicized story of the convenient marriage of Viennese military and American Colt Firearms must have garnered attention—and made some souls nervous."

He smiled at Zsuzsa who was slumped in her chair, her eyes half closed. "Miss Ferber understood that something vital had been told to Harold Gibbon—by Zsuzsa Kós. So she encouraged me to talk with our Zsuzsa. Harold's last word—the name 'Zsuzsa'—was the key.

Last night I had a long talk with our beloved Zsuzsa, who'd had long conversations with Harold Gibbon. She told him something, but what? Whatever it was began the chain of events that led to his murder. Last night Zsuzsa, recollecting, mentioned that she'd been on the underground train and thought she'd spotted young György walking off at a stop. A casual observation, not one she considered important. It confused her because she thought he'd returned with his aunt to Russia. Something we'd all been led to believe. That tidbit, a throwaway remark shared with Harold, drove Harold back into the kitchen at this café, accelerated his questioning, and suddenly it all made sense to him. But it also made someone realize the dangerous game was over. Harold had to die."

At her table Zsuzsa cried out, but János Szabó touched her hand protectively. Ivan Farkas pointed a finger at Vladimir Markov. "You, sir, played a role in the deaths of Cassandra and Harold. Just today the authorities have learned that your absent wife doesn't come from a Russian village but from a small Serbian village in Montenegro. So your nephew György is…"

At that moment, Vladimir Markov, sputtering in anger, darted away from the wall where he stood and rushed into the center of the room, paused, uncertain, and yelled out something inarticulate. In Serbian? In Russian? I had no idea what it was. With those words hanging in the air, a hysterical look on his face, he pushed over a table, smashed glassware, and toppled chairs. Barreling his way, he shoved a man who attempted to confront him. He yelled in English, "I am an innocent man. Such madness there is in this hotel."

As he hurled himself through the scattered tables, heading to the doorway, a calm and deliberate István Nagy extended his right foot, catching Markov off guard, and the man crumbled to the floor. Nagy's body trembled, but the look on his face was triumphant, proud. Immediately Inspector Horváth and Ivan Farkas were on top of Markov. Screaming and defiant, he was hauled into the lobby.

Stillness in the vast room, save for some incoherent mumbling from Lajos Tihanyi. When I saw his face, he was smiling broadly at me. Still grinning, he saluted me. When I looked at Bertalan

Pór, he was also smiling. Pór tapped his friend on the shoulder but addressed me. "Lajos was right. He *did* see what you heard."

Suddenly, unexpectedly, and a little embarrassing to me, the two men started to clap. Others nearby, watching, joined in. Even István Nagy, standing now and grinning exuberantly, bowed to me.

Winifred winked, whispering, "Really, Edna." And the two of us started laughing.

A chandelier overhead sputtered, and the lights dimmed. A hissing sound, spitfire, and a whiff of something burning filled the room. But then the lights came back on.

I announced to the table, "This hotel is a death trap."

Zsuzsa, in a trance, glanced up at the sputtering light fixture and roused herself. She grabbed the edge of the table and pulled herself up, one hand resting over her heart. Her eyes flashed and whatever she was trying to say was lost in her swallowed tears. János Szabó, concerned, put his hand on her lower back, coaxing her back into a chair, but Zsuzsa's eyes swept the room as all of us nervously watched her. Her hands flew up in front of her face, fingers spread out, grotesque, as she gripped her face. The old man reached for her hand, but she shook him off. We waited, anxious, as madness enveloped her. A long screech, a raspy sob, then in a labored voice, in choked English, she spoke to the room.

"I murdered them all. I was the one. Me. Only me. It was my fault. I know that now. Death followed me into this café. I murdered them all."

Chapter Twenty-one

Paris was waiting for me, but I delayed. I ignored a terse telegram from my mother, now arrived in France. She had plans, she announced, and I needed to be at her side. The communication rankled, finally, not only because I could detect her hectoring voice through the abbreviated wire, but also because I was long used to her assumption that her unmarried daughter would be at her side. My sister Fannie was married with a family now, and I was the dedicated spinster.

Simply, Budapest got in the way. Its brisk, sulfurous air, its—well, I'd discovered a wonderful freedom in the ancient city. For me—only for me. A city, I realized, that made you cavalierly dismiss guilt you shouldn't have to begin with, laugh off the piddling shame that others pinned on you, and allowed you to celebrate the baby steps you learn to take on your own.

I'd experienced a sea change during my short time in Budapest, especially traveling with a feisty Winifred Moss. I'd watched her reinvent herself on the arms of two painters. A woman who reached back into her soul to rediscover her own squelched humanity. The encounters with Harold Gibbon and Endre Molnár and the two Hungarian artists had jolted me away from the airtight confines of a punishing mother. I breathed now, drunk with a lightheaded freedom as I moved alone through the wide avenues of Budapest. Sitting by myself in a sidewalk café, a cup of coffee in front of me, reading a French newspaper, I celebrated my own day of independence.

I felt grown up. At thirty it was about time. After all, Lajos Tihanyi, though a scandalous artist, had painted me in red. With a daisy in my hand. Delightful. Really. A daisy.

My mother, though loved, could wait. The Eiffel Tower would still be in the same place. Moulin Rouge would tantalize with the dark red flowing curtains. The gardens at Versailles would still be in lavish bloom. Paris would still look like the postcard picture I carried in my mind.

Of course, my rebellion was a soft one, lined with velvet. My suitcases were packed and I had a ticket for the long train ride to Paris. But not yet.

First, Winifred and I needed to relish a late-night supper with Endre Molnár and Ivan Farkas, both men filling us in on the events that followed after Markov's spectacular arrest. Zsuzsa's spotting of young György led to a search orchestrated by Inspector Horváth, and the lad was caught boarding a train south to Bosnia and Herzegovina. Apprehended as he settled into a train compartment, his face covered with a fake beard, his head covered with a red Turkish fez, he battled Inspector Horváth's men, a vigorous fistfight, and he unsuccessfully tried to swallow the cyanide capsule he'd slipped into his mouth.

"The anarchists don't leave home without them," Ivan wryly noted.

"So he was the murderer?" I asked.

Ivan nodded. "Yes. Actually his name is Bogdan Prpić, a Bosnian Serb, and, yes, a relative of Vladimir Markov, though not a nephew. But cherubic György, that skittish, infatuated boy, is really a nineteen-year-old rabid assassin, connected to Serbia's Black Hand and the monster Apis, the man behind so many of the bombings. There are groups of such young boys, fiery, zealous, crazed, trained in bomb-making and murder, ready to sacrifice their lives for the Serbians enslaved by Austria-Hungary. The annexation of Bosnia by the empire was the last straw. Such hatred."

"He admitted to the murder?"

Again the nod. "And proudly, I might add, the boy puffing up his chest. It seems the news of the marriage had incensed Dragutin Dimitrijević of Serbia, and orders were given. Austria's army is weak, old, its armaments outdated. Howitzers from the Skuda factories, arms from the German Krupp works—not enough to satisfy the warmongers. So the radicals feared any American connection. The marriage had to be stopped."

Endre looked puzzled. "But I still don't understand Markov's role in this. I mean, he was at the Café Europa for years, a loyal, likeable man, trusted. He loved Budapest."

Ivan nodded. "All that's true. But from interrogations I gather that he was drawn into the conspiracy, unwittingly at first, the result of his wife's family, radicalized Bosnian Serbians. He hated them—wanted nothing to do with them. He was torn between his family…and Budapest. He was afraid when György—Bogdan—was purposely placed in his kitchen, but he had no choice. Perhaps he was threatened. Or his family was threatened. They would kill him—without question. Reluctantly, he found himself agreeing, and then, I suppose, sympathizing, locking into the rightness of it. A man torn, really. A sad, sad man, jailed now. All he ever wanted was his job at the Café Europa—his pride and joy. He did adore Budapest." A quirky smile. "How could you not? He *did* love his job."

"It's just that he found that deadly cause more attractive."

"It happens." Ivan shrugged.

Endre spoke up. "So Markov admitted carrying the note to my rooms?"

"Yes, finally. Cassandra liked him, trusted him. He claims he did it as a favor. He never expected a murder *that* night. But when young Bogdan learned of it, the plan for the murder fell into place."

Endre shook his head. "Seduced into being an accomplice."

"He should have known it would end in disaster," I said.

Endre looked contemplative. "But such anarchists willingly give up their lives as long as the cause is won. And it *was*—the marriage with the firearms dynasty was stopped. They did what they wanted to do. Their plan worked."

The conversation turned to Zsuzsa. "Sad, that story," I commented.

Zsuzsa's slipping into insanity that night in the café stunned many, though we'd all watched it evolving in the days leading up to that dreadful night. The singer blamed herself for the tragic events, sitting nightly in the café and accosting anyone—even strangers, newcomers to the café—and telling them she was a murderer.

"For a few gold coins," she said over and over. "Judas Iscariot. I sold an American girl into a marriage, and so they had to kill her." Then she'd weep. "And then they had to kill my poor Harold, a man who loved me."

One night Endre and I sat with her, but she resisted our efforts to lead her out of such sadness. It was too late, of course, because her scattered mind, a jumble of memory and desire, had decided her destiny.

"Doomed, all of us," she whispered, her eyes dancing. "We are melancholy people, we Hungarians. We are forced to sob through our days. We wait to die."

"No," Endre had told her, holding onto her wrist lovingly, "that streak of melancholy covers us, yes, but we smile through it all, holding onto a glimmer of hope."

She'd laughed out loud. "All Hungarian men are beautiful fools and liars." She winked at me. "That's why we women are so sad."

Endre rhapsodized about the fields of sunflowers and intoxicating Tokay wine and bathing at Lake Balaton and wild Gypsy orchestras and the way a barge slowly crawled up the Danube under a moonlit sky—a ramble of lyricism that Zsuzsa ran away from with a dismissive growl.

"And beautiful women," Endre added. "Like you, dear Zsuzsa."

Zsuzsa faced me. "I told you—beautiful fools and liars."

That night, alone in her room, that tiny cubicle paid for by the doting János Szabó, Zsuzsa tried to end her life. But it was a feeble attempt, a bit of loneliness sweeping through her, and luckily she reached for the telephone—which, as the Fates had it, decided to work that night. I shuddered at the thought of what might have happened, given the capriciousness of electricity and communication in the ancient hotel.

A day later Winifred and I visited her with chocolate and flowers as she lay propped up in her bed, the door ajar so her admirers would not be inconvenienced, and she teared up immediately. She'd made a decision, she told us.

"I am going back to my grandmother's village where I will live quietly, away from"—her hand trembled as she stretched it out toward the small window overlooking the back alley—"this. Budapest. I will find quiet, and die there. I'll wait out the war there. Harold's war. His prophecy."

Then, in an abrupt shift, she pointed a finger at me, her voice sharp, raspy. "You thought it was me, didn't you, Miss Ferber? You thought I murdered Cassandra. Yes, I hated Cassandra because she refused to fight her parents. She gave up Endre Molnár. No Hungarian girl would relinquish that man." She chuckled for a long time. "You've seen him, haven't you? Are American girls that foolish? Hungarian women live for love, not politics."

When I told him what she said, Endre scoffed at that idea. "She's gone back to that village a hundred times and then returns to Budapest. She'll be back at the Café Europa, singing her songs, the cabaret songs. This city gets into the bloodstream, it intoxicates, it's a narcotic. Once you're touched by Budapest, no other city will satisfy."

A day later I said goodbye to Bertalan Pór and Lajos Tihanyi in Tihanyi's studio. A sad parting, true, but both men kissed my hand too much, bowed too much, so much so that the moment translated into some comic vaudeville routine, some parody out of a Buster Keaton stage antic. All of us at the same moment suddenly stepped back from the scene, bursting out in laughter.

Bertalan Pór remarked, "When you go back to your country, no one will kiss your hand, Miss Ferber."

"I may actually miss it."

"Then you must return to see us."

Tihanyi revealed the portrait in red he'd been working on, still unfinished but galvanizing, dramatic, something that took my breath away. Yes, there was Edna Ferber, the American, captured on canvas, but of course it wasn't me. Rather, it was a slender woman with a bony face, my black hair cascading over my shoulders, that infernal red jacket over a blue blouse, open at the neck. But the face was elegant, sculpted, with eyes both melancholic and fierce. It startled, quite. And that infernal daisy in my hand. A daisy? I asked again because he didn't answer me last time.

"The beginning of a life," Bertalan Pór told me, reading from his friend's scribbled note.

I believed him, emphatically.

Bertalan Pór said the painting, once finished and mounted in a gold frame, would be shipped to me in America. "But first we must display it in a gallery window. On the Váci. You are famous here now—people talk of the American woman who solved the murders." He waited a heartbeat. "Your Hungarian father would be proud of you."

I choked up, looking away for a moment. "Come to America," I told them. "See where I hang the painting in my home."

Both men shook their heads slowly.

"What?" I'd asked.

"If we don't die in the war," Bertalan Pór said finally.

I shivered. "Oh, God, no. Please don't say that."

Both men looked at each other. Tihanyi was saying something but he was frustrated. He squeaked out a sentence. His friend translated.

"Lajos has gone to a Gypsy fortuneteller. She told him he would die in Paris. Alone in a studio there."

"No," I told him. "No." Then I turned to Bertalan Pór. "And you?"

"I'll be an old man in my small apartment on Rákóci, the solitary painter. I will die there."

"Will you marry?"

His voice got solemn. "I was meant to live alone." Next to him, Tihanyi was laughing. "Lajos is the lover, Miss Ferber. The women chase him in the park. But he tells me women look at me on the street. They want to love me."

I grinned. "Perhaps you should listen to your friend." I nodded at Tihanyi. "You see what I see."

"Maybe." Pór's word was wistful.

I watched the two men as they left me, and I knew, to my soul, that the fortuneteller was telling them what they already believed.

I said goodbye to Winifred a few days later, and thanked her. She'd taken me from Berlin—and my mother. In that generous act she liberated me, this feisty, dedicated woman who'd been so horribly treated in London. She'd allowed me my own voice. She drifted lazily through her days now, renewed by her stay in Budapest. She'd opened herself up to the friendship of three men, all so different. Lajos the deaf mute, Bertalan the gentleman, and Harold—Harold the gadfly. Maybe four—Endre, too. Within the week she was headed to Dubrovnik for a summer of sun and rest. Then, she said, it was back to London to rejoin the suffrage protests, the battles, and the marches in the streets. The jails, the taunts of narrow-minded subjects of the king, the full ferocity of British intolerance.

"When we next meet, dear Edna, you and I will be able to vote in elections. I promise you that. In England and in America."

I frowned. "But we have to vote for men who will still see us as invisible."

She chuckled. "That's why I march in the street. That way they have to see you—step around you."

"Or run you over."

"That, too." A flick of her head. "Another way of being noticed by myopic men."

We laughed a long time before we hugged goodbye. She watched me climb into a taxi headed for the train station. When

I looked back to wave, she was gone from the sidewalk. I felt a chill. I knew to my marrow that I'd never see her again.

On June 28, a Sunday, I sat next to my mother at the Grand Prix races in Paris, bored, watching horses trot the circuit, a meaningless redundancy that stultified me. But, according to my mother, an obligatory event, given the weight the Parisians placed on the annual spectacle. Elegant women in pearls and hobble skirts slithered by, demanding that we notice them. But my mind drifted back to Budapest.

"Why are you smiling?" Julia Ferber grumbled, unhappy. "You're staring into the skies."

I didn't answer her. My world back there, precious, beautiful. Salvation. Mine alone.

At one point we watched French President Poincaré enter his elaborate box, accompanied by a retinue of attendants, and for a moment the crowd gaped, waved. He offered a royal wave. But then the President abruptly rose, calling some orders, and the entire party disappeared. A humming swept the crowd, nervous. Some rushed out, others stood and questioned others. My mother kept nudging me—what happened? Tell me. Unseemly, I assumed, such a departure in the middle of this event.

Outside in the buzzing, frantic streets, we heard the news.

Archduke Franz Ferdinand and his wife Sophie, the Duchess of Hohenberg, had been assassinated as they climbed into an automobile in Sarajevo, Bosnia.

The French president, a nephew of Franz Josef, had business to deal with. The next day the newspapers were filled with the horrible accounts of the doomed couple, shot to death by a nineteen-year-old Bosnian Serbian, an anarchist named Gavrilo Princip, rumored to be a part of the feared Black Hand. Other young men—boys really, though fanatical—were apprehended, some trying to kill themselves but failing. Cringing, I thought of György—Bogdan Prpić—stabbing poor Cassandra in that midnight garden and then, in disguise, shooting Harold Gibbon. Harold was right, of course. For days Paris squirmed and debated and argued and lamented the fortunes of the heir to the Austro-Hungarian throne.

Franz Josef, that old man I recalled unfondly from his painting on the dumbwaiter, said, "Is nothing spared me?" He issued an impossible burr-under-the-saddle ultimatum to Serbia, because it was assumed Serbia orchestrated the heinous deed.

That was all we talked of, my mother and our friends and—everyone we met. But not me, I hasten to note. The day's cruel headlines—those grim photographs of Franz Ferdinand and his wife Sophie—plunged me back into Budapest. Into the Café Europa. The heir apparent's last words to his wife: "Take care of the children, Sophie." A photograph of the skinny, wiry Princip wrestled to the ground, screaming defiantly, "Long Live Serbia."

I was tired of Europe now, and changed my plans. I was tired of shopping on the Rue de Rivoli or on the Rue St. Honoré. Silly baubles to carry back home. A few weeks later, the end of July, we sailed on the North German Lloyd ship mysteriously named the *George Washington*. Exhilerated, happily striding onto the outflung gangplank, I was ready for home now—Chicago and New York, my short stories, a novel maybe. A smooth voyage, with German efficiency and regard. Yes, ma'am, *Das is Gut*. More infernal kissing of the hand. But then, as evening approached, alarms sounded, waiters dropped dishes, cabin attendants disappeared, and someone knocked on our door and demanded we go on deck immediately. Lights dimmed, portholes closed, cigarettes forbidden on deck. Nervous, I bustled about, found myself packed in with a crowd of frightened voyagers.

War had been declared.

Germany was at war.

Franz Josef had ordered an attack on Serbia, which precipitated a wide-scale conflagration. England, France, Russia. Allies, sides taken. Germany's Kaiser declaring war. A French traveler kept screaming, "*La monarchie dèclare la guerre á la Serbie.*" The German steward begged her to be quiet.

The ship slipped through the frigid Atlantic waters while we were told to spend the night on deck.

A French gunboat was in pursuit of the *George Washington*. Crying, moaning, groaning, silence, as we huddled there. The night was cold and misty, a drizzle, nothing but the slap and hiss of waves below us. Hunkered down with slickers and great coats, hats pulled over damp cold faces, we stared out into the dark foggy night. I waited for the first blast, the cannon roar, the ball of fire rolling across the hull, the ship tilting toward our deaths. Involuntarily, I flashed to the image of the *Titanic* disaster two years back, and shivered.

Perhaps I slept for a few minutes, though sleep it hardly was. My mother wept and I had to turn away from her hold. In my fitful dream I was back in Budapest. In Tihanyi's paint-spattered atelier. In the Café Europa listening to Zsuzsa wail her songs. Endre Molnár with that moustache and deep-set eyes, one eye enticingly lazy. And the bodies of Cassandra Blaine and Harold Gibbon, the first causalities of the world war Harold predicted. Archduke Franz Ferdinand might be the public face of this new and awful war, but not to me—two innocent Americans presaged that horror. A boy named György—named Bogdan. Bogdan—Endre told me it meant "Given by God."

Horrible.

In the morning, exhausted, we crawled into our beds as the ship slid through calmer waters, headed to America. America! Later I found myself on deck, wrapped in a blanket, my face covered with a scarf, staring back toward Europe. Gone, all of it, I told myself. That crusty old world of the dying empire. The haughty nobility in their decorated gold carriages pulling up in front of Gerbeaud's, the red carpet stretched out ceremoniously. Gone. The courtly manners, the exquisite protocol, the aristocratic snobbery, the dark world of privilege and dismissal. Gone, all of it. What would be left after the war? Europe picking itself up from debris and chaos and slaughter. Gone. *Küss die Hand.* The bowing. Gone. Would there be an Endre or Bertalan or Lajos left to remember? Gone, the world of Victoria and Franz Josef and Tsar Nicholas and Kaiser Wilhelm II. Gone.

Count Frederic von Erhlich.

Gone.

I turned to face what I imagined to be America. The sun was rising. I was going home. I thought of John Donne's line: "O my America my new found land." Home! No one would kiss my hand, but the cabbie in New York would snidely call out, "Hey, lady, you in or out? Make up your mind." That made me smile. No bowing, but the hot dog vender on the corner of Michigan Avenue would drop cigarette ashes on the grilled wiener as he spread relish on it. The counter girl at Woolworth's would ask me, "How's tricks?" A fistfight would erupt at Wrigley Park over a baseball call. "Nuts! Attaboy!" A run of lovely American lingo. "B'gosh. Oh yeah? Get lost! Hey fella. So's your old man. Hey, wisenheimer, pipe down!" It was the heartbeat of the pavement, the lively pulse humming from a landscape that stretched on and on. America! From the Atlantic to the Pacific.

I was going home.